10/29/23

The WITCH of WETHERSFIELD

To Kitch,

Enjoy the read ~
based on a true
story of Colonial
Connecticut! Best Wishes!
Katherine

ALSO BY KATHERINE SPADA BASTO

Days to the Gallows: A Novel of the Hartford Witch Panic

Vestal Virgin: Chosen for Rome

The WITCH *of* WETHERSFIELD

A CUNNING WOMAN

Katherine Spada Basto

PAINTED TURTLE PRESS

For my husband Ron,
who is always there for me.

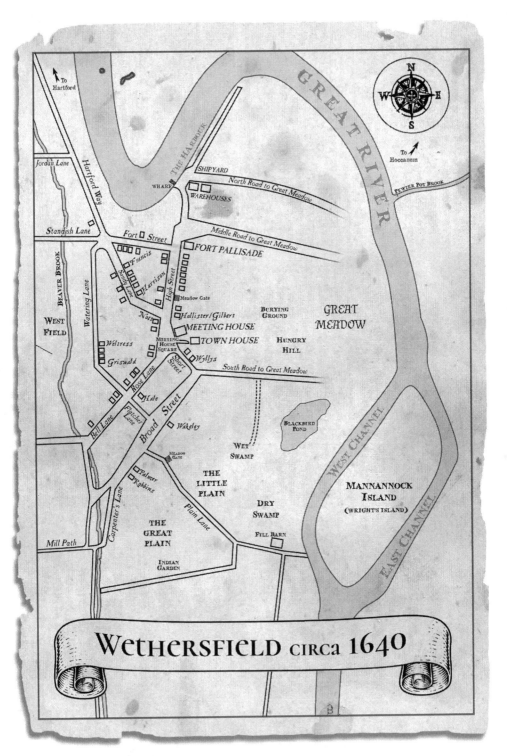

To Hartford

GREAT RIVER

N
W E
S

To Hoccanum

PEWTER POT BROOK

Jordan Lane

THE HARBACK

SHIPYARD

WHARF

WAREHOUSES

North Road to Great Meadow

Hartford Way

Standish Lane

Fort Street

Middle Road to Great Meadow

FORT PALLISADE

Francis

Beaver Brook

Watering Lane

South Lane

Harrison

High Street

Meadow Gate

WEST FIELD

Nott

Hollister/Gilbert

BURYING GROUND

GREAT MEADOW

MEETING HOUSE

Weltress

MEETING HOUSE SQUARE

TOWN HOUSE

HUNGRY HILL

Griswald

Rose Lane

Short Street

Wyllys

South Road to Great Meadow

Hale

Broad Street

Bell Lane

Fletcher Lane

Wakeley

BLACKBIRD POND

WEST CHANNEL

Palmer

MEADOW GATE

WET SWAMP

Robbins

THE LITTLE PLAIN

MANNANNOCK ISLAND

(WRIGHT'S ISLAND)

Carpenter's Lane

Plain Lane

DRY SWAMP

EAST CHANNEL

THE GREAT PLAIN

FILL BARN

Mill Path

INDIAN GARDEN

Wethersfield circa 1640

Part 1
THE DEPARTURE

CHAPTER 1

Bristol, England
September 1651

The first warning bell rang out. Officers and common folks alike milled about the Bristol City Dockyard, as Katherine Gilbert, heart pounding, bent to kiss her mother farewell. A fresh, stiff autumnal breeze from the east brought them closer to an embrace. It would be but minutes before Katherine boarded the ship.

The *Peacock,* moored on the Avon River awaited its voyage. From the Avon it would float into the Bristol Channel, down through the Severn Estuary Gorge, and then at last, enter the green-grey waters of the open Atlantic. Katherine gazed at the ship, its brown hull bleached and caked with salt, rocking side to side like a cradle.

This will be my home for the next two months, she thought. She quelled a pang of anxiety. Alone but not alone, she had her books, her notes, her secret things…

Katherine's mother gently pushed her away so she could admire her only daughter.

Long legged and straight backed—still unmarried at age twenty-five—Katherine wore a dark woolen cloak, brown waistcoat, a half- apron over her dark skirt and new tanned leather boots. She straightened her freshly starched mobcap patting down its winged sides. It all made her look and feel like a proper Puritan woman but for her thick auburn hair that never stayed properly put in a cap.

"Did you remember everything?" her mother asked, her thin voice cracking. "Are you sure you want to go? It's not too—

"Aye, Mam. What's done is done. Everything is packed and ready. The only thing I'll be missing is you."

Her mother drew close again. "Did you bring the Lord's good book with you?" she asked.

Katherine laughed. "Of course, Mam. I have my Bible right here in my satchel." She lifted her thick cloak and exposed the worn leather bag slung over her shoulder.

"What about the *other* book? her mother asked. "Tell me you've left it behind."

"What other book?"

"You know, Kat. That horrid book by the astrologer, Lilly. The man you met in London. The man who reads charts. *That* book!"

"Aye, Mam. Rest assured, I'm leaving that behind," she lied.

"Remember God is giving you a chance for a fresh start to get your life right." She gripped Katherine's arm. "And please, no further mention of the war. We've seen enough these last years what with poor King Charles beheaded and all." Her mother shook her head, sniffed the cool breeze, and eyed the docks where soldiers stood about in small groups. "And remember, your father's side of the family in New England come from good Puritan stock. No one of them needs to know how you were raised by me in Lancashire."

Katherine nodded, but said nothing. She had heard this talk before.

The sun slanted down from behind clouds, and she blinked in the glare. Her mother was right. She needed to leave the astrology and fortune-telling behind. She shook the thought off because after all, wasn't that why she was going to New England? Her Puritan relatives in a far-off place called Wethersfield in Connecticut Colony awaited her.

"Please give your cousins Josiah and the Gilberts my sincere thanks. And I know I'll hear from you. You will write now, won't you?" Her mother wiped a stray tear from her eye.

"I will, Mam. I'll write you every detail of my life in Connecticut." She studied her mother's small blue eyes squinting up at her. Katherine had heard many stories about this new country, and of the colonies ruled by Puritans seeking freedom of worship. People who left England to start anew, just as she was doing now. She had heard the rumors about New England: the wild snowstorms, the howling of wolves, native savages, even tales of—witchcraft.

But it was too late to change her mind. Her ticket was paid, her trunk safely stowed on board.

She quickly checked her satchel one last time to make sure she had her cousin Josiah's letter. This would serve as her identification. Once settled in her berth she would read it again.

The ship's bell began to clang for the second time.

"High Tide Up!" shouted the Harbor Master.

She was ready with everything she needed, including her most prized possession, the book *Christian Astrology* signed by William Lilly, famous court astrologer to the king. She would conceal it amongst her other books, including a collection of ballads, along with her own native chart, transits, and an ephemeris to help her cast others' charts. In her satchel she also carried her snuff tin. She would sneak a dab as soon as she got on board. For her hands trembled and her heart beat a fast rhythm. One good sniff would certainly go far to calm her nerves, she thought.

Katherine's mother took a deep breath as more tears formed in her eyes. "This is it then, Kat. May God bless you and keep you safe. And watch that mouth of yours. Don't let it run off before the rest of you can catch up."

They embraced a final time. The wind blew up again raising small whitecaps on the water. Seagulls screeched careening in circles about the ship; the river's rushes bent down to bob in the breezes.

"Follow the laws over there, daughter." Her mother shivered and retrieved a cloth from her pocket dabbing at her eyes and nose. "You'll get your life right this time."

Katherine began to make her way along the quay toward the gangway. She turned to wave to her mother. "Fare-you-well, Mam. Many thanks for the extra coin so I could get a better berth." Her mother stood solemn, suddenly appearing small and helpless.

"Godspeed child!" She clasped her chest with one hand and with the other hand waved.

"Aye, Mam— and don't fret!" she shouted as she swept into the press of other passengers boarding the ship.

CHAPTER 2

Katherine waited in line with her ticket in hand. She stood behind families with restless children groping at their mother's skirts and a few single adults like herself, making sing-song small talk about the weather and the voyage ahead. Finally, it was her turn. A tall man with a cheery, weather-beaten face, bushy beard, and twinkling blue eyes greeted her. He held a worn book in his hands. "Welcome aboard! Captain Daniel McAllister at your service. Kindly state your name, age and association."

"Katherine Gilbert, age twenty-five."

He searched for her name. His long fingers thumbed through the thick ledger. "No Goodwife in front of your name, eh?" His eyebrows arched up.

"No, Captain, still a maid."

"A maid you say? A comely lass like yourself? Indentured as well, I presume?"

"My plans are to live with my relatives, the Gilberts in New England. Connecticut Colony to be precise."

"You don't say?" The captain roared out a hearty laugh. "Any relation to the Gilberts from Yardley?"

"Aye, Captain. 'Tis the same family."

"Good people these Gilberts. Stubborn but decent, God-abiding folk." At last he found her name and checked it off with a tick, as Katherine presented him her ticket.

"Do you hail from Yardley?" he asked.

"I was born in Yardley but spent many years in Lancashire, as well as London. I served with the war efforts up in Yorkshire."

"Seems like you've gotten around and seen much for a lass."

Pushing, poking, then impatient rumblings behind her began to grow louder.

The captain urged people to remain quiet. "There's a place for all of ye, if ye stay *still*."

He beckoned Katherine forward. "Go on now. Your berth is just past steerage. He pointed toward the aft-deck. "Straight this way, then down the hatch. Turn left and there you'll find it."

Katherine, relieved to be cleared for passage and on board, stood on the deck's edge, retrieved her new white kerchief from her apron pocket, saved for just this moment, and waved the cloth toward her mother.

Others about her shouted their goodbyes to family and friends, tears and cries mingled with Godspeeds, joyful proclamations, and well-wishes.

•➤•

The climb down the narrow stairs made Katherine's legs wobble and body sway right to left. She grasped the wooden siderail and stepped with care.

Her berth was the last area off a small, dark corridor smelling like bilge and making loud, creaking noises. She could hear water gurgling from just below. a small wooden door indicated the entrance to her quarters. Before she entered, she dug deep into her satchel and pulled out her snuff tin. The ship lurched left and a ray of light pierced through a prismed window illuminating the top of the tin. She looked at the tin and beheld her large hazel eyes, thick brown-red hair that stuck out from the sides of her cap, and the sprinkle of freckles across her small pointed nose.

She quickly opened the tin, took a pinch out, and sniffed it up a nostril. Closing the tin just as fast, she dropped it back in her bag. The mix of tobacco, lavender, and other herbs calmed her nerves.

Katherine opened the door and immediately noticed how low and curved the ceiling was and how tiny and dark the room appeared. A pallet stood on the right with her trunk underneath. One small round window hole brought in scant light.

Then she heard what sounded like twittering coming from the opposite side of her bed.

"Why—!" exclaimed Katherine.

"Why, nothing!" she heard a tinny voice say.

"What were you expecting? A berth fit for a queen?" another voice asked.

Katherine, her eyes now accustomed to the semi-dark, peered at two figures sitting along the other side of the cabin.

"There must be some mistake," she said. "I paid extra pounds for *private* quarters."

"And so did we. Or should we say, our master paid our way," answered a voice.

"Master?" Katherine cringed with the thought.

"Aye. Indentured servants we are. We have our papers right here. Serving for seven years we are in Boston. Then according to the master's contract, we will be free!"

"I'm free now," Katherine said in a boastful manner. "And I'd like to be free from the likes of both of you."

She heard loud laughter. "Well, you won't be free of us. This is our quarter too. You had best get used to us." There was a pause. "Who are you, anyway? There's no cause to act like you are better than us. You've got more nerve than grace, I'd say." The women chirped together like two sparrows in a bush.

"I am Katherine Gilbert, going to my cousin's house in the New World. Aye, I'm a step above you two, and I have a mind to speak with the captain about your coarse manners." She sat on her bed, crouched over, and retrieved her snuffbox from the bottom of her satchel. She put a finger through the tobacco mix and sniffed it up a nostril for good measure.

She regarded the two women. They might be sisters for all she knew. Was it the thin strands of mouse-colored hair showing from their caps? The pasty skin that looked like lumpy pudding? The cheap homespun they wore? Or the floral perfume that made Katherine feel sick of a sudden?

At least the snuff was taking effect.

"I recognize the accent now. From up north, are you?" she heard. Two pairs of eyes watched her carefully.

"Lancashire actually. I spent many years in London and then up north in York working the war efforts. And I recognize *your* accents. East London, if I am correct?"

"And you would know, wouldn't you? Likely spending time walking with them bright women of the night. We know your kind," said the forceful one. "Helping the army? Ha!"

"How dare you voice such thoughts to me?" Katherine felt her neck stiffening. "I told you my name, now what are yours?"

"I am Ann Mary," announced the more vocal one. "And this is my cousin Elizabeth. We call her Nellie." Ann Mary stood and extended a small hand, a hand that looked raw and calloused. Katherine thought that Ann Mary might have been pretty once, but life had turned her features cold and lifeless. Her skin was blotchy, her thin lips peeling, but her eyes held a mischievous twinkle.

Katherine refused to shake that hand.

Ann Mary withdrew her hand with a huff. "If you think we will bow to you we won't. You are not royalty, and we won't treat you as such."

Nellie, smaller than her cousin, stood up. She also had blue eyes that held an element of surprise in them. Katherine could make out the same twinkle in the half-light.

"If you won't shake my hand, I'll curtsy to you anyway." Nellie grasped the corners of her homespun dress and bent her knee full to the ground. Both cousins burst into a gaggle of laughter.

"Ha! She truly thinks she is royalty. Nothing but a servant herself, I bet." Ann Mary said with a chuckle.

Katherine bent to peer out the small round window. The *Peacock* was veering down the Avon River, moving at a fast pace.

She turned to face her fellow passengers.

"What do ye know?" she said. "Rest assured, someday I shall be mistress of mine own house."

CHAPTER 3

Katherine hauled herself up the hatch stairs and stomped across the deck in search of the captain. Most likely he would be steering the ship out to the open waters. Crew members were beginning to unfurl the sails and moved cargo into the proper positions as ballast. She was determined to get the single berth she had paid for— and expected.

Passengers gathered on the fore and aft decks, leaning over the bulwark, speaking to one another, anticipating the long journey ahead. Katherine brushed through the crowd and noticed a distinguished looking older man sitting on a bench holding a compass in his hand.

He turned to her, blinked, nodded, and glanced out toward the riverbeds. Then he turned back toward her. He squinted and signaled her over with a wave of his hand. "Good day," he said as she approached. "I do think I know thy face from somewhere. But where?" He peered up into her eyes, studied her face, and then glanced down at the rest of her.

"You say you know me?" Katherine asked. "Why, I know you not." She thought the man odd. "Who are you?"

The man tucked his compass into a pocket, leaned on the rail, his cane to one side, and looked ahead. He was stout with a florid complexion and a neatly trimmed grey beard. He had the reassuring smell about him of beaten leather and pine. "There's no mistaking your face— those pale hazel eyes and auburn hair. Could it be you were at Mr. Lilly's talk in London? He was signing books. Was that you waiting in line?"

Katherine stared intently at the stranger. She brushed her hand along her satchel as the ship rolled down the high-tide river. "Perhaps."

"Please sit." He motioned his hand to a small bench. "We have but a few minutes before the river meets the sea." The stranger mumbled about not having worthy sea-legs for the trip. "Let me introduce myself. I am James Robson."

"I am Katherine Gilbert." The two sat together listening to the screech of gulls diving up and down near the ship. She took out her snuff tin, opened it and pinched a bit for her nostril.

James glanced at the box, but said nothing about her actions. "Why are you leaving England? Running away?" he asked her.

"You might say that." Katherine gazed at the vast opening horizon as she searched for the right words. "Running from the horrors of this war. Aye, I'm leaving it all."

"Where to?" he asked.

"I have cousins in the New World. Left England years ago. They settled first in Boston and removed to Connecticut Colony. That's where I go. And yourself?"

"I head to Boston where an uncle resides. I, like yourself, escape the ravages of this bloody war." He paused. "Did you lose kinfolk?" he asked, glancing into her eyes.

"Nay," Katherine replied. "I worked with the sisters up north in Yorkshire—Pontefract Castle to be precise. Now it's no more. This was my last duty after being stationed in London for a time."

"You don't say. Trained in the healing arts? Ministering to the soldiers?"

"Aye, trained in the laying on of poultices, setting bones with splints, cleaning wounds and making myself useful. But I could not suffer the heartache any longer. To see men with amputated limbs— torn apart like our country— the agony of it— and the thought of the King's head hanging on that pike at London Bridge, it haunts me— aye, 'tis why I leave my home."

"Hush dear girl," James said softly "Let no one know of your Royalist leanings." He gently slid a silver flask from his coat pocket, uncapped it, and took a long sip. "Here." He handed her the flask. "Drink in the name of our good King Charles. God rest his soul." Katherine accepted it willingly, and took a deep gulp. The brandy warmed her while the snuff calmed her. She exhaled a long, deep sigh as the ship rocked gently back and forth.

"And remember… Cromwell is our new Regent. The Rumps rule Parliament now."

"And I'm free of it all!" Katherine lifted her arms to the waters.

James's face reddened from the wind and the drink. "Tell me, what will you be doing in the New World?" He drank again from the flask. "And by-the-by, did you plot the astrological aspects for your voyage and life ahead like Mr. Lilly suggests?"

"Aye, indeed I did," she said with pride. "All the signs, aspects, and transits look favorable." Katherine noticed some crew members and remembered why she had come aboard the deck. "Perhaps we shall speak later. I have business to attend to," she said to James and abruptly took her leave.

She approached a crew member, a disheveled young man who looked as slippery as the deck. "Excuse me, please direct me to the captain. I have important business I need discussing with him."

"With those strands of hair glowing like threads of fire from your cap? Don't you know a woman looking like yourself on the deck of a ship can bring bad luck?"

Katherine waved the comment away. "Never you mind. Enough of the superstition. But if you truly believe this well enough, I'll bring thee that bad luck, lest you take me to the captain—immediately."

Clearly startled by her words, the sailor pivoted around and headed toward the foredeck. Katherine followed at his heels.

The captain stood afore her, hands on his hips, his face ruddy from windburn. "What is it?" he demanded. "I'm a busy man."

Katherine pulled out her worn ticket receipt. "See here." She pointed to the stub. "My ticket says 'single berth.' I'm paid up."

The captain snatched it from her hands. "Indeed," he murmured and then grumbled, "Why, you are a demanding one, trying to strike a bargain."

"No bargain, Captain. I make certain I get what I pay for. There will be no steerage or hold for me on this voyage."

"I see." He glared into her eyes and made huffing noises under his breath. "How tough a lass you are. It will serve thee well in the New World."

"Aye, Captain. I may be lanky, but sturdy I will always be. I'm quick on my feet. Why, I have lifted soldiers to my back and carried them across hill and vale. I've even—" She stopped of a sudden. Why was she revealing this now? Was the captain a Royalist as well?

"Quick on your feet and quicker with your tongue, eh? But aye, I see you're a good lass, a good subject of the Realm."

"So you will find me a proper berth?"

The captain nodded. He steeled himself and met Katherine's eyes again.

She knew her eyes held power. They often turned from hazel to brown or a green-grey depending on her mood. They either frightened people or drew them closer— and it was clear to her— they were working again. Now she would use every ounce of her powers to set things right—in her favor. Whether one did her bidding— by fear or awe— she didn't care. She was determined to get what she wanted.

•—•—•

She sat alone in her new cabin. It was located in the stern of the ship near the captain's quarters. "This way I can keep an eye on you myself," he said. "You'll have naught to complain about." Her trunk and belongings had been retrieved and were placed underneath her pallet.

Sighing, Katherine unraveled her cousin's letter from her satchel. She blinked in the waning light of the sun to see the inky scratches on the torn paper:

> *Dear Katherine,*
>   *On behalf of the Gilbert Family, we pray your voyage and journey go well. I have a copy of the ship's timetable. Based on the arrival time, I will make certain someone will meet you at Wethersfield Harbor.*
>   *When you arrive to Boston, go directly to the White Hart Tavern, stay the night and upon the morrow, the shallop The Breeze will sail to New London. Show this letter to the captain and crew of the shallop. This is to be your identification. Once in New London, you will take the boat to Saybrook. Then you will embark up the Great River to your new home.*
>   *Godspeed on your journey.*
>   *Your cousin,*
>   *Josiah Gilbert*

Everything had to go as planned. She could ill afford any delays. She brushed through her satchel and found the Almanack written by

Mr. Lilly for the year of our Lord 1651. She plumbed through the pages and found what she searched for:

Autumn 1651

'The great benefactor, Jupiter is in close aspect with the Evening Star along with the planet Mercury overseeing safe travels. The planet Mercury closely aligns with the above planets, indicating this being a fine time to make plans and execute them.'

She shut the Almanack confident her timing was aligned with the stars.

Katherine was on her way.

CHAPTER 4

Wethersfield, Connecticut Colony
Autumn 1651

Josiah Gilbert paced the floorboards near the hearth of his-soon-to be old home. He had received word from the Harbor Master that Katherine's ship had arrived early to Boston. He also held a letter just arrived from his cousin Richard. He read the letter and found it disturbing.

As if he did not have enough worries. He had his new house to make ready these next several months, his banns of marriage were posted on the meetinghouse door, and within a fortnight, he would be a married man.

And now this letter from his cousin, a letter that contained a warning about Katherine. Josiah shook his head and stomped his legs back and forth. Finally he sat on a stool in front of the fire and thought for a time. It helped his mind to stare at the bright, crackling flames. Perhaps he should share this letter with his brother Jonathan in Hartford, or his wayward brother, Thomas in Windsor. Or maybe he should dash the letter into the fire and forget it.

He reread it again:

Dear Josiah,

I pray this finds you well and that you receive this letter in a timely manner. This letter serves as a warning, a warning about cousin Katherine.

I do not know how good she is, but I do know she has a reputation for ungodly acts, impulsive and disruptive behavior. If I were you, I would have nothing to do with her. She's no good, Josiah. Drenched in sin she is— May the Lord forgive her, because I cannot. Mark my words she is trouble. You have been warned. She is from the ilk of the cunning folk-folk not to be trusted.

I pray your marriage to Elizabeth bears much fruit and joy in the Lord's good graces. You need not burden yourself with a woman who followed the troops. May God's Providence continue to bless you and the Gilbert family in Hartford and Wethersfield.

With love,
your cousin,
Richard.

Now Josiah was determined not to have his cousin stay with him; not when he made ready for his nuptials. She'd not be interfering with his plans—not if he any say.

He slammed the kitchen door shut. He decided he would discuss this matter with Elizabeth, his betrothed. She always knew what to do. Mayhap Katherine might stay with her until she was settled elsewhere, he thought.

Josiah walked the half mile to Elizabeth's house and pounded on the door with one hand, holding the letter in the other. Elizabeth opened the door. "Why Josiah, whatever is wrong? You look pained. Come in." Her almond-shaped brown eyes twinkled at him. She always made him feel better.

He entered the hall noting the fresh smell of lavender and the cleanliness of her family home. He found a stool near the fire, sat down, and brandished the letter to her. "This letter arrived today. The ship's servant boy delivered it to me."

"What doth it say? Bad tidings from abroad?" Elizabeth pursed her lips and wrinkled her nose, concern on her face.

"Depends. My cousin Katherine is to arrive any day. Her ship landed to Boston early." He sighed and stared up at the ceiling.

"I recall you mentioning your cousin. Why are you troubled that she doth come early?"

"'Tis the point, Elizabeth. She will be here before our nuptials. I refuse to have her stay with me—" He paused. "Or with you and your family, the more I think on this. We have enough to prepare for our wedding day."

"Cannot she stay with your brother Thomas and his wife Lydia up in Windsor?" she asked.

"With *them*?" Why, we wouldn't want Katherine to learn about their past, now would we? She easily could be of the same ilk herself."

Elizabeth looked at him in dismay. "But that's all in the past, isn't it?"

"Doesn't matter. They are criminals." He sighed and stared down at the rushes covering the floorboards.

"What about your brother Jonathan in Hartford?"

"My brother is far too busy with his warehouses along the Great River. He's busy fixing up the Hollister house with us. He has no time nor inkling—" He paused for a breath. "Here," he gave the letter to Elizabeth. "Read what my cousin writes about *her*."

Elizabeth took a moment to read the letter and shook her head.

"Why Josiah, it is but a simple affair. Of course your cousin must come and stay. We have an obligation to show her Christian charity." Elizabeth, always a kind and generous soul, knew how to calm his hot temper.

"I suppose," he said rather sullenly. "But I'll not have her staying with me—or you. We know her not, Lizbeth. What are your thoughts?"

Elizabeth sat in the chair closest to the fire and reached for the bag on the floor next to her. She retrieved a bundle of yarn and her knitting needles. The clack and clicking of needles began, settling down to a steady rhythm. Would he ever get used to it when they married? At the moment this was the least of his concerns.

"Knitting helps me think," she said, as if she knew his thoughts. He said nothing, just pondered the few choices available. "Let me think on this matter," she said. "Would you like a cup of mulled cider to take the chill off?" Elizabeth set her needles and yarn down to fetch a mug, then ladled out a portion and handed it to her fiancé.

"I thank thee, good woman." He looked around. "Where are your parents, Lizbeth?

"They are at market today."

"What say you? Any thoughts for me to think on?"

Elizabeth poured herself a mug of the hot drink, sat back down, and took a careful sip.

"Aye. I have an idea. I have heard from Ann Griswold that Captain Cullick is looking for help." She paused, a small smile forming at the creases of her heart-shaped mouth.

"Captain John Cullick of Hartford? Secretary to the Colony? Soon to be Commissioner to the Colonies, I hear? Why, he's a wealthy man, one of the wealthiest in Hartford." Josiah stood and helped himself to more cider. "Surely he has enough help."

Elizabeth shook her head. "Never enough help, Josiah. His house is the grandest in all of Hartford—besides the Wyllys house, of course. They claim that due to his demanding nature, he has trouble retaining help. They say his root cellar has many rooms. Imagine! And his stately home along the Little River is just far enough from Wethersfield."

Josiah gazed at his soon-to-be wife in astonishment. Where did she come forth with such ideas? He grabbed onto the thought and remained silent for a time. "Aye, my dear, this is a providential idea. How shall we proceed?"

Elizabeth hummed under her breath and began to clean up by the fire. "Let us drink up and be off to your house. You can hitch up your horse, and we shall make way to Captain Cullick's house for a visit."

"Now?" he asked, his eyes widening.

"Now!"

"So be it," he said, as he quaffed the last of the cider.

·•·

The couple walked the half mile at a pace to Josiah's house; then they hitched up his farm horse to the small cart readying for the two-mile trip to Hartford. Being Market Day, the town square would be bustling with townspeople bartering and buying goods. Hartford's Market was always on a Wednesday; Wethersfield's Market was on Thursday.

Josiah knew that Elizabeth's idea held merit. His cousin Katherine needed to busy herself, to have a position, and to have her own life. With her own wages she could stay where she pleased.

The cart rambled down the road to Hartford bumping into hardened ruts and clods of dirt. Josiah and Elizabeth snuggled together in the bracing chill of the late autumn air. Josiah pondered his good fortune—to have such a helpmeet as Elizabeth.

At last, Captain Cullick's home came into view; the grand house stood by the east bank of the Little River, a rivulet that flowed into the Great River. It boasted a lovely view; along the river's bend were willows and oaks hanging over the banks, their branches stretched out toward the lightly flowing waters. The stately home, burnished brown with whitewashed trim, had two full floors and diamond-paned windows. In the back of the house a widow's walk— as well as the Great River— was in partial view.

Both Josiah and Elizabeth had heard of the captain's reputation for strange behaviors, including unannounced fits of temper and odd habits. He was known to curse after a few rum toddies. Oftentimes people would watch him atop his walkway looking from his spyglass with serious intent—as if waiting for an enemy attack. People would laugh out of his earshot about his arrogant, odd ways, but Captain Cullick was a man to be reckoned with. No one wanted to get on the man's bad side.

The couple tethered the horse and cart to a nearby post, walked up the stairs, and stood huddled together on the stoop. Josiah lifted the iron knocker against the oaken door.

"Art thou ready, Lizbeth?" he asked, feeling unsure of himself.

"Aye, as ready as I'll ever be."

Josiah banged the knocker up and down three times and shivered as they waited to be received.

CHAPTER 5

"May I help you?" A servant dressed in a blue-grey woolen skirt, white waistcoat, black cap, and black shawl peered out from the open door.

"Is the captain in?" Josiah asked.

"Aye, so he is. Busy in his study. What's this concern?" She watched the pair closely with narrowed eyes.

He promptly removed his hat. "My name is Josiah Gilbert. This is my fiancée, Elizabeth. We heard the captain is looking for some help."

The servant nodded. "Would you both be in need of work then? Captain Cullick could use another man round this house." She boldly observed Josiah's muscled arms and strong wide chest.

"Nay, 'tis for my cousin Katherine. Please tell the captain we would like to see him."

The servant shut the door, and so they waited. Elizabeth shuffled in her boots trying to keep warm, stomping away the chill. "This was my idea. I hope we are doing right by coming here," she said under her breath.

"Too late," Josiah whispered as the door opened wide.

"Come in, please," the servant girl said. "The captain will see you now."

The pair lingered in the hall for a moment admiring the Great Room that lay on their left. Neither Josiah nor Elizabeth could take their eyes from its grandeur. Blue and white Dutch tiles graced the border of two large hearthfires on each side of the room. Porcelain figures from the East sat on a mantle. Maps and paintings hung on white wainscoted walls. Bells of different shapes and sizes hung from the ceiling near a grand light fixture with several candle sconces attached to it. A large open dining room could be seen on the right.

Josiah knew that only important people could live in such splendor. People who had money and power— like the captain. Like his brother Jonathan. Someday it shall be my turn, he thought.

They followed the young servant now scurrying down a thin corridor. She led them to a heavy wooden door and knocked briskly.

"Send them in," a gruff voice shouted.

"Here you be," said the young woman, who bowed, then let them into the room.

Captain Cullick stood with his back to the pair looking through a spyglass out the window. Shelves displayed leatherbound books and medals sparkled in wooden frames. Racks of firearms hung on one wall. Many more different-sized bells with cords and ropes filled each nook in the room. His wide desk was scattered with maps and trinkets. Two chairs sat empty in front of his desk. An hourglass stood on the table near him. The captain abruptly picked up the hourglass and turned it over.

He pivoted round to face Elizabeth and Josiah. The captain, of medium build, was short in stature but broad in the shoulders. He scrutinized them with small, grey-blue eyes and bushy eyebrows that arched, then descended into what looked like a thick, overhanging frown. His shock of unruly dark hair had strands of grey. Not old but not young, the captain had a heaviness about him, as if he still carried his battles around.

"So, you're the young Gilbert, eh? Your brother Jonathan is an upstanding man." He stood staring Josiah down and pointed to the chairs. "Take a seat young people, please. I'll do the standing." Josiah and Elizabeth promptly followed the captain's orders.

"Aye, Sir. Many thanks for your kind words."

The captain nodded, his thin mouth trembling.

"Very well. I hope you are more like Jonathan—but if you are anything like your brother Thomas and his wife Lydia— you can leave this instant!" The captain paused, mumbled something under his breath, and then said, "Never mind. What can I do for ye today?"

Josiah cleared his throat. "If I may, Sir. I hear you are looking for help. We speak on behalf of my cousin, Katherine Gilbert. She will be arriving soon from England. As Elizabeth and I plan to marry in the next month, Katherine will be in need of work. Room and board as well, Sir."

The captain pivoted to the window again, staring out toward the Great River in the short distance, silver-blue and calm. He bent down and fumbled with the latch of a small cupboard behind his desk. "One moment… if you please."

Josiah heard the clinking of a glass and saw the captain lift something up. They watched as his head flew back and heard a long sigh from his mouth as he dropped the glass back into the cupboard.

Captain Cullick licked his lips, turned to the pair, and sat down in the simple, high-backed wooden chair behind his desk. "Tell me, Goodman Gilbert, what qualifications does your cousin hold?"

Josiah thought for a moment. What did he *really* know about Katherine? Not much, he thought. But he knew he must give an answer.

"According to her letters and that of her mother, she was trained to minister to the army, caring for the wounded during the height of the Civil War."

"Ah, trained in the healing arts, eh?" The captain coughed and continued. "What side was she on, man? Is she a supporter of the Royalists, or a follower of Cromwell and his Rump Parliament?" Cullick's face glowed a bright red, and he began to huff.

This time Josiah knew how to answer. "I am certain she followed Cromwell's troops," he replied. "Just the fact she's chosen to come to New England, willing to work and to start a new life here, tells me she's been on the right side all along— the Puritan side."

"So… she comes because she's a Puritan in heart, soul, mind and body?" The captain lightly mused, "How old is the lass?"

"Nearing her mid-twenties, I was told."

"That old, eh?" The captain chuckled to himself. "Still young enough to be trained into a right servant girl. Do you think she takes orders well?"

"I am certain, Sir, given your status, that Katherine will not only take orders well, but will be much obliged by your generosity and good graces," Elizabeth answered.

The captain's bloodshot eyes blinked bright and his thin mouth rose to a half-smile. "When can she start?" he asked.

"As soon as she arrives, Captain. It should be any day now. We will bring her right around," said Josiah with relief.

"Aye, then I can look her over," said the captain. "Decide her suitability. Decide if she fits in and where she will fit best. Aye, bring her around. If I approve of her, she can board with the other servants. This house, should you be interested, holds a special quarter for them. We have plenty of room—and plenty of work." The captain found a paper, inkwell, and quill on his desk. "I'll write something up now. A quick contract. What say you, Gilbert? Would two years be appropriate for your cousin—as indentured to me?"

"Aye," said Josiah. He grabbed for Elizabeth's hand and held it tight. With Katherine working for the captain, they need not anguish over her anymore.

The captain finished his writing, let the ink dry, and passed the paper to Josiah. "Sign here," he ordered. "This will be our evidence."

Josiah signed the paper with not much of a glance at the writing. "So, it is settled then," he said, rising from his chair.

"Aye, bring her about. I will be here. My battle days are over. The only battles I fight now are the ones in this house."

"We are much obliged, Captain," Elizabeth said.

"Aye, Captain, grateful for your kindness," said Josiah.

"And I wish for you two great happiness in your married life together. Invite me to the ceremony. This Colony needs good news— and more babies!" With that he turned his back to the couple and proceeded to look out the window.

The interview was over. Katherine had a job —and a new master.

"What a fruitful meeting," Elizabeth said as they journeyed home. "I like the captain. He will do right by Katherine."

"But will Katherine do right by him?" Josiah wondered aloud.

CHAPTER 6

November 1651
Connecticut Colony

The shallop ribboned its way up the Great River carrying two dozen passengers. Katherine watched flocks of geese overhead flying south. The day being overcast, the river looked as grey-blue as the sky. Here she sat, chilled and tired, almost to her final destination.

"How close are we now?" she called to the ship's captain. As the ship rounded the bend in the river, Katherine pointed to a large, looming rock on the left. "And what's the yonder rock?" It brought to mind the stories she had heard as a child, the rock where the Lorelei lived, the sirens who sang to sailors, then lured them to their deaths.

"They call it the Rocky Hill," the captain shouted back to her, concentrating on the sails. "It's the only hill about this area made from rock. We steer clear of it, but 'tis a landmark to know we are not far from Wethersfield."

For a time, Katherine thought she might arrive earlier than scheduled, but the sail up the Great River had taken longer than expected. Between the boat getting stuck on stubborn sandbars and winds that becalmed the waters, she was surprised to be on time. Not late, but not too early either.

Today a breeze from the southwest pushed the craft further up the Great River. The crisp air invigorated Katherine's spirit.

"Wethersfield is but a league away now," chimed an old woman bundled in a cloak. "My grandbabies await. 'Tis been far too long." She sighed and smiled at Katherine.

Past the bend the river became wider, and on both sides, Katherine beheld vast tracts of farmland with small houses near the river. A long, sandy island set in the center of the river could be seen on the right; it was laden with oak and pine trees. Houses and farms appeared on one side of the island; the other side lay fallow.

"An island, imagine!" Katherine said aloud. "And people live there as well?"

"Aye. It's called Wright's Island. The natives call in *Manhannock*, or the Island of Merriment." The old woman chuckled. "They return during the growing season to help with the planting."

Katherine of a sudden felt a knot in her stomach, then a flutter of second thoughts passed in her mind. Would her cousins welcome her? Could she truly be the person she had become of late? Drops of sweat beaded around her temples, and she gripped her hands together. A case of the nerves was upon her.

She quickly found her snuff box for a pinch. She also realized she needed a wash-up. After all her travels, she smelled like fish, salt, and cheese.

The ship sailed close along the west bend of the island gliding onward. Across the river Katherine espied more meadows and tracts of now-fallow farmland.

"We follow the bend north, then around the loop, and head down south to the harbor," shouted the captain.

Katherine took in the new sights. The vast abundance of land and waterfowl, even in the stark November grey, appealed to her love of nature. She dug through her satchel and found her packets of seeds: English lavender, mugwort, thyme, wormwood. She hoped her cousin would allow her an herb garden. In turn, she would make herself useful with her healing arts. Back home her poultices and cures were well known. These thoughts reassured her.

The small ship traversed the north bend of the river and sailed south toward the harbor. Katherine watched the row of small, dark brown and grey squares getting bigger. She now recognized them as a large, wooden blockhouse with a palisade and several warehouses. Groups of people cluttered along the docks waving white cloths came into view. A bell clanged over and again.

She noticed one great warehouse; in front of it was a half-built ship held by pulleys and ropes. Throngs of men sawed wood, measured pieces to nail, and then banged mallets against the ribs of the ship. The smell of fresh pine and pitch tar filled her nose. Her stomach grumbled with hunger. The only thing she had eaten all day was a hard tack biscuit, a piece of cheese and a half glass of warm ale.

She thought how fine it would be to share her first meal in New England with her cousins. She had much to tell of her voyage, never mind all the questions she had for Josiah. She drew in a deep breath. Perhaps Wethersfield will be right with me... for I see how hard these people work, she thought.

The shallop loomed ever closer to the bustling dock. The townsfolk seemed almost as excited as she felt, waving, smiling, welcoming people, welcoming ships with much needed supplies. She realized that like back home, ships to harbor was always an exciting event, breaking up dull routines in a life of drudgery.

She immediately took a liking to all the activity along the harbor. For a moment she felt at home. But, she mused, how much more land this country had— more trees, more resources—and far fewer people. She breathed in the fresh, crisp, late autumn air and felt a wisp of freedom flow through her cap on the breeze, something she had not felt for a long time.

·—·—·

Katherine finally departed the shallop thanking the captain and his crew. She stood on the dock watching and waiting for her cousin. Was anyone anticipating her arrival? After a time she leaned against a post; her trunk lay heavy at her feet.

Then she noticed a young boy observing her with interest. He approached her cautiously. "Would thou be—Katherine—Gilbert?" he asked, squinting as he looked up at her. She stared down at the child.

"Aye, that would be me," she said, feeling tired, worn, and irritated of a sudden. Did they think so little of her as to send an errand boy?

"You look different than I thought."

"Well, nothing a good bath and scrubbing won't do to wipe any differences away," she said, heat rising at her neck, a vague annoyance setting in.

The boy searched the harbor. "Wait here. I'll let Goodman Gilbert know you've arrived."

With these words he raced down the dock and ran toward a path leading away from the harbor. While she waited, another ship arrived bringing more folk down to the docks. The heavy scent of cinnamon, clove, and nutmeg filled the air. "Ship in from the West Indies," she heard someone shout out. From the loud clamoring noises, Katherine knew many people were waiting for this ship's arrival.

She heard a dog bark, turned from the ship, and watched a man counting staves for newly built hogshead barrels. He raised his head and noticed her stare. "Aye, we make the staves right here in Wethersfield. We get a pretty-pence for these exports. In demand they are. Keeps everything tight and secure this way." His chest puffed out with pride.

Katherine nodded and smiled. She knew from everything she had seen at the harbor thus far these Wethersfield townsfolk were industrious. Would they accept her skills with the poultice, the charms, the healing herbs?

She stood, waited, and continued to wait, moving her head back and forth, becoming restless, and more anxious. The clacking, banging, and bustle along the harbor was chiseling her nerves. Perhaps she should have remained in Boston, where people were more timely, more civilized.

A woman brushed by her and bumped her basket against Katherine's side.

"Excuse me," the woman said, and turned to behold her. "Why, ye are new around these parts I'm guessing? Rough travel for you, eh?" The woman eyed Katherine from her rumpled, now dirty cap, to her blackened boots.

"Aye, that's right." Katherine gazed straight ahead to the placid river eager for her cousin to arrive.

"Can I help thee find your way? Do you know whereabouts you go?" The woman's clear blue eyes, fair hair, and round pink cheeks brightened Katherine's spirits. This woman at least, cared enough to want to help, she thought.

"I await my cousin. He's received word my ship has arrived. Over an hour I have waited, I will have you know." She stomped her foot, then stared down to her sodden boots, and shook her head. "Perhaps 'twas a mistake coming here."

"What's your cousin's name?" the pretty woman asked. "I live here in town. My name is Katherine Palmer. I await my husband Henry, who is purchasing some lemons and limes from the Merchant Warehouse. The fruit just arrived off the ship. Need them for those rum toddies my Henry enjoys. And they say they prevent sickness and plague."

"My cousin's name is Josiah Gilbert. I am Katherine Gilbert. I presumed he would be waiting for me. I plan to stay with him for a time until I get settled."

A smile stretched up on Katherine Palmer's face. "I do hope you stay in Wethersfield. It seems providential we share the same name. No matter, everyone calls me Kate." She brushed a lock of her thin, yellow hair from her forehead and tucked it under her cap.

"People back home called me Kat."

"Well, I like the looks of thee, Kat. I can tell already you are a smart lass and will do well here in this rugged, crude land we call home." She paused and cast her hand toward the river and then over the harbor. "I welcome you to this new land, and may God bless thee in your new adventures. I am honored to be your first friend in Connecticut Colony."

"And I thank thee Kate—for greeting and welcoming me as such." What a relief to speak to someone from the town, someone who truly welcomed her to this colony. For a moment Katherine didn't feel so alone.

"Once you are settled, Kat, perhaps we shall see one another at market." Kate cocked her head to the side. "You see, sometimes I go to Market in Wethersfield, sometimes in Hartford, and sometimes both!" She smiled warmly. "Women in this colony need their distractions, 'tis true." She placed a small hand to Katherine's arm. "I will be wishing you well now, Kat. Hoping your cousin arrives soon."

Katherine could only hope the same.

·—·

She did not have to wait much longer, for minutes later, a tall dark-haired, handsome young man came toward her. He tilted his beaver hat in greeting. He seemed to have a half-smile on his face. His brown eyes darted side to side. Was he nervous, annoyed—or both?

"You must be— Katherine?" he asked.

She nodded in relief.

He began to carry her belongings to a large area where horse-drawn wagons and ox-carts stood. She heard shouts from farmers and merchants ordering servants to lift goods onto their wagons. He stopped and turned towards her. "I am Josiah. Welcome to Connecticut Colony," he finally said. "I apologize for the waiting." He cast his eyes downward to his boots. "I was bartering tools with a neighbor."

"I understand you are busy," said Katherine, not caring in the slightest what he was doing. Josiah's pace quickened until he pointed out his wagon.

Sitting atop a seat in the front was a small woman bundled in a dark cloak. She had black hair, an upturned nose, pale skin, and striking brown eyes. "Welcome, Cousin Katherine, we are happy you made the trip safely. God has been good to us Gilberts of late." The woman smiled down at her.

"Let me introduce the two of you," announced Josiah. "This is my new wife, Elizabeth. We married a fortnight ago. With all the messages I received regarding your ship, I thought you would be early. In time for—"

"I did not know," said Katherine. "Nor could I control the tides nor the weather. But please let me congratulate you both on your nuptials." She felt even more like an outsider now, an intruder into her cousin's new life as a married man.

Josiah heaved her trunk onto the wagon and came around the front to help Katherine up to the seat next to Elizabeth. Elizabeth, unlike herself, smelled like fresh lavender and lemons. How embarrassing to know she smelled like fish, tobacco, and rotten cheese. And the way Elizabeth turned her nose up and looked away from Katherine—

Josiah clambered up into the driver's seat and with a whiplash to the horses' backs, he shouted, "Get on now!" With that command the wagon rumbled out from the harbor heading down the High Street toward the town center.

On the east side of the street, acres of meadows stretched down right to the river's edge. Flocks of ducks paddled silently through the water, letting the wind's currents swirl them about. A shaft of bright late afternoon light pierced the clouds. "Great wide tracts of land I see," Katherine said. "Must be very fertile soil in the spring."

"Aye, especially after the spring flooding," Josiah replied. "The river floods the meadow plains each year. We are indeed fortunate."

A row of two or three houses with acreage for farmland lay on the right side of the road. Imagine living in such houses with views of the meadowland, Katherine thought. She knew her seeds would thrive in such rich soil.

"Do you work crops in the meadows, Josiah?" she asked.

He nodded. "Aye, and we Gilbert brothers have purchased the old Hollister homestead. We will be passing by it shortly." The horses clopped on until Josiah pulled on the reins and shouted, "Whoa!" The wagon stopped at a road that intersected the High Street to the right. "Look this way," He pointed to the left. "You'll see the Hollister plot." He pointed a finger toward a notice in front of the grounds. "We plan to build the Gilbert homestead soon. I intend to get it ready; my brother Jonathan comes down weekly from Hartford and works the land; other times he manages his warehouses in Hartford. Your other cousin, my brother Thomas from Windsor, will also contribute with the labor. We will be building the house come spring."

Katherine realized the land Josiah and his brothers were purchasing was perfect for her future herb gardens. She would have everything she needed to make her salves and poultices. She started to feel welcome at last, beckoned by the land around her.

"I look forward to meeting my other cousins soon."

Then Josiah pointed to the right. "This here is John Nott's store. He's the local joiner. Right next to the store is Sadler's Ordinary. Across the road is the Meetinghouse, the Town Office, and the burial ground."

"Nice to live in a small village," she said.

He took an abrupt turn right onto the road with a sign posted, 'The Sandy Lane.' And sand there was, for sandbags lined the sides of the street. "Helps with the spring flooding. Makes it easier to get to Hartford. You'll see a lot of these sandbags around town."

"And what lovely farms grace this road," Katherine added.

"Three acres a piece; 'tis a fortunate location. Close to everything. And we Gilberts own acres of land in the meadows as well."

Katherine turned to Josiah and Elizabeth. "Is your present home near the Sandy Lane?" she asked, her stomach beginning to grumble again.

Elizabeth reached into her bag and offered Katherine a small oat cake. "Something to tide you over. Until we get you settled."

The Sandy Lane took a sharp, steep bend as the wagon heaved up the small hill. Then it flattened out onto a straight road. Katherine turned around and beheld the pink-grey, late afternoon light, the wide expanse of the meadows, the sounds of water fowl settling in, small birds chittering in the bushes, and in that moment felt peace. She knew this was why she had come so far—to find her place among this fertile land and her new family.

The wagon kept rumbling along the road until it came to another crossroads. A wooden sign weathered from the elements was shaped in the form of an arrow with the words burnt into it, 'Hartford Way- 2 miles' pointed straight ahead.

Josiah kept to the road. To Katherine it appeared that they were leaving Wethersfield. Josiah prodded his horses onward. "Ye must live on the outskirts of town, I presume," Katherine said. "Either way, it's lovely about these parts." She breathed in the clean air, so much cleaner than the dust and grime in Lancaster and London.

"Aye, hold onto the rail," he commanded both women. With one more lash against the beasts' back, he pushed the cart forward never taking his eyes off the road. They were on the Hartford Way passing wagons headed home to Wethersfield.

Why Hartford? Why now? She wondered to herself.

"Are we going to Hartford to visit your brother, Jonathan?" she asked Josiah.

"You'll see," was all he said.

Part II

THE DUTY

CHAPTER 7

The wagon crossed the bridge over the Little River. Several fine homes graced the bank of the Little River that flowed onto the Great River. One could see to the east the Great River behind the houses, glowing in silver-blue light.

Josiah steered the wagon toward the front of a stately home. "We stop here," he flatly said.

"Is this cousin Jonathan's house?" Katherine asked. "He's done well for himself, I see."

Josiah mumbled as she heard him calm his tired horses with soothing promises. They would have fresh water and oats to tide them over soon. What about her? She was treated with less care than her cousin's work horses. All she could think of was how tired, hungry, and dirty she felt and looked. Perhaps a nice hot meal was waiting for her in this wealthy person's home. Mayhap her cousin wanted to introduce her to folk from Hartford. All she could do was wonder— and wait.

"So, you are set then?" Elizabeth reached over and patted Katherine's arm. "All will be well—once you are settled."

"Settled? I'm set for naught but a hot meal, a wash-up, and a comfortable slumber," said Katherine tired of the delays. She needed no further attack of her tight-wound nerves.

Josiah jumped off and tethered the wagon to a post near to the house. "I will be but a few minutes," he called out, as he rushed up the stairs, and boldly knocked on the door. As the sun set, shadows darkened along the Little River. Yet glimmers of light remained; they cast thin, gentle rays onto the surface of the calm waters.

She bundled her worn cloak about her and shivered. England was never this cold in November. The frosty air and brisk winds were something else she would have to get used to. But she could not shake off the chilly reception she had received from her cousin; a tiny spark of anger burst open inside her. The beating of her heart quickened. Did her cousin and his new wife forget she carried Gilbert blood? Blood that carried that anger right to her heart and mind? An anger that could turn ice cold or flaming hot? *Where* were her cousins taking her?

The door opened, words were spoken, and just as quickly, the door shut again. Josiah returned to the wagon, wiping his brow and checking on the horses. Then he dragged Katherine's belongings up the few stairs to drop them on the stoop.

"Where are you taking my things?" she asked, confusion and panic in her voice. "Am I to spend my first night here?"

Josiah said nothing, as Elizabeth attempted to soothe Katherine with calming words. "The man who lives here is wealthy, Katherine. He's a prominent person in Hartford. Used to be a captain in the Indian Wars. Captain Cullick is his proper name."

Captain Cullick? She had never heard of the man. Why was she here—now? Too tired and angry, she could say no more—not yet.

Josiah came around the wagon and helped Katherine alight to the ground. "Here you be."

"Here I be? Here I be nothing, Josiah. Was this your plan all along— leaving me to a stranger's whim?"

Josiah refused to look at her; he just stared down at the ground. "Let's get you inside. The wind is picking up." He shivered and clutched her elbow. "The captain is ready to meet you." Tightening her mouth to a grim line, Katherine steadied herself— for what she knew not.

While Elizabeth waited in the wagon, the cousins entered the grand house. Down a long hall they walked, Katherine barely keeping pace with Josiah. At last they faced a closed door and Josiah knocked— hard and furious.

"Come in," cried a loud voice. The pair opened the door and entered. "Ah," the captain announced, lifting his head in greeting. He pointed to the two chairs in front of his desk. "Please sit. I see you finally brought your cousin around." He stared at Katherine while she sat, fumbling with her hands. "Can I get you both a hot drink?" The captain took a long sip from his own tankard.

"We're fine," Josiah said, speaking for Katherine. "My cousin has been anxious to meet you."

"You don't say, Goodman Gilbert? And I thought her sentiments might be to the contrary." The older man grinned, seemingly amused by his own words. "So Katherine, tell me a little about yourself, your background... please."

Why should he care about her background? The gall! It is not his business, she thought.

"I am twenty-five years of age, sir," she replied in a hesitant voice. "Trained as a nurse, I ministered to the soldiers during the war and made myself useful in the healing skills of the poultice, the salve, and the drink. I helped save many a man. And for this I am proud."

The captain peered down from his high-backed oak chair, and studied her face as if it were a map. "War? What side were you fighting for, lass? What side did you minister to?"

She paused. How should she reply? Should she be honest with this stranger? An answer appeared in her mind that she considered true.

"I took no side, Sir. I ministered where I was needed."

"No side, you say?" He shook his head back and forth." In war everyone must take a side."

"I did not and would not, Sir. I did what I was told."

"Call me Captain, please," he reminded her. "So, you did what you were told? Now that's what I like to hear." A slight smirk appeared on his face. "You're a maid who can follow orders. Good. Then it's settled." He drank from his mug, then banged it down hard against the desk. "Settled indeed." He wiped his mouth with his sleeve.

"Settled, Captain?"

The captain looked to Josiah who awkwardly clutched his hat. "I'd best be taking my leave, Captain. I will be back to check on my cousin come the morrow." He nodded to Katherine. "You'll be fine here, cousin."

"Good man you are, Gilbert. You run off now with your bride. Katherine is in good hands. Godspeed."

"Godspeed," said Josiah, quickly donning his hat and fleeing the room.

Katherine, almost in tears, could not stand the silence, the unknowing, the heaviness of this room, this house. "Please, Captain, I know not what this means. Even why I am here." Second thoughts of coming to Connecticut Colony filled her mind. Sorrow and anger mingled with the salt of her tears, starting to flow from her eyes onto her face. She clenched her fists hard.

"You know not why you are here?" the captain shouted. "Your cousin told you naught?"

"Nay." Katherine sniffed and let go a large sob.

"Hold onto yourself, girl. I allow for no womanly displays, especially…hysterics. Enough now. Conduct yourself with dignity."

What could she do in this very moment? Scream? Curse? She felt trapped, unable to escape with nowhere to go. "Then tell me, Captain, why *am* I here?" She sat up straight and wiped her eyes.

"Why? Your cousin and his wife recommended you to my service—since they knew I was in need of help around this house. Why, your cousin never told you he signed you on for two years of servitude, including pay once a fortnight, room, board, and victuals? They thought it best for them—no— I mean best for you."

"Best for me, Captain?" Katherine repeated, shaking her head. "Nay, not for me."

The captain stood up and thrust his hands to his hips. His eyes narrowed. "This is a display of ingratitude. You ought to be relieved your cousin thought highly enough of you to find you work— and to work for *me*. I allow no such displays of self-pity. I thought you were a tough lass. And I know you don't want to be a burden to your kin, now do you?" His lips quivering, he leaned close to her face.

Katherine sat in the silence of deep twilight. She had nothing to say to her new—master. This was not predicted in her astrological consult.

A knock sounded against the door.

"Aye, proceed in," the captain ordered.

A young girl of about eighteen, with light brown hair and light brown eyes, was dressed in a servant's grey skirt, black cap, white shirt, and apron. She looked at Katherine with alarm—staring at her now thread-worn cloak and dirty cap.

"Katherine, this here is Elizabeth Bateman. We call her Betty. Betty, welcome Katherine Gilbert, our new help."

"'Tis a pleasure." Betty clasped her hands together and blinked her eyes nervously. "Shall I take the new girl to our quarters, Captain?"

"Aye, Betty. That's my good girl. Show Katherine around and then take her up to the servants' quarters—and make sure she has a full servant's dress, clean and starched. She will be needing it soon enough—tomorrow in fact."

"Tomorrow, Captain?" Katherine asked, still shocked by this unexpected turn of events.

"Aye, tomorrow. Your duties begin first thing on the morrow. Betty will show you about, and teach you the routines. As you can imagine, routines are important to me. Discipline, routines, drills, smiling faces. We have no time for indulgences."

Captain Cullick leaned back in his chair looking satisfied. He waved a hand. "Now be off, both of ye."

CHAPTER 8

"Follow me," Betty said to Katherine after they departed the captain's study. The pair turned left down another narrow hall, passing the dining room on the right—a grand room with a grand table that filled the area and windows that looked out to the side of the house. Betty showed her the kitchen and the keeping room, a vast area in the back of the home that had everything that was needed: kettles, pots, hooks, cupboards, platters, and two large hearthfires for cooking. The back door of the kitchen led to the well and outhouse. "Cook is on her break," Betty said. "She will be returning shortly." Betty grabbed a tallow and lit it from the fire.

Then she took Katherine to the end of the hallway where two shut doors awaited them. The door on the left had the words *Root Cellar* with an arrow pointing down. The other door said *Servants*, the arrow pointed up. "Here be the stairwell down to the root cellar and a pantry," Betty explained, noting the door with the downward arrow. "This other door leads up to our sleeping quarters in the loft. Come now, I'll first show you the cellar."

They made their way to the root cellar down the winding wooden staircase that creaked under their feet. "There's quite a chill down here," said Katherine, her boots pounding the steps that echoed loud in the cold air.

"Tsk, tsk, complaining already, I hear," said Betty, cupping the tallow with care.

Katherine shivered, hoping her sleeping quarters were warmer. She thought descending these stairs seemed worse than the entirety of months aboard a ship, the bouts of nausea, the frustration and delays. Now she felt trapped. Was this the shining destiny Mr. Lilly foretold in her astrological predictions?

"There's a fire always going in the kitchen, and throughout the many hearthfires in this house," said Betty. "Part of your service here is to help keep them alight. But it looks like you are in need of a good meal. Nothing like hot victuals to get color back to the cheeks. We'll get you up to the kitchen soon."

Betty showed her about the main root cellar where vegetables like onions, carrots, parsnips, and yams were stored. Labeled hogshead caskets filled with dry goods and crates of drink lay stacked along the sides of the room. Herbs drying hung from the low ceiling swinging in the cool, stiff breezes.

Katherine trudged behind Betty back upstairs to the kitchen. "Here's Cook at last," Betty said, pointing to a woman dressed in dark blue and white. "Cook, this be our new help—Katherine's her name."

"Indeed." Cook, a stout, red-cheeked woman with a warm smile, eyed Katherine's soiled cloak, cap, and boots. She pointed to the table board. "Sit. I have a nice bowl of pottage awaiting you. Along with a thick crust of bread and fresh cheese."

While Cook ladled out the victuals, Katherine sat at the long, sturdy table, breathing in the fragrant smell of meat, peas, and onions, ready to pounce like a spider on the food. As she waited, she noticed the gleam of the hanging pots, the bright kettles, the freshly-shined pewterware. Everything in the captain's kitchen had its place—neat, tidy and in order.

"Here you go, my dear." Cook laid the steaming trencher platter in front of her and gave her a spoon and cloth. "Eat up. You'll feel better with some nourishment."

Unsightly as she looked and felt, Katherine could not resist stuffing the stew and bread into her mouth. Betty and Cook watched her wide-eyed as she devoured her meal. Let them look, she thought, as long as I can eat.

After she had eaten her fill, the questions began.

Where did she hail from? How old was she? Why was she here?

She wondered where she should begin, and how much of the truth she should tell them. "I am twenty-five and hail from the north of England. The Gilberts are my relatives."

"Is that so?" said Cook, wiping sweat from her ruddy face.

"Seems both my cousin Josiah and wife care naught for me," Katherine mumbled, self-pity returning once again.

"But *we* care and have need of you," said Betty. "We have been short of help for weeks; ever since the last girl left in tears. Fired by the captain, for what we still don't know. You are welcome here, Katherine, as long as you are not afraid of work—and you obey the captain. His temper can be fierce."

"Who else works for the captain?"

Betty waved her hand about in the air. "He's got domestics that come and go. Many are seasonal. Many have come…and many have gone." She twittered like a sparrow.

Katherine drank the rest of her pint of ale and smacked her lips. "I'm not a whit afraid of work. Never was."

"So, it is settled then. We are grateful to have you here," said Cook, her face softening. "Betty, show Katherine to the sleeping quarters. On the morrow after breakfast, you will receive your work duties. Rising is four-thirty, often before the captain's vexing rooster crows up the dawn."

"Aye," said Betty. "You will need your rest. I'll show you the grounds tomorrow. 'Tis a beautiful view of the Great River."

Betty lit another small tallow and led her to the door with the arrow pointing up. "To think I now have company and someone to make my burden lighter strengthens my faith. Why, I have been praying for this help for weeks. God hath answered my prayers. Divine Providence, I should call it." She smiled warmly at Katherine.

At least this girl, younger than Katherine by a few years, was happy to welcome her to the household. Someone appreciated and needed her. But Katherine was anything but happy. She was resigned to accept her fate—for a time.

As they climbed the winding steps to the loft, Katherine asked Betty, "Is there privacy here?"

"Aye, a bit. The loft is partitioned, so you and I share one section. Cook and any extras have the other area. I will be no bother to you, Katherine. I try to keep to myself. The captain works me hard and I get through the days. Having another set of hands will help."

"So there will be *little* privacy for me." Katherine mused.

"I'll give thee your privacy—if you give me mine." The two stayed silent as they trudged the final stairs to the landing. "Here we be," Betty said with a flourish. "Follow me."

All seemed quiet above the rest of the house. Katherine, for a brief moment, felt some peace. Maybe it was because she was so tired. All she could think of was sleep. She could not remember her body feeling this dull and heavy.

Betty stopped at the first door on the right, opened it, and raised her tallow. "This is where we sleep." The room under a great eave had a small window looking out to the grounds and to the Great River. The light of a waxing moon shone pale. A pallet lay on each side of the room. Near each pallet stood shelving and a few cupboards. A worn Bible sat on a small table. A chair stood near the table with a fresh set of servant clothing draped over it. Fresh rushes and sprigs of dried lavender graced the floorboards. A chamber pot stood in a corner of the room.

Under her bed she noticed her trunk and bag. She touched the quilt atop her bed and felt the soft, down feathers. At least the captain made certain his servants slept well. This is the warmest welcome I have received since landing in Connecticut Colony, she thought.

She thought again. Tomorrow would be her first day of work. All must go well. On the surface, nothing must appear amiss. She would work to fit in. And no one must know she was determined to make a plan to remove herself from these bonds she had never agreed to— for she deserved this not! She vowed to herself silently that the right plan for her would come— and if it wasn't Mr. Lilly's plan—or God's plan— it would be *her* plan. For if this was God's plan for her—she would think no more on such notions.

"Thank you, Betty. I am grateful for your kindness. But now I can think of naught but sleep."

Betty held the candle alight and smiled at her. "Aye, I'll let you be. I have some cleaning up to finish downstairs. You get your rest. Tomorrow you'll get a good wash-up, breakfast, and then I presume, you will meet the captain's family. Sleep in peace. You need to be fit for your first day of service."

Katherine fell onto the pallet as Betty shut the door. Just as quickly she sat back up and pulled out her satchel. She felt inside it to make certain all her things were in place. She reminded herself to check Mr. Lilly's astrological forecast on the morrow for the winter months ahead. She shook her head with tired disbelief. How could such a betrayal have happened? She needed hope and renewed faith in Mr. Lilly's uncanny predictions. "No matter," she told herself. "I am here. Tomorrow I'll find time to review my astrological aspects. And no one needs to know—anything."

She shrugged off the mounting anger towards her cousin and the captain, took off her boots, clothes and cap, and changed into a shift. She lay her head atop the soft pillow, taking comfort in the familiar scents of lavender and pine until sleep blessedly and finally overcame her.

CHAPTER 9

I n the still of dark she heard the loud, persistent tinkling of a bell. Someone was shaking her. "Time to get up, Katherine." Betty hovered over the bed, a tallow in her hand, and then lit another in a wall sconce. "'Tis morning. Here, I brought you some hot cider."

Half asleep, Katherine lifted her head. The lull of the quiet was what she needed. More sleep, not noisy bells, not at this hour. The steam and scent of the cider filled her nose. She stretched out her hand and grasped the mug.

"There's warm water in the basin here in the corner. There's a new cloth on the stand for a wash-up. God knows you need it." Betty's nose twitched in disdain. "Your servant dress is ready. Drink up now, wash, dress, and come downstairs for breakfast. You'll need a hot meal to start your first day." While Katherine sat and sipped her cider, she heard Betty muttering about everything they had to do today. "Be quick about it. The captain likes us ready by first light." And with those words, Betty departed.

She admitted to herself the cider tasted well enough, and she had slept soundly her first night in the captain's house. Still in her shift, she walked to the window and stared out at the grey sky to the east, beginning to brighten with sharp rays of pink and gold light. She glanced down to the faded outline of the captain's now fallow garden, dead stalks lying like a patchwork quilt about the grounds. She vowed to herself she would find a way to leave this place—even if it meant saving for a return passage home. Later in the day, she thought, she'd find time to review Mr. Lilly's *Almanack* that helped her follow the moon's phases and astrological signs. She shook her head to cast these intruding thoughts away. She had work to do.

Quickly she removed her shift, then washed away the grime, dirt, and odors from her skin. The warm water soothed her, briefly letting her forget the shock and horror of yesterday. After drying herself, she dressed in her new servant's attire—a woolen grey skirt with a white waistcoat and apron— then fixed the starched black mobcap atop her head. A small, pewter looking glass hung against a wall. Katherine regarded her new self, and was pleased with what she saw— with the exception of dark rings around her swollen eyes. She tucked her thick hair snugly into the cap, squeezed her cheeks, and pinched her wide mouth to bring bloom to her lips.

By the time the sun began to rise, she was ready. Her footsteps pounded down the spiral stairs, pounded with an angry determination. She opened the door to the hall and rushed toward the kitchen. She vowed to herself once again, she would make a better life. Until then, she was at the mercy of Captain Cullick.

She entered the kitchen. The smell of fresh bread baking and the sound of bacon spitting grease from a large pan made her stomach rumble. "How now? A good morrow to you, Katherine. You look right pleasant and prim in your new dress. Did you sleep well?" Cook asked, hanging a kettle of water on a hook that hung over the fire.

"Aye," said Katherine, rubbing her eyes. "I need more of it though."

"You will have plenty of rest and sleep when you're dead and gone," Cook said laughing, busying herself flipping the bacon. "But sit for now—have your meal. You will need your strength to keep up with the captain's demands."

In front of the blazing fire, Betty bent over stoking the flames with a poker. "Girls, sit. Eat," demanded Cook, face aflush from the heat.

Katherine decided she liked the no-nonsense Cook and kind-hearted Betty.

A young lad of about sixteen waited near the tableboard. "Here is my son, James," said Cook. "He helps me as he helps the captain. Works the grounds when he is needed and runs errands. James, welcome our new help... Katherine's her name."

The young man nodded and smiled graciously.

"You can call me Kat," she said. "They did back home."

Betty, Cook and James looked wonder-eyed at her.

"Why of course, Kat," Betty said. "The name suits you."

"And 'tis a pleasure to meet you, Kat," James said before abruptly taking his leave.

Cook placed a platter of hearty victuals in front of her: a rash of bacon, hot biscuits with a slab of butter, an egg scrambled and a great slice of cheese. Katherine thought this the finest meal she had partaken in months. All at the servants' table!

"Do you always eat this well?" Katherine asked, a mouth half full of biscuit.

"Captain makes certain of that. He can be generous with his help—when the mood suits him," replied Cook. "Just take care not to anger him...." She fanned her brow with a cloth. "Just do as you are told, Kat. You will be fine."

As Katherine stuffed the last morsel into her mouth, James returned. "The captain will see you now," he told her. "He's waiting." A fresh case of the nerves overcame her. She needed her snuff box, but that would have to wait. She stood, wiped crumbs from her fingers, pressed down her apron, and then fixed her cap.

"Follow me," said James as he led her to the captain's study. He knocked hard and smiled at Katherine. Then he left her waiting. Alone.

"Come in," she heard.

Captain Cullick was awaiting her. Alongside him stood an attractive woman, heavy with child, and a young, pretty dark-haired girl of about fourteen. A small boy of about two ran around the room chasing a ball with determination.

"I take it you slept well your first night?" the captain asked.

"Aye, Captain. Slept well enough," she answered.

"Sit down, girl." He pointed to the chair in front of his desk. "This is my wife, Elizabeth. This here is my daughter Mary, from my deceased first wife. The young girl smiled widely and nodded. "And my son, John." He pointed to the chubby toddler running about. Katherine thought that little John was the only member of the household who could create disorder—and get away with it.

The captain's wife smiled kindly down at her. "Welcome. We are relieved to have new help."

Katherine decided now was the time to explain herself. "Please, I mean no offense. But I never signed on for this position."

Before Elizabeth had time to reply, the captain began to pace the room. "Elizabeth, take John and Mary out. Now! Let him run about elsewhere, I've got business to attend to here."

Elizabeth grasped John's chubby hand and left with Mary, who grinned at Katherine on her way out the door. Then Captain Cullick approached Katherine. He bent down close to her; she could smell the scent of bacon and egg on his breath. "*You* didn't sign. But your cousin did in your stead. He signed two years for your services. Told me you were in need of a job." He returned to his desk, rustled through a pile of papers and retrieved a wrinkled form that he thrust at her. "Here— see for yourself."

There was cousin Josiah's signature—her own relative signing her to two years of indentured servitude. She shook her head in disbelief. She would comply with the captain's orders—for now.

"Are ye satisfied?" he asked her. She remained silent. "Today, for your first day, you will follow Betty in all she does. Learn from her." He fixed her a narrow gaze. "I will especially require your help next week. I have invited some prominent folk for midday meal. Do not disappoint me, Katherine. If you have further questions, ask Betty or Cook. I need not be disturbed."

He turned his back to her, and moved to the window looking out toward the river. "And—" the captain cleared his throat. "One more item—after a fortnight of hard work, you may earn an afternoon off. All depends upon your performance. Wages are given every Friday. And remember, part of your wage goes for food and board."

"Is that all, Captain?" she asked, feeling weary and ready to leave his dreadful study. He pivoted about and faced her again.

"That's all for now, lass. I expect to see you serving the dinner platters and drink to my guests next week. Stay in the background— stay silent as death itself." He chortled, huffed, and bent down to his cupboard, where he retrieved a noggin of something, and drank it heartily. "The less you say, the better for you... and for us all." He smacked his lips.

She stood and made ready for the door. The new servant skirt was stiff and hard to move in. She would get accustomed to it, she thought, but would she ever get used to the captain's harsh, demanding tones? Katherine resolved she would bide her time. What would Mam think? The thought of saving enough shillings and pounds for a return passage filled her mind.

And hadn't Mr. Lilly warned her of 'watching her impulses to further herself—that might cause vexations amongst others?' How could she possibly further herself as a servant in Captain Cullick's house? But she had no time to think, for Betty was scrambling down the hall toward her, calling her name, letting her know there was much to do—at once.

CHAPTER 10

A week later there was a knock at the door. The house was dusted and polished to a shine; everything was prepared in exact accordance with the captain's orders. The house smelled like fresh lemon, rosemary, pine, and roasting meat.

"Answer the door." Captain Cullick's voice echoed down the hall. Katherine promptly opened the door and greeted the three men waiting to be received, practicing what Betty in jest called "the meek and welcome bow." But beneath her meek exterior, Katherine's emotions raged. She clenched her hands together hard, knuckles bone-white, and gritted her teeth as if she wore a horse's bit, preventing her from her normally wide-mouthed smile.

She welcomed the men in, and stepped toward the back of the hall. Betty and James joined her to form a greeting line. A stocky, broad-chested man thrust his cloak and beaver hat into her waiting arms, whilst the rest of the servants received the other men's cloaks and hats. They hung them on nearby pegs, and then returned to their line formation.

The stocky man eyed Katherine with small, narrow black eyes, as if she were livestock to be assessed and graded. She shuddered and felt her neck go stiff. Why was he staring at her? She heard the captain's boots pounding the hallway floor coming closer. He spread his arms wide in welcome. "How fare ye, men? 'Tis always a pleasure to see you."

"Indeed, John. 'Tis always good to visit," said the tall, older man with flowing dark and grey hair. "The Goodwife sends her well wishes from up north, for God's good Providence to the family." He handed a small package to the captain. "A gift for the new babe coming soon."

"William, many thanks. 'Tis an honor to have such a distinguished judge in our presence today. Girls, James—this here is Judge William Pynchon come all the way from Springfield." He turned to the younger man. "And Katherine, this is Samuel Wyllys, soon to be a magistrate I hear. Just finished studying law at Harvard."

The young, thin man nodded, color rising to his cheeks, and he flashed a dim smile at Katherine and the others. "Nice to be here again," he said. He cast his gaze about the rooms. "Captain, your furnishings are rivaling my own family home for the most distinguished in Hartford. And from all I hear, you will be Commissioner to the Colonies soon. Huzzah! From a Magistrate and Secretary to the Colony, to now Commissioner." Samuel Wyllys's eyes beheld the captain in high regard.

The stocky man with crow black eyes and short-beaked nose was clearly a man of authority. His eyes continued to bore into Katherine. "I see you have new help, Captain. Haven't seen the likes of this maid round these parts."

"Let me introduce you," the captain said. "Our new help's name is Katherine Gilbert, cousin of Josiah, Jonathan, and Thomas. Just arrived from England and was in need of work—so I was told. Josiah signed her on for two years of service. Providential I would say, considering our second babe is on the way." He turned to Katherine. "This here is Major John Mason, a true hero of the Pequot Indian War. We've fought

many a battle together. A braver man I have never known." He patted
the man on the back heartily.

"'Tis truly a pleasure," Katherine heard herself say, not meaning it
a whit.

Katherine knew naught about any Indian wars and wasn't certain
she wanted to hear anymore.

Major Mason narrowed his eyes; the sun's reflection from a
window made them look red— almost devilish, so Katherine thought.
"Thank you for the kind introduction, Captain. Surprised you left
off any mention of witches," he said, a slight grin to his face.

Katherine shuddered.

Witches?

"We'll save that talk for later," said the captain, as he led the men
toward the Great Room's hearthfire.

·-•-·

Katherine busied herself setting the tableboard in the dining room.
The pewter was polished, dust swept up, and everything in its proper
place. After the table was set with the captain's finest pewterware,
Katherine rushed back to the kitchen.

Betty was helping Cook with the meal. "What would you have me
do next?" she said out of breath. She knew she must present herself as
confident and assured, even as sweat formed on her brow and palms,
heart beating to a quick pace.

"Help us here first," said Betty.

"Will the mistress be at table?" Katherine asked, arranging items
in the keeping room.

"Nay, she's in bed. Doctor's orders until she gives birth. Lying-in
for the time."

A loud tinkling of a bell sounded. "Remember," Betty said to her, "one bell means to get prepared. Two soundings of the bell, 'tis time to serve the captain and his guests." After several minutes of preparations, the sound of two bells clanged.

At the savory smell of Cook's meat pies, Katherine's stomach grumbled. But before the pies were served, she had to ladle the first course, steaming vegetable soup into bowls, along with a fresh piece of brown bread on the side. She cautiously approached the open doors leading to the dining area, then carefully placed the tray on a nearby serving side-table. The men, all seated, looked to her with anticipation waiting for the soup.

"At last!" said Captain Cullick. "I am famished. Major Mason, will you kindly say grace?"

The men bowed their heads. Katherine did the same.

"Lord God, we thank thee for the bounty of this day. We thank thee for the peace that can only come after many battles. May we, the righteous of this Colony, see to the battles. Dear Lord, with your help, we conquer all evil. Amen."

A chorus of quick amens resounded, and Katherine began to place the soup bowls afore them. After the men had finished, she cleared the table as Betty entered with the main victuals. "Return the bowls to Cook. Then come back to join me." Betty whispered. "Are you alright?"

Katherine nodded. She hadn't dropped a morsel or spilled a drop of anything. Her hands stayed calm and steady…the steadiness that had helped her when she ministered to the wounded back home. If she could witness an amputation or apply a tourniquet, she could do this chore.

She hurried to the kitchen, took a deep breath, scraped the plates, and placed the soiled dishes into a large bowl. Then she returned to help Betty with the serving of the savory meat pies.

"Betty," announced the captain. "High compliments to Cook. Not a one in Hartford can surpass her meat pies. Here." He reached in his pocket. "A pine shilling for her talents." Betty, flustered, took the coin and left Katherine alone in the room. She waited by the serving table lest she was needed.

"So… William, what's the good word from Springfield? Any updates on the Parsons' trial?" Captain Cullick asked. All eyes were on the judge from Massachusetts.

"Aye. Hugh Parsons sits in jail awaiting trial. His wife remains hysterical— maniacal in fact. Hugh will be tried as an accomplice to murder of their infants, and charges of witchcraft are in order."

"Witchcraft? You don't say?" Major Mason murmured. "Like a plague… it seems to spread."

"And this is why I need to ask you gentlemen for advice," continued Judge Pynchon. "I know that you, Major, and the Captain have served on jury trials convicting the Carringtons and Goody Basset of the crime of witchcraft and entertaining Satan. I've gone through many of the depositions myself against the Parsons and need to know if we have enough to send them to Boston for trial." He looked to young Samuel Wyllys. "And with your fresh mind, ideas, and knowledge of the law—between us here—I will get the advice I need."

Captain Cullick leaned over the table, lips trembling. "Right you are, Judge. No need to worry. Let's look at the evidence here. Two infants gone, most likely taken by the hands of the parents. The wife accuses the husband of murder. Yet she is guilty as well. It's infanticide, it is. And both must pay—with their lives." He pounded his fist on the table rattling the silverware. He frowned with his eyebrows knit together as if he were the one preparing for a fight, panting with quick breaths of air.

"Indeed," said Major Mason, nodding in agreement.

Judge Pynchon slowly took a sip of beer. "So then Major, what is *your* advice pertaining to this matter? I know in the past we've disagreed over the treatment of Indians. Let us leave this behind for the time." Katherine glanced at Judge Pynchon and saw something in his eyes. Was it sorrow? Compassion? It was hard to tell. She stood stock still.

"I say waste no time, Judge. Hang them both as witches," said Mason. "For the sake of the lost infants. For the sake of Massachusetts Colony. Hang them!"

"First the evidence must be reviewed and then a trial with witnesses will follow. "I think the wife too sick to cooperate, I'm afraid," said Judge Pynchon.

Captain Cullick looked askance at Katherine. "You girl, bring us more beer."

Jolted from her thoughts, she straightened up, brought the pitcher to the table, and refilled their mugs. Just then Betty entered with the dessert on a tray—pumpkin souffle with a whipped topping. "Perfect timing, Bette," the captain said. "This talk has worked my appetite up for something sweet."

Betty served the dessert, as Katherine cleared away the remaining platters.

She scurried off with the plates on a tray, now realizing she dwelt in the house of one who condemned others as witches and cared for naught that they went to the gallows. She shivered and tried to cast the thoughts away.

Something about Major Mason scared her as well—the black, unflinching cold eyes that were haunting— and the smug pride he took in calling himself a condemner of witches.

CHAPTER 11

After the captain's guests departed and the platters were washed and dried and the tableboard and utensils cleaned, Katherine finally had time to speak with Betty alone. The pair sat in the loft resting for a while. "You never told me that Captain Cullick sat on witch trials, and condemned people to the gallows," said Katherine.

"The captain is a fair man and if he sees fit to hang a witch, what can I do but my work?" replied Betty.

"Have many been sent to the gallows around these parts?" Katherine asked, suddenly feeling a pang of nerves set in. She reached into her satchel for her snuff box. As she pulled it forth, the Lilly book fell flat out to the floor.

Betty stared down at the book before Katherine could grab it back up.

"*Christian Astrology!*" exclaimed Betty. "Pray tell, do you do astrology—for other people as well as yourself? Do you...tell fortunes?"

"Why would you think that?" Katherine asked, as she picked the book from the floor. "I study my own chart which helps me map my future."

"Did your chart predict you would arrive at Captain Cullick's as a servant?"

Katherine's eyes sparked with anger, and she gritted her teeth. "Nay, of course not! There are writings in my notes though, that say I may be surrounded by false friends."

Betty blinked. Her eyes rounded. "I would ne'er be a false friend to you Kat, rest assured."

"Tell not a soul." Katherine removed her snuff box. "Tell not a soul about this book, nor my readings— nor my habits. That's what true friends do. Keep secrets."

Betty drew closer. "You can trust me. And could you... would you... read my native chart? Make predictions for me and my future? Please?"

"Aye, if I can trust you, I will."

They were interrupted by the sound of the captain's bell, this time an incessant clanging that offended Katherine's ears. Vexing bells, she thought. I would like to throw them all into the river. "What now?" she wearily asked.

"I know not. I just know we are needed," Betty said, and dashed out the door.

Katherine knew she must do the same, but she decided not to rush. She would have her much needed snuff break first before she faced the captain. Finally, she was ready. Down the loft stairs she flew until she found herself knocking on the captain's door.

"Enter," she heard the order. Betty stood alongside James and Cook. All eyes were on Katherine. "I demand promptness from my servants," the captain reminded her. "Tarrying in one's room is not allowed. Why, I could withhold your wages. But for now, never mind." He paused, his sharp narrow eyes bearing down on her. "My company was quite satisfied with your work today. All of you."

Betty beamed with pride at Katherine.

Captain Cullick stood, reached for the hourglass, turned it over, and addressed the servants. "I will be leaving tomorrow for a fortnight or so, heading upriver to aid Judge Pynchon with the Parsons' trial. Needs more of my advice and expertise, so he says. I still carry my duties as a magistrate. I'm obliged to offer my ideas and expertise. In the meantime, see to the Mrs. And to your chores. I expect a fine report about all of you." He stiffened up like a soldier.

He focused his attention on Betty and James. "You two may leave now. Give my praises to Cook. Katherine, please stay behind. I need to speak with you in private."

After the others left, Captain Cullick asked Katherine to sit. "Rest at ease," he ordered her. She waited, running her hands along her skirt pressing the wrinkles away. She smoothed her cap on the sides and made eye contact with him.

"What now, Captain?" she asked.

The captain narrowed his eyes at her—again. "Your cousin and his wife stopped by to see how you were faring."

"Why did not you use one of your *bells* to call for me?"

"You were busy with the dishes in the kitchen. I did not want to disturb your work."

"He is still my cousin." Katherine cared not a whit about seeing her cousin. But she boiled inside realizing Captain Cullick thought her menial chores more important. And how she wanted to tell Josiah what she *really* thought of him. She would have her chance— someday.

"They were in a hurry. Headed out to Windsor to visit those *other* Gilberts, Lydia and Thomas."

Katherine grimaced. "You'd think they would want *me* to meet the other members of my family."

"Lydia and Thomas? Visiting those thieving, no good lying, ne'er-do-wells? Not on my watch. You are to stay here! Are you not appreciative of your new home? Forsooth, girl… you are an ungrateful lass."

"Do you consider Josiah, this cousin of mine and his wife welcoming me warmly?" she asked, knowing it was a useless pursuit of her question.

"They got you this position, didn't they? Be thankful for what you have. I will have no ingrates among my staff. Toughen up lass! They came and inquired of your wellbeing. Isn't that enough?"

No, it wasn't enough for Katherine. She wished she had never set foot on the shores of this rude settlement. She *would* save her pine shillings for a passage home, however long it took her. The sand in the hourglass flowed fast. Would this meeting ever end? At last, the captain waved a hand. "That is all."

"Godspeed on your journey upriver, Captain," Katherine said, relieved he would be gone for a time.

"And stick to your work. No use meddling, now or anytime, whilst you live under my roof."

CHAPTER 12

Captain Cullick was away upriver. During this time with the captain gone, Katherine felt lighter and freer; she even found herself humming the tunes of her favorite ballads from the Old Country, singing like a high-pitched sparrow. She also found some time to make notes on her astrological aspects, and since Betty had asked her, she began to draw up Betty's nativity chart.

It was a Wednesday, Market Day in Hartford. Cook asked Katherine to take a basket to find some woolen goods, as the weather was becoming colder and windier with each passing day; light bits of snow now covered the tops of roofs, trees, stones, and roads. She wasn't accustomed to such cold and biting winds. England was warmer—in so many ways.

But there was a beauty to the stark greyness of Hartford: the sharp rocks glazed with ice, the shiny morning hoar frost, the silver-smooth ribbon of the Little River, and behind the house, the Great River swirling with eddies of thin ice and ripples capped by small, blue-grey wavelets. And for Katherine, Market Day harkened back to home, where townspeople would gather for gossip and to barter goods. She looked forward to her little outing and to get away from the captain's house.

Meetinghouse Square, where market was held, wasn't far— just a short walk along the Little River Highway. She turned right toward the meetinghouse and passed the local tavern filled with people sharing news and taking a break from their work-a-day. She took notice of the stocks, the pillory, and the dreaded whipping post alongside Market Square, a grim reminder of the punishments for law breakers.

Finally, she arrived to market. In one corner stood cattle lowing; in another, horses pawed their hoofs snorting steam through their nostrils. Dogs ran about the square while cats ambled warily in search of a discarded morsel. The fragrant smell of roasting meat, onions, sweet potatoes with molasses amid thick smoke filled the air. Here at Meetinghouse Square, it was but steps to the landing where rows of warehouses sat along the Great River.

Here she felt like she was home. She could go bargain with whom she chose and pretend for a time she was someone other than a servant. She pulled her dark, hooded cloak closer around her to keep the river chill away. She espied a woman displaying baskets full of skeins of wool, yarn, homespun, and containers of brightly colored dye made from the juices of plants.

As she began to walk toward the wool table brushing past chatting townsfolk, she heard a faintly familiar voice. "Kat—how now?" She turned and recognized Kate Palmer from Wethersfield, the woman she had met on the docks.

"Kate! A good morrow. 'Tis a pleasant surprise to see you."

Kate's gold hair was smoothed tight in her cap. She wore a lavender skirt under a thick brown cloak. It complimented the bright blue of her eyes.

"So—we meet again, Kat. I have not seen the likes of you in Wethersfield. I have been watching for you. And here you be." Kate smiled as the friends drew close.

"Aye. Can you tarry a moment, Kate?" asked Katherine. "Let me first make a bargain for some wool and yarn."

"Of course."

After a time, Katherine returned to Kate, her basket filled with wool stuffs.

The pair walked together toward the Great River. "What happened, Kat? When we met, you were waiting for your cousin Josiah." Kate stared down at Katherine's dress. "And you're wearing a servant's dress?"

Katherine sighed. "My cousin Josiah arranged an indentured position for me at the home of Captain Cullick. Delivered me there with ne'er a warning, a bath, nor a meal. Signed me on for two years he did!"

"You? Indentured?" Kate Palmer's mouth was agape. "For two years you say? Why, the gall of your kin. I looked for you at Market in Wethersfield, watched for you down at the harbor. Thought maybe you took one look at our crude settlement and decided to leave. If I had known—"

"Aye, Kate. At least you've been thinking of me. I never got a true look at Wethersfield. Just glimpses of the vast meadowland and the open farms close by. Seems a lovely town."

Kate Palmer stamped her foot. "This is hogwash and I will do what I can to find another place for you, away from that beast of a captain. All of Hartford is afeared of him… so they say."

"I will bide my time," said Katherine, patting the stiff, raw wool further into her basket. "Little did I know the captain condemned people to the gallows—for witchcraft!"

Kate grabbed Katherine's arm. "Hush, make no mention of this lest others may hear."

Katherine glanced about the Great River's edge; no one was about.

"Just be careful what you say," Kate warned her. "And to whom. Townspeople love gossip—it's like food for them—nourishes the vexations and stirs things up. Makes them feel alive. Have no part in it."

They found a bench nearby and sat watching settlers on rafts and Indians paddling canoes and traversing the waters in wide circles. Several thin, frosted sheets of ice floated down the river, but boats still sailed on it. Not for long, Katherine thought— and shivered.

"Answer me this, Kat. Art thou a churchgoer? Have you gone to Meeting here in Hartford yet?"

"Twice I attended Meeting in a month. And twice I fell asleep." Katherine laughed aloud.

Kate looked askance at her.

"Kat, you'd best not give these folks any reason to suspect you. Go each week from this moment forth. A Sabbath breaker is viewed as a criminal. My Henry and I attend meeting each Sabbath in Wethersfield along with the children." Kate paused. "Though we care more about the meeting *after* the service. There we discuss news, the weather, crops, seeds…farm topics of sorts."

"So you and your family attend meeting for the show of it?" Katherine asked.

"Aye. It's a way to keep our place in the community and to keep the scolds' tongues from wagging." Kate leaned over and whispered to Katherine. "We have other gatherings too. Gatherings of a different sort." She stared off toward the river.

"What gatherings?"

"Celebrations of sorts. We call them merrymeets. Cakes, ale, songs."

"Aye," said Katherine wistfully. "I know of these merrymeets from the Old Country. I miss a good frolic, although 'tis best in the spring, isn't it?"

Kate nodded, and the friends had a brief chuckle.

"Would you care to attend?" Kate asked. "I could let you know, now that I know where you are staying."

She was being invited to a merrymeet! Katherine gasped at her friend.

"Think about it, Kat. It's one of the few pleasures we have. 'Tis better than just attending quilting bees, muster days, and corn husking. 'Tis a tedious life here at times, so my Henry and I look forward to a little merrymaking."

"Perhaps," said Katherine, thinking about all the chores she had left in the day. "I will think on your invitation. Mostly, I'm thankful to have you as a friend, Kate."

"And I feel the same, Kat." A tall, lanky man with dark wavy hair approached them, signaling to the pair. "That's my Henry," Kate said. "I must go now." She took one of Katherine's hands. "I'm glad we found each other. And I know we shall meet again soon."

CHAPTER 13

Windsor, Connecticut
December, 1651

After the midday meal Josiah and Thomas sat at table, while Elizabeth and Lydia cleared off the platters. The brothers glared at one another, their bodies stiff, backs arched like cats.

"Why didn't you introduce Katherine to us?" Thomas asked. "She's *our* cousin too. To think you dropped off our kin at Captain Cullick's house as a servant? Indentured for two years? By God's work, Josiah, you have got the Gilbert heart of stone. What say you?"

"I received a letter from cousin Richard in England."

"And?"

"He warned me about Katherine. Wrote me of her ungodly ways. Wrote that she followed the troops—in a wanton way— if you must know."

"So now you believe everything you read? You gave her no chance, Josiah." Thomas shook his head in disgust.

Josiah immediately regretted telling his Windsor relative of Richard's letter, of Katherine's arrival, or what he and Elizabeth had done. Why would Thomas, or for that matter, Lydia, understand their actions? Both of them had been convicted of petty crimes and sent to the workhouse

for a time. Wasn't that how they met? They had brought shame upon
the Gilbert family. They were nothing but trouble. He would ne'er be
the one to introduce Katherine to his brother.

Thomas continued. "You profess to be a Christian. Yet you throw
our own relative to a salty dog like Captain Cullick? Everyone knows
he arranges rum-running from the Indies weekly." He lifted his mug
and drank the remains.

Josiah felt his jaw tightening. "Perhaps *you* would offer room and
board to Katherine?" He spat her name out in disgust. "Since your old
boarder Henry Stiles was shot at the autumn muster." He clenched
his fists. "I was sorry to hear of the accident."

"I say it is not your business ruminating over that!" said Thomas,
eyes and face glowering. "The man who shot him received a fine. It
was but an accident. Now for some unknown reason, rumors claim
Lydia had a hand in it. Something about preternatural causes—"

"Lydia? Why, what sorcery is this? She wasn't even present at the
scene of the accident." Josiah dreaded such conversations with his
brother. But collect his monthly dues from Thomas he must. The
Hollister land in Wethersfield must be paid in full soon.

The women joined the men in the Great Room, a threadbare
space with few items of any worth and scant light. It is dark, thought
Josiah, like Thomas and Lydia themselves.

Lydia carried a pumpkin pie, and Elizabeth brought out bowls
and spoons. "Something to sweeten the mood," Lydia said cheerfully.
After she knifed them each a slice, the two couples ate in silence.

"So…tell me, Lydia," Josiah finally asked. "What are people saying
about you *now*? 'Tis never good, is it?" He grunted and swallowed a
smooth bit of the pie.

"Keep out of it, Josiah. 'Tis not your business," Thomas replied.

"I can speak for myself, husband," Lydia said.

Josiah studied his brother's wife, her dark round eyes, cream-colored skin, angular cheeks, puckered mouth, arched eyebrows, and nut-brown hair. She was a handsome goodwife— and she was trouble.

"I pay no mind to rumors and gossip," Lydia said. "Hodgepodge and rubbish I say. I ask you, Josiah, pay no mind to the gossipmongers and scolds. They know naught of the truth."

Josiah had heard enough. "The truth is, I am here to collect the monies owed on the Hollister land. Pay up lest I report you to the new Constable of Hartford, our own brother, Jonathan."

Thomas leaned forward and placed both hands on the table. "You don't say?" He stood up and clasped Lydia's shoulder. "Perhaps, wife, it's time we make ready to visit our brother Jonathan in Hartford to congratulate him. And perhaps it's time to visit *our* cousin Katherine as well. 'Tis no crime to be charitable."

"Visit Katherine?" Josiah asked. "Why—"

"Why not?" Thomas replied. "There's no harm in showing Christian kindness, now is there? If you won't bring our cousin to Windsor, we'll go and meet her ourselves."

Josiah stuck out his hand. "Just give me the coin owned me."

"So much for family charity," mumbled Thomas, making his way to a locked cupboard. He found the right key hanging on a nearby peg, unlocked the small cupboard door, and retrieved a pouch rattling with coins.

"Here." He threw the pouch clear across the table. "Your precious money. Good riddance until next month. For a brother, you strike a hard bargain."

Josiah shook his head. "What's fair is fair. I will be back again next month." He grabbed Elizabeth's arm. "Come, wife, we mustn't tarry—"

"Rest assured," shouted Thomas. "We will make it clear to cousin Katherine that we *truly* are her kin in word and deed."

"Just pay pay your monthly shillings," Josiah said, as he and Elizabeth abruptly left the house.

·–·

The next afternoon someone was knocking on the front door of Captain Cullick's house. Katherine hastened to the door and opened it. There stood a man and woman dressed in worn clothing grinning at her. The man lifted his oiled hat and smiled. His dark yellow hair, as greased as his hat, hung down to his shoulders. The woman, dressed in a mustard-colored skirt, black cloak, and donning a broad black hat nodded. She's pretty, thought Katherine, but for the hard lines running down her angled cheeks.

"A good morrow," Katherine said. "Can I help you? Captain Cullick is away on business."

"Is that so?" the man asked. "Chasing natives...or witches?" The pair chuckled, huddling together in the cold. "Actually, we are looking for Katherine Gilbert."

Katherine stared in disbelief. "Aye, that would be me."

"Good. Let me introduce myself. I am Thomas Gilbert, brother to Josiah and Jonathan. This is my wife, Lydia. We are your *other* cousins. We heard you worked for the captain. How are you faring with the man? Have you met our other brother Jonathan yet?"

How bold of the man to ask! Katherine's eyes and mouth grew wide. "'Tis a wonder to meet you both. I have been in service to the captain for over a month. I am learning the job and learning the captain's likes and dislikes. And nay, I haven't had the pleasure yet of meeting Jonathan."

"You'll meet him soon enough, I am sure," Thomas said with a laugh. "Jonathan is an unforgettable presence in Hartford."

"We try to come down for Market Day in Hartford once a fortnight, so here we are," said Lydia. And we would like to take you to the tavern up the road for a pint. As a welcome. Would you care to join us?"

"Captain Cullick has gone north upriver," she replied. She knew this was not the time to head to the tavern for a pint. She had work to do. The captain's staff, including the Mistress, were watching her closely. "I've no time today. Just a few minutes to spare," she told the couple. "Let me run in and tell the other servant girl I have visitors. You can wait for me by the bank of the Little River."

After speaking with Betty, Katherine ran to meet the couple, but not before taking a pinch from her snuff box. Her nerves didn't need to leave her now. She found her cousin and his wife on the riverbank lingering under a willow tree. "'Tis well met," she said, slightly out of breath. "Seems right to finally have caring kin come looking for me."

"How is it with the captain?" Lydia asked, looking about. "Does he treat you well?" Lydia's eyes darted back and forth as if danger lurked close by.

"He's a stubborn man. Likes to think he is fair-minded being on trials for accused witches. Forsooth, I see little of what he blathers about in these parts—the worry of conjurers, devils, witches—why, the only devil I have met in Hartford is your brother Josiah!"

The words fell from her tongue. But the couple laughed as if they agreed and understood her plight. Thomas pulled a leather-covered flask from his pocket, unscrewed the top, cocked his head back, and took a deep drink. "In honor of you, Katherine," he said. "Ahh, fine indeed."

He wiped his mouth, and handed her the flask. "Here," he said. "Have some. It will keep you warm." She politely took a sip. Fire burned down her throat, a fire coated with syrupy molasses that sweetened the flavor.

"Here ye be." She handed the flask to Lydia who quaffed down the rum with a loud gulp. "The kill-devil," Lydia hissed. "It always gets me." She pointed to Thomas. "Him too." The pair burst into another round of giggles. Then suddenly they both grew serious of a sudden and watched Katherine closely.

"You can come live with us in Windsor, you know," said Thomas. "You are always welcome. We are in need of a boarder. Lost our last one to an accident." He spat on the ground and shuffled his feet.

"Accident? I am sorry," she said, the drink helping her warm to the sentiments. "On your property, was it?"

"Nay," said Lydia wiping her mouth. "A gun went off at the Windsor autumn muster. Our boarder, Henry Stiles was shot by John Allyn. He's the son of an important man in Windsor."

"Accidents can be tragic," said Katherine. "I hope it was resolved."

"The son was merely fined," said Lydia. "We have had trouble with him since."

"Seems that trouble follows us," Thomas said.

Katherine understood this well for she knew what trouble was like. Isn't that why she'd run from England, as if this land was a shelter of sorts?

"Still, we would love to welcome you as a boarder, cousin," he said.

Katherine stood for a moment unsure of how to respond. "I will think on it," she finally said. "I've got my own reputation to keep."

"We understand," said Thomas. "Why don't you come for a visit up to Windsor? We would enjoy speaking with you further. Lydia can make supper. I can fetch you and bring you back."

"I would like that," said Katherine. "But I must return to the captain's now. And I thank ye both for the introductions and brief meeting."

"'Tis our pleasure," said Lydia, while Thomas grinned in agreement. The pair turned and headed in the direction of Hartford's Tavern.

•—•—•

"Kat," Betty asked, when she returned to the house. "To whom were you speaking? 'Tis a good thing the captain's gone. Bad news is… I hear he's supposed to return any day now."

"My cousin Thomas and his wife Lydia came down from Windsor. Made me feel welcome for a change." The rum had warmed her insides. But the news about the captain's return jolted her. "Any day you say? Seems like he just left," she said.

"Aye, 'tis always the case. Mind you, we have much to do in preparation for his return." She thrust a basket into Katherine's hands. "Here are some of the captain's knives, dull from overuse. See to it they get sharpened down at market. Go to the blacksmith's tent. He will fix the blades up right." Betty handed her a pine shilling to cover the expense. Katherine had her own scant savings to spend from her very first wages.

Her thoughts swirled around her meetup with Thomas and Lydia. Should she move with them north to Windsor? What she really wanted was to review Mr. Lilly's *Almanack* for 1652. Even with the captain gone, she'd not had a moment to look at the predictions for next year. At least it gave her something to look forward to.

•—•—•

Meetinghouse Square bustled with its usual weekly activity as townspeople scrambled for the goods they needed. She espied the blacksmith's tent. She watched him giving demonstrations in a stall used as a makeshift forge. Inside the tent various knife sizes and kitchen items were for sale or barter.

A short line formed in front of the tent. Katherine waited patiently while a tall, thin man in front of her kept turning around, addressing a black mastiff pup tethered to a post by a thick rope. "Silence, Titus. Be still." She noticed the scar on his cheek immediately; clearly, he was a fighting man. He was dressed in black and his hair and hat oiled down by grease. His knee- high, black-buckled boots looked like weapons with spurs and other sharp objects hanging off of them. He had a familiar bearing.

The dog persisted in barking. The man limped over to the beast and spoke to it sternly. A thin, older woman with delicate, birdlike hands grasped his arm. "A good day to you, Marshal. 'Tis cold but clear for early December. And a rousing huzzah is in order for your new position. There's no better man in Hartford suited to be our constable. We are all safer now because of you. May the Lord continue to protect us from strangers and sorceries."

The marshal nodded and bowed slightly to the woman. "And rest assured, Goodwife Smith, I will work tirelessly for the good people of Hartford—and Wethersfield. Townspeople no longer need to fear the uncanny power of strangers. Neither should they fear those whom the devil calls his own." He reassuringly patted the elderly woman's arm, and the pair smiled in mutual admiration at one another.

So this was her *other* cousin, Jonathan Gilbert—now Marshal of Hartford. Should she introduce herself? Katherine thought quickly. She decided she had met enough Gilberts for one day. Now was not the time. Soon enough, she thought.

CHAPTER 14

March 1653

Over a year had passed since Katherine started service for Captain Cullick. She managed to get her chores done on time; she wrote to her Mam; she even put wages away for her future, whatever her future may hold. She kept her head down, like an ox in the field, and worked hard. She even found time to visit her cousins in Windsor, meeting their growing brood as well. She refused Thomas and Lydia's offer to board with them; something told her to keep to her plans.

Of Josiah and Elizabeth, she had seen little. She heard that the Gilbert brothers finally built a new home on the old Hollister property in Wethersfield. She even met her respected cousin, Marshal Gilbert, who took an immediate liking to her. Katherine shared the same sentiments. Here was a man who commanded attention. He told her, "I am the Marshal, Katherine. My word is law round these parts."

She told her cousins scant about her past. Why bring up the memories? They would ne'er understand; she knew that Captain Cullick and his household wanted her to fit in—something she now worked hard to fulfil.

Meanwhile she worked in secret on Betty's chart. Just the other day Betty asked Katherine again when she was to read her fortune.

In exchange, Betty offered to do Katherine's work for a day. "I will finish your tasks and even give up my afternoon off," she promised. "I need answers. You know of what I speak."

Katherine knew that Betty was in love with Will Chapman. Hadn't she seen the man lingering behind the trees and bushes on the banks of the Little River waiting for Betty? She also heard that Captain Cullick complained to the local magistrates that Betty was violating the law that forbade dependents from making a motion of marriage. The captain refused to accept Will as Betty's suitor, and Betty wanted answers. Katherine reassured Betty that they would find the right time and place—out of the captain's earshot.

Today Katherine had a great amount of spinning to do. Her reputation as a master spinner and knitter was growing. Captain Cullick's wife, now with two young children, pressed Katherine to knit more scarfs, hats, woolen gloves, linens, and booties. Always more, never enough. But Katherine enjoyed the art of the knitting needle, spindle and wheel. During the war, she had sewn, knit, and spun much for the cause.

Mistress Cullick even set up a special room for her to spin and knit. This gave Katherine time to be alone, to think, and to pass the time without the captain barking orders at her. The whirl of the spinning wheel or the clicking of knitting needles helped release the tension and the drudgery of her days. When all her other chores were finished, she'd often spin the afternoon away. Because she spun briskly with a rhythm she knew well, she could find some peace in the house—even for just a few hours.

Katherine had mostly empty baskets of wool beside her as she quickly pressed her foot on the spinning wheel's treadle. She hummed along with the wheel's rhythms keeping to a brisk pace. The door opened, and Betty entered with more skeins of wool. Her eyes popped wide open with surprise. "Surely, thou could not have finished with the first batch of wool? Upon my word, I have never seen the likes of such a swift spinner!"

"Aye," said Katherine, enjoying the attention. "I made a name for myself back home. I spun and wove cloth for the wounded. My skills were widely known," she boasted. "And tell the Mistress the yarn is ready for the weaver."

"But how?" Betty asked. "How can you spin so?" Then in a low voice she mumbled, "Methinks sometimes you have help, Kat. Methinks sometimes it's magic. I get dizzy watching the wheel spin so fast." She dropped the new wool into the baskets and came closer to watch.

"Magic? Why that's hogwash." Katherine laughed as the wheel turned. "There's no magic here. I work hard at my arts. Makes me feel useful and keeps my hands busy." Katherine wondered if Betty was envious of this skill, a talent that often got her away from the more menial tasks in the household.

"You are a woman of many talents, Kat. Skilled where others are lacking." Betty bent close to Katherine's ear. "Tell me, when will you read my future?"

Katherine kept her foot tapping the treadle holding the spindle aright. "Soon Betty, soon."

⤙—⤚

The next day was the Sabbath. The captain demanded his staff go to meeting each week, and Katherine knew any excuse to miss the lengthy service could incur his wrath. Today was no different; only she had decided that today she would refuse to attend. She rested in the loft making some astrological notes for Betty's reading.

Suddenly, Betty bounded into the loft room ready for meeting. The household staff was allowed to wear their finest clothing to meeting, the one day the servants' dress was given a rest.

"Are you ready, Kat? The captain is asking for you."

Katherine sat up on her pallet and shook her head. "Nay, I will not go today. Tell the Captain I'm ailing with head pains. He need not know the truth."

"The truth being you don't feel like it? Is that it? You will be considered a Sabbath-breaker, upon my word," exclaimed Betty.

"No one need know the truth but you. I am ailing today and that's that." She continued, "You also need to know I'm preparing your reading—your fortune, Betty. So tell not a soul of me staying here today. I *know* how you and Will feel about one another. Rest assured your fortune will speak truth for you."

"Aye, this is what I've been waiting for," Betty said, her eyes brightening. "I need to know if Will is the man for me. It's just that the captain thinks otherwise."

"Remember Betty, it's not what the captain thinks. It's what the spirits doth know."

"Aye, Kat. I'll cover for thee today and make certain the captain believes you are ailing."

"I trust you. It will *all* come a-right."

·—•·

Finally the time and place was determined. It would be on the morrow, Katherine's day off, and Betty would meet her in the root cellar. It was quiet and cool in the vast cellar, and they would have the privacy they needed. Betty would meet Katherine during her break at the chosen time. If anyone knocked or disturbed the reading, Katherine and Betty knew to say they were gathering vegetables for Cook.

The next day near the noon hour, Katherine walked down the hall carrying Betty's astrology chart with her notes tucked in her apron pouch. She looked in both directions, opened the door to the cellar, and made her way down the thick wooden steps holding onto the rail. Although she hoped for some payment, she realized Betty's offer to do her chores was the best Betty could do; it just irked Katherine that back home she'd received good money for her readings.

She waited anxiously at the bottom of the stairs. One lone wall candle flickered shadowed light. At last, she heard footsteps.

"Kat?" a soft voice called out.

"Here."

Betty stood afore her, holding the bright nub of a lit tallow in a candlestick.

"Are you ready?" Katherine asked in a whisper.

"Aye, as ready as ever."

Katherine pushed the thick wooden door open and felt the rush of a vast, cool breeze. The room was dark; Betty located a wall sconce that held a candle and lit it with her tallow. The smell of onions, yams, and potatoes filled the crisp air. Cold, hard vegetables lined the shelves in neat bundles, some in baskets, while some like garlic and smaller onions hung on twined rope from the ceiling. A small ladder lay against the shelves, so one could reach the top row. Thin shadows bounced against the walls.

In another area of the room a large covered hogshead barrel sat empty; servants used this for discarded peels and vegetables gone by. It was the next step before the compost pile the captain maintained out back. Two small chairs near the barrel indicated a sitting place.

"Here, let's use this as a table," Katherine suggested, pointing to the barrel. Then she noticed Betty's hands trembling.

"Why are you shaking so? Put the candle down, you are making it sputter."

Betty carefully placed the candlestick on the flat top of the barrel.

"I am afeared of my fortune. And my future. Perhaps Kat, I should be asking *God* about my life—not *you!*"

"Nonsense. We agreed, Betty. I did not spend these many months casting your chart for naught. And I've prepared myself to receive the spirit—for your sake," she said, glaring at Betty who now looked like a quivering rabbit.

How dare Betty question her? The two pulled the chairs close to the makeshift table.

"Do you pray to God before you begin?" Betty glanced about the root cellar, eyes askance, looking around in dread at the shadows appearing on the walls.

"Of course, I pray to God," Katherine replied. "I pray in silence. And I pray you do the same now." She bowed her head.

"I will, Kat. I will," said Betty, who bowed her head, folded her hands, and shut her eyes.

After a brief moment of silence, Katherine pulled out the parchment and unfolded it. Betty's eyes loomed large, her mouth rounded, and she stared down at the paper. She blinked and bent down to study the strange symbols on the paper. "What is all this?" she asked.

"Shush now."

Katherine dug again into her pouch and retrieved a small, round magnified glass. She put it up to her eye and continued to study the marks and notes.

"Tell me, Betty, what is it you seek to know?"

"I thought you already knew."

"Tell me again. Ask aloud." She lifted her head and stared directly at Betty. "The spirits are with us now."

"Spirits?" Betty's round face now looked long and distorted. Again, she glanced around the cellar as if the root vegetables had ears and eyes, heads and limbs.

"Go on."

"It's about my relationship with…Will."

"Aye, Will. What would you have the spirit made known to you?"

"Why, we love one another. The captain forbids our union. Is he for me? Will we marry? I want to know. I need to know." She sighed, looking forlorn.

Katherine carefully noted all of Betty's astrological aspects. She had studied each detail over time, recalling bits and pieces from the Lilly book. "I see your moon is in the sign of Virgo, the earthy mother. And your sun in Capricorn bodes well with the Virgo moon. You will have harmony in your marriage. And you will have many children."

She held the candle up. "And I see the position of Venus, the Morning Star, is close to Mercury, the planet of news. But it has an affliction with the planet Saturn, indicating setbacks. It will take hard work on your part."

"I already *know* about hard work," Betty said with a whine, then stiffened up and asked her, "Tell me, what else do you see?"

Katherine closed her eyes, breathed in the cool cellar air, and shook her head. "'Tis not meant to be, Betty. 'Tis about the timing. Will is *not* the man for you." She opened her eyes and stared straight into the face of the shivering servant girl.

"Will… not for me?" Betty repeated slowly. "This I cannot believe." She shook her head. "But if not Will…then who?"

Katherine took a deep breath. "Now is the time I go to my own prayerful state of mind…to get the answer you seek. Grab ahold of my hand." She reached a hand out to Betty still shaking from the prediction. Katherine shut her eyes again, and she began to sway back and forth. When she began to speak again, her voice sounded lower, slower, and more pronounced.

"You will marry…rest assured…you will marry a man named… Simon." Her eyes abruptly opened and watched Betty who looked as though she had seen a specter.

"Simon? Who is Simon" I know no Simon." Betty slumped in the chair, clearly dismayed by the answer. Her lower lip curled into a stubborn pout. "But I love Will, and he loves me," she said with a sob.

"So you say. But the spirits speak otherwise. Thou shalt marry a man by the name of Simon."

Betty stood and brushed off her skirt as if she was trying to rid herself of this answer, then began to mumble about lies…

"I expect my payment, Betty," Katherine reminded her. "In the form of work, as you promised. I toiled at this task and you haven't shown any appreciation—nor thanks."

"I think *your* fortunetelling is nothing but blather," Betty cried. "I won't believe this, not for an instant. I love Will…and Will loves me. Nothing will stop us from being together…not you… nor the spirits…nor the captain!"

"So you say."

"I say the devil take you and your spirits."

Now sobbing in earnest, Betty grabbed the candlestick and stormed out of the root cellar, leaving Katherine alone in the shadows.

CHAPTER 15

Katherine folded her notes and stuck them deep in her pocket. Then she snuffed out the wall candle, shut the root cellar door, and proceeded up the stairs. She could not understand Betty. How dare she respond in such a manner? Her fellow servant and friend had asked— nay— begged for an answer to her love query. But it had not been the answer Betty wanted.

Everyone knew that Captain Cullick complained to the local magistrate about Betty and Will, that Betty was violating the law, the law that forbade dependents from making any motion toward marriage. Could Betty not see that this Will was *not* for her?

The stars and the spirit had spoken.

She was only the messenger. But people wanted fortunes that aligned not with the stars or the spirit, but with their own desires. She thought next time, if someone asked, she'd tell them to find the answers for themselves. But now it was too late. The reading was over—and Betty wasn't happy.

Climbing the stairs, she heard the loud, tinkling of a bell. *The bell* that sent her scurrying up the stairs like a stray cow being called back to the fold. Captain Cullick, face red and wrinkled up in a twist, awaited her at the top of the stairs. "Do *you* know what upset Betty?

Did *you* say something to her? She ran past me in tears shouting, "Tis not true!'" He pointed a thick finger at her. "My household needs no disruptions. Nor do I. Take care, Katherine. Your business is— my business is— *your* service to *me* and *my* household. Lest you forget." His stocky figure shook in a fury, his hard mouth trembled.

She cast her eyes down and sighed out a long breath. So the captain knew nothing of the true reason for the meeting. "Aye, I've been consoling Betty. Women's matters, if you must know."

"Women's matters? Bah! Pooh! Keep to your job, maid. That's all that matters in my house. Stay the course." He reminded her, "You have less than a year left."

Katherine shrugged her shoulders. She felt trapped. Back home she had made a name for herself with her fortunetelling. She prided herself on her accuracies.

"What are your plans today?" the captain asked, hands on hips glaring at her.

"'Tis my afternoon off," she said. "I have personal matters to attend to—that are not your concern." She tossed her head as the words flew from her mouth; it was too late to take them back. Katherine realized she needed to control her tongue, the tongue that lashed out like a serpent. Mam had warned her—time and again.

The captain took a threatening step toward her. He frowned, brow and eyebrows furrowed together. His hair looked to stick out on end. "Everything and everyone in my household is my business. *You!*" He wagged that finger again to her face, the smell of sweet rum on his breath. "Are my business." His voice echoed clear down the hall.

There was never winning a battle with the captain. He always had the last word. Crossing the man was a dangerous affrontery. He saw enemies everywhere. Katherine knew she did not need to be one of them. "Of course," she said, placing her hands over her apron pockets where her pouch lay hidden, "I will take care not to get in your way."

⊷

The afternoon was cold and foggy, so Katherine dressed warmly, fastening her hooded cloak tightly about her neck. After the captain's rant, she realized how little she cared about the affairs of *his* household. She was counting the days until she was free. She knew she had months left, not years anymore. Could she endure the humility? Now she realized how foolish she was to read Betty's fortune—yet Betty had sworn silence. That she'd tell not a soul. Katherine believed her friend. Would Betty keep her promise?

She walked to the back door of the kitchen so she wouldn't be noticed. But alas, she heard footsteps running briskly behind her. "Wait… Katherine!"

She turned to see the bright-eyed daughter of Captain Cullick, who now looked like a young dog begging for a scrap.

"What is it, Mary? I am off of the afternoon."

"Can you—would you—read my fortune?" the young girl asked in a whisper. "Please?" She seemed to pant in anticipation of an answer.

"Shush, Mary!" Katherine put a finger to her lips. "Why would you think—?"

"Please," she begged. "Please… *I* need to know my future."

What had Mary heard? She wondered.

"What nonsense is this? Who is filling *your* head with such notions? I do not read fortunes or anyone's future." Katherine scoffed and shook her head back and forth.

"But—" Mary insisted.

"But nothing. I'm off for the afternoon. I know naught of such notions."

With that said, Katherine burst out the door and headed toward the Great River.

All seemed quiet along the river. Clouds and fog hung heavy with moisture that settled down like a dark pall. Katherine longed for some peace. The winter cold was breaking in anticipation of spring; ice floes floated downriver heading south. She strolled along the banks past the many warehouses lined up near the landing until she found a large boulder to sit on near an oak tree.

She thought of Mam. It had been months since she'd last heard from her. After her unexpected turn to the captain's house, she had written Mam of her plight. The letter Mam wrote back gave her encouragement and hope, for Mam had her own trials in this life.

Mam told her to finish her service, and then she would be free—free to return home— or free to start her own life somewhere else. '*Save up your coin, Kat. You don't know when you will need it, or what you will need it for. Keep your head down and may God keep thee safe. Expect the best and you will get it.*'

Katherine always felt reassured thinking of her Mam who believed in her.

No matter how many mistakes she made.

·•·

Determined to complete her two years, she thought of Mr. Lilly's forecast for next year: '*There will come to pass through the unseen world, many hitherto unknown events that may work in your favor. In the meantime, until Jupiter and Mercury align, trust no one.*'

Had she made a mistake trusting Betty? She wiped dew off her face, and shook the thoughts from her head.

She had work to do this evening.

She returned through the back door to find Cook preparing the evening meal. The Mistress was also present, reviewing the menu for the night's supper. Katherine brushed by them and feeling chilled, felt in need of a good sit in front of the kitchen hearth.

"Good day, Katherine. I hope you enjoyed your afternoon off," said Cook.

"Aye, the fog left me wet and hungry. I'll dry off by the fire," she said.

The Mistress's eyes narrowed to Katherine and then she turned to Cook. "The supper menu sounds just right. I approve. The soup will be perfect for such an afternoon." Cook blinked and took a slight bow toward the captain's wife.

Then Mistress Cullick turned to Katherine who sat shivering by the fire. "After you warm up, have a bowl of soup to nourish yourself. Then get yourself prepared. The captain has requested to see you in his study. He is waiting."

·—·

After a quick bowl of soup and a change of dress she was ready. She stood in front of the captain's door, knocked loudly and heard the commanding voice say, "Come in."

She turned the knob, and pushed the door open. The captain stood afore her, examining an astrolabe in his hands. As she stood waiting, she looked with wonder at the miniature ships in bottles, compasses, the tangle of maps, papers, and books strewn across his desk. The large hourglass sat on a nearby table, no sand moving through it.

The captain lifted his head up and placed the astrolabe down on his desk. He looked tired and drawn, his grey-blue eyes glazed over like icy rocks. "Please. Sit down." He pointed to the chair in front of the desk and promptly sat in his own. He leaned over and fixed her with a stare.

"Tell me…what do you do in your idle time?"

"Captain, I have very little idle time. I never stray too far. I run errands for the Mistress, go to Meetinghouse Square on Market Day to pick up goods and—"

"Is that all?"

"I take walks along the river, stop in at the tavern. Knit and spin. I find common ways to rest."

The captain cleared his throat. "Common ways, eh? There's nothing common about the accusations set against you." He started drumming his fingers with a fixed rhythm on the desk.

"Accusations, Captain? I don't understand." Thoughts swirled in Katherine's head. Could it be Betty? Or Mary? Or even worse—both?

Captain Cullick stood up, moved to the center of the room, and began pacing the floor as if he was back on a ship's quarterdeck. Hands behind his back, he paced in silence. Katherine felt unnerved of a sudden. She never could abide much heavy silence. It made the air thicker— harder to breathe. Finally he circled around to her chair towering over her, legs apart, hands on his hips. "Attention!" His voice broke the silence. "Tell me Katherine, is it true you read—fortunes?" He glared down into her eyes squinting to watch her reaction. "Answer me—did you—yay or nay…read Betty's fortune?"

Katherine kept still, but inside she fumed. In England she would have received payment and a good meal. She'd only told Betty what she saw. How dare Betty? She has betrayed me. How will I get myself out of this tangle? So much for thanks, she thought.

"It was but a game, Captain. I only tried to help." There. She admitted part of the truth.

The captain drew closer to her face. "You *only* tried to help," he repeated, lowering his voice, disgust on his breath. "You are leading my domestics, and for fact my daughter, down a dangerous path of perdition. Why, this could rise to the crime of witchcraft— in the eyes of the authorities. We folk in Hartford put our faith in God, not fortunes. Bah!" He pounded a fist to the air. "I should have known better—you...you... Gilbert!"

"Betty begged me," she pleaded. "'Tis not just *me*."

"*You* are the source of this, Katherine. We need to cut the head off the snake. Further, do I need to remind you again of my importance in this town? Lest you forget, I was asked to be a magistrate in many court cases of great importance, as well as Secretary to the Colony and soon, Commissioner to the Colonies. I need no bedevilment in my own home!" He hovered over her shaking with fury. "So, *this* is why you are a Sabbath breaker and at times refuse to enter God's house of weekly worship. Forsooth, methinks you might be a witch—or one in league with the devil. What did you say to Betty that upset her so?"

"Ask Betty yourself."

"Let it be known, I will have no entertaining Satan and his minions in my home. Do you hear me?" His voice boomed aloud and rattled the bells hanging from the walls. "I have sat on many a trial. Mayhap I will be sitting on yours soon enough—"

"I made a mistake, Captain. The first in many months. I would like another chance to redeem myself," she said, her fingers twisting in a fury.

"Redeem yourself? Whilst my servants and daughter stir with the idea of fortunes—waiting for you to predict their futures? Bah! Pooh! Balderdash!" His thick eyebrows descended over her, displaying grey hairs that looked as sharp and pointed as little needles. "I am now ordering you to gather your effects. On the morrow you will leave my house. I have a right mind to report you to the authorities." He paused, turned his back to her, and stood by the window. He placed a hand on the hourglass. "Your time is up here, Katherine. You are on your own. And because you *have* been hardworking—" He walked to his desk and retrieved an envelope. "A pound for your leaving."

He thrust it at her in disgust.

"You will be gone on the morrow, bags packed, and out of my house. Lord knows what will happen to you. I want you and your devilry far from my residence. What will people think of me housing a fortuneteller? In a God-abiding town such as Hartford?" He shook his head muttering, "Why, the authorities might think I am harboring a witch!"

Part III
THE DESTINATION

CHAPTER 16

The next day Katherine stood with her scant belongings outside Captain Cullick's house wondering what to do next. She would not plead with Josiah to take her in. She always could head north to Windsor to Thomas and Lydia's house. Or maybe stay with cousin Jonathan? She thought mayhap she would find Kate Palmer, to abide with her for a time. Or perhaps it was time to return home. She was never one afraid of work; it was just her mouth that got her in sore trouble time and again.

She surveyed her surroundings. It was Market Day, a sunny, crisp day in late March, a day that brought townspeople to Hartford from Wethersfield and Windsor. People bustled about the square busy stocking up for their larders. She glanced back at the captain's house for the last time, thankful to be free from his rule.

She started out south toward the road to Wethersfield carrying her satchel and lugging her trunk behind her. She had given this New England a chance and received little, with the exception of a few weeks saved wages and a hefty dose of humble pie.

As she made her way out of Hartford following the rutted, mud-soaked road, she heard the clip-clop of hooves and the bumping rattle of a cart behind her, then a booming voice that shouted, "Whoa!" Quickly she stepped off the road to let the wagon pass.

"Whoa, I say!"

The cart full stopped.

Katherine looked up to see a man grinning down at her. His muscled body, red rough hands, and weather-beaten skin clearly indicated he worked the land. Yet his small, light blue eyes twinkled with a good nature she had rarely seen in Hartford. The sun bore down on them, and she squinted up to get a better look at the man. He raised his hat to her, and pushed back a thin mess of yellow hair that revealed a wide forehead; then he flashed her a broad smile.

"Where would you be headed, Goodwife? Do you need some assistance?"

"I am no Goodwife," she replied sullenly. "I am still a maid, if you must know. I am on my way to Wethersfield."

The man perked up. "Why then, you are in luck. Live in Wethersfield myself." He jumped from his cart and lifted her trunk to the back of the wagon. "Come around the front. Here, let me help you up." Before she could reply, his hands were tight round her waist, and he lifted her to the seat next to his, as if she were a bushel of apples.

"Get on now," he shouted to his team of horses, as other wagons awaited the same passage behind them. He cracked a small whip to the horses' backs, and the cart rambled off towards Wethersfield. "I have yet to even know the name of my hazel-eyed passenger. Do tell." He leaned close to her, smelling like leather, horse and hay.

"I am Katherine Gilbert," she said. "I have been under the service of Captain Cullick for over a year now. He is no longer in need of my work."

"Gilbert, eh? Related to Josiah, the Marshal, and Thomas? Same family?"

"Aye. And you haven't as yet told me your name?"

"Name's John. John Harrison. A shoemaker by trade I am, but mostly these days a farmer and a part-time merchant. I busy myself with crops, trading, the price of seed, and working the land." He smiled and glanced at her, waiting for a response.

"And since you called me Goodwife, shall I call you Goodman?"

John let out a loud laugh. "You can call me a good man surely, but as to being married, I am not. A bachelor I am." He kept his eyes straight ahead to the road. "I have been a lone-man round these parts, causing vexation to my neighbors and townspeople. Gossips too. Why— I was almost fined for being solitary. No wife, no family! Well," he clicked the reins back and forth, "I won't make a match with someone just because of pressure from townspeople. All the young maids with few brains in their pretty heads batting their lashes at me? Nay, I'm a stubborn sort, I am. But they all like me well enough during harvest season." He let out another roar and laughed aloud. "Where do you hail from?" he asked her.

"I hail from Lancaster up north England. I lived in London for several years. Sailed from Bristol Harbor; my Mam got me a better berth. London was too crowded, dirty, and dangerous to sail from." She carefully chose her words. She'd not tell him her involvement in the Civil War—not yet.

"I see you're an independent sort," he said.

Katherine realized she had also met someone with an independent spirit like her own.

"So where to then, Katherine?" John was back to the matter at hand. "Josiah's house?"

"Nay, I think not. 'Twas my cousin and his wife dropped me off at Captain Cullick's house over a year ago, contracting me as a servant for two years. I expected better. I could ne'er take the rules, the duties, the gossip, and the gruffness of that captain. I am glad to be gone from Hartford."

"So where to?" he asked again.

"Perhaps it's best to take me to the harbor. A ship to Boston might start me on a trip back home. Or perhaps to the house of my only friend, Kate Palmer." Katherine shook her head and covered her face with her hands. "You see, I don't fit in round these parts. I am not welcome."

The man stared hard at her. "Not welcome? Surely, you'd be welcome to my home. I have a cottage round back; my native farmhand Joseph often uses it when he and his family stay on the island—*Manhannock* —they call it."

"The Island of Merriment? I remember seeing it on the sail upriver." Katherine smiled at the thought.

"Indeed. The Wangunk people work hard—and deserve merriment." He laughed heartily. "As we all do." Katherine thought for a moment. She watched John, taking in every bit of him. Could she trust him?

"Can you cook?" he inquired.

"Aye. I enjoy the preparation of victuals. I spent many an hour in Captain Cullick's kitchen. My training at the residence and my training back home have served me well." Katherine puffed her chest out, took a deep breath, and sighed. Here was a man taking a genuine interest in her. "I will accept your offer for a time—maybe a moon's time or so. Then I will seek passage back to England. Townspeople in Hartford are already talking about my fortunetell—" She stopped short and gasped for a breath.

"Fortune?" John repeated. "Never you mind. 'Tis fortune just brought us together. Being a farmer, I take no notice, have no time for idle chatter. My ear is deaf to gossip; don't believe in it and never will. Something I stay far away from. Never could abide by it, if truth be told."

Katherine sighed again. Here was a man who perhaps *really* could understand her.

"I thank you for your offer, John, and 'tis just for a month."

But John was humming a tune, lost in his own thoughts.

•➤•

The wagon made its way south out of Hartford until it came to a fork in the road. Arrows on a wooden sign pointed to Fort St. to the left, Standish Lane to the right, and another to the Watering Lane and Sandy Lane. "We take the Sandy Lane," announced John. 'Tis the direct way home."

"Sandy Lane? Why, my cousin Josiah took me up the lane when I arrived. 'Tis lovely with the views of the meadows and the river."

"Aye, then you will like my homestead," John said with pride. "It's the house close to the corner of Sandy Lane and the High Street. I bought it several years ago in the late '40s. Man named Abbott sold it to me. Over three acres at a fair price. My land's an envy of Wethersfield—so they say." He chuckled to himself. "'Tis a perfect location, for I also own and lease land in the Meadows."

Suddenly one of the horses buckled. His hoof was stuck in a rut of thick mud. The cart slowed as the horse threw back his head and strained to lift his hoof. "Here, Katherine, jump down and see for yourself, whilst I care for this horse. I shan't be long."

Katherine recognized her chance. For a moment, she truly felt free from the captain's demands. Could she be herself with this John Harrison? She would but stay a few weeks, so she would make the best of it.

She let herself down from the cart and ran along the Sandy Lane, getting dirt and mud to the bottom of her skirt. She ambled to the curve leading down to the High St. There it was on the left, a white, clapboard house on a small upland slope, surrounded by a railed, zigzag fence with a gate. In the back she could see a great barn; the barn was flanked on one side by a rowed apple orchard, and on the other side a stand of pines, oaks and shrubs. Near the trees stood the cottage, several sheds, and a privy.

A vast ditch encircling the farm was filled with muddy water. She heard a cow lowing and some chickens fretting, running to and from the barn. A pig squealed, making the chickens cluck louder. She rushed by the house to the High Street where the Great Meadows opened afore her. The melting snow and rains of early March carried the smell of fresh and marsh water mixed with rich soil. Hundreds of rushes swayed in the breezes as if to welcome her. In the far background the Great River loomed, shining a bright blue-grey, calm today, with wavelets of small whitecaps pressing up and down. The river and meadows were almost in John's backyard!

"What do you think?" she heard his voice. "What say you to my humble abode?" She turned and ran back, as John led his horses closer to the gate.

Out of breath, eyes shining, she turned to the young farmer. "'Tis perfect. And glorious!"

John smiled and nodded in approval. Then he gestured toward the deep trenches that traversed the property. "What thinks you of my glorious ditches? They may be unsightly, but these ditches keep the water from entering my house. My neighbors and I took suit with the town years ago. The meadow starts flooding this time of year; I need not live on an island. One year I had to use a raft to paddle to my door."

"'Tis most practical, these ditches." Katherine laughed.

"And that's who I am. 'Practical John' they called me back home. You see? You already know quite a bit about me. More than I know about you."

"There's time for that," was all she said.

Katherine breathed in the scent of coming rain. She could smell wet loam, livestock, manure and hay, and suddenly realized this was the happiest moment she had experienced since she'd arrived from England.

"I am honored you'll be staying for a time. It matters not what others think. I'm a man of my word." He nudged closer to her. "Wait here while I settle the horses and feed the rest of my hungry children."

"It feels right," she said with hesitation. "For a time. But how can I thank thee, John? This is the first time I have felt free since landing in Connecticut Colony." She began to sob in earnest.

"That's enough now… here, here. There will be plenty of work on this farm. And you will meet other workers soon enough. You are welcome here."

Katherine stifled her tears and threw back her shoulders. "I will help in any way. Make myself useful. But know I shall never be called servant again."

CHAPTER 17

April 1653

S everal weeks passed. Katherine sat in the cottage behind John's house writing a letter to her Mam. The simple cottage suited her. A small hearth with a brick chimney gave her warmth and comfort. Beside the pallet stood a small dresser with two drawers. A wall sconce hung over a round table. On the table lay a mysterious circle of small, smooth stones and feathers, no doubt collected by the native farmhand who sometimes stayed there.

Most of all, Katherine relished her new privacy.

After finishing the letter, she read it again:

Dear Mam,

I am not longer under the service of Captain Cullick in Hartford. Mam, it was dreadful being a servant. My own kin rejecting me and selling me off as an indentured, as if I owed them my life.

But good news, Mam. I have found another employer by the name of John Harrison, of Wethersfield.

He pays me for my work, and I make do. Goodman Harrison is alone on his farm, so I help him with the chores. I am saving up for passage just in case my present arrangement does not last. I hope you fare well. May God Bless and keep you.

Yours, with love, Katherine

She sealed the letter and decided to carry it to the farmhouse. John had promised on the morrow to deliver it to the shipmaster down at the harbor. John also had leather goods to export. Katherine in turn, promised to cook him supper as a way of thanking him.

Katherine thought a fine, frothy stew would please John on a cold day. It was something she could do to repay him his generosity. She gazed east at the Great Meadow, soaked and glistening from the early afternoon rains. The spring flooding was all about them, filling in the ditches and slowly inching up the Sandy Lane toward the house. The setting sun behind her cast deep hues of red, orange, violet and gold—a gold that shimmered off the waters and lit the landscape in blurred light.

As she set foot for the farmhouse, she noticed a shadowy figure ambling over the slight knoll. He was walking towards the cottage. "Who goes there?" she asked, peering into the settling twilight.

He seemed a younger man, she thought, maybe twenty years of age. He was tall and wore a dark-brown leather coat and leather breeches, with a colored blanket draped across one shoulder. Beads glowed from his long, dark plaited hair that hung together like strands of twine. Around his waist, shiny belts of purple and white shells glittered in the pink-gold light. But it was the young man's eyes that held her attention. They were black, round, and full of wonder.

"Who are you?" she asked.

"They call me Joseph, Joseph Hawk Wing. I am from the Wangunk Tribe. I work for Harrison man. He is good man to me. And you?" He studied Katherine from her cap to her muddy boots.

"I am Katherine Gilbert. I *also* work for Goodman Harrison now."

"I see. And I see red hair shining from cap. Red hair—fiery heart." He thumped a hand to his chest.

Katherine laughed. "'Tis true, so they say."

Joseph pointed to the cottage. "You stay there—now?"

"Aye. Until I take my leave."

"My cottage," the young man said.

"I understand," she said. "I was led to believe you were gone."

"I'm back." He pointed toward the Great River. "I stay on island. With my own people. In winter we Wangunks go on Great River south to Mattabassett."

"What brings you here now, Joseph?" she asked.

"Harrison man owes me money," he said. "I do many chores. He pays me with goods, sometimes coin. This way—my people get what they need."

"Come, let us go together to Goodman Harrison's house. He told me about you."

They made their way to the whitewashed door and knocked. The astounded look on John's face when he opened it—to see them together— amused Katherine.

"Well now," John cried, "who have we here? I see you have already met. Come in!"

The Great Room in the farmhouse boasted of a grand hearth with a blazing fire. It was a large, open room, with John's small study and large bedroom on the right and a staircase that led to a loft. The smell of hops, onions, garlic and mutton wafting from the kitchen filled the room. "Was I not supposed to cook the stew tonight? In honor of you delivering this letter tomorrow to the harbormaster?" asked Katherine, surprised. She reached into her apron pocket and handed him the letter.

"Hmm—" He turned the letter over and looked at the writing. "Of course. On the morrow. And never you mind about supper. I have been cooking for myself all these years. And I haven't starved yet."

Joseph stood blinking and waiting, his long lanky frame stiff at attention. He was too polite to interrupt. Finally, John reached for a pouch sitting on the hearthfire mantle, and handed it to him. "Here you be. Make sure you enjoy the merriment on the island this summer. This money will help." Joseph nodded in thanks and smiled.

John turned to Katherine. "You will be seeing more of Joseph in the coming weeks. He's helping with the planting. He is a loyal worker." John beamed with pride.

"I'm honored," said Katherine, already liking the Wangunk.

"Same," said Joseph, concealing the pouch in his breeches. "I go now. Thanks to Harrison man." He made a short bow, opened the door, and departed.

The couple was alone at last.

"You and Joseph will get along fine," said John. "Rest assured, he will be a great help to you, as he is to me." He walked to the bubbling stew and gave it a great stir with a wooden spoon. "Sit, Katherine. I wonder would a mug of brewed beer suit your fancy tonight?" Before she had time to respond, John had ladled her out a pint from a cask in the corner of the room.

She sat drinking her beer at the long tableboard watching him serve her the savory stew.

"I thank God for my blessings, with you counted among them," John said, as he held up his mug and drank heartily. "Now, let's eat." The pair remained quiet until the tasty stew was finished. When she gazed up from her empty bowl, she noticed John staring at her with intent in his eyes. "So— tell me Katherine, what were you running from in England—that you ended up here? Why did you come?" He smiled, waiting for a response.

Katherine paused. "My Gilbert cousins made me an offer. I assumed they would find a proper place for me. Instead, I was taken to Captain Cullick's to live life as a servant for two years."

John's blue eyes widened and he became serious of a sudden. "You mean your own kin wouldn't take you in? And they claim they be Christians? Hogwash!" He grumbled in disgust. His eyes met hers again. "So... tell me, Katherine—"

"Please call me Kat. That's what they called me back home."

"Tell me Kat, if you would, the real reasons you left your old life behind. Who were you? Who *are* you?"

Thunderstruck by such questions, Katherine thought a moment. How should she respond? Should she be truthful with him? She decided she would.

"Aye, I'll tell thee the best way I can. I trained and ministered to the wounded soldiers in the Civil War, and I left trying to leave it all behind." Fumbling with her hands, she twisted them together in a hard knot. "I witnessed much suffering and pain—both physical and of the mind. Why, men were brought to me missing arms and legs. I tried to save many—as many as I could. And I did save some but others, nay. So I came to escape the ravages of the war. Came to start a new life. I have always been a fighter." She looked down shaking her head, and studied the veins on her hands.

"I see," was all John said. He seemed shocked by such news. Was she right in telling him? "And can ye tell me what side of the war you were on? I think not of you as a supporter of Cromwell and his Roundheads."

"In my heart, I will never be a true Puritan."

All was silent for a moment.

"Then you are a Royalist, eh?" The white teeth and wide smile were gleaming again.

"Aye, so you might say. It broke my heart to see the head of King Charles on that pike at London Bridge. The sight will forever be with me—as well as the sights and worse, sounds of the wounded, and the cry of the dying. To see my beloved England torn in two…I sought to leave it all behind." She covered her face and let out a sob in remembrance.

"And behind you shall leave it. I apologize for my intruding," John quickly added. And then he burst into another wide grin and slapped his thigh. "Why, glory be. If the truth be known, I share your sentiments as well. I always believed in the Great Chain of Being— with a monarch in charge. I think we share this belief, Kat. I hope that the poor King's exiled son finds his way back to the throne. It will set things right—there— and here." He stopped for a moment. "And no one needs knowing about it either. Best keep this to ourselves."

"Then tell me, what brought *you* to Wethersfield?" she asked, feeling relieved.

John smiled warmly at her. "Opportunities of course. I landed in Boston years ago with my brother Richard. I heard tales in the taverns of the fertile land in a small town called Wethersfield, took my chances, and removed to this little settlement. I bought, as I told thee, this parcel in 1647, and I plan on purchasing ten more acres in the Great Meadows. The land was what brought me here." He stopped to gaze at her again. "And God brought you here to me."

He let out a cough and cleared his throat. Katherine decided this was her chance to be even bolder with him. "Tell me, John, what astrological sign were you born under?"

"What? Sign born under what?" His voice echoed and bounced around the corners of the room. "You believe *that*?" He leaned over and seemed to be counting the cluster of freckles atop her nose. "Let no one know of this, Kat. 'Tis dangerous, such knowledge."

She asked the question again.

He answered with his own. "What sign of the sun do *you* think I was born under?"

Now he wore that mischievous yet innocent grin on his face. Katherine realized that John seemed to be making merry of it all—clearly something that was lacking in Connecticut Colony.

She took note of his broad shoulders, thick neck, wide-spaced eyes, tousled hair, wide forehead, and strong jaw. "I would say John, you were born under the sign of the bull, stubborn but kind, a lover of the earth and all that grows." She smiled at him, proud of her prediction.

John's face paled. "Why, I do have a mid-May birthday. How did you know?"

"I know these things," she said, puffing her chest out a bit.

John seemed to find some amusement with Katherine's pride. "Tell me then, what star were you born under?"

"The sign of the archer, Sagittarius. I take my bow and arrow, shoot, and hit my mark. 'Tis all about the aim, the timing, the patience. But under this sign, my mouth can run amuck and get the better of me. I need to keep quiet—my Mam warned me as such."

"The archer, eh? I can see that in thee." He raised his eyebrows. "Though I don't believe in such hodgepodge." He stopped speaking to bring over a pudding cooling aside the hearth.

"But *I* believe in it," she said. "If the Bible says, '*God created the heavens and earth*,' then all the planets and all their movements are created and blessed by God. 'Tis correct." She nodded, feeling sure of herself.

"'Tis enough," John said of a sudden. "You do what you want with my stars and your stars, but take care. Tell no one of this interest. Mayhap they may think you are a soothsayer—or worse, a witch!"

"A witch? Nay!" She shook her head aghast to hear the word. Again.

"Take care, my merry maid, there's been hangings round these parts. Alse Young of Windsor was hanged in 1647. Then in 1648, it was a Wethersfield servant, Mary Johnson. She admitted to carnal knowledge with the devil, and that he helped her with her chores. She repented, but was still hanged on the gallows for 'entertaining Satan.' And just two years ago, my neighbors John and Joan Carrington were taken to the gallows—and hanged as witches. I knew them well. Tragic for those who doth know the real truth."

"Your neighbors? Hanged for witchcraft? What did they do? What was the real truth?"

"Hard to fathom, but John Carrington traded a gun to the Indians; 'tis all the man did. The authorities thought the gun *bewitched*. Thought it could be used for killing white settlers. Carrington was an honest carpenter. After his first wife died, he married Joan. She, being much younger than he, was an object of suspicion. She joined him on Gallows' Hill in Hartford, leaving a young babe barely months old. Authorities claimed his three acres up the road. God help us 'tis a warning no one is safe!" His shook his head, shoulders drooping low, as he fixed his gaze on a floor plank.

"'Tis truly a tragedy, John. I'm heartsore for you, and for the Carringtons...and their young child." She decided she would admit something else to him. "Aye, this astrology led to my troubles at the captain's. Another servant asked me to read her fortune, and she was not happy with the message."

"Fortunetelling? Nay, take heed, Kat," John said in a low voice. "You've left the war behind. Leave this astrology and fortunetelling behind as well. As far as your healing, townspeople are always in need of remedies. You can prove useful in this manner. But best remain silent and keep these *other* things to yourself. As far as me being stubborn, yes— in a manner—but I'm a kind, understanding man. Do what you will, but take heed. People in this town talk."

Katherine smiled. "I am certain they are already talking about your new boarder."

"And if they are?" He stood and bunched a fist into the air, his broad mouth opened wide. "I will quell the gossip if I hear any. Just take warning. Do not give townspeople fodder for talk. Read what you will, study what you must, but keep quiet, Kat…if you truly want to stay in Wethersfield. You have been warned."

CHAPTER 18

The next morning dawned bright and sunny. John explained he had work to do in town helping out a friend with a barn-raising, and making some trades down at the harbor. He would be gone most of the afternoon, so Katherine had the day to explore. She decided since the weather was drier, she'd make her way to the Great Meadow. She would find the land John mentioned he was to buy soon. And she wanted to see again the Hollister tract of land, land that her cousins now owned, and the new house they had built. It just happened to be right across from the High Street, across from the Sandy Lane.

She pulled her worn boots on and walked down the Sandy Lane, breathing in the fresh morning air. She noticed all the places that Josiah had pointed out years ago; on the corner of High Street and the Lane was John Nott's goods and furniture shop. And next door to Nott's store was the town tavern, Sadler's Ordinary. Across from the Ordinary were the Meetinghouse, the Town Green, the Town Office and the Hollister land, now the Gilbert land.

Katherine found a gate to the meadows and gently pushed it open. Here a small path led to different plots; arrowed wooden signs bore names such as James Wakeley and John Barnard; they identified who owned what.

At last she found John's sign indicating his land. She longed to help him with the planting, but in the back of her mind, she still thought it best to return home. She felt like an outsider, a single woman boarding with a single man. She looked out toward the river, her mind torn with decisions.

"Cousin." She heard a voice call out from behind her.

Katherine spun sharply about.

There was Josiah glaring at her. "Josiah," she gasped. "You startled me."

"You are back," he said, frowning. "Removed from the captain's house I hear, for—"

"Aye, the same house where you and your wife left me, dropped me off like a box of common goods."

"I knew you would never last in Captain Cullick's service." Josiah shook his head. "You come with no station in life." He spit on the ground and spread his legs in a fighting stance, as if he might spring a knife—or wield a stick at her. "In fact, you bring shame to the Gilbert family. Fortunetelling and astrology? 'Tis a wonder you were ever considered a member of the Gilberts. Now I truly doubt it."

"And you have never treated me as such. I survived, no thanks to you!" With her fists clenched, she glared back at him. I'll hold my ground, she thought.

Josiah sneered. "What are your plans now? Why did you not come to your kin first? People are talking, what with you staying with the unmarried Harrison, wondering if you are bundling together yet. Are you setting your sights on the man? Well, he's too good for you. If I were you, I would book passage back to England. The war is over."

She stomped her boot hard, and pointed a finger at him. "How dare you? What business is it of yours where I stay and with whom

I stay with? *Cousin* Josiah, you have shown me naught of what they call true Christian charity. I will not listen to such blather. I go free… where I may. And you keep away or—"

Josiah removed his hat and snickered. "Or what… *cousin?*"

"Never you mind," she said, brushing past him to head back to the gate. She had seen enough of the Great Meadow for now.

·•·

Katherine and John sat quietly at the tableboard sipping her chicken soup. She was not in the spirit for talk, for too much filled her mind.

"Why so quiet this eve? The soup is good," John murmured, his head low, eyes on her.

"John, 'tis time. Time for me to leave. I'm not wanted around these parts."

"Leave? The devil you will—"

"But I must. I have enough saved to book passage to England. Spring will turn to summer, and I will be forgotten…like a weed. Mark my word."

John looked incredulous. "I daresay not. Did something happen to set your mind so?"

Should she tell him about the encounter with Josiah? Was it worth the effort? In her mind, it was.

"On my way to the Great Meadow, if you must know, I encountered Josiah, my cousin. He told me people are talking about me—about us. My removal from the captain's house has caused sparks in this town. 'Tis all my fault. I am already bringing you tidings of woe. You will forget me soon enough."

She thought in her head and heart this was so. She had tried—and failed.

"This is nothing but idle gossip and right meddling. I do not, as I told thee, listen to such hogwash. And neither should you!"

"I do appreciate the genuine kindness you have shown me these weeks. I don't want to be a burden to you."

John pushed back his chair, stood up, and came toward her. He rested a hand on her shoulder and gazed down at her. "I won't let you go. I have waited my whole life for you!"

Katherine stared up at the burly farmer shocked by his blunt words. "What are you saying, John?"

He grabbed a vase filled with violets atop the table and thrust them toward her. "I am saying, Katherine, I want and need you—for my wife. Over a month has passed...but I knew that day we met, you were the one for me. You may be feisty, your auburn head of hair high among the clouds and stars at times, but you bring life to my dull existence." He took a breath and wiped his forehead. "You see, I am hoping you will grow to love this farmer. What say you?"

Katherine glanced about the Great Room in a house she now felt was a home of sorts. In just a month, she realized her feelings for John had developed into a deep caring, a bond that she truly never had experienced before. Aye, there had been others, but John was different. She had grown to love his deep voice, his hearty laugh, his broad chest, strong shoulders, and steady ways. Here was a man who needed a helpmeet.

He sat down on a bench next to her and grasped her hand. "Will thou take me for a husband, Kat? A perfect team we shall be. And once I nail our banns of engagement to the meetinghouse door, the townspeople can say naught; they can talk all they want, but why should we care?"

He rose, grabbed Katherine's waist, lifted her into the air, and swung her about, her cap flying off her head, unloosening her thick hair.

"Stop," she squealed, dizzy with the spinning.

"Not until I get an answer—the right answer." He laughed and continued to twirl her about.

"Put me down," she demanded. He followed her orders, and then sat down waiting for an answer, while she tucked her hair back into the cap.

She knew she liked this man; he amused her with his ways, his earthiness, but also his independent devil-may-care attitude that matched her fiery spirit. He had helped her a month ago; she knew he would do so again if need be. John was a trustworthy man fit to be her husband.

"Aye, John. I will take thee for a husband." She leaned over and wrapped her arms round his thick neck. Then she lay her head against his chest. "I have found you, and I have found my home."

— • —

The next afternoon John burst through the farmhouse door as Katherine swept the floorboards and dusted the furniture. "The banns are up on the meetinghouse door," he said out of breath. "I just posted them for all to see. I will soon be a marrying man. And I'll be proud to call you wife."

"What will people think?" she asked him.

"Why should we care, Kat? We are a right team to be reckoned with. I am a respected man about this town. And take no care about gossips. They always need *something* to talk about."

"Aye." She laughed, nodding in agreement. "And now they have it."

The pair embraced and then Katherine continued to polish up the pewterware and strew fresh rushes onto the floorboards.

"I will find a magistrate to marry us, Kat. Then we shall set a date." John hummed under his breath, as he ladled a mug of cider for himself.

"Will my cousins be invited?" she asked.

"Invite whom you will. I say when the magistrate is full ready, he can marry us on the Green. If there are bystanders, so be it. This is between you, me, the magistrate, and God."

"A spring wedding? I need a proper dress to wear."

"Worry yourself not. If thou would wear plain homespun, I would still think thee the finest lass in all the Colony. You bring me smiles, Kat, while most in this town bring me frowns."

"I will do better than homespun, John. If we can trade goods for materials, I will attend to the making of my own dress."

"And that's what I love about thee, Kat," John replied. "A self-sufficient lass if I say so myself."

"Aye, and I respect the same in my husband-to be." The word sounded odd on her tongue. Husband? It seemed a dream to Katherine. Maybe this is what Mr. Lilly meant when he told her that she might receive an unexpected windfall.

Katherine Gilbert would soon be a marrying woman.

What would her dear Mam say now?

CHAPTER 19

Josiah stormed into the house like a wicked wind. "As if it wasn't bad enough to see Katherine roaming free in the meadows, but now to read the wedding banns nailed to the meetinghouse door? Not only will Katherine marry… but she is to be our neighbor as well." He griped to Elizabeth who sat silently rocking nine-month-old Benjamin.

"You are waking Ben with your loud banter, Jos. Forsooth, please, no sense vexing us all with your complaints. Mayhap you need a tonic to calm your nerves."

Following her suggestion Josiah filled a noggin with rum and swilled it down. The fiery liquid settled him. He pulled up a stool next to Elizabeth watching Benjamin's small chest rise and fall. Ben's eyes stay closed, but his long lashes fluttered as if he dreamt.

"Why such anger?" Elizabeth asked. "Are you ashamed of your cousin still? Why deprive her of the good will to marry? Why not wish the couple well? Don't you think it is time for a change of heart?"

"Change of heart?" Josiah shook his head. "She never completed her service to the captain. And she was removed because of fortune-telling. Now she is taking advantage of John Harrison. What spell did she conjure on the good man? That's what I'd like to know." He cleared his throat and groaned.

"John pines for companionship, as God hath put forth. 'Tis natural. He's found himself a helpmeet," Elizabeth said. Benjamin stirred as she opened her blouse, found a cloth nearby, and settled the babe's searching mouth against her nipple. "And people change, Jos."

"So, what do you propose I do…to make it better?" he glumly asked.

"We owe it to Katherine and the family to attend the wedding ceremony. When is it?"

"I happened to see Rebecca Smith in town today. She-who-knows-everything told me they will be married in a fortnight. The third of May to be exact. I am certain it will be announced next meeting."

"Then," Elizabeth said, rocking the baby, "we must go. 'Tis time to set things a-right. Once married, Katherine will no longer be a worry or concern to you. And we ought to give thanks to Goodman Harrison, for he will make a fine husband. Mark my words, he will make a fine goodwife out of her. I think it's time to make amends."

"Aye," said Josiah, the liquid fire warming his blood. "You are right, Lizbeth. I will try."

·—·—·

John found the Magistrate, Samuel Wyllys, who agreed to marry them on the Wethersfield Green. Katherine remembered the quiet, young man from Captain Cullick's, and how she had served him and the others their midday supper.

The planting time had begun; most people were preoccupied with the price of seed, what to plant, and how to prepare their gardens and fields for the season. Wheat, corn, beans, onions, cucumbers and turnips all had their place in Wethersfield gardens and fields.

John returned home with a bolt of fine linen he traded for down at the harbor. Katherine knew she could sew together a proper wedding dress. She busied herself by twisting some old grapevines together forming a small circlet, weaving in bright purple and white violets to wear after the service.

John had a stiff black doublet, black hose and breeches, a long-sleeved white shirt, and polished buckled shoes, along with his oiled steeple hat. "Aye, I'm wearing my steeple hat," he said. "Just in case these old Puritans make a fuss."

"What about food, John?" She had learned that after a Puritan wedding, guests were invited to the new couple's home bearing gifts, but the newlyweds must graciously provide the meal.

"We'll make a few platters beforehand. Invite folks over. Maybe even your cousin, Josiah?" John's eyes held a twinkle. "Isn't it time you made peace with your family?" He smiled at her and gave a wink. "You should be thankful you have kin round these parts, Kat. A grateful heart never hurt anyone."

Katherine drew close and leaned her head on his shoulder. "*You* are my family now, John."

John sighed a breath, his eyes gleaming in the candles' reflections. He pulled her to him. "You will have naught to worry about. This merchant farmer will always keep guard for you—against the wolves and bears roaming about—beasts and men." He bent down and kissed the top of her head. "You need not worry about anything."

"Aye, and a grateful bride-to-be I am," she said.

·—•—·

On the third day of May 1653, the pair stood on the Wethersfield Green encircled by a ring of townspeople. Some were invited guests, others bystanders. It was a brilliant day for a wedding; the May sun beamed down in thin splashes of light; the sky was bright blue. New shoots of pale green appeared on trees, bushes, and plants.

Two days earlier on May the first, Katherine remembered to tie colorful ribbons to the spindly but erect pine tree aside the house, as May Day was her favorite celebration back home. She would ne'er be able to dance the Maypole in Wethersfield, but she could dress the tree with bright ribbons of red, gold, green, and white. John never made a mention. He was too busy with the preparations for the wedding day.

Josiah stood in the circle, glaring at his cousin, wondering how she managed to capture the most eligible lone-man in the Colony. Elizabeth stood beside him holding Benjamin in her arms. Josiah held open the worn Gilbert family Bible. His brother Jonathan stood nearby, beaming in pride. At least his wayward cousin had found a proper place and a proper husband, he thought. Goodwife Rebecca Smith, the town gossip and scold, joined the circle along with her elderly husband. Kate Palmer, Katherine's first friend, with husband Henry, stood close by along with some of John's farmer friends and neighbors.

Magistrate Wyllys, dressed in a black robe and wig, smiled at the couple and had them state their vows, and they announced their 'I dos.' The magistrate then opened his Bible and said, "The reading today is from the Book of Proverbs, Chapter 31, verses 10-12. *'Who can find a virtuous woman? For her price is far above rubies. The heart of her husband doth safely trust in her, so that he shall have no need of spoil. She will do him good and not evil all the days of her life.'"*

The magistrate slapped the book shut and eyed Katherine. "And what dost thou say to this?"

"He shall trust me, and have no fear of evil from me."

"And you, John Harrison? What say you?"

In a solemn voice John said, "To me she is far above the price of rubies. I trust her well."

"So be it," said Magistrate Wyllys. "Before I pronounce you man and wife, I ask you, Katherine, to announce what psalm you have chosen to be sung at next meeting—in honor of both of you."

During the last week, Katherine had thought long as to what psalm she would request. Of course, this meant she and John would *have* to attend on the next Sabbath; she dreaded thinking about the four-hour meeting. All those people eying them, the newlyweds.

She straightened up and took the paper from her wedding pouch. "I have chosen Psalm 27." She opened the paper and began to read: *"The Lord is my light and salvation; whom shall I fear? The Lord is the strength of my life; of whom shall I be afraid? When the wicked, even mine enemies and my foes came upon me to eat my flesh, they stumbled and fell. Though an army may encamp against me, my heart share not fear. Though war may rise against me..."* She lifted her head and paused to fix her eyes on her cousin Josiah.

"Hmm, very well...thank you, Katherine. Your choice of this psalm is duly noted. You may stop now," said the magistrate. The small group of attendees seemed to sigh together, relieved she read no more.

"It pleases me to announce," Magistrate Wyllys said, "by the laws of God and this Colony, I, as presiding magistrate, pronounce you man and wife." He paused and looked around. "And please stop by the Town Office to duly record your names and date with the Town Clerk."

A loud huzzah rang out among the small group, and clapping could be heard.

John reached over and grabbed one of Katherine's hands. "Please," he shouted. "All here are invited back to our house for the sack posset and hearty victuals including the wedding cake, baked by my…" he turned to Katherine, "…my wife." He grasped her hand hard and beamed out to the group. "Goodwife Harrison."

Katherine squeezed his hand back. Here was a man who was proud to call her wife.

·—•—·

The wind lightly pushed the small band of Puritans who followed the newly married couple home. After stopping in at the Town Office, they crossed the High Street, and headed up the Sandy Lane. A few stragglers joined the party. The group totaled about twelve. Even old Goodwife Smith joined her friend, the Marshal's wife Elizabeth, and together they proceeded with their husbands lagging behind.

John opened the gate for the group and with a sweep of his hand pointed to the door of the farmhouse. "Come in! Welcome," he said merrily. He escorted the group into the house and to the tableboard. "Please gather round. My bride will make the sack posset."

Katherine went to stoke the embers of the hearthfire, and retrieved the posset's ingredients: ale, eggs, cream, and port wine. She also had managed to find a few cinnamon sticks at Market, and had grated the spice in a small bowl. Kate Palmer joined her in the making of the wedding drink. She cupped her hand to the bride's shoulder. "I'm happy for you, Kat. Relieved as well, that you found yourself a fine man. Aye, he's a right one for you. Many townspeople are pleased he found a bride…and many maids are envious." She giggled and gazed about the spotless sitting room. "Now this farmhouse is your home. Soon you will be knitting caps for a new babe."

The pair stood in front of the kettle cracking eggs, stirring, pouring the wine and cream into the brew until it began to bubble.

"Let it simmer," Kate suggested. "In the meantime, I will serve the cold meat, cheese, and vegetable platters to the guests. After they eat the dinner, we can serve the posset and cake."

The small crowd mingled about the tableboard cackling like hens, exchanging pleasantries; everyone but Josiah who sat glum and stiff, his eyes glowering at the bride. After the meal the wedding cake was served, a vanilla cake stuffed with sugared almonds, walnuts, and sprinkled with ground lemon peel.

Finally the sack posset was ready. Kate Palmer poured out the brew and cups were lifted high. Rebecca Smith, the scold, stood and proclaimed she would like to make a toast. John rushed over to help the town gossip from her chair.

"To the newly-weds… good health… and fortune. And may you have many healthy children together." She drank from her cup, her hand trembling. "I have a request," Goodwife Smith said with a flourish, "Let us sing together the psalm Katherine hath chosen for meeting next week. Why Katherine would choose a psalm about 'thine enemies,' I know not. For we are not enemies, but friends. Shall we sing *now*?" She looked about the crowd, eyes twinkling, pleased to be the center of attention.

Katherine stood up, tippled from the sack. "Sing Psalm 27? Why, I declare we shall *not*!"

Most of the party lifted their heads and stared mutely at the bride. John seemed amused with the untoward behavior of Katherine speaking up on their wedding day.

"What hast thou planned for us now, Kat?" his voice echoed across the room.

"Why I'll sing thee a ballad dedicated to the month of May, 'Tis a tune from the old country." Watching with pleasure the stiff, somber faces of the Puritan guests, she smiled a toothy grin and began to sing:

"Go no more a rushing…oh maids in May…
Go no more a rushing… maids, I pray;
Go no more a rushing, or you'll fall a blushing,
Bundle up your rushes and haste away."

"Maids in May? Go a rushing? Bah! Katherine, you are no longer a maid," said Josiah, frustrated with this wanton display. Her impudent behavior made him even more glad he'd never let her set foot in his house.

Katherine frowned. This was her home now. Josiah was fortunate to be a part of the celebration. She bit at her lip and waited. "Then I'll sing ye my favorite ballad from the North. This is for you, husband."

She lifted her wedding dress with one hand, and raised her mug toward John with the other. All eyes were on her as she sang in a lilting voice:

"A bonny fine maid of a noble degree
With a hey down down… a down down
Maid Marian called by name
Did live in the North, of excellent worth
For she was a gallant dame.

The Earl of Huntington, nobly born,
That came from noble blood
To Marian went, with a good intent
By the name of Robin Hood.

With kisses sweet
Their red lips do meet
For she and the Earl did agree
In every place, they kindly embrace,
With love and sweet unity…"

Katherine glanced about the room and took a mock bow. She expected applause or maybe huzzahs and cheers from the group.

Henry Palmer chuckled under his breath, and started humming the tune; he seemed to enjoy the merriment of the moment. John sat gazing longingly at her, undaunted by her boldness.

Now Goodwife Smith slowly stood again, and was coaxing her old husband up from the bench. "Jacob, cover your ears," she ordered. "We can no longer tarry here. Ballads are forbidden in Connecticut Colony, especially ballads about love and maids carrying on in May. Forsooth—'tis dreadful—such behavior. Pooh!" She shook her head, wobbled unsteadily, and rolled her eyes toward the ceiling. "You and I will hear no more of such blather." She looked over and nodded to her friend Elizabeth. "I shall see you at market soon."

"But—" said Katherine, surprised. "'Tis only an innocent ballad about love. Should I not sing of love on my wedding day?"

"We have rules and laws regarding singing anything but psalms, Goodwife Harrison," said old Goodwife Smith. "Perhaps it would behoove you to sing Psalm 27—even if it is about thine enemies. Good day." The couple made their way to the door.

"I will sing what I want!" Katherine shouted. "This is my house too, lest you forget. How dare you people try to despoil my wedding day?"

Goodwife Smith turned around, and her small blue eyes narrowed. "You don't want to sing psalms about thine enemies," she intoned, "lest you accumulate even more enemies than you have already. By the by, we all know what happened to you in Hartford at Captain Cullick's. And here be your husband trying to make an honest goodwife out of you. When will you ever give up your wayward notions? Do you not care what others think of thee? Forsooth!"

Katherine thrust her hands to her hips. "These are but rumors, Goodwife Smith. Gossip and hearsay. I steer clear of gossips and scolds; far too many round these parts." Her hazel eyes glared with a cold fury, and her wide mouth was set in a hard line.

John crossed the room to the front door, his face reddening. "Rebecca, this is neither the time nor place. It is a time for celebrations, not accusations. My Katherine is starting a new life with *me* now. She is leaving *that* behind." He bent down and stuck a finger in Goodwife Smith's pinched face. "And so should you."

CHAPTER 20

After Goodwife Smith swept herself and her husband out the door, those who remained slowly gathered up their belongings making ready to leave. Josiah approached Katherine, his eyes dark with ringed shadows. He wished his cousin a brisk huzzah, and left with wife Elizabeth and little Ben.

The Palmers were the only couple left at the celebration. Kate Palmer was tidying up, chittering like a nervous bird.

"Please, Kate," said John. "Sit and enjoy what's left of the cake and posset." Her husband Henry proceeded to quaff the rest of the sack posset from his tankard, and licked his lips.

"Come Kate, we must go. Let's leave the newly-weds alone to themselves." He stood and made way to the door. "A long life to both of ye," he said with a broad smile. "And to much happiness…and many children as well." He approached Katherine. "I enjoyed your singing. The wife and I never have a problem with song." He gave a shout to John. "If you need some extra work done on the farm, let me know."

"I will need some shelving for my herbs and simples," Katherine reminded John and Henry. "A nice, new cupboard would suit me fine."

Kate Palmer ran to her friend. "I will see you on Market Day next." She winked. "We will talk then. I am so very happy for ye both." The two friends embraced.

"You are a true friend, Kate," Katherine said. "Many thanks for your help. Amid mine enemies, you are true."

Finally, the Palmers left and the couple was alone.

"Why am I not allowed to sing in mine own house, John? Why? How dare they? How dare anyone try to stop me—on my own wedding day no less? The gall! And after witnessing our vows and eating our food? These people have no shame!" She was starting to get herself into a fluster.

John approached Katherine and touched her hand. "There be rules on the outside, wife. Rules we must follow."

"Rules? When I was back in England, I sang to the boys all the time—"

"Sang to the boys?" John asked. "What boys?"

Katherine quieted with the question. Should she share more slices of her past with him? He was her husband now. "I speak of the men I ministered to during the war. I was trained, as I told you, as a sister to nurse the wounded soldiers. So I sang to them, the hopeless and helpless—and the dying. I tried to lift their spirits as best I could. With the help of God, I saved many. The others—"

John raised his eyebrows, his face serious now. "Was there a special—a special somebody in your life—before you met me? Tell me, Kat. I need to know."

Katherine stood and walked to the hearth briefly staring into the dying fire. "Aye John, there was someone I cared for." She sighed and retrieved a poker to stoke the embers. "But that is all in the past. I came to this colony to leave it all behind— the war, the pain, and the heartache." She turned and drew closer to him, and rested a hand on his broad shoulder looking into his eyes. "Don't you see John? There's only *us* now. There's only you and me." She grasped his warm hand. "I left everything to come to this roughshod colony with few expectations. But I found you. If not for you, I'd be on a ship returning home." She sighed, then looked back to the fire.

John seemed relieved. "And I will never let you go, Kat. You are my bride, my goodwife, my helpmeet."

Katherine swung her hips about and bowed to him in dramatic gesture. She began twirling herself about the Great Room. "And what can I do for you, my Lord?"

John's wide face cracked open a wide smile. "Sing for me again, my Maid Marian. Your Robin Hood awaits."

···

After she cleaned up and prepared for her wedding night, Katherine stepped outside and breathed in the twilight air. The farm was quickly becoming a part of her. The spring air smelled of fresh rain and meadow, clean and delicate. She listened to the sunset twittering of birds settling in for the night. She stood near the kitchen door and gave thanks to Providence.

Then Katherine saw the shadow of a man walking up from the High St. coming around the side of the house. He looked as if he were planting seeds along the farmhouse. Katherine decided to be bold and walked toward the intruder. "How now? Who goes there?"

The stranger turned out to be none other than Joseph Hawk Wing. He stepped forth from the shadows carrying a small jar in his hands. "Joseph comes to bring gifts, brings protection from my tribe, the Wangunks. For love and future. Blessings to you and Harrison man!"

"A gift for us? Why—"

Joseph displayed the open jar. "Tobacco. I drop it around the farm. Good luck for you. Protection, fertility. Will keep out bad spirits." He continued to carefully sprinkle the herb about the back door to the kitchen.

"How thoughtful of you and your people." Katherine said, honored Joseph and the tribe had remembered the day. "Please do come in when you are finished."

As she made ready to walk the steps to the house, Joseph stopped and approached her. He dug deep inside his leather breeches and pulled out a pouch. "Here." He handed it at her. "Joseph knows what you like—Joseph knows!"

"Joseph!" Katherine said, surprised at the gift. "How did you know?"

Joseph chuckled to himself nodding his head. "Joseph knows."

What could Katherine say? She grabbed the pouch and stuffed it in her pocket.

"Thank you, Joseph. Come in when you are finished. John will be delighted to see you."

⋅—⋅

A few minutes later a soft rap sounded at the door. She let Joseph in and led him to John, who was still sitting at the head of the tableboard eating the remains of the wedding cake.

John turned his head and grinned. "Well, Joseph, what say you?"

Joseph bowed slightly before John. "Me—and my tribe—wish you happiness with Goodwife Katherine. Here...is a gift." He slung a small black satchel off his shoulder. He pulled a leather pouch out and reached inside, revealing a belt covered with deep purple and white shells. "Wampum. For you on your wedding." He offered the belt to John.

"A hearty thanks to you and your tribe," John said. "You are a good people. Would you have a piece of wedding cake? 'Tis good." John patted his stomach.

Joseph shook his head. "I go now…back to the island. But first, you are both invited to the Island of Manhannock to make merry in June, first day of summer. Strawberry Moon Festival. Come join us." He opened his hands toward them. "Much food and dance."

Katherine felt a stir for another celebration. "That sounds like a delightful festival. What say you, John?"

"Perhaps…perhaps we shall go. But for now, I have enough worries about merriment on my wedding night."

Joseph laughed aloud and gave a whoop. "You will be merry. You are a good man. You have good wife now."

He made his way to the door and let himself out.

CHAPTER 21

On the next Sabbath, Katherine and John sat in the front pew of the Wethersfield Meetinghouse, listening to Reverend Russell preach about the sin of pride. Afterward the congregation would intone the Psalm Katherine had chosen in honor of her wedding. Katherine wrung her restless hands together as John's stomach growled. The newlyweds desired to be any place but meeting on this Sabbath Day.

"Ahem." The Reverend Russell cleared his throat, his eyes searching the faces of the stern Puritan attendants. "Tithing man." The reverend pointed to a young boy asleep, slumped over in a pew. "Tap the young lad. I'll have no person, young or old, shut their eyes and ears to the word of God." The tithing man abruptly made his way to the pew and tickled the young offender under the nose with the tip of his fox-tail stick.

The reverend began reviewing his notes. "Let us rise to sing Psalm 27 to honor the newly formed bond of husband and wife, John and Katherine Harrison, please stand and face the congregation to receive your blessings from the Freemen, Believers, and members of this church."

Turn to face the people? As if sensing her fear, John grasped Katherine's elbow. "'Tis won't take long. Smile and sing, wife. And sing loud," he said in a low voice.

The newlyweds faced the congregation with a flourish. And sing they did, with such passion that both old and young took note. Katherine did see a few pairs of eyes narrowed at her. Was it jealousy that she had married the one solitary man in Wethersfield? Was it disbelief? Or worse, judgment?

Could not these townsfolk be truly happy— for John at least? Were they willing to give Katherine another chance? Even be happy for them? Instead, Katherine felt like daggers burned bright afore her eyes. Would this suspicion of her ever end?

John nudged her. He already had an uncanny way of knowing when a case of the nerves fell upon her. Just the bulk and heaviness of his body kept her spirit strong. She leaned against his solid frame. "This is almost over," he said in a whisper. "We are almost to the end."

•—•

Finally it was over. Katherine, readying to leave, wrapped her dark green cloak about her and shivered. Townspeople began to gather on this fine spring day waiting to encircle and welcome the new couple—husband and wife—to the church.

John stepped up glowing with pride. "Katherine, let me introduce some townsfolk." He gestured to a short, staid couple dressed in black. "Here be Michael and Ann Griswold. Live on the Watering Lane. And meet the Robbins from the Broad Street— they live next to the Palmers. They are important members of the community." The two couples nodded and expressed their welcome.

Other people joined the circle. John stretched his arms out. "Here be some of our neighbors. Joan and Robert Francis live but a few houses up the Sandy Lane." The pair nodded silently at Katherine. The wife arched her thin eyebrows, turned her nose up, and pursed her lips. "And here's John Goodrich, and here's Samuel Beldon, other important member in our community. Good people, I say."

Important members? Katherine began to feel her face aflush. She couldn't contain her emotions or words any longer. "I don't understand. Are we not ...*all* important members of this town?"

"Of course," John quickly said. "'Tis just that—"

Katherine noticed Ann Griswold squinting her dark eyes, shaking her head, and frowning.

"We heard you worked in Hartford for a time," Goodwife Griswold said, "serving Captain Cullick in his household. How did you ever—?"

John interrupted. "Aye, so my wife did. But the past is the past, so let it be. My Katherine has begun a new life with me. Any more questions can be addressed to *me*, her husband."

"Respect must be earned in this town. Never forget that," said Mrs. Robbins, peering her nose down at the couple. "But you know this, Goodman Harrison."

John glowered in silence at the shocked observers. Katherine, instead of cringing in shame stood firm, clenched her fists together, and felt like pounding perfect Ann Griswold, with her perfect, little shiny face. How dare this woman speak as such? And Mrs. Robbins commenting as well? But she decided for John's sake to keep quiet.

The pair walked home for the midday meal before afternoon meeting. She did not— and would not— return to meeting that day. She had seen enough and heard enough from all the *important* people in town.

·—·

After meeting Josiah mounted his wagon and held tight to the reins awaiting Elizabeth. He had watched his cousin with her new husband surrounded by a group of people, welcoming them to the community. He wasn't one of them. Imagine his cousin, once a servant, now mingling with Wethersfield's finest? He reckoned Katherine was trying to make way with the leaders and distinguished townsfolk, the same way she had warmed up to his brother Jonathan. Was she trying to prove she was worthy of being one of them?

He spotted Elizabeth chatting with friends. The sun beamed across the town green, alighting the great elm's treetop that towered over all else. He waited, tapping his foot. All those people round the couple! Bah! He refused to join them— for a hypocrite he'd never be—not for Katherine.

He knew of her past, but not the details. Who knew what she *really* did for those soldier boys—to ease their pain? He shuddered. He shook his head in bewilderment, pushing away such thoughts. But they kept returning to his mind. How did she ever entice a farmer like John Harrison to marry her? What spell did she cast on him? Josiah wondered.

He watched Elizabeth come forth from the crowd holding Ben in her arms.

"What took thee so long? My stomach's a-growling," he complained.

"I had to push my way through the people—and I should ask why you are sitting here like a rough-hewn stone? And what think ye of the beautiful psalm Katherine chose to sing at meeting?" Josiah helped his wife and Ben to the wagon.

"Beautiful?" He huffed. "I think not. My cousin is a schemer and a deceiver. Mark my words, she is no good."

"She is trying, Jos. You must as well," Elizabeth said, as the horses stirred, and the baby began to wail.

"I have tried, but she's a pox on the Gilbert name."

"And to say such words after meeting," his wife mused, shaking her head. She placed Ben against her shoulder and began to pat the baby's back to quiet him down.

Josiah snapped the reins to the restless horses' backs. "On with ye," he shouted, his mind and stomach on his nooning meal.

CHAPTER 22

Mid-June, 1653

Katherine burst out the back door of the farmhouse and ran toward John who was pitching bales of first hay from the wagon. "John," she said, out of breath, leaning against the wagon. "I am late by over a fortnight. No wonder I have no appetite. I would say husband, it looks like we are going to have a baby!"

She did not have to wait long for a response. John let out a loud *huzzah* that echoed across the field down to the High Street and throughout the neighbors' yards. He grabbed Katherine by the waist, lifted her up, and spun her around several times as he was wont to do.

"Nay, John, stop. You'll make me dizzy." She paused. "And the baby." She listened to her own words, stopping to think of what she just said. Could it truly be so? Katherine, now a married woman, with a young one on the way?

He put her down gently. His eyes remained on hers, his mouth open wide with wonder. "I just knew it wouldn't take long. You're strong, Kat. Strong enough to give me a son." He gazed at her with great anticipation and reverence.

"That's for God to decide. I would love a girl child to teach her my arts. And I must write to Mam with the news."

John drew her close to him and wrapped her in his arms. The smell of fresh mown hay and the scent of elder wafted in the June breezes; the aroma of fresh new clover calmed her mood.

"If it's a boy, I'll teach him to cobble, farm, and to trade. And if it's a girl, you'll teach her the arts of your cooking, knitting, and spinning." He laughed and patted his own stomach. "Just the talk of your cooking makes my belly to rumble."

"I shall bring thee your supper, John. The pottage is almost stewed."

"Aye, and you are a right helpmeet and a good wife, Kat."

Katherine smiled at her husband. "And what a father you will be. Let's not tell a soul until my belly starts to ripen."

John wiped stray pieces of hay from his damp forehead. "You bring happiness to my days, wife. Soon I shall start building a new room near the kitchen so you can feed the babe with ease." He was already thinking ahead. "Of course, the new room will be the birthing room. I'll hire out Henry Palmer to help with the new addition—*for* the new addition." John laughed aloud, as he was wont to do; he found his clever jokes amusing and never ceased to be entertained by them.

"And don't forget to remind Henry of my much-needed cupboard and shelving for my remedies. 'Twill be good to have my herbs and salves lined in proper jars," she mused, "now that my garden is planted."

But John, no longer listening, was back to his work, only this time she heard him humming his now favorite tune, *The Ballad of Maid Marian*, the song she loved and knew so well.

⋅•⋅

While John was eating his midday meal, Katherine reminded him of the invitation from Joseph and his people. "Tonight's the celebration, John. 'Tis the twenty-first of June."

"Aye, so it is. I have arranged for Joseph to pick us up at the harbor. He'll canoe us to the island—and take us home again," he said, eating his stew in mouthfuls. "They'll have shad roasting over the fire and strawberry cakes for dessert. I shan't ever refuse an invitation for a meal. And remember Kat, we go as guests, not participants."

Katherine knew that Wright's Island, as the settlers called it, had homesteads and plots that the white man sowed and reaped in season. Yet the natives called it *Manhannock,* the Island of Merriment and spent time there during the growing season. To think that settlers and natives existed together on the island brought her some peace. She looked forward to the celebration.

·•·

Late in the afternoon the couple walked arm and arm up the High Street to Wethersfield Harbor. There they would wait for Joseph to take them to the island. Katherine carried a basket of strawberries from the farm as an offering. John carried a rucksack filled with utensils, small cups, and pans as gifts. He also included some leather strips and a few pairs of shoes he had cobbled.

She'd worn colorful clothes: a dark violet skirt, blue shawl, tan waistcoat, and a freshly starched white cap. The attire blended well with the red-brown of her hair. John wore a red doublet, brown breeches, and a small brown hat adorned with a hawk feather. He was freshly shaven, his face smooth, and he smelled like lime and lemon.

The harbor seemed quiet this afternoon with only a few folks strolling about. As the couple awaited Joseph's arrival, Katherine espied Josiah, with wife Elizabeth holding their child, standing a short distance away. Katherine nudged John. "Look who stands nearby but my cousin and his family."

John stiffened. "This is a perfect time, Kat. 'Tis providence, I say."

"Perfect time for what?"

He looked down at her and frowned. "Now that you are my wife—and I your husband—I will allow no discord with your family. 'Tis not the man I am to hold a grudge. Let us make amends. There must be peace in the family. I will hear naught else of this. Let us make haste."

They approached the Gilberts, and John greeted them. "How fare ye? Nice to see you kin down at the harbor this first day of summer." His eyes warmed at the sight of young Ben in Elizabeth's arms.

Josiah eyed Katherine's colorful dress. His furrowed brow and pursed mouth indicated his disapproval. "'Tis a pleasure. Where do you go—dressed as such?"

Katherine stood mute as John stepped forward. "Each year my native farmhand invites me to the festival on the Island. This year I have my wife who joins me." He put his arm around Katherine.

Josiah remained quiet, and shook his head in dismay.

Katherine bristled, not wanting to speak. How dare John demand this from her? Her pride was strong; after all, she had done nothing wrong. She was the one wronged. Why should she apologize to kin who sent her into servitude? She held that grudge close to her heart. Mayhap it was time to put it behind her; or at least try to act that way.

"Cousin Josiah," she began, "I know we had a rough start—I certainly did—but let us declare it bygone. Perhaps 'tis time for a new start." She glanced about the water, waiting nervously for Joseph's canoe.

"Aye," John said. "Now that I have taken Katherine for my wife, we want peace in the family. What say you two come round to dinner tomorrow to our house. Bring little Ben of course."

Elizabeth, coddling the baby grabbed Josiah's arm. "Nay," she flatly said. "We would like you newly-weds to come for supper at our place, our new home on the old Hollister land. What say you, Josiah?"

What could he say? He could hardly say no. He shrugged. "That would be fine." He stared hard at Katherine, his eyes giving her what looked like a warning. "Now that you are properly married—to one of Wethersfield's finest men—I would say God is giving you another chance. If He in His goodness has granted you another chance, I can do the same."

John took a deep breath, grasped Josiah by the shoulder and said, "What is past is past. Aye, you are a good man, Josiah; I am proud to call you kin."

"And I as well," said Katherine, eyes cast downward. What could she say— or do?

"How's late afternoon on the morrow?" Elizabeth asked.

"Aye, we will be there. Shall we bring a dish?" John asked.

"Bring something sweet," Elizabeth replied.

·•·

Katherine fumed silently as Josiah and his wife wandered away with the baby. Here was her husband telling her what to do. But she realized he was right. If she was to live like a proper goodwife, it was best to make amends with her cousin. People talked enough. She needed no more gossip about her.

Joseph finally arrived and helped them into the ochre-colored canoe. Katherine crouched in the bow while John sat in the middle, his hulk of a body and heavy rucksack sufficient as ballast. Joseph handed him a paddle.

"What is this?" John asked in jest. "My farmhand making *me* work?"

As they paddled toward the island, John announced of a sudden, "That was good to get *that* off my chest. All will be well now, Kat." With that he patted his belly and announced with a flourish he was ready for victuals. "Resolving family matters always makes me hungry. Frees up my nerves to eat more—"

Katherine smiled taking in the sights and sounds along the Great River. She noticed a ferry departing the island and pointed.

"That's Thomas Wright's ferry. He owns a good part of the north island. Perhaps we will take the ferry back?" asked John.

"No," shouted Joseph. "I will paddle you back to the harbor."

The canoe skimmed the far northside of the island. Katherine saw a large dock where several boats and rafts were moored and tied up with strong rope. A few men fished off the dock; others fiddled with tying up the crafts. Along the sandy beach a row of canoes and paddles were lined up in perfect order. A lone heron waded nearby ready to spear its prey.

She noticed that a small path wove around the island surrounded by thick clusters of pine and low-growing oaks. Lilies and wildflowers grew along the edges. The sun was lowering in the sky sending gold and white shafts of light onto the crystal-blue waters of the Great River.

Once landed John and Joseph hauled the vessel up onto the sand. Katherine, holding her gift basket of strawberries, looked with wonder about the island. It was clear that Thomas Wright and other settlers had claimed the north side of the island; the natives occupied the land south. She could hear a faint drumbeat and breathed in the smell of fresh bread, roasting corn, and whiffs of tobacco smoke.

"Come," said Joseph, signaling the direction they would take. "We follow the path." A few stragglers stopped to stare at the colorful settlers accompanying Joseph. The sand path was narrow and rock-strewn, causing Katherine to tread lightly. Dense green pine branches hung over the path, as if they welcomed her into a new world. The three walked in silence, dappled light breaking through the trees. Squirrels leapt across branches and ran down the tree trunks scolding the visitors.

The path continued as the sounds became louder. At last, they came to an opening and found themselves in a great clearing. Now Katherine saw up close the small round huts that dotted the land alongside low-lying dwellings covered with bark. She watched a group that had formed a great circle and then heard a loud whoop and shouting.

"What are they doing, John?" she quietly asked.

"It's a wrestling match. Let's take a look."

Sure enough, two greased, half-naked men were rough tumbling, grasping and grabbing at each other. One man stood nearby watching their moves.

Joseph pointed to the man along the side. "He's the judge. Wrestling is a serious game," he told Katherine proudly. Then he reminded them it was time to meet his family. They walked by some older children who were practicing their juggling skills. A few stray dogs ran back and forth in the Indian camp, tongues lolling, spurred on by the smell of roasting lamb on a nearby spit. A woman cranked the spit, turning it over, and brushing the meat down with a mixture.

Then the smell of fish filled the air. "At last," said John, taking in a deep breath. "I can smell shad roasting."

This past April and May, Katherine had seen the silver fish swimming like tiny dolphins up the Great River. The shad, after spawning, would return downriver to the ocean once again. Townspeople and Indians counted on the abundant fish for food, and watched for the schools to swim upriver. She had seen people fishing daily from boats or along the river's edge. The yearly shad run was a reason for celebration.

"Fish and lamb—all for the feast tonight. Then real celebration begins," said Joseph. He led them to a small hut with smoke rising from a hole in the roof. "Come in, meet my wife." They entered through a leather curtain, and a young woman stood and greeted them. She held a sleeping baby to her chest.

"This is my wife, Nya. This is baby Daniel. Daniel Hawk Wing. First baby."

Nya bowed to the pair and welcomed them with a faint smile.

"You know Goodman Harrison. This is his wife, Katherine," said Joseph.

"You are honored here," Nya said.

An older woman sitting nearby grinned, displaying an almost toothless smile. Other children ran about the hut, tugging at their elders' shirts and chasing one another. How free they are, how happy they seem, Katherine thought. She truly felt welcomed by the family and Joseph's tribe. She glanced over at John. He was beaming with pride.

Katherine extended the basket of strawberries to Nya. "A gift of the season. For a new mother." Nya blushed, and nodded her head in thanks, her long, straight black plaited hair staying in perfect place, her deep black eyes filled with emotion.

"So grateful," she said.

John, in turn, handed out his gifts from the rucksack to Nya, making a clamor that almost woke the baby. So, what's for dinner?" John asked. "And what time does it start?"

"John, 'tis rude to think only of food," Katherine said, nudging him. But with all the aromas about the camp, she was hungry as well.

"We go out— soon," explained Joseph "Find a place around fire. Wait for lamb, roasted shad, strawberry cakes and more. But first... my tribe has gift for new bride of Harrison man. Sit, please...sit."

They found only straw mats, so they sat down on them. An adolescent dressed in warrior costume began to softly play a flutelike instrument. Wind blew through the open curtain sending the river smells of fish, sand, and dirt into the hut. The breeze was filled with summer's arrival. It soothed Katherine's nerves.

Joseph ducked outside and soon returned carrying a bundle in a bright-colored cloth.

"What can this be?" John asked. "Could it be food?" He released a hearty laugh.

"Patience, Harrison. Here, this is for your wife." He placed the soft, warm bundle into her arms. She opened the cloth to reveal a tiny black kitten that looked up at her with the blue eyes of a helpless innocent.

"'Tis a kitten. Oh my!" she whispered.

"He's very young. Will be powerful. His name is Hoccanum."

"Hoccanum?" she asked.

John and Joseph began to speak together in a flurry of words from the native Algonquin language. Katherine stood in wonder at John's talent. "Hoccanum is a river just north of us. There they found a cat with kittens near their fishing spot," John explained.

"That's right, Harrison. I teach you well. You teach me well." Joseph looked to Katherine, cradling the kitten. "Hoccanum River, good fishing grounds... flows to the Great River. Onto the ocean."

Katherine peered down at the new life only a few months old. The kitten, listening to the words and feeling her heartbeat against him, began to knead the cloth and purr with vigor.

"You see, he likes you already," Joseph said.

"Can we keep him, John...please?" she asked.

"I could use another mouser about the farm. Aye, consider it done."

Katherine beamed. "Many thanks, Joseph. To you and your family."

"His mother—good fisher and mouser. Hoccanum will be more than good mouser. And when you have first child, he will protect."

"It's all settled," said John. "Now, let's eat."

They departed the hut with Katherine carrying the kitten. The drumbeat continued as the western sky turned pink and then to shades of grey. Swallows circled overhead dipping down close to the island and then soaring upwards again.

A procession had begun around the fire with elders dressed in bearskin robes, fox-skin cloaks, and feathered headdresses of flaming red, white, and black. Loud chants, whoops and cries filled the air. The dancers circled the blazing firepit, thumping on drums or shaking rattles, dancing one deep step in front of another, bending low, and then reaching up to the sky.

When the dancers stopped, everyone sat and waited. A fully costumed elder with a headpiece of gold, red, white, and black feathers greeted the crowd. "In the name of all our Manitous, I welcome you. This is a time of peace and harmony with the white man. We thank the Manitous for the peace—and for the food we eat today. Let us give thanks...to earth, sun, and sky!"

A large whooping cry with howls and screeches arose as the drums beat rapidly, shells rattled, and horns tooted.

The Elder lifted his arms up. "We raise our prayers up to the sky where Manitous receive. We welcome the summer when the south wind rules, so—let us eat!"

And what a feast it was! Roasted lamb, shad roasted on wooden boards, corn cakes, asparagus and for dessert, strawberry cakes, sweet biscuits, and pies. They even drank a light, frothy strawberry ale.

When the feast was finished, Joseph came and stood over the couple. "You like?" he asked, his dark eyes filled with pride.

"Not like. Love," said John, wiping his mouth.

"The meal was delightful," Katherine agreed. She could not help but think on the difference between this ceremony with that of Sabbath Day. These natives who had so little expressed joy in the dance, the food, and the celebration of life, compared with the staid Puritans, always scolding and gossiping.

"Will you stay? More dancing, more drumming. We dance until sun up," Joseph said. He fixed the two hawk wing feathers on his small headdress. Katherine smelled the tobacco and sage smoke rising from the fire; it was beginning to lull her to sleep.

John stood and stretched. "I would say 'tis time for us to return to the mainland. Katherine…and Hoccanum are tired."

Joseph stood with a smile and nodded. "Joseph knows. You two… having child."

Katherine gasped. "How did you know?" She snuggled Hoccanum closer to her belly.

"I know. Joseph knows." He smiled. "I will take you back."

It was hard to leave the merriment, but Katherine *was* tired. In all her years she had never seen such a true outpouring of life and goodwill.

The three walked the darkening path back to the dock. Hoccanum was asleep again, curled into the blanket. "This was quite a celebration, Kat." John said. "Your eyes were wide with wonder watching the dance."

"And I never knew you had such talent—speaking a Native tongue."

Suddenly they espied a man on the dock. He stood with a torch in one hand, the other hand raised to his forehead. He peered intently toward their direction. "John Harrison," the man called out in a low voice. "I thought it was you." The group approached the beach area as Joseph found his canoe and made ready for the trip across the river.

"Why Michael Griswold, 'tis a surprise seeing you out on the island tonight," John said.

"And I could say the same for you— making merry with the natives, eh? And bringing your new wife along, I see."

Katherine shivered at the man's tone, and drew Hoccanum closer.

"What say you?" Goodman Griswold coughed, cleared his throat, and waited.

"I say 'tis the right time to mind your tongue, Michael Griswold. *And* your business. That goes for your wife as well—the scold that she is," John said in an angry voice.

"And I have a right mind to report you for slander."

"I could say the same."

Goodman Griswold quieted with the words. "Only making sure mine eyes doth not deceive me."

"Never mind your eyes. I will have none of your tongue." John grabbed Katherine's arm and the two made their way to the canoe where Joseph awaited them.

CHAPTER 23

The Hollister house was now the Gilbert Homestead. Perfectly situated on the High Street across from the Sandy Lane, Josiah could view the rising of the sun east over the Great River, and to the west watch John Harrison's barn weathervane spin about in the ever-changing breezes.

But Josiah could see it no more, for today he was putting the last touches on a new stockade fence. He'd erected it along the side of High Street, so little Ben, almost ten months now, could toddle about; the child was attempting to walk. With a fence protecting Ben from the busy High Street, there would be no danger he might crawl or toddle away from the homestead.

Josiah's brother Jonathan, Marshal of Hartford, had a room ready for his visits to Wethersfield. The same was true for brother Thomas. Each brother had five acres of land, and Josiah refused to plant, weed, plow, or bale hay on any land but his own.

He swept the back porch clean of mud clods, old bits of hay, and dust; now that the spring floods had abated, he replaced some rotting planks from the porch and house with newly seasoned wood.

Josiah wasn't sure how he felt about Katherine and John coming around for supper this afternoon. He admitted to himself that he liked John: the man was honest, forthright, amiable, and quick with a kind word. Now that John was married to Katherine, what could he do?

As Elizabeth reminded him, peace between the families would make life easier for everyone. After all, they were neighbors now. Only the High Street separated the families.

·—•—·

Katherine and John strode down the Sandy Lane. Katherine carried a basket filled with the last of the strawberry crop. The setting sun cast a bright light to their backs giving Katherine some much needed strength. "I wonder what Elizabeth is cooking up for supper?" John asked. His mind was already on the food, Katherine thought. She shrugged, thinking about having supper with her cousin.

The pair crossed the High Street and followed the path around the stockade fence toward the back porch. Katherine, startled by the great expanse of the two-storied farmhouse, stood in wonder at the improvements made to the old Hollister abode.

"Why, I wouldn't recognize the house now. Those Gilbert men have spruced up the old place," John remarked.

Both Josiah and Elizabeth awaited them on the back porch, Elizabeth holding ten-month-old Benjamin; he still wore his long dressing gown. It was clear he had many months to go before his breeching ceremony.

"Welcome," called Josiah, sounding almost pleasant. "What do ye think of the new fence? I will whitewash it next week."

"What do you need the fence for?" John asked roughly.

"Privacy. And little Ben needs roaming room and soft ground to fall on. We need not have him near the busy road."

"I have to say, Josiah, you Gilberts always think ahead," John said. "Either way, you are a wise father."

Katherine and John climbed the three steps leading to the back porch, then turned to view the Great Meadow at dusk. A flock of red-winged blackbirds silently alighted on swaying rushes, paying homage to the peace settling over the meadow. A few sparrows chipped and chirped in the tall grasses. Frogs began singing from the marshes near Blackbird Pond. The sky, pale orange and pink, slowly began to shed its colors.

"Let's all go inside. The meal will get cold," Elizabeth said.

The back door led to a homey kitchen that smelled like cinnamon spice and freshly baked bread. They followed a short hallway that led to two open Great Rooms. A staircase led straight up to the second floor. Rugs covered some parts of the floor, while rushes lay on the exposed planks. Elizabeth's womanly touch had created a warm feeling about the place.

"Please sit at the tableboard. Let me take your basket," Josiah said, maintaining a gracious manner. "Sit. I'll light more candles about the room."

Elizabeth had settled Ben down in a great wooden ring with wheels and a seat. To watch him trying to push himself about in his long gown, and listen to his babbles amused Katherine. She gestured to John, "Wouldn't it be wonderful to have something like this—when *our* child arrives?"

Elizabeth turned from the boiling pot she was stirring. "When your child arrives? Why, Katherine, John, I am so pleased." She called for Josiah. "Jos, we have news. Cousin Katherine is with child. Ben will have a new cousin."

Josiah returned, eyes wide, mouth agape. "How providential. We are happy with the welcome news." He promptly joined the Harrisons at the table.

Elizabeth began serving up her chicken stew with warm bread and asparagus from the garden.

"Would thee kindly say grace, John?" Josiah asked.

"Praise be to God." John's voice rang out as all bowed their heads. "Let us give thanks to the Lord, and give thanks for new life and for the blessings of kin. For which we are grateful. Amen."

They began to eat in earnest, little Ben taking the opportunity to wheel himself about in his wooden ring. He smiled, gurgled, and tried to get words out that sounded like he had his mouth filled with soap bubbles.

"What a precious child," Katherine said. She already loved little Ben's spirit; he was afraid of naught.

"He's learning a lot these days. Already said his first word, and that was 'Mama,' not 'Papa.'" Josiah laughed.

"He will say Papa soon enough. And once he starts talking, he'll never stop," said Elizabeth, rolling her eyes and laughing. "Ben certainly keeps us busy."

After the meal, Katherine helped Elizabeth clear the platters and prepare the dessert. They mashed the strawberries, sliced the small cakes Elizabeth had baked earlier that day sideways in half, stuffed them with fruit and smothered them with the whipped cream.

John dove into the sweet treat murmuring this was the best strawberry cream he had ever eaten. "The strawberries are from your garden, John. Right delicious I'd say. Take some credit," Josiah said, grinning. He seemed to be enjoying himself—for a change.

⸱⸱⸱

It was approaching Ben's bedtime. Elizabeth picked him up from his roaming ring and cuddled him close to her breast. "Such a good boy," she cooed. "Why not show our guests how far along he is—and if I may boast but a moment—he is readying to walk. Just watch him toddle and try to walk a bit."

She set Ben on the floor, his long gown brushing against the rushes on the plankboards. His plump arms stayed steady as he balanced himself, his legs firmly planted on the ground.

"Katherine," said Elizabeth, "call to Ben. Open your arms wide and he'll come toddling to you."

Katherine opened out her arms and called to him. Ben looked up, smiled, and began to waddle toward her.

"Only a few more steps, Ben," shouted John, cheering, "Aye, he will do it!"

Josiah looked on with pride.

Ben kept his eyes on Katherine, smiling and reaching out with his arms. But then he stumbled and fell, his chubby legs giving way beneath him. His arms went straight out afore him, protecting his face. Then they heard the scream—an ear-piercing screech.

"Ben, Ben!" Elizabeth ran to her son. The child lay face down, his gown flung over his head. He was screaming and howling in anguish.

Katherine stood. "Is he hurt?" she asked. "Don't move him yet." She examined Ben's legs and body, then slightly lifted his head; they were untouched. But something was keeping his right arm stuck to the floorboards. She saw it immediately. "He has a large splinter in his arm. Don't move him," she repeated.

Elizabeth began to sob. "I told you to sand the new floorboards, Josiah Gilbert. Now my only son is injured. Should someone fetch Dr. Rossitier in Hartford?"

Here was Katherine's chance to be useful. "No, no time. All of you—do what I ask. Elizabeth, gather some soft bits of bread. Soak them in a small dish with milk." She looked to John, whose cheery countenance had gone ashen. "Find me a piece of charcoal in the hearth. It needs to be warm. Use the small shovel to grind it and lift it up. Then add it to the poultice Elizabeth works on." John, mouth open wide, followed her orders. "Josiah, I'll need some clean cloth, just enough to bandage the wound. I will also need some vinegar and boiling water." She took a breath in, and wiped her forehead with her arm sleeve. "Hopefully, the poultice will loosen the splinter, and then I can extract it."

She stayed with the sobbing child, soothing him. After Josiah returned with a small clean cloth, they lifted Ben carefully up by a few inches. His screams pierced her ears.

"Who has a knife?" Katherine asked. "The splinter is still attached to the plank."

John came over and swiftly lopped off the remaining wood. As Josiah gently held Ben, Katherine observed the wound. The splinter was large and sharp. It protruded from the child's arm; he yelped in pain when she poked it to see how deep it had penetrated the boy's skin. She said naught, but knew this to be a serious wound.

When the poultice was ready, Katherine cleansed the area with the vinegar and hot water. Ben screamed with the application of the vinegar, but responded to Elizabeth's familiar, soothing voice. Katherine then gently spread the area with the milk-soaked bread and warm charcoal before carefully wrapping the cloth around the wound. "This will help loosen the object so when the time is right, I can remove it. 'Tis simple really and hopefully with little pain to Ben. Now all we can do is wait."

But in Katherine's heart, she knew that it wouldn't be simple. The splinter was lodged deep inside the child's skin. She asked Elizabeth, "Do you have a silver needle? I may need one. Also, a flax thread. We don't know how the wound will look after I remove the object."

Elizabeth scurried about collecting the items. Ben, calmer now, listened to the voices around him and stayed quiet; still, his eyes shone with fear. Josiah looked down at his precious son, fear in his eyes as well.

"Let us remove the poultice now," Katherine said in a commanding voice. "'Tis time." She unraveled the poultice carefully, while Ben remained still, his little chest heaving as he whimpered, tears awash down his face. He seemed to understand she was trying to help. "The skin has softened. I can easily extract the offending object. All will be well." Working with care, she loosened and slowly pulled on the three-inch splinter, but a small bit remained under the skin. "Now, everyone, grab ahold of Ben while I work on this."

She gently tugged on the piece of wood and Ben screamed, his face as bright as a raspberry. "Steady now, Ben…steady." With one long, straight pull, the jagged piece of wood slid out from the child's arm. "It is out!" Katherine held it up to the candlelight.

"Thanks be to God," she heard Josiah say.

Katherine, upon viewing the wound, knew her work was not done. A part of the skin lay open and blood trickled from it. "This must be sewn up now. Do you have any healing salve or balm?" she asked Elizabeth, who had returned with the needle and a long string of flax.

"Here." She placed the needed objects before Katherine. "I will look for a salve in the cupboard."

"And I will clean the wound again with the vinegar cloth… just in case. We need no infection."

She briskly set to cleaning the open wound while Ben shrieked. Katherine then carefully prepared the suture. Both Josiah and John hovered about the child watching Katherine with fascination. She tied a surgical knot to the end of the flaxen thread. She studied the wound; it was uneven with jagged edges.

"Are ye ready to help me? Get me more hot water!" She glanced at the two men. They both looked as helpless as two abandoned pups. Josiah nodded numbly, while John leaped up to retrieve the fresh water. Then she dipped the needle into the vinegar and hot water mix; this would serve to cleanse the needle sufficiently. She threaded the needle with precision. "One of you hold Ben's legs; the others, get behind him and hold his head."

Elizabeth returned with a jar of ointment. "This is all we have. Balm of Gilead."

"That will do," Katherine said. "Draw close to your son, Elizabeth. Speak to him and tell him all will be well." She had the needle ready, the pointed tip glistening in the shadowed candlelight. "Someone… bring a light and hold it over me."

Josiah gasped. His much-maligned cousin readied to stitch up his son. He brought forth a tallow, lit it in the hearth, and held it carefully over his son. Calmly, Katherine continued to give orders. "John, I need you to hold the skin together tight while I suture; nay, don't pinch too hard. Ben needs no lasting scars."

John, Josiah, and Elizabeth watched silently as Katherine stitched Ben's arm. Her fingers moved with a rapid spin of efficiency. A few times Ben whimpered and cried, but he lay still, as if he knew someone was helping him. Around the wound she quickly stitched, cooing softly to him.

And then it was over. The seven simple stitches were perfectly wrought, as neat as any stitches on a new dress.

"All will be well," Katherine said at last.

"Will there be a scar?" Elizabeth asked, placing a hand on her forehead.

"Nay— I doubt it. I'll return in ten days to remove them. Just try to keep Ben from itching or pulling at them. He is a brave boy." She got up and kissed the boy's forehead. Ben was becoming more and more sleepy, as his eyelids drooped, and his head dropped to his chin.

"How can we thank thee?" Elizabeth asked her.

"Aye, cousin," said Josiah with relief.

Katherine was also relieved this ordeal was ending and ending well. "You have thanked me well enough, cousin, inviting us to supper. 'Tis the least I can do." She paused. "And methinks Ben is trying to thank me as well. He's making babble talk."

John and Katherine left the Gilbert House, and made their way home to the Sandy Lane.

"Kat, you fill me with wonder. Every day I learn of another talent God gave you. How blessed I am to call you wife." He embraced her heartily.

Katherine was pleased. She was finally getting the approval and attention she so desperately desired—and needed.

CHAPTER 24

February 1654

Over eight months had passed, and Katherine's time was drawing nigh. She sat knitting beside the front window waiting for John. Outside a light, soft snow fell calming her nerves. The tiny white flakes sparkled down like starlight then disappeared into the air.

Smiling to herself, she thought how as the months passed, and her stomach widened, so her reputation as a healer with nimble fingers and quick thinking took on a new life in Wethersfield. Townspeople of Hartford and Wethersfield were claiming she used a tourniquet on young Ben's arm preventing him from bleeding to death. Even Kate Palmer told her many goodwives were exclaiming, 'Goody Harrison sewed the boy up perfect.'

If they only knew the truth. The truth that she had staunched the bleeding of soldiers' arms and legs, twisting rags tight to amputated limbs in just the right manner. The thought jarred her. This was to be a happy time. She need not recall the horrors anymore. John— and townspeople needed her. Over the last months, when a Wells, Francis, Griswold, or a Talcott needed a simple or a salve, they often sent a young one to request the remedy. Katherine always obliged.

These days she knew well enough to keep quiet about astrology and fortunetelling. She would predict no more, for she was a goodwife now, soon to be a mother. She would draw a chart up for the new child—but she'd tell not a soul—just Kate.

Recently she had decided on Kate Palmer as midwife for her soon-to-be birthing time. Kate had experience birthing babies. Just thinking of Kate being present for the delivery quelled her unease.

Today she had sent John to the Palmer's house on an errand to give Kate warning it could be any day now. She shifted uncomfortably in her chair grasping the bottom of her sagging belly. For although she herself had helped birth babies in England, she needed help with her own.

·-·-·

John lumbered through the door and stood in the hall, his scarf, coat, and hat speckled with snow. He bore a large sack slung over his shoulder. "Wife," he cried, "I've got news!"

"By the by, John, I am right here knitting by the window," she called out from the Great Room. "Tell me, did you speak with Kate?"

"Aye. She's ready anytime. She's got her satchel packed. Henry will watch the household when your time is upon us."

John took in a deep breath, puffed his chest out, and approached her. "I have got other news, Kat."

She stood up and first took notice of the wet snow dripping onto the floorboards. "Forsooth, you will flood us out. Tread your feet at the door, and I'll hang your coat by the fire."

John's eyes gleamed and his breath came quick. "A bit of water matters for naught." He grinned, a slight mischievous half-smile, removed his hat, bowed, and announced in a serious tone, "Goodwife Harrison, you are now looking at the newly chosen Town Crier of Wethersfield. Chosen by the Freemen of this fine town. And if I could lift thee and twirl thee about I would, but I wouldn't want my child—or wife— to go dizzy."

"Town Crier? My word," she said. "My heart rejoices for thee. Now hand me your coat. I'll fetch thee a mug of hot soup and you can tell me more."

They removed to the hearth after Katherine hung his coat and hat to dry. "This is a paid position, Kat. We'll soon be adding more money to our coffer," John told her.

Katherine stirred the soup of beef and barley. She was pleased for him and for her. They could use the extra shillings. She ladled a mug of the soup for John.

She saw the light of joy—and pride— in his eyes. Townspeople considered him trustworthy. He was a well-respected figure in Wethersfield. How proud she was of him!

"Tell me about your duties," she said, as the two settled down for some soup. "In England, our crier gave us news and entertained us as well. He told many stories."

"Indeed," John replied, sipping his soup. "Let me show you my Crier dress." He pulled out blue breeches, a dark blue coat with shiny brass buttons, buckled shoes, a fresh new broad hat—and a large brass bell. He dug deep into the sack. "One last item—a ledger. I am to keep records of all my cries."

"What type of news must you cry?" she asked.

"Whatever is posted. The authorities and townspeople post queries, notes, and sundry items to the Meetinghouse door. I am to check daily, usually around the noon hour. I will cry out for lost items as well… and news from Hartford, Wethersfield, and Windsor."

"How were *you* chosen?"

John burst into a torrent of low unabashed laughter. "Come now, wife. What thinks you?" Before Katherine could answer, John shouted, "They like my voice, Kat. It carries!"

They both giggled together with the thought. "'Tis true. What else?" she asked him.

"They claim I was recommended due to my patience and amiable ways. And I've got a pair of strong legs to strut myself about the Green."

"Aye, all true." She got serious of a sudden. "But what of the farm? We will have our firstborn with us soon enough."

"'Tis winter so we can do chores in the morning. With the extra money, I can hire more help. As long as you make me a hearty break-fast each morn."

"Aye, so I will." She smiled. "But now I order you to dress for the occasion. I want to see and hear you as our new Town Crier."

John grinned, took up the sack, and changed in the new east-facing room off the kitchen. He and Henry Palmer had built the room with tender care because it would soon serve as the birthing room. Henry also built a cradle for the newborn, and after he was finished, John had the joiner, Goodman Nott carve small sunflowers onto each side, down at his shop on the High St.

At last John came forth from the bedroom, chest expanding with a newfound pride. The brass buttons shone on his jacket, and complemented the bell that jangled when he walked. When Katherine saw him, her eyes and mouth rounded.

"Why John," she exclaimed, "all the young maids scurrying about the green will take notice; aye, they will stop and flutter their eyelashes at thee. And how envious they will be of me—"

"Never mind envy. Let me cry now." He began to pace the floor-boards, his jacket swinging along with the bell. "Oyez, Oyez! Hear Ye, Hear Ye, gather around good people of Wethersfield. Katherine, wife of Town Crier, John Harrison of Wethersfield, is set to give birth any day. Oyez Oyez!" He rang his bell and stomped about the floor, enjoying his practice. Even Hoccanum chased the new Town Crier about the room, finding curiosity in John's shiny brass buttons and shiny bell.

Katherine smiled.

The Harrison stock was rising.

CHAPTER 25

February, 1654

The week after his new appointment, John walked to the meetinghouse to check on the notices nailed to the door. It was a warm February afternoon; the sun was strong for this time of year.

He espied a notice nailed to the door. In a young child's writing, it said, 'Lost cat. Yellow and white with green eyes.' Is this it? he thought to himself. For my first cry? He grinned and straightened his broad shoulders back. The request was as fair as any.

He yanked the notice, stuck it in his pocket, and walked to the green. People ambled about taking a break, while young children played tag or catch. He found a tree to stand under, pulled out the notice, and started to ring his bell, shouting, "Oyez, Oyez," then called out for the lost cat. No one seemed concerned or interested, except for one small girl of about eight. She approached him, her white cap slanting off her head.

"What can I do for thee, young one?"

"That is *my* cat that is lost. Cry the news *again,* please." The child looked so forlorn, what could he do? He cried the message another time, announcing to the crowd that here was the cat's owner. "If ye find the animal, give it to—" He leaned over to her. "And your name?"

"Mary Brown" she proudly said.

"To Mary Brown. This sweet child wants her cat back." He patted her on the head. "I have done what I can, Mary. All we can do is wait."

The child gazed up at the man with the clanging bell and hugged tight to his pant leg. "I am grateful, Town Crier. For you." With those words, she ran off down the green. Such a sweet child, he thought. But John knew that the forest wilderness near them held predators— like wolves prowling along the wood's edge—sometimes veering even closer.

Then he noticed a group of young boys giving him crisscross looks whispering among themselves. The tallest one pushed a smaller boy forward. "Go on," he said in a command.

The boy approached John.

"What can I do for ye?" John asked.

The boy shuffled nervously, twisted his fingers together, and narrowed his eyes at John— as if he was ready to charge the Town Crier. Either that or run in the opposite direction.

"I…we have a question for you."

John heard loud bantering as the group of boys moved in closer to listen.

"Ask away, young man." He knew he had an amusing way of responding to people. This was no different.

"Umm…"

"What, tongue-tied already? Speak it out," John said, laughing at the game.

The boy took a deep breath. "Is it true…umm…is it true…your wife really doth read people's fortunes?"

"What? How dare you, you little rascal!"

The boy turned and ran to his friends who patted him on the back.

The group pointed at John. The tallest boy spoke up. "Everyone says your wife reads fortunes. If 'tis true, she speaks with the devil, and that means she's a witch!"

John felt his face afire. "Get on home with ye before I find a sharp stick to switch your behinds. Get on before I cry out for your parents. Where did ye learn such lies? Begone!"

How dare they be so bold? Is this what townspeople were saying about his Katherine—still?

He recognized one of the boys as Michael Griswold's son. He had a right mind to speak to Goodman Griswold. Surely, he would never approve of his son's behavior.

Before the group disbanded, two of the younger boys started chanting, "Goodwife Harrison tells fortunes, Goodwife Harrison tells fortunes." John's neck and ears burned red.

"Get now," he shouted, losing patience. "There will be no more slander—nor idling on the green."

The boys laughed and ran away toward the river.

John was finished with his duty. He had other things on his mind. For Kate Palmer was staying at the house until the baby was delivered. He had no time to tarry.

He strode across the High Street, and made his way in a huff up the Sandy Lane. How dare those young scoundrels insult his wife? If the town was rife with rumor about his Kat, he would defend her name. He did not understand how people could not—nay, would not—let go of her past. They clung to it like a spider her prey—wrapping it tightly in a web, always keeping it close—even though it was dead.

He opened wide the split rail fence to let himself in; all seemed quiet in the farmhouse. He entered through the back. The birthing room door was closed. He knocked gently. He could smell something familiar, a pine or juniper scent. Kate answered the door. "Come in… come in quiet now."

There was his Katherine lying abed, eyes half shut, holding a mewling bundle swaddled in her arms.

"By God's grace, what have we here?" he asked. "Do I have a son? We'll name him John of course." He peered over her trying to get a peek of the new baby.

"John." Katherine gazed up to her husband's astonished face.

"I came as soon as I could."

Kate elbowed him out of the way. After bundling up bloodied sheets she turned to John. "She couldn't wait—I mean your new—daughter."

"Daughter?" John thought of the sweet child named Mary from the Village Green. "God hath seen fit to bless me with a daughter? Why, I am a happy man, the happiest in the Colony! Let me have a look at the wee one." He pulled up a stool and gazed down at mother and child. Then he pushed back the swaddled head covering. "Look, she's got my light hair. A golden tuft of it."

"And wide forehead." Katherine smiled. "She's a Harrison all right." She sighed, relieved but tired. "The pains started a few hours back— I thought the labor would last—at least until you finished your job crying."

"Is she healthy?" he asked.

"Aye," Kate replied. "She came into this world screaming, with a fine set of lungs in her."

"Ah Kat, she's perfect," said John, his eyes tearing. And was the delivery long, Kate?"

"That child wanted out and into this world. 'Twas an easy delivery over in a few hours."

"Let me hold her now." John gently pried the tight bundle from Katherine, too weak to resist. He rocked the child in his arms, cooing with delight at his firstborn. Although her pinched, red face looked like a squashed berry, she was his.

"Why don't we name her Rebecca? In honor of my mother."

"'Tis a beautiful name," Katherine replied, drifting to sleep.

John smiled down at his daughter. Rebecca tried to open her puffed eyelids; she seemed to listen to his words.

"She knows I'm her papa," he crowed.

Then Rebecca started to wail—a good lusty cry.

"I told ye she had good lungs," Kate said, smiling.

Katherine reached out a hand to John. "Here, let me soothe her."

He returned the screaming bundle to Katherine. He was a father now and the townspeople should know the news. Promptly he left the house, took out his bell, and rang it loudly up and down the road, shouting, "Hear ye, on this day, a daughter hath been born unto John and Katherine Harrison. Oyez, Oyez."

CHAPTER 26

September 1654

Katherine rocked seventh-month-old Rebecca to sleep in her arms. Hoccanum, over a year old, slinked around her feet purring for milk. He was an independent, do-as-he-pleased cat—unless he wanted something.

John was down on the green crying out news. What gossip was he privy to? What did the other goodwives whisper about her? It was envy, that was all. She brushed it from her mind, focusing on Becca's needs. She had no time to consider what townspeople thought of her. She had John— and the baby now.

By afternoon the late September sun sparkled and cast dappled shadows on the changing leaves that seemed ready to burst forth with color. Finally John arrived home, tired and hungry from attending to business at the harbor. Katherine settled the baby in her cradle and served John some leftover venison stew. He didn't seem to mind considering how fast he ate the meal.

When he finished, he stretched his arms back and yawned.

"How did the crying go today, John? Any news?" she asked.

John blinked, wiped his mouth with a cloth, and frowned. "I have some distressing news." He shook his head in disgust, mumbling something about the unfairness in life.

"What is it? Tell me."

"It's about Lydia, Lydia Gilbert from Windsor. Your cousin Thomas's wife."

"Aye, what about Lydia? She minds well her business these days from what I hear about her. She is raising those boys to be fine men. No easy task."

John nodded. "'Tis true, wife. But it makes not a difference. Lydia has been indicted on charges of witchcraft."

Katherine sat shocked by the news. "Lydia? Witchcraft? Why, I never—" She wrung her hands together, then stood and faced her husband. "Why John? What crime hath she committed?" Lydia besides Marshal Gilbert, was one of the few people from the family she liked. Often Lydia would visit the Harrison home after market to catch up on the news.

"She's being blamed for the death of Henry Stiles—from three years ago."

"The death of Henry Stiles?" she repeated. "Everyone knows that Thomas Allyn held the gun. And the man *admitted* his guilt; it was but an accident and he paid his fine. Only a fine! Was he even put in jail three years back? Nay, it was called a 'homicide by misadventure.' Forsooth, this news vexes me!" She wrung her hands into knots, and twisted them together. Her legs began to shake and wobble.

John grabbed ahold of Katherine's arm and held it tight. "Sit wife. I insist." She sat again, frustrated and angered over such distressing news. "Listen to me, Kat. No one is safe when accusations, however fanciful, begin. I warned you about what happened to my neighbors, John and Joan Carrington. Hanged, both of them, for trading with the Indians. A nine-month-old child was orphaned." He put his hands to his head.

Katherine glanced over at Becca sleeping peacefully in her cradle. "Tell me, what *evidence* do they have against Lydia?"

"Evidence? They have little evidence from what I hear. The authorities in Windsor charged Lydia with entertaining Satan—and with Satan's help killed the body of Henry Stiles— by means of witchcraft."

"Satan helped Lydia kill a man we know was killed by another? She shook her head in disbelief. "'Tis not true!""

John pulled himself closer to her. "Of course, 'tis not true. But the authorities and townspeople *believe* it as true. That's all that matters, isn't it? 'Tis but a tale, but tales in this colony take on their own life. They are calling it *spectral evidence.*"

"Spectral evidence? They indicted Lydia on this basis?" The more she heard, the more disgust and fear she felt "Why, if they can accuse Lydia of bewitchment years after the crime, no one is safe." Gooseflesh pricked her arms with a chill. A shudder went through her back and neck.

"This is my point, wife. The less you say, the less fodder people can conjure against you." John lowered his voice. "I know not—when this madness —if ever—will end."

"I understand it not."

John pounded his fist on the table stirring Becca from her sleep. "Thou art not meant to understand, Kat. I hardly understand but I make no matter or fuss about it. What can we do?"

"What of Lydia's sentence...if convicted?"

"Aye. Lydia will most likely be sentenced to die atop Gallows Hill in Hartford—hanged by the noose on a branch of the Great Elm. I am sorry, Kat. Mayhap your cousin Marshal Gilbert can save her?"

Katherine had heard enough.

"I am in need of air," she said groaning, as she ran out the back door.

"I knew I shouldn't have told thee." he yelled, following her. "Can we forget this talk?"

Katherine found a place alongside the barn and leaned against a side plank, breathing fast, and hoping not to retch. She knew that Lydia, a friend and relation, was innocent. Yet Katherine could not speak up for her, lest she be accused of something as well. She felt powerless and heartsick for Lydia, Thomas, and the family.

Katherine had much to lose. She could do naught but pray and hope for her friend, a relative of sorts, now accused of witchcraft, a friend who could soon be swinging by a noose in Hartford.

And they called these acts Divine Providence? She would call it a sacrifice, a way to rid the town of undesirables. She would never understand the minds of these people—and as John suggested— it was not worth trying.

CHAPTER 27

November 1654

Josiah still didn't really know how he felt about Katherine. What a commotion was made over little Ben's injury. To be sure, Ben's wound did heal fully with barely a scar on his arm. Now townspeople flocked to her for remedies. Katherine was even advising neighbors about their children's health. She has the experience, he thought. What is all the fuss?

But he had no time for thoughts of Katherine. Today was a day he dreaded, for this was the day his sister-in-law Lydia was set to hang. He shrugged his shoulders. What could he do? The only action required of him was to attend the hanging out of respect for his brother, Thomas, who would not be present.

The plan was to meet up with his brother Jonathan in Hartford, and together they would make their way west, by procession, up the road toward Albany, to the great hill with the great elm atop it that towered over the land. He clenched his stomach.

Josiah knew *not* what Lydia had done; he wasn't sure he cared. Deep in his heart, he knew this guilty verdict to be wrong. He never liked Lydia, never liked Katherine; both were trouble—brash and low born—everything a goodwife was not. Women like Lydia and

Katherine talked too much, had too much to say. Unlike his Elizabeth, who knew when to speak and when to remain quiet.

But Katherine's and Lydia's husbands could not control them— they dare not try. But did Lydia deserve death? He shook the thought from his mind. He did think of this day as, 'the Will of God,' something he would never understand— and didn't have to.

He arrived at the Hartford Meetinghouse Square riding his bay mare. The November sun slanted bright rays through the otherwise cloudy, cold day. He looked around for Jonathan amid the growing number of people who would proceed to the gallows. Some people would walk, while others rode on horseback, or in a cart. Vendors had already gathered on the square, hawking oat cakes, apples, roasted corn, and other tasty bites. He noticed many people primly attired in their solemn black and white Sabbath dress ready for the spectacle.

He finally espied his brother waving his arms "How now, Josiah? 'Tis good timing. I will take up the lead in the procession. You can help me by taking up the rear."

A loud bell began to clang and the slow sound of a drum, low and steady, pounded like a heartbeat until everyone was lined up. Many of the wagons, pulled by teams of oxen or horses were already filled with people—including children.

Marshal Gilbert flailed his arms about giving orders. People whispered in small groups awaiting word. Soon all became eerily quiet. Josiah noticed Kate Palmer standing with another woman. Had Katherine sent her so she would report back the grim news?

Josiah took up the back of the procession. He got a quick view of Lydia being dragged out of the dugout of a prison, young boys throwing clods of dirt at the condemned woman.

"*You* bewitched a man unto death. *You* caused the gun to fire. Witch!" they taunted.

Josiah kicked the ribs of his restless horse onward. The procession had begun.

The group came to a crossroads and turned left onto the Road to Albany. More people along the way joined the somber group of Puritans. More vendors lined the road on each side, luring walkers in for a sweet or savory bite to eat. He decided he had to keep his eyes straight forward to stop his distracted mind. When the large group finally reached the bottom of the great slope of the hillside, he couldn't help but look up. For there was the great elm, with a ladder hard up against its trunk, and a crisp noose dangling from a thick branch.

A small path wove its way around the hillside. An area to park wagons and post horses had been cleared on the opposite side of the hill. "Riders, dismount and guide your horses up the path and tether them. Carts and wagons up the back side of the hill. Walkers, follow the path," Marshal Gilbert shouted.

In great anticipation, the crowd began to gather willy-nilly around the tree. Whispers like little hisses could be heard. Josiah, after posting his horse, joined his brother among the spectators awaiting the announcement. The creaking wagon carrying Lydia was brought to rest under the great tree. The team of horses whinnied, pawed the ground, and snorted; they seemed reluctant to move forward, as if they sensed that tragedy awaited.

"Gather around," the Marshal shouted. "We shall now receive the Word of God from Reverend Stone of Hartford."

People bowed their heads and clung tight to their Bibles—and their children— as the elder minister droned on in prayer.

After the prayer, Josiah noticed Major John Mason, dressed in shiny black and wearing a large steeple hat, take a step forward. He also noticed a man waiting along the side wearing a black hood with slits for his eyes, nose, and mouth.

The hood of the executioner, he thought.

Major Mason began, "Good people of Windsor, Hartford, and Wethersfield. As you know, the authorities accumulated a good deal of evidence against the prisoner, Lydia Gilbert. We now know that Lydia befriended Alse Young, another one of Windsor, who was hanged in 1647. Naught has changed." The Major paced near the tree. "Ye know, good people, we ferret out the witches so you, the chosen and law-abiding citizens can live in peace." A loud huzzah sprang up among the spectators.

"Where's all the evidence against Lydia, Major?" a brave soul shouted. "Why her? And why now?"

Major Mason frowned and glared slowly about the group but could not locate the offender. The crowd was stirring and becoming restless. "This woman has been convicted. There are pages testifying to the spectral evidence against her."

Spectral evidence? Josiah shivered at the thought of it. Lydia had no right to haunt others. And would she haunt others beyond the dishonored grave she would be tossed into following the execution?

"The prisoner has been convicted of the crime of witchcraft. 'Tis all you need to know," the Major concluded.

Hands tied, waiting in the wagon, Lydia stood tall. She was dressed in a drab brown skirt, white blouse, tattered brown coat, and wore a faded white cap atop her head. Reverend Stone and Major Mason turned to face Lydia, who regardless of the crisp cold breezes, had sweat glistening upon her pale face; her red eyes rimmed in dark shadows. Josiah could hardly recognize her.

"The time is nigh, Lydia Gilbert, for you to speak your final words on this earth. Speak, Lydia, or forever go to your peace," Reverend Stone intoned.

Lydia's eyes blazed through the crowd like kindling to a flame, as if she searched out her husband and her children, but none were present. Her first action surprised Josiah. She requested her cap be placed in her bound hands. The authorities obliged her final request, took it from her head, and handed it to her. She grabbed her mobcap in a fury, threw it to the wagon's bottom, and stomped on it. "I denounce this cap. I refuse to go to my death in it. I'll wear this dreaded cap no more." Her hair was pulled up, but Josiah could see the wild brown and grey strands flowing freely from her hair knot and neck, hanging down her face.

"I may not be a perfect Goodwife, but as God be my witness—I am *no* witch! I had naught to do with Henry Stiles's death three years past. Who will believe me?" She looked out to the crowd. "I am an innocent woman being brought to slaughter like common livestock." She glared at Major Mason. "*You* may not need me, but my husband and my children—*they* need me."

The crowd remained silent.

"Are you quite finished, Goodwife Gilbert?" asked the Major.

"Nay," shouted Lydia. "I say unto all of ye, upon my death… rest assured, I see naught but trouble… schisms, plagues, aye… death in these towns. And you people," she screamed, "have brought this upon yourselves."

"Nay, you brought *this* upon yourself," Major Mason said, pointing at her.

Lydia's curse caused Josiah to shiver. He grabbed his thick coat and pulled it tight around him.

"You have had your time, Goodwife Gilbert 'Tis now over," Mason said.

A drum began to pound in earnest. The noose hung limp as the executioner climbed the ladder and secured it around the condemned woman's neck. She stood in the wagon under the tree, and then she began to beg for mercy.

But it was too late. The executioner stepped from the ladder, walked to the team of horses, gave them a strong switch on the back and shouted, "Get!" The horses bolted forward leaving Lydia to swing by the rope. At last Josiah heard what he thought sounded like a snap.

It was over. Josiah looked askance at the body swinging from the tree, feeling a wave of nausea overtake him. He glanced away in disgust. Was it because he had just witnessed the hanging of his sister-in-law, or was it because he also secretly wished it was his cousin Katherine?

⊷·—·⊷

Late that afternoon, Kate told Kat the news. "No one could save Lydia," she said. "Not the marshal, nor her own husband."

Katherine cringed thinking of the hanging, relieved she was not present. What Kate shared with her next shocked her even more. "Lydia cursed all three River Towns, and prophesized about schisms and plagues on the Colony. What can all this mean?"

"It means a woman was hanged for not enough reasons that I understand," said Katherine, crying in earnest now. "It means no one is safe."

CHAPTER 28

March 1656

In June of 1655, the Harrison's second daughter was born. Named for Katherine's mother, Mary had Kat's red-brown hair, light brown eyes, and a demanding temperament.

"She's all you, Kat," John said, smiling.

"Excepting her stubbornness—she gets that from you too," Katherine said with a laugh.

Today little Mary was nine months. And the Palmers had invited Katherine to Market Day in Hartford. At the last moment, Katherine decided to take Mary along. She wanted to show off her second child.

She found her cloak hanging from a peg near the door, and picked Mary up from her cradle, then wrapped her in a woolen shawl. Rebecca, now two, was asleep in her crib. John was at work in his shed cobbling, so she made her way to tell him she was leaving for market. She could hear the quick pop-pop-pop of his awl punching holes in the leather that sounded like a woodpecker banging on a tree trunk.

"John, I'm leaving for market and taking Mary with me. She needs some bloom to her cheeks. The fresh air will do her good. And don't forget to feed Becca when she awakens."

"Aye and then Becca will help me round the farm," he said, with a twinkle in his eyes. Rebecca now two, with blonde hair and blue eyes, loved to stand aside her father watching him work. Like a shadow she followed her father everywhere.

The Palmers were waiting for her, their wagon and team of horses parked near the fence. Kate reached down for the baby, as Katherine lifted herself up to the front seat. The three began the journey to Hartford. This March the weather had been dry, and although warming, the winds blew brisk. "Come now," Katherine said, soothing the waking baby. "We are almost to market."

The road to Hartford was clogged with wagons, horses, teams of oxen, and travelers walking on foot. Mary began to stir from the sudden lurches forward, and then the sudden halts of the wagon. Henry's shouts of "whoa" and "get on" further rattled the restless child.

Katherine had an idea. "Why don't we get off here, Kate? 'Tis close now. We can walk to Market Square and meet up with Henry after he parks the wagon and sees to the horses."

Kate turned to Henry. "Would you mind?"

"Mind? Why should I mind? You women need your time together. And I need mine." He pulled the reins back and shouted, "Whoa!" to the horses, causing a fuss from the wagons behind them. The pair, with Mary, descended from the wagon.

"Look for us at market," Kate said to Henry. "And don't tarry long at the tavern."

They began the short walk to market. Katherine was especially thankful for the boots John had recently cobbled her. The burnished leather, now softening and stretching round her feet, provided comfort and strength to her stride.

She had in mind to purchase some new spice jars for her herbal cupboard—and an almanac for the new year; planting time would soon begin. She and John both followed the moon's phases and astrological signs for planting as many townspeople did as well, but would ne'er admit it.

Kate mentioned she needed a pair of candlestick holders, so they walked to the blacksmith's tent to have a look about. Mary, alert now, reached down with her chubby fingers, wanting to touch the shiny silver, iron, brass, and pewter implements on the table.

Kate laughed and commented that Mary already had an interest in silver. "Truly, she's a merchant's daughter," she said smiling.

While Kate was deciding what to buy, Katherine espied the peddler's table nearby and noticed a small stack of what looked like almanacs. She saw some unusual jars as well. "Kate, we will meet up later. I need to get my supplies."

Katherine headed toward the peddler's table and quickly purchased the almanac and a few jars for her growing herb collection. Suddenly she heard a familiar voice addressing her.

"Why, if it's not Katherine Gilbert herself. How *now*?"

She turned to her right and there stood Betty Bateman, Captain Cullick's servant, the servant whose fortune she read, the servant who got her removed from the job. Katherine noticed Betty was no longer in servant's attire. Was she free of the captain? Kat grimaced and held little Mary tight to her chest.

"Well Kat—Goodwife Harrison I hear—and now a mother… let me congratulate you." Betty tossed her head and stared intently at mother and child. "Why, 'twas not for me, you would never have met your husband. Mayhap I deserve thanks from you." She bent close and poked a long finger under Mary's chin.

"Thanks? Should I thank thee for spreading gossip about me? Betraying me? Why I never—"

"And perhaps I owe some thanks to you…after all this time." Betty cast her eyes down and batted her thick lashes. Was she blushing? Katherine wondered.

"Thanks?"

"Aye. Your fortune came to pass. I *did* meet a man named Simon."

"And?"

"We are betrothed. Set to marry come October. You see, I no longer work for Captain Cullick." She brushed her olive-colored skirt and thick brown cloak back and forth. "Simon—Smith is his last name. He hails from Long Island. And he's a rich merchant, just like I hear true of your own husband. Isn't everything turning out grand for the both of us?"

Mary began to fuss and fret. She was getting hungry. "You have not told anyone about your fortune…coming to pass?" asked Katherine.

"Why not? 'Tis all true. You said I was to marry a man named Simon. And it's all coming to pass. Now that I no longer work for the captain, he's well pleased I'm marrying Simon. Wait until I tell the captain I saw you and the baby. We are friends now, you know." Betty leaned over and brushed Mary's cheek with her finger. "I will never forget that day… you and I alone in that root cellar with you telling my fortune."

"And I ask you again, Betty, tell not another soul of what we speak."

Betty nodded in silence.

"I must go look for my friend," Katherine said. "A true friend." And then abruptly, she turned her back on her servant friend, who had turned on her years ago.

CHAPTER 29

March 1657

"Breathe, Kat!" John could hear Kate Palmer coaxing Katherine through the long hours and labor of their third child. This time they all hoped for a boy.

John waited in the farm's Great Room trying to keep Rebecca, now three, and Mary, two, entertained with wooden toys, corn dollies, rag poppets, and silly songs. How they laughed at their father's roaring voice, wide grin, and watched his every move and expression.

But John's mind was on the new baby. It hadn't been an easy pregnancy for Katherine, made worse by the baby wanting to come early. He listened to Kate Palmer urging Kat to breathe, to push, to let go. He also heard his wife struggling with stifled yells, cries, and heavy panting breaths. He thought that perhaps a nip of the spirits might help calm him. He found a bottle in the cupboard and downed a long gulp.

He dared not approach the birthing room with his two daughters in his charge. He was assigned the role of nanny to the girls, ordered to keep them busy. Once the baby was born, he would let the girls in to see their new brother—or sister.

How he prayed for a son. He loved his two daughters, Rebecca so like himself in looks and temperament, and Mary who showed that headstrong bossiness like her mother. She never liked second place and could be willful at times.

"Where is she? Where is Mama?" Mary now demanded. She toddled toward John, stuffing a clenched fist in her mouth.

"Ah, Mary…methinks you need your dolly." John jumped to pick up the discarded doll from the floor. Mary looked straight at him as if she knew this was a ruse. "If you must know, Mary, your mother is busy in the next room."

Rebecca joined her younger sister. Then she spoke up. "Why is she in the other room?"

Both girls had seen animals giving birth on the farm but were still too young to understand. John tried to explain they would soon have a new baby sister or brother.

He found a poker and stirred up the embers in the hearth, feeling restless himself. He wiped his brow and shuddered. Was everything alright? John felt out of sorts, being the only man in the house and helpless to do much for Kat.

Suddenly everything seemed too quiet. As he glanced toward the birthing room, the door softly opened, and Kate stood beckoning him with her hand to come nigh.

"What is it?" he asked her in a whisper. "Am I a father for the thrice time? Is it a boy— or girl?" He tried to peek inside, but Kate blocked his view.

"She's bleeding bad, John. And the baby's not quite ready." Sweat dripped from her face, hair, and cap. Her hands, apron, and skirt had dashes of blood on them. "I am afraid I cannot staunch the bleeding."

"Then let me in!" he shouted, attempting to push his way past a very pale Kate. "I'm her husband. I must see my wife!" Mary began to cry in earnest.

"Nay!" Kate held a palm to his chest. "Saddle your horse, and ride to Hartford this minute. There is no time to waste. Fetch a doctor. Check for a doctor at the Tavern. Ask the tavernkeeper. I can't save her myself. Hurry lest she bleed to death."

John swept up his now sobbing daughters and placed them into Mary's crib. "Lie down together, girls. Be good and quiet. Your papa will be right back."

Mary started to scream for her mother, but John turned away, pulled his cloak and hat from a wall peg, and dashed out the door. He saddled and mounted his horse, kicked her in the flanks, and began to gallop toward Hartford. The evening was cool and windy, with fog rising, but John knew the way and would let naught stop him from his task. He vowed naught would happen to his Kat—or unborn babe.

·⤳·

He heard from the tavernkeeper that Dr. Rossittier was out of town. But he had a suggestion for John. "Check the stables behind the tavern. Our newly appointed governor, John Winthrop Jr. just had his supper and is preparing to take leave. He has experience and might be able to help."

John found the governor watching the stable boy saddle up his horse who munched on fresh oats. "Please, Governor. I am John Harrison from Wethersfield. You must come now," he said out of breath. "My wife is in the throes of childbirth. The midwife claims she is bleeding unto death. You must try to save her—even if it means losing the baby."

"Aye, Goodman Harrison. You are in luck. I have my doctor's satchel with me this evening." The governor smoothed down his scant mustache and short cropped beard. "Stable boy. Assist me in mounting my horse." He looked to John. "I will follow you, Goodman. Let us make haste!"

Governor Winthrop was always ready to help a townsperson in need. He had ministered to many people using his medical skills. He always kept a ledger on his person, listing all those he served. His skills as a physician were well known; townspeople rarely minded that he used information such as astrology to plan treatments; they never minded as long as the end result was that they were healed of their maladies.

··•··

Kate Palmer was in a panic. Two young girls screaming, their mother bleeding, and at last, she saw the baby's head begin to crown.

"Where's my baby?" Katherine screamed again and again.

"Keep breathing," Kate said calmly. "The doctor will be here soon."

"Doctor?" asked Katherine, wavering between bouts of pain, then fading out into grey-black shadows. "Where am I?" she asked.

"You're in your home giving birth. 'Tis no time for sleep now. There's work to do." Kate rinsed a cloth in cool water and placed it on Kat's forehead. She gave her a sip of valerian tea, something to calm the distressed woman down and ease her pain.

While Kat pushed, Kate cleaned as best as she could, changing bloody linen and then rushing to check on the girls. Thankfully they were quiet now, so Kate put fresh water in the kettle to boil, and ran back to Katherine.

"John will soon be back... with the doctor."

"Why—?" Katherine asked, and then dozed off into a fitful slumber.

··•··

"Papa!" Kate heard Rebecca shout from the crib. She stuck her head out the birthing room door. Sure enough, John bounded into the house with the doctor following behind him. Governor Winthrop carried his black satchel, and the two made their way toward the birthing room.

Kate was shocked to see the new governor right behind John. But this was no time to gawk or gasp; her best friend could be dying. "I thank God in His mercy," she said, pushing John aside. She pulled the tall, thin wiry man into the room and slammed the door shut.

·—·

This was no time for hard feelings. John went about settling the girls down to bed, then cleaned the kitchen, and stacked up logs by the hearth; anything to keep busy. He felt helpless, but knew he had done all he could. Katherine's life and the baby's were in God's—and the Governor's hands.

Then he heard a cry—a small, sharp cry. And then the cry became lusty and full. The baby had arrived at last. But what of Katherine? Had she survived the ordeal?

Finally Governor Winthrop came forth from the shrouded room. "Glad tidings, Goodman Harrison. You wife hath delivered unto you a healthy child." The governor looked tired: his hands trembled as he wiped them down with a clean cloth.

"And my wife, Governor? Did she…did you… save her?"

"Aye, so she hath survived. 'Tis God's good Providence this child be delivered unto thee and Katherine."

"Can I go in now to see my wife and baby?" John asked, relieved to hear such good news.

"Aye, in a moment. Goodwife Palmer is cleaning the baby. Your wife has lost a goodly amount of blood. Her strength hath diminished…for the time." The governor's kind brown eyes held a look of compassion.

"Can I go in now?" John asked again.

"Soon. I must warn you I have other news. Although Katherine and the baby survived—" The governor paused for a breath. "She will ne'er be able to carry or birth a child again. I'm pained to share this news, John. For the sake of your family and Katherine's, this must be her last."

John nodded numbly, thanking the governor, shaking his hand, then digging in his pocket for a pound note. "We are obliged to you, Governor and honored by your esteemed presence. We can't thank thee enough."

"'Tis always my pleasure and duty to help out in a crisis," Winthrop said. "I must take my leave now. And please say naught of this to your wife…until she gathers her strength."

With that the Governor departed, and soon John hastened to the birthing room.

There she was sitting up in bed holding their new bundled baby, whose squished little face was red and wrinkled as a plum.

Kate could not contain the tears any longer. "Come closer John, and meet your new daughter. She's puny now, but look at the fighting spirit in that little face," she said.

John wiped Katherine's brow, kissed her forehead, and did the same to the babe. "She's got your fighting spirit for certain, Kat. I thank God in His goodness!"

"Are you disappointed, John? That I didn't give you a son?" Kat asked.

"Disappointed? Why I am delighted with this child. Have you thought of a name?"

Katherine hugged the baby tight to her. "Nay, I had boys' names in mind. What say you?" She watched John with tender love in her eyes, as she noticed the color coming forth to his face.

"What say you to Sarah? 'Tis a strong biblical name."

"Sarah is a lovely name," said Kate, fussing about as she prepared to take her leave.

Kat gazed down at the baby. "Aye, 'tis lovely… Sarah." The baby turned her ear toward the voice.

"I am well pleased and relieved, Kat," John said, knowing once she was well, he would share the news from Governor Winthrop.

"Next child will be a boy," she said. "I promise."

"Promise me naught," John whispered, "but that thou will recover and stay by my side as my helpmeet. I need you wife—and so do our girls."

"Aye, and promise you'll never leave me." She tightened her grip on little Sarah. Her voice was fading. Sleep was overtaking her. "Kate, thank you. Don't know what we would have done…."

"God hath His hand in this," said Kate, standing at the door. "All is well here with the Harrisons. I must return home to my own family."

Katherine gently closed her eyes unable to fight sleep any longer.

"Rest now, wife." John took his newborn daughter from Kat and rocked her in his arms.

CHAPTER 30

The week after Sarah's birth, while John was out crying and doing business, a knock sounded at the door. Katherine sat rocking her newborn to sleep. The girls were napping, so she rested the baby against her shoulder and quietly rose to answer the door. "Why, Governor Winthrop, please do come in. These March winds are fickle. No need to stand out in the chill," she said, patting little Sarah on the back.

The Governor took off his hat and stood looking at her with concern—or was it a look of caring? His wise, brown eyes and thin lips seemed to speak to her, even before he spoke. She stepped aside and he entered the farmhouse. "I have come calling to see on your health, and the health of your newborn."

"Sarah's her name and we are both doing well. Thanks to you." She turned Sarah's face to the governor, and the baby yawned, her head resting on Katherine's shoulder.

The governor smoothed his thin beard to a point several times, and watched the child with satisfaction. "After the scare last week, I am relieved you are both hale and well," he said.

Katherine felt a flush to her cheeks. She nodded to a chair by the hearth. "Please sit, Governor. Would you care for some cider with an oatcake?"

The Governor beckoned her to the chair instead. "Please, Katherine. You suffered an ordeal. I will help myself." She pointed to the cupboard and told him where they kept the mugs. He retrieved one, and proceeded to fill it up with the warm drink, then took an oatcake from the side board. He sat on the settle watching Katherine attend to her infant.

"Where's John? Is he out readying the land for spring planting? 'Tis a blessing the floods have finally receded."

"John is out crying the news. I told him after work to fetch me an almanac down at the warehouse. I need my almanac for my work." She continued to rock the sleeping baby.

"I received mine yesterday," Governor Winthrop said, sipping his cider. "'Tis important for my work as well."

These words interested Katherine. She glanced at him wondering what she should ask next. "I know you are not only governor, but town physician round these parts. Do you use astrology for your healing purposes? Do you follow the sun and moon's progressions?"

The governor's eyebrows shot skyward and his long thin nose perched downward. He seemed at a loss for words. "Only for healing purposes—and for planting," he finally replied. "But ne'er do I use it to predict the future or outcomes. Why do you ask, Katherine? What do you know of the movement of the stars? From what I hear, you have accomplished some healing work yourself around these parts."

"Aye, so I have," she said, proud of her work with the plasters and poultices she was adept at making. "I had experience during the Civil War ministering to soldiers; I tended to amputations and surgeries of all sorts. I studied Mr. Lilly's book and almanac—"

"You mean the London astrologer who predicted the death of King Charles I?"

"Aye, 'tis the same man. I advised the barber-surgeons of the best time to cut, sew, stitch, remove—all according to the moon and sun signs."

"I see," the governor said. "'Tis useful knowledge."

Perhaps he is unaccustomed to women who are knowledgeable in the healing arts, she thought. But he seemed genuinely interested.

"For healing, astrology is necessary for the doctor and the nurse," the governor explained. "Timing is critical." He swallowed the last of the oatcake and drank from his mug. "Did you know the father of medicine, Hippocrates, wrote, '*A physician without knowledge of astrology has no right to call himself a physician?*'"

Katherine's smile widened and her hazel eyes rounded. Here was the Governor of Connecticut Colony admitting his broad knowledge of the arts to her. "I am certain, Governor, you have studied many of the great works by alchemists…such as Paracelsus and John Dee?"

"Indeed. I'm surprised you know of such works. I have delved into alchemy—'tis a very useful art." The Governor smiled, seemingly impressed, then prepared to take his leave. "I write daily in my ledger; I collect recipes for healing, and of course, make note of mine own remedies as well. Please feel free to share any with me."

"I shall," she said, honored to think the governor could gladly use some of her remedies. She walked him to the door. "And I thank thee for the visit and for saving my life—and Sarah's."

"Did John share with thee the news?"

Katherine knew of what he asked. "Aye, so he did. Governor, I give thanks for what God hath provided me: a good husband and three beautiful daughters. I am healthy, and although I will bear no more children, I am happy and grateful for my life."

"Aye, so I can see that," said Winthrop, looking relieved, his eyes now twinkling and a smile filling his thin face.

They stepped out to the front porch. As she bid the governor a good day, they turned and saw Joseph coming from the cottage carrying a bouquet of snowdrops, violets, and crocuses. The native workman bowed to Katherine. "For Goodwife Harrison. To feel better and to brighten the home." Then he stared long at the governor.

"Why, bless you, Joseph. And you know who this is—he who helped with Sarah's birth and pays us a visit today?"

Joseph's eyes opened wide and he bowed, saying, "I know. Governor Winthrop. My tribe, Wangunk says you are the best leader in Colony for them— to them. You are wise."

"The Wangunks are a good people, Joseph. Wangunks deserve respect," said Governor Winthrop, reaching a hand out to shake Joseph's.

"My tribe and I thank the good governor."

"I try for fairness around these parts."

As Winthrop readied to take his leave, John came ambling up the hill, waving a packet in one hand and swinging his bell in the other.

"How now?" he shouted. "Good to see you, Governor… Joseph." He kissed Kat on the cheek and handed the packet at her. "I found you an almanack for 1658. We are sure to be ready for the planting season. And Kat, you've received a letter from England." He pulled it from his satchel and handed it to her.

"Thank you, husband. The yearly almanac always makes things easier."

The governor smiled and nodded in agreement. "Well then, I shall be on my way. Just checking on your wife and beautiful daughter, John. You are a blessed man."

"I thank thee, Governor. Can you stay for supper?" John asked politely.

"Goodwife Winthrop will have supper ready soon," the governor replied.

"I don't know about the rest of you, but I'm ready for mine."

"John, bring the baby inside. I'll be right in after I read the letter."

As the group dispersed, Katherine ripped open the letter from England. She read the official notice that her mother recently had died from heart trouble. Inside the envelope was a heart-shaped locket, a remembrance from Mam. She thought she'd give it to one of the girls—someday. Although saddened by the loss, Katherine was relieved that her mother knew of her marriage to John, knew of their family and good fortune. Mam could go to her death in peace.

CHAPTER 31

July 1660

In the three years since Sarah's birth, Katherine and John increased their land holdings and their coffers as well. Thomas Gilbert, Lydia's husband, died in 1659. He had never been right after his wife's death.

But what grand news came from abroad; it spread like a swarm of bees throughout the three river towns. For a king had been restored unto the throne of England. The son of Charles I was crowned King Charles II; he had returned triumphant from exile in France, and thus began what the people called, 'The Restoration.' Although Katherine and John shouted in private, "All hail to the new King," and toasted him mightily, the Puritans in town were none too pleased with the new 'Merry Monarch.'

And if this wasn't troubling enough to the Puritans, a great church schism took hold in the towns of Wethersfield and Hartford. 'Hearts against hearts, neighbors against neighbors,' people proclaimed. The new half-way covenant that allowed membership to the unbaptized, divided the people. Many of the Wethersfield supporters of the Reverend Russell, those against these new notions, were readying to take leave to Hadley, Massachusetts, including old Captain Cullick.

Thomas Bracy was another such person. The young man had signed the petition in favor of the Reverend Russell, and decided his fate lay with the Russell followers. Today he had spent the morning at his friend Samuel Well's house across from the Harrison farm. They discussed the imminent move, for Thomas planned to join the Wells party on the journey north.

After the meeting he stood aside the Sandy Lane wondering if he should walk back home or head to the meadows to check on what few of his crops remained. As he made his way readying to cross the road, he wondered if the rumors were true, that the Harrisons be witches. He did not have to wait long to see evidence of his belief that the Harrisons used preternatural means to gain the wealth townspeople claimed they were amassing.

He saw a cart approach the Harrison house loaded up with hay and driven by the Harrison's native worker. Bracy blinked his eyes twice. For atop the haystack, he saw a red calf's head, its round brown eyes and long eyelashes blinking at him, with its ears sticking straight up. He mumbled a prayer and continued to watch the cart at the gate.

Thomas knew what he had seen: a calf's head atop the haystack. Now it had vanished. In its stead on the hay-load was Katherine Harrison herself, glaring at Thomas, hands on hips.

"So, thou art a witch and a conjuror after all, Goodwife Harrison," he shouted out.

Katherine quickly jumped from the cart and confronted Bracy with her finger pointed to his face.

"How dare you make such claims?" she said. "You speak any further of these lies—"

"But I saw with mine own eyes that calf's head staring at me," he said. "Where did it disappear? Where is it now?"

"You, Goodman, speak naught but hodgepodge. You saw naught but my hair and hay; methinks thou art envious and a right meddler."

"I know what I saw, Goodwife."

"You saw naught. And lest I hear more lies, I will get even with you, mark my word!"

To young Thomas, Katherine Harrison's eyes looked like two burning embers ready to spit fire at him. Even her freckles, those devil's spots, glowed with unnatural light.

Bracy bristled, alarmed by the curse Katherine had laid upon him. He could say no more and hastened to take his leave. But he knew what he had seen: the odd image of the calf's head. He turned about and headed back to the Town Green. He tried to push that woman's words from his mind—but he would not soon forget what he had seen this day.

·•·

On his way to the Green, Thomas Bracy remembered that Goody Harrison was friends with Goody Palmer, and the scoundrel, James Wakeley. Rumor had it that Kate Palmer, her husband Henry, and James Wakeley attended forbidden Merrymeets in Hartford.

Bracy assumed Katherine Harrison did as well.

They all seemed busy doing the devil's bidding, all being Sabbath breakers. People took note of who attended Sabbath each week and who was missing; Thomas ne'er saw them much at all. For if one truly loved the devil, how could one pray to God? And everyone knew Katherine Harrison and James Wakeley had married up— James to a rich, older widow and Katherine to John—a wealthy man now with much land and great holdings.

That night as Thomas prepared for bed, he wished his father Martin a good eve, kissed his mother, and promptly got into bed. He thought not to share with them about his encounter with Katherine; his parents were already saddened he would be leaving for Hadley soon. Why upset them further?

All was quiet for a moment as Thomas lay in bed. But not for long. For when he opened his eyes next, there was Goodwife Harrison alongside James Wakeley, whispering together at the end of his bed. They seemed to glow, as if some preternatural, otherworldly light shone from their bodies. He remained still, afeared to make a sound. He thought Katherine Harrison's curse was truly upon him. He listened to the voices conspiring against him to 'slit his throat.'

"Nay," said a voice that sounded like Katherine's. "'Tis best to strangle him. That will keep the tattler quiet."

Thomas grabbed onto his neck and began to pray in silence. But the prayer did not stop the fiends. Of a sudden, his body felt as if he were pinched here and there, painful afflictions that pulled his hands from his throat. He felt a body atop his, pushing him down.

He groaned aloud, groaned again, and screamed out. Screamed until his father arose and came to help. When his father asked him what was wrong, Thomas could not speak—not until his father laid a reassuring hand to his forehead. His mother came rushing into the bedroom.

"What is the matter?" she asked.

"They want my life! They pinch me. They try to strangle me." He pointed to the end of his bed. "See? Goody Harrison and James Wakeley are here—and they want my life!"

His mother ran out of the room, shocked by his words, and retrieved a cool cloth for his forehead. Thomas had always been a sensitive child. "'Tis but a nightmare...that is all," she muttered to herself.

Or so she thought. For the next day, his family saw the markings on Thomas's arms and legs, the result of painful pinches and hard squeezes. "Now I *know* they be witches," declared Thomas, "and they have cursed me."

"'Tis a good thing you will be removing to Hadley soon," said his mother, shaking her head. "They will not be able to catch or curse you. You will be safe up north—once you cross the river."

"Aye," said Thomas. "I am ready to leave this accursed town behind."

·•·

Thomas was not alone in his desire to leave Wethersfield. The next day John Graves, a farmer who planned to remove to Hadley, happened to be leading his cows to graze in the meadows. He had heard the rumors about the Harrisons being witches. Why not let his cattle feed near the Harrisons' land, nay, on their land? His cattle always grazed peacefully wherever they went; if something went amiss with the cattle, he would know for certain the Harrisons were meddling with Satan.

He tied his cattle to the cart rope, keeping them tight together by making thick knots in the rope—something he did often. He watched his cattle, waiting for them to feed. But they merely stood and fed not. They stared at him blinking their long eyelashes. Without a movement from either Goodman Graves or the cattle, the tight web of knots suddenly began to unravel afore his eyes. He started up retying the knots, only to witness them loosen up—again.

In a short time, his cattle seemed spooked, as if they had seen or felt something upon them— like a specter, he thought. Invisible yet powerful, like a wind full of malice. With the knots refusing to stay put, John Graves's cattle, usually placid in grazing, fell to running away from the Harrison's toward the meadow with such speed, the oxen yoke went a-flying, and Goodman Graves was in the awkward position of having to chase them.

My cattle never acted in such a manner before, he thought. 'Tis clear that the Harrisons *are* witches who curse anyone or anything that trespasses on their land.

John Graves felt relief it would be but several weeks before he and his wary cattle would leave for Hadley. He was convinced the Harrisons had put a spell on their land—and his cattle.

CHAPTER 32

August 1660

In addition to the great church quarrel and the departure of disgruntled townspeople to Hadley, a sickness came upon Wethersfield during the summer of 1660. No one could explain the cause of the illness, nor name it; only that it weakened a person with fever and wasted the body away.

Both Katherine and Kate Palmer were doing a brisk business with their simples, plasters, and poultices. Henry and John had carved out a bigger cupboard in the kitchen for Katherine's herbs. John's influence down at the warehouse allowed him to purchase special glass and pewter containers for her collection. She had them neatly lined and labeled on shelves in the expanded cupboard.

Just the day before Kate Palmer had told Katherine she needed to deliver a simple to Mrs. Robbins— the matriarch of the well-placed family— who happened to live next door to the Palmers on the Broad Street. Would Katherine care to join her?

"Aye, I will come with you. John can watch the girls for the time. I will bring a plaster for Mrs. Robbins's fevered head."

Everyone knew how the Robbins family had suffered these last two months, losing daughter Mary to the sickness. Now Mrs. Robbins had taken to her bed, ill with the fever herself. Katherine thought about the Robbins's grand house, perfectly shingled, white-washed with yellow trim, and set with diamond-shaped window panes.

A starker contrast between the Robbins and Palmer homesteads she ne'er had seen. Although the Palmers settled their land first, the Robbins treated them like trespassers. The Palmers' mean, faded grey dwelling seemed to lean toward the road as if it should fall. Henry, it seemed, had no time, nor inkling to fix his own home.

"I've always wanted to see the inside of the Robbins house. 'Tis so grand looking on the outside. Reminds me of Captain Cullick's—" The words flew fast from Katherine's lips.

Kate ignored the mention of Katherine's old master from Hartford. "Grander on the inside, in fact. Far grander than most around these parts." Kate hung her head. "But we own property on prime land so they say. Perhaps someday we shall sell it for a pretty price; I know Goodman Robbins doth desire it." Kate's face brightened. "And they always request my physicks. Appreciate my skills, so they say.… but ne'er do show it in public." She shrugged. "I know the Robbins will honor your healing ways." She embraced Katherine. "Aren't we the pair? I will see you at noon on the morrow."

·⊷⊶·

Katherine finished up the last stitch to her scarf, an autumn gift for John, tied an end knot, and shooed Hoccanum from the threads. He rolled on his back, paws grasping for the yarn. "Why Hoccanum, you little devil! You will twist yourself up in this skein. Shoo!"

Hoccanum slinked away looking for another means of getting into mischief. He was a restless roamer, a mouser, and her daughters' favorite distraction. He tended to draw closer to Katherine and turned his nose up to the others, unless a bowl of milk, or a dried piece of fish or meat was offered. The cat knew how to strike a bargain; if he thought a morsel might be coming, his purring became a steady hum and then became louder as he wrapped his black tail around the willing giver, as if this slight gesture was a gift unto itself.

Katherine readied herself to leave, gathering her basket of salves, ointments, and a fresh plaster. "I'm going now," she called out from the back door of the kitchen.

John and the three girls waved. He knew how to keep them busy; work became an amusement, a game with John in charge.

She made her way to the Broad Street. The sun was bright and hot, the blue sky cloudless, a perfect August day. She hummed to herself, singing old ballads, glad to be away from the farm for a time. She walked past James Wakeley's house and saw him out front. She waved to him, and noticed how he stared at her with a odd look.

"Going for a visit to Kate's place, are ye?"

"We are ministering to Mrs. Robbins. They say she's ailing." He nodded his head and wished her a good day.

At last, she found herself knocking on the Palmer's narrow, grey door. She heard bumping and jostling noises inside. "Stop! Nay, you *did* do that!" she heard Kate shout. The sound of boys roughhousing among themselves—all four of them —was boisterous and loud.

Kate opened the door. "How now, Kat? Art thou ready?" Kate turned around in the scant hallway and shouted, "Henry, I'm leaving for the Robbins's house. Get these boys back to work in the meadow. We need no idleness today." She heard a loud grunt from inside.

"Aye, I'm ready." Katherine smoothed down her skirt and straightened her cap. "I have brought one of my well-known plasters. Known to pull the fever up and out every time."

Kate hurried to check her bag. "I've got what I need to aid Mrs. Robbins in her distress as well."

The pair approached the white door with the overhead lintel painted a bright yellow. They huddled together as Kate carefully pressed the door knocker down several times. A girl who looked to be in her late teens answered the door. Her wide-set blue eyes, clear skin, and tiny sloped nose reflected a soft, refined manner.

"Hannah, a good day to you," began Kate. "May we visit your mother for a time? We are here to help." She pointed to Katherine. "You know Goodwife Harrison from up the road—the Town Crier's wife. She's come to aid me."

Katherine smiled and kept silent.

"Did my mother request this—?" Hannah asked, abruptly cut off by Kate Palmer pushing her way through the door right past the startled girl. "Why...please stop...Father come quick," she called out, but it was too late. Both women stood in the center of the grand hall. The sunlight seemed to enter from all directions beaming down on the two visitors.

Mrs. Robbins was in the Great Room to the right, lying on a makeshift cot, gasping for air. It appeared Mr. Robbins was in the parlor to the left. Katherine swiveled her head back and forth, surveying the rooms; the grand hearths in each had delicate Dutch tiles framing the fireplace, with exquisite glass figurines gracing the mantles. Light brown wainscoting surrounded the walls. Freshly picked sunflowers sat in vases, their heads turned toward the light. Katherine took in the views of this glorious household, and the pair made their way to the ailing woman.

Mrs. Robbins began to moan under the light quilt atop her. She opened an eye and glared at Kate. "'Tis you?" she asked.

Hannah had returned with her father. They stood at the entrance of the room, disapproval on their faces. Hannah held her arms crossed, shaking her head back and forth.

Kate ignored this and spoke with Mrs. Robbins. "We are here to help," she said. "'Tis what thou requested." She lifted up her basket. "I've brought you my rue simple. It will help sweat out this fever."

Mrs. Robbins blinked and pointed a finger at Katherine. "Why is *she* here?"

"'Tis Goodwife Harrison from up the road. She brought one of her healing plasters for you as well."

Mrs. Robbins, sweating and panting, shook her head. "I know her…*not!*"

Kate leaned over and whispered to Katherine, "She's fevered. Pay no mind."

But Katherine responded, "Of course thou know me, Mary. Why do you reject me—when I am only here to help you? Quiet now." She took out her can of salve and began to rub it on the ailing woman's throat.

Mrs. Robbins groaned as Kate wiped the sick woman's brow of sweat. Katherine dug deeper into her bag. "Here is the plaster. Put it on her forehead." The woman's face, pale as the whitewashed walls, turned the other way.

Mr. Robbins and Hannah moved further into the room. Mr. Robbins, frail and standing with the help of a cane spoke out. "You have thrust your way past the threshold of my home. And, remember, Goodwife Palmer, the complaint I submitted against you years ago in '48. As God be my witness, I shall do it again. Now leave!"

The women ignored the man's pleas.

"Forsooth! We are only here to help your wife," said Kate, sighing. She shook her head and made a tsk tsk sound— as if to scold the old man.

Hannah, now frantic, began to cry in earnest.

Mrs. Robbins stirred again in anguish. She threw her arms out to the side. Mustering her strength, the sick woman slowly lifted her body, leaning up on the cot. She looked like bones strung together under a white shift. She pointed directly at Kate Palmer. Her eyes, glistening with the light of one who is sick, spoke slowly in a low, rumbling voice. "Get out!" Then she fell back down on the pallet.

Hannah rushed to her mother's side, speaking words of solace to the agitated woman. "You heard her. Remove yourself at once, lest I call the constable."

"But—" Kate Palmer argued.

"Ye are not welcome here." John Robbins reminded them. "Ye bring sorrow unto my house. Begone."

Once again, Mrs. Robbins stirred. Every movement seemed to weaken her body, but not her resolve nor her spirit. She made another effort to speak, and now she spoke low and clear. "Get thee behind me, both of ye!" She lay back again, panting for breath and tossing about on the cot.

Mr. Robbins hobbled toward them and jabbed a finger at Kate. "And I say for the last time, get thee out. You are naught but a pair of lowborn crows. You have vexed my ailing wife, and now you vex me with your impudence. And to enter my house as such? Aye, my wife speaks *truth* in her illness."

The pair gathered their belongings and fled from the house, but not before Katherine took a long, lasting look about. After Kate scurried home, Katherine began to walk back to the farm. She turned toward the Robbins house for a last look. Hannah and her father stood with hands on hips glaring at her from the stoop.

"We don't want or need your cures. We know your kind. We have heard what people are saying about you. Good riddance," she heard Hannah say.

Katherine shrugged her shoulders. She was *only* trying to help.

She shook her head in dismay thinking about what she would tell John. The walk back was long enough to think of something.

CHAPTER 33

The day after the visit to the Robbins's home, Katherine and John were out in the barn cleaning, their three girls running about helping with chores. Suddenly they all heard a great cry, "Kat, Kat!"

There was Kate Palmer rushing up the hill toward them, her cap flaps loose and slapping the sides of her head, her face aflush. "Kat, I need speaking with thee…alone." Kate gulped for air. "'Tis urgent."

John agreed and began to entertain the girls with funny faces and loud, cow-like bellows to give them a distraction.

Kate and Katherine ambled toward the farmhouse and sat on the back stoop. The day was hot and sticky. Kate fanned herself with her hands wiping sweat from her face. "Have ye heard the news?" she asked.

"Nay," said Katherine. "I have heard naught. What now? I've got work to do."

Kate was silent but a moment. "Mrs. Robbins is dead! Dead! Died sometime this morning. James Wakeley just told me. Why, his wife Alice went for a visit today, and Mrs. Robbins *just* died. According to Alice, her body became soft and then stiff. They know we were the last people to visit her. They think we hexed her."

Katherine shook her head in disbelief. "Actually then, Alice was the last person to see Mrs. Robbins alive. And by the by…did you stop at the Robbins's house to get the truth?

"Aye, so I tried. For when I stepped out from mine own house, Mr. Robbins approached me. Claims we agitated the wife, upset her bodily functions, and gave her a simple that sped up her demise. He claims we cursed her unto death. What say you?"

Kate's eyes pleaded for an answer. Katherine stared back frowning. "And so…they are saying we together bewitched the woman unto death? Forsooth! This is naught but lies. Why the woman was most clearly on her deathbed. We tried to make her better not worse. So this transpired *after* we did a good deed. How people can think this… it vexes me so!" She felt a tightening in her stomach and her fists clenched. She really did need a snort of snuff.

"What shall we do?" Kate asked.

"We do naught. We are innocent, so there's nothing needs being done."

"But I am the Robbins's next neighbor. What if they report me to the authorities?"

"You have a witness, and that witness is me. Naught happened that we caused. Wipe the guilt and worry from your face, Kate. We merely visited upon a sick woman whom we tried to help, and she died—from the wasting sickness— anyway."

"So *you* say."

"I say correctly. We have naught to worry over," Katherine said, trying to reassure her friend.

Kate laid a veined hand on Katherine's arm. "I feel some relief now. We *were* just trying to help."

"Aye, 'tis true. And stay to it, Kate. The woman was sick…and then she died."

"You are right, Kat. We did nothing wrong." She paused. "So… what say you come with me and my Henry, along with James Wakeley to attend the Harvest Merrymeet in Hartford? We want you and John to join us. Remember we meet on the South Green? What say you?"

Katherine watched her friend in silent shock. How could Kate be thinking as such? "Nay, I will not go. 'Tis taking an unnecessary risk. Especially now." She thought Kate a fool to think on such matters.

Kate Palmer's eyes retained their pleading look. "These people— James, Rebecca Greensmith and others— are *my* people. Our gatherings mean much to me. Even James agrees that leaving his old wife home... where she belongs... provides him some distraction. We are clever, Kat. Will you come?"

"Nay, I won't go," Katherine repeated with stubborn firmness. "Go if you must, but take care. From what I hear, some of those Hartford folk are trouble. And I need no trouble!"

Kate put an arm around her friend. "These gatherings give me strength to know there are others who think like me— like us. I, for one, will take my chances and go next month. By then, any fervor over Mrs. Robbins will be long past. Both Henry and I enjoy the sack, the ale, and cakes, the songs in season. We need to make merry."

"And I need to finish cleaning the barn—"

"Tell not a soul of what I have shared with thee, not even John. We shall speak again soon." Kate straightened her cap flaps and calmly made her way back to the road.

⋅—⋅

"What's the good word, wife?" John had a giggling Sarah on his back, while Rebecca and Mary tied a rope around his neck, pulling him like a stubborn cow. Katherine, hands on hips, looked upon her laughing family enjoying these few precious moments of merriment.

Should she tell John? She wondered. As the Town Crier he would find out soon enough.

"Kate needed more valerian for a simple," she said.

John lifted his head, as Sarah pulled back the 'reins.' "For Mrs. Robbins, I presume?"

"Don't know," Katherine lied again. "I gave Kate the answers to some of her herbal queries."

"Good," said John. "Mayhap old Mrs. Robbins will heal. In the meantime, we have got much work to do in preparation for the harvest."

Suddenly Katherine remembered she had left the cows grazing at the Dry Swamp in the Great Meadow. It was time to get them back to the barn. Hoccanum often accompanied her on her walks if he was bored or so inclined. Today he seemed ready for an adventure. "Come, Hoccanum, let's get the cattle." The cat stretched and sat up to attention.

She told John she would be right back to help with the hay. The cattle had grazed through the night, likely ready to return home. Kat grabbed a small pail, and a long, thin rod made of birch that she used as a cattle switch and began her walk to the Dry Swamp.

The sun was afire today. She wiped her forehead pushing away bits of dried hay, sweat, and the news of Mrs. Robbins's sudden death. Clearly God had other plans for the poor woman. All Katherine could do was get on with her daily life—and get her cows back home.

She walked the Broad Street, careful not to look toward the Robbins house, lest they be watching for her. Hoccanum stayed close near her on the road, keeping to her legs. Only when she arrived to the Meadow Gate and began to open it, did the cat rush through to prowl and stalk about the rustling cornfields. He enjoyed pouncing upon an insect or a mouse, even grabbing fish from Blackbird Pond, but today the flocks of meadow birds commanded his attention,

She walked toward the Dry Swamp. The Harrison cows were nowhere to be seen. She found herself following Hoccanum. What had happened to her cattle? While she searched the area for the cows, a flock of blackbirds circled around overhead and landed on the swamp's reeds, searching for bits of seed to eat. With the whoosh of the movements, Hoccanum became a wild creature of a sudden, waiting, stalking his prey, then pouncing.

As one blackbird flew so did the others. Katherine watched the cat race down the Dry Swamp toward the Fill Barn. Now, *he* was gone as well "Hoccanum, Come Hoccanum!" she shouted over and again. And then a great rumble of crashing and lowing could be heard—from a distance.

Suddenly she saw her cattle appear, clamoring to get to her. Tails up, eyes bulging with fear, they looked spooked. When she saw Hoccanum running hither and thither between the cows' legs, she understood and laughed. "Hoc, you clever cat! You are better than most sheepdogs from the Old Country."

She joined the cattle by the meadow gate waiting to return home. "Aw, 'tis just a cat." She calmed the disturbed cows with her voice. "You will be back to your stalls soon enough."

•—•

Joseph Dickinson just happened to witness Goodwife Harrison calling out near the Dry Swamp. He had heard, 'Hoccanum, Come Hoccanum.' What could it all mean? But when he watched her cows dash toward her with great vigor, nay violence, he thought it strange. Aye, he had heard the rumors about Goodwife Harrison's curses, her fortunetelling, aye, her predictions that had come to pass. And now this. Goodman Dickinson stood in great wonder at such a spectacle.

Never in his years had he witnessed a herd of cattle almost crash through the Dry Swamp to get to their mistress. This woman hath strange and unearthly powers, he thought. 'Tis true what they say. She doth meddle in witchcraft.

He saw his friend Phillip Smith walking the road toward him. Goodman Dickinson would most certainly share what he had just witnessed with his friend.

·•–•·

Samuel Wells stood outside the back of his home on the Sandy Lane, readying to bring his cows back from the meadow. When he heard the familiar sound of cowbells coming up the road, he saw that the Wells herd was making their way to the house. He noticed what looked to be his Harrison neighbor's cows following close behind. The whole of Sandy Lane was blocked with impatient bovines.

Then he saw her. Aye, he espied Katherine Harrison crouch down with her pail right next to his prized milking cow, and then she vanished from his sight. It appeared to Samuel that Goodwife Harrison was milking their finest cow!

Samuel attempted to cross the road to tell Goodwife Harrison to stop the theft. Instead, his feet stuck fast to the ground. He could not move a muscle, nor speak a word— for he was dumbstruck.

As he watched Goodwife Harrison arise again to lead her cows to the barn, he seethed with anger. He was certain she had put a spell on him, preventing him from coming closer. When he could no longer see her, his legs began to move again.

He had a lot to tell his friend Thomas Bracy about what just happened. He would share the news on their way to Hadley just a fortnight away.

•—•—•

Wethersfield was now abuzz with the news of the death of Mrs. Robbins. John found out through a townsperson later in the day, and confronted Katherine about her visit to the sick woman's house with Kate Palmer. "What happened, Kat? People are talking. Getting suspicious of you—*and* me. Rumors are flying. What say you?"

"I say we tried to save her. God had other plans."

"Tried? You need to *stop* trying, wife. We have enough on this farm to worry about, and with my expanding business, it should keep us all busy enough." John grimaced, clearly tired of the rumors and gossip.

"Through my healing I have brought money into our coffer. Isn't that something? My work brings extra means to our home. Besides Mrs. Robbins, I've done good for this town. Whether I'm appreciated or not… I don't know; I just know my healing skills are needed here."

"Needed? We need you, Kat. And my heart doth pain with such worry and burdens. Promise me you will stop these visits— for my sake?"

"I will try. But if someone needs me…I will do what I can for them."

John folded his arms together. "Forget these people. In their eyes, one minute you are a healer, and the next a witch! *You* can't save this town. Your family needs you more."

Kat huffed. "I will be whoever I am."

John was resigned to his wife's stubbornness. "Be yourself, Kat. True, but keep your mouth still. You don't know who's listening round these parts."

She remembered Kate sharing Lydia Gilbert's last words on the gallows; that this Colony would suffer plagues, schisms, and heartache. It all seemed to be coming to pass.

CHAPTER 34

June 1661

Almost a year later Katherine stood spinning at her wheel. The girls ran about the house chasing Hoccanum. Kat tried to explain to four-year-old Sarah not to grab Hoccanum's tail. "'Tis not a pull toy, Sarah. He's a live animal." The child was relentless, laughing to herself, stretching her hand to yank the cat's tail, even falling as she reached out toward the wary feline.

John finally arrived home. He wore his summer Town Crier dress with a light half-cloak and hat for the season. He was returning from a long morning. "Wife," he shouted, "I have news. 'Tis history!"

Katherine smiled. Her husband was always the first to know. "What news today?" She took her foot off the treadle; even the girls came around gazing up at their beloved papa.

John began ringing his bell and announced, "Let it be known that our esteemed Governor, John Winthrop Jr., has at last departed our shores for England to meet with King Charles II. He leaves to secure a charter for our colony. His return is hence unknown." He dropped his voice to its normal resounding pitch. "Aye, according to the news, he had quite the send-off in Hartford. The authorities even hired a trumpeter for the occasion." He paused and proclaimed, "God save the King. And God save our good Governor!"

"'Tis all good, John. But what doth this mean for us? Who will be charge now?" she asked, foot back on the treadle, the wheel whirring with a new frenzy. She gripped the thread tightly, pleased to think of Governor Winthrop meeting with the King and bringing the colony a new charter. But she knew with the governor gone, his calm presence would be sorely missed.

The girls stood staring at their father. "Yes, Papa. What does it all mean?" asked seven-year- old Rebecca.

How grown she acts… though she still be but a child, thought Katherine.

"Here's the rest of the news," said John. "Governor Winthrop has appointed none other than Major John Mason in charge." He peered over at Katherine. "What say you to *that*?"

She remembered Major Mason from years ago and frowned. Could she ever forget the day he came to Captain Cullick's house for midday meal? How his talk revolved around witches? She decided she would cast a chart for this day, to review whether this would be an auspicious or inauspicious day for Governor Winthrop's journey. And for a new Acting Governor to the Colony.

"I say Mason is a poor choice for governor. What doth he truly know of running a colony? The man has natives and those he deems witches on his mind. He is dangerous, John. I don't trust him."

"Witches," Rebecca said. "What is a witch, Mama?" Her three daughters stood wide-eyed, waiting for her answer.

"There are no witches," she said. "Only bad people who call other people names."

"It's bad to call people names," Mary repeated. "Papa taught us that."

"And if Papa catches you calling people bad names, why I will report the lot of you to our new Acting Governor Mason. He shan't be pleased," said John glancing over at Katherine with a wink.

"Nay, Papa. We try to be good…every day," Rebecca reminded him.

Katherine paused the wheel. "John, stop scaring the girls. 'Tis no time to jest or make light of this news. Governor Winthrop is gone—for how long we know not. I will pray for his safe journey and return."

John pulled up a stool and sat by the spinning wheel. "And you, my dear, must take care…*we* must take care. Remember the old expression, 'When the cat's away, the rats doth play.'"

"Are you calling Major, nay, Acting Governor Mason a rat?" Grinning, she put her foot back on the treadle, the spinning wheel moving at a steady pace.

"Aye, and you know 'tis true," said John. "Time to keep our heads down and our mouths shut tight. We need no trouble. The shadow of Mrs. Robbins still looms large over you and Kate."

·—·

The day was perfect for laundry. The girls loved to help throw the clothes into a steaming vat of hot water, lye, and a dose of lavender oil for a clean scent. Rebecca, already an expert at the washing board, scrubbed the clothes down the correct way. She was so like her father—determined, exact, and thorough.

The wind blew in warm breezes from the south that hinted at hotter days to come. Flocks of geese settled over the Great Meadow, gliding onto the waters of the Great River, others landing along the river's edge looking for nesting spots. The swamps and ponds were filled with tadpoles and frogs, dragonflies, and red-winged blackbirds claiming their roosts. And with each passing day, Wethersfield became greener and brighter with new life.

Today, Joseph and his family worked alongside the Harrisons on the farm. There was weeding and planting to get done. But today Joseph approached the family with a scowl on his face.

"Joseph, is something wrong?" Katherine asked. Usually John's worker was happy, content with his lot. Today was different.

"We Wangunks…do not like Mason. He hates natives. My tribe is afraid of him."

John joined in the conversation. "Afraid? You have no reason to be afraid, Joseph. You and your people are like family to us. Governor Mason has no power here. And Governor Winthrop *will* return, so be it."

Joseph shook his head. "Mason hates natives…and some women… he thinks witches." He looked in all directions as if the town militia were coming for him. Then he watched Katherine. "You are healer. *You* be careful." His dark eyes glared at her, his brow furrowed, and his lips set firm.

Kat laughed, trying to lighten the mood. "Why, with Goodman Harrison here to protect us, what worries have we?"

CHAPTER 35

December 1662

Joseph was right. With Governor Winthrop gone and Major Mason in charge, a witchcraft panic struck Hartford like a plague. An eight-year-old Hartford girl had sickened in March, accusing others of pinching and choking her. Soon after, eight-year-old Betty Kelly died in fits of torment.

After Betty's death, a young maid named Ann Cole of Hartford began speaking in strange tongues, and then the accusations flew from her lips. They swirled around Hartford like a nor'easter blows snowflakes—fast and hard.

Katherine, although relieved this was happening in Hartford, knew no one was safe with Mason as governor. How she longed for sensible Governor Winthrop to be home again. Only he could put a stop to this madness.

But still this was a quiet and fruitful time for the Harrrison family. The farm was flourishing, and John's trade down at the warehouse— and his trade with the natives— was bringing in extra money. His hides, leather goods, crops, and now exports, commanded much interest.

Yet Kat remained worried. For in June one Mary Sanford of Hartford was hanged for a witch; her husband was acquitted and left the colony. Now many people sat in the Hartford jail awaiting trial. News of strange Merrymeets in Hartford filled the talk of town gossips. How relieved she was she had never attended those gatherings. But her friends Kate and Henry Palmer, as well as James Wakeley, attended regularly.

When she spoke of her worries to John, he dismissed her concerns. "We have naught to fear, Kat. Minding our business keeps our heads above the din. And look what happens when we mind *our* business? The money is flowing into our coffers."

"And what of our minds and hearts?" she asked.

"We are bringing in plenty of coin, Kat. That should soothe your heart—and calm your mind."

These words soothed her little. And she found little solace that the Wethersfield gossips and scolds had turned their attention to Hartford, and away from the Harrisons. In their fickleness and spite, they could well turn back again.

·-·

One December evening after the girls were put to bed, and John was snoring aloud in the loft, Katherine sat knitting by the hearth. She heard a quick rapping to the door. For safety's sake, she eyed John's musket standing erect in the corner of the room near the door, just in case.

The wind blew fierce this December eve. Who could this be? She thought maybe someone had fallen ill and was in need of a plaster or some strong drink. Either way, the knocking sounded urgent.

She found a tallow, lit it, then slightly opened the door and peered out. Tiny snowflakes whipped around the house in a frenzied dance, white against the blackened sky.

"Kat, Kat," she heard a soft voice cry. "Let me in." A restless horse whinnied from near the fencepost.

She recognized the voice.

"Kate, what brings thee here so late? Come in from this wind. The girls and John are asleep." Kate Palmer stepped inside shaking from the cold. And when Katherine saw her friend, she could see the fear in her eyes. Kate was ghostly white and covered with snow.

"Do you need a remedy? Are you alright?" Katherine asked.

Kate rubbed her hands together and shook off the light snow gathered on her boots and cloak.

"Kat, I have but minutes—"

"Minutes?"

"Kat, we have been warned out."

"Warned out? What do you mean, warned out?"

"Henry and I—the family— James Wakeley too. We have been warned out of Wethersfield. Given notice by an authority, one privy to information. Told us to leave immediately. That we are in danger here. The wagon is packed. Henry and the boys are waiting."

"Why, Kate?"

"Rebecca Greensmith speaks against us now. Thinks she can save herself by accusing others. She sits in jail speaking drivel to the authorities. Never did I think she'd turn on us. Why, she's even accused her own husband of being a witch."

"What doth Rebecca say?" Kat asked. A series of gooseflesh prickles coursed up and down her arms and neck.

"She claims Henry and I, along with James Wakeley, attended her Merrymeets in Hartford. All a part of Ann Cole's accusations." She hung her head in disgrace. "Aye, so we did. And Rebecca was quick to bring up the demise of Mrs. Robbins, and even included your name as one who attended these celebrations." Kate's breathing was quick and her red eyes rimmed with tears.

Katherine knew Kate was afeard for her life.

"'Tis a pack of lies. I never set foot on the Hartford Green. But go if you must, for your own safety." Suddenly she thought of something. "Wait here." She rushed to one of John's money boxes hidden behind a loose brick near the hearth, and counted out three pounds in shillings. Then she found a thin belt of wampum shells. "Here," she told her friend. "Take these for good measure."

Kate's eyes opened wide as she placed the items in her coat pocket. "We are grateful, Kat. And I am grateful for our friendship all these years."

Katherine felt tears filling her eyes. She thought of Lydia and now Kate. At least, she thought, Kate would escape—and live.

"So, this be it, Kate. Fare-you-well on your journey. Where will ye go?"

Kate drew close. "Tell not a soul, not even John. We head toward the border of Rhode Island. We hear they are more accepting—of differences."

Katherine embraced her steadfast friend. "I'll miss you, Kate. Go well."

At last Kate pulled away, and fixed her strained blue eyes to Katherine. "Kat, your name was mentioned by Rebecca Greensmith. No one is safe. 'Tis a warning."

"True," Katherine said, already feeling the loss of her friend. "No one is safe."

CHAPTER 36

June 1663

Two years passed and Governor Winthrop Jr. was finally returned home. He had secured the charter for the colony from King Charles II, granting Connecticut more rights and freedoms. Now he sat waiting at a corner table at Jeremy Adams's Tavern in Hartford, waiting for Acting Governor, Major John Mason.

Major Mason was late for their meeting. The governor grumbled to himself in disgust and drank the last of his pint. He scratched his long nose, wiped his forehead, then began to drum his fingers on the table. Where was the man? Should he order another pint— or leave?

Gone for two years he had returned to discover that four people had been hanged for witchcraft in his absence. While he was busy attaining the colony's charter in England, the magistrates and the ministers could not quell, nor control the Hartford Witch Panic that had lasted a year, resulting in many accusations—and deaths.

What to do about these quarrelsome folk of Hartford, Wethersfield, and Windsor he knew not. He thought that when a problem arose in the towns, witchcraft became a convenient accusation and answer. Although he was well acquainted with the alchemical arts and had knowledge of the occult, he knew of no physick nor remedy to mend the rifts in these towns, no alchemical potion to set things right. In the meantime, he would demand answers.

The serving girl came by and asked him if he cared for another. He assented with a nod. He would wait with a heavy heart for Major Mason to explain how this witch hunt had happened.

A candle flickered its last breath at the table. He'd ask the girl for another one. He needed some light between him and Mason—if the major even showed. The noise from the tavern rose slowly, while the fragrant smell of roasting meat on a spit filled the air.

"Major," he heard. "'Tis good to see you. Looking hale, hearty, and determined as usual."

The governor turned to espy the tavernkeeper, Jeremy Adams, slap Major Mason on the back and lead him to the table. "Here we be." Adams stood with a proud smile on his face, his wide girth expanding under a wrinkled white apron. "'Tis an honor to have two such noble personages under my roof. Sit, Major." He looked to the Governor. "Welcome back, sir. Huzzah to you on the news of the charter. 'Tis good to have you home." As he turned to leave, he announced, "And if either you be wanting a meal, our minced pies are fresh today. On the house, considering—"

As the tavernkeeper waited for an answer, Mason hung his cloak and hat on a nearby peg and took a seat. "Aye, get me a pie—or two."

"I am fine," said the governor.

The tavernkeeper took his leave as Governor Winthrop prepared to speak.

But Major Mason was determined to have the first words. "I reckon, Governor, you be calling round to assess my two years as governor in your stead?" He leaned over the table, his black eyes boring into the governor's expression of shock. "Before you venture speech, ask the people in Hartford what they think. Why not ask the tavernkeeper, Goodman Adams, what he thinks of my handling in such matters? Before you speak, know that the people respect me, and I in turn did honor the good people of this town by doing my duty."

"I want an accounting, Major. Four people were executed in my absence. For witchcraft. You..." he leaned close to the major, "... have some explaining to do." He pounded his empty pint hard on the table, prompting the serving girl to scurry over to remove it. She set a new pint in front of him. "And before I listen to your rantings, remember *I* am the governor once more, lest you forget." He realized his voice was getting louder. The tavern had gone quiet. Winthrop smoothed the hairs of his thin mustache and beard in place, and waited for an answer.

"Why don't you question the ministers? And the magistrates. *I* merely followed orders."

The old soldier was dodging the issue, refusing to take any responsibility. He was still considered a hero by the people—as he had been in the massacre against the Pequots—and he considered that he still deserved the glory.

"*I* appointed you governor in my stead," said Winthrop. "*You* could have stopped the hysteria—the unnecessary hangings. Methinks you have more blood on your hands, Major."

"Unnecessary hangings? Blood on my hands? You simply do not understand, Governor. While you were dining with King Charles II in his court and visiting the Crowned Heads of Europe, meeting with royalty, traveling the Continent..."

"Go no further, Major. I obtained the charter for *this* colony. I never planned to be away these two long years. But ne'er did I think such goings on would occur in my absence." Winthrop paused.

"Why did you not delay the trials? Why not wait upon my return?" He wrung his hands together, then wiped his forehead. The heat of the hearthfires was bringing on a sweat.

Mason surveyed the room, and took his time before he made eye contact with the governor. "The jury gave their verdict. Is not that enough?" He smirked with smug satisfaction.

Jeremy Adams arrived with the two steaming meat pies.

Governor Winthrop sat repulsed watching the major stuff his mouth like a gluttonous swine. The man had little decorum. Mason seemed to care more for his savory meat pies than for the distasteful subject of witch-hangings. As Winthrop watched him devour the food, he could not help but compare the refined elegance and dignity in dining he experienced at the Court of King Charles II, to the coarse-mannered rudeness of the major's display. He was losing patience.

In between bites, Major Mason stared up and said, "Why, if you had seen that young girl, Ann Cole, in her fits and ravings, you would think different. You see, after the death of little Betty Kelly, Ann was not right. Those who practiced the dark arts in Hartford—they possessed the maid to the core. Do you not care she was made *well and whole* after the witches were hanged? They can harm her no more. But methinks you care naught for these truths."

"I say 'tis wrong to believe the rantings of young girls." The governor drank from his mug.

Mason continued. "Once Betty died and Ann began her accusations, we had no choice. This was our evidence— and thus our duty— to stop this vexing scourge plaguing Hartford."

"But *you* could have quelled this panic. Instead, you gave full rein and believed a young, ranting maid and a delirious child who saw specters in her fevered state. I expected far better, Major Mason."

Mason stuffed more of the meat pie in his mouth. "Sacrifices must be made, Governor," he said between mouthfuls. "Instead of being grateful we purged this community of witches and those who consorted with Satan—you condemn *me*? Ha!"

"I asked for an explanation. That is all."

"And I gave my explanation. You are back in charge. Do what you deem fit, Governor. I wash my hands of this."

Governor Winthrop straightened his spine and prepared to take his leave. "I can't bring the dead back, but by my word, rest assured, any accused from hereon in will get a fair trial."

Major Mason's eyes darted back and forth, and he refused to look at the Governor. "Go speak to the jury," he said in a low voice. "Discuss this with our esteemed magistrates and ministers. Speak with Marshal Gilbert; they all worked to convict these dangerous misfits who brought death unto Hartford. I need no blame. I did nothing wrong. Leave be."

Governor Winthrop rose abruptly, stomped his boots, and went for his cloak and hat.

Jeremy Adams sensing something was amiss rushed to the Governor's side.

"Is all well, Governor?" he asked, concern on his face.

"Aye, put the pints on my tab."

"Have no worry." The tavernkeeper smiled. "'Tis on the house tonight, remember?"

"Much appreciated, Goodman Adams." He turned to Mason. "Major, I thank you for your time."

Mason nodded as muscles started twitching on one side of his jaw.

As Goodman Adams lumbered off, Governor Winthrop made a promise to himself; this would never happen again—if he could help it. He knew he was just one person; as governor he could never be on a jury, but he could be a magistrate. He vowed that he would make certain to study all the evidence against the accused. Ann Cole's testimony sounded like the rantings of a disturbed maid. Balderdash is what it is, he thought.

Mason wiped his mouth with a cloth, looked up, and narrowed his eyes at the governor. "Witchcraft is real, Governor. It always lurks close by...when and where you least expect it." The corners of his mouth lifted to a half grin.

"So you say," Winthrop said, leaving the deputy governor alone at the table.

·—·

Josiah and Marshal Gilbert watched Governor Winthrop storm out of the Adams Tavern in a huff. "He doth look angry. I can't blame him. Look at the travails he returned home to," Josiah said, as he and his brother ambled about Meetinghouse Square.

"Slow your pace," the marshal ordered. "My thigh wound aches today."

The marshal's limp was more noticeable, so Josiah walked with care. "What say you about the witch panic, Jonathan? Four people brought to the gallows? Did you believe the maid Ann Cole in her rantings?" He paused to let his brother catch his breath.

"Aye, so I did. 'Tis a good thing the likes of Katherine Palmer and James Wakeley escaped with their lives. Warned out of town, I hear." The marshal peered over at his brother. "Hmm...what concern is it to you, Josiah?"

Josiah looked his brother boldly in the eye. "Many were accused. Rebecca Greensmith even mentioned Katherine Harrison as one who attended the Merrymeets. She even accused her of a witch."

"Our cousin?" The marshal arched an eyebrow and glared at Josiah.

"Aye. 'Tis her I speak."

The marshal shook his head in disbelief. "Why would I accuse my own kin? Those others—the likes of the Greensmiths—she *admitted* to familiarity with Satan. He leaned on his cane. "Everyone knows by now I have a soft place in my heart for cousin Katherine. She's a clever one...hard working...and wealthy now— so they say." Marshal Gilbert grabbed a hold of Josiah's arm. "What do *you* have against Katherine anyway? Tell me."

Josiah felt as if he were on trial now. "Years ago, I received a letter from cousin Richard. Warning me about Katherine."

"Cousin Richard? Nonsense."

"People are talking in Wethersfield, Jonathan. About *her*. The rumors fly—but ne'er an action is taken against her. We have Rebecca Greensmith's words that Katherine did attend a merrymeet or two—"

"And those words you profess to believe are from a convicted witch—a lying woman—now a dead one. Forsooth, Josiah, our Katherine is different. She made foolish choices years ago, but she's a goodwife now, settled with a family."

The brothers continued their walk about the Square, Josiah taking great pains to change the subject.

CHAPTER 37

August 1666

Three quiet and prosperous years passed for the Harrisons. Now Katherine was worried again. After the spring rains a long drought had settled upon Wethersfield parching the land. Earlier in the day, she sent John down to the meadow to inspect their wheat and corn crops. She stood waiting by the front gate, shaking out clothes and linens, then folding them into a basket. They had no extra water for washing.

Rebecca now twelve, Mary nine, and Sarah seven, did all they could to help around the farm. Today Joseph had taken them down to the Beaver Brook, he carrying a yoke with pails on either end, while the girls lugged their own pails with ladles to fetch any water they could find. Sunflowers wilted on the farm, the pole beans drooped low on the vine with leaves as thin as parchment paper, and the stand of pines near the cottage began shedding dried yellow needles. Hoccanum had even lost his passion for the hunt, choosing instead to roll in the dust and shake himself off.

A dry hot, southerly breeze blew dust and dirt about the Lane. Several people on horseback passed the house kicking up more sand. A man shaking a cowbell pulled three cows up the lane; they looked skeletal, their ribs protruded, and their parched tongues hung from their mouths. This drought, Katherine thought, has taken a toll on everyone and everything.

At last she saw John trudging up the road, rucksack across his shoulder, swinging to and fro at a pace. Head down to the ground, he made his way up the hill. "How now, John?" she shouted, waving a cloth in the air. "What news?" She paused to gape at her husband. "Why, what's all this?"

John stood afore her, his hands and face blackened like charcoal. It took him some few moments to catch his breath. He reached a hand into his rucksack and pulled forth what looked like burnt nuts. "Look, Kat, look what is upon us."

"What is it?"

"'Tis the blight, that's what. We have blight on the corn and worse—the wheat crop has the *blast*. The drought has damaged most of our crops and killed our yearly earnings on our exports. I reckon we'll be lucky to get but a few bushels an acre this year." He leaned against the fence placing his hands to his face and hair.

"John, come to the back of the house and we'll wipe this off you," she said in a demanding tone.

"I won't use what little water we have for a-washing. We must save what we have," he said, shaking his head back and forth.

Vexed as she was that John had touched the blight and was covered in it, she was relieved to see Joseph and the girls coming down the lane with buckets of water.

"Why does Papa have black on his face? Papa needs a bath," Mary shouted. Like her mother, Mary tended to say whatever was on her mind.

"Nay, take the water to the barn. The animals need it more than I," John said. He turned to Katherine. "I have more concerns than blight on me. After I'm cleaned up, I will take myself to the harbor and see if a deal can be made to compensate our lost exports."

"We lost some of our crops last year to a similar blight," she said.

"Aye, and it took only a small share of our totals. Not much can be saved from this year's crop though." Before they went into the house Katherine grabbed his rucksack, walked to the road, and dumped what damaged grain was left.

After his wiping down John removed to the harbor to discuss the problem. Katherine was relieved he was acting himself again, realizing that the life of a farmer depended on the weather, timing, and a bit of luck. Together they would find a way to bring in the lost monies. "We will have to make do," she said to herself.

Meanwhile she asked the girls to feed the chickens and churn the butter, then told Joseph he could take the rest of the day for himself. She began supper preparations. And she had confidence that the Harrisons would figure something out. They always did.

·➤·

Upon returning home John announced that he had worked out a deal with the merchants at the harbor; together they would get through this drought. John told Katherine they would make do by selling other goods. "Don't forget our trade with the natives," he reminded her. "I have received many valuable strands of wampum for the tools and extra leather hides from my workshop."

The girls gathered round the table as the family readied for supper. After the prayer, Katherine served up fish stew and hot biscuits, one of John's favorite meals. She watched him as he took his first bite, then slumped in his chair.

"Kat, I'm too tired to eat. 'Twas a long, hard day."

"Go rest in the bedroom. Your supper can wait. I'll bring thee a warm platter later." John got up and shuffled toward their bedroom, his feet dragging as if he pulled heavy weights. Meanwhile, the girls and Kat ate in silence.

All was quiet as she put the girls to bed. Rebecca used the loft now for her own room, whilst the two youngest shared the back room. After the girls were asleep, and before she scraped the dishes, she stepped out for a snort from her snuff tin. The news of the day had brought on a fresh case of the nerves. The tobacco mix along with other fragrant herbs soothed her. She looked out at the farm, dark beneath a crescent moon that cast but faint light. An owl hooted from a nearby tree. Calmer now, she thought, we will survive this. Aye, the astrological transits in the almanac indicated some challenges ahead, including an eclipse of the moon, but that was a fortnight away.

"Kat, Kat," she heard John suddenly cry out. "Kat!" She tucked her snuff box in her pocket and ran into the house. Finding a tallow candle in a candlestick, she lit it to a dying ember and made her way to the bedroom. She bent over John's face that shone with sweat. She placed her hand to his forehead. "You're feverish, John. I will make thee a poultice— and a strong drink as well."

"Water, Kat. Water!" His lips did look dry and parched. She rushed to the kitchen and ladled him a mug from their reserve. After helping him drink the cool liquid, she returned back to the kitchen, took out her mortar and pestle, and began grinding up feverfew, valerian, and mullein; this would serve to bring the fever out and to heal his clogged nasal passages from breathing in the blight.

When she brought the hot drink and poultice to him, John was sitting up in bed.

"Here. Drink this. It will bring the fever out and the color back to your cheeks." John drank the hot liquid, murmuring how he did not need it, that he was already feeling better.

"Lie back. Let me apply this poultice to your chest and throat." John lay down as Katherine carefully placed it on him. "Breathe in," she said. He attempted to take in a deep breath but began to shudder and cough. "We are purging your lungs from the blast," she said.

John groaned. "Kat, these are my crops. I'm heartsick. They are like my children. We depend on them,"

"Now you can depend on me. Keep the poultice on. The herbs will help you sleep through the night. And you will sleep alone. I'll bed down with Becca."

"Kat." John's glazed eyes met hers. "I know not how I survived all those years alone without thee. God has been good in His Grace and Mercy to us Harrisons."

"Aye, so He has."

"Before you go…" John whispered, "…sing to me the way you did on our wedding night. Sing me *The Ballad of Maid Marian.*"

She smiled. "I will sing thee the ballad my only and true Robin Hood." And by the time Kat had finished with the song, John was deep in sleep.

·•·

The next morning John's fever still lay upon him. His face was as pale as the inside of an onion, with red patches on his cheeks. Rebecca delivered him a fresh poultice for his chest, while Sarah and Mary brought him watered-down cider and good cheer. All three Harrison girls were learning from their mother the healing skills that would serve them well in the future. "Rebecca, please milk and feed the cows, then tend to the horses," Katherine said. "Sarah, Mary, feed the chickens and clean the coop."

She heard John calling her name. She rushed to the room and saw him sitting up in bed. He had removed the poultice. "What's for breakfast?" he asked. "I'm hungry." Kat nodded in relief. For John to feel like eating 'twas always a good sign.

"I'll scramble you up some eggs. The food will settle well with thee today." As she quickly cooked the eggs, she could hear John's chest rattling and wheezing; he was working hard at clearing his throat. After the meal she would make a fresh comfrey salve to put on it.

She brought the egg scramble and fed John a few bites. She thought his eyes seemed clearer, brighter than the dull glaze of yesterday. He raised a hand indicating he was done. "That's enough—for now," he said, moaning as he lay back on the bed of down feathers. Katherine promptly took the dish and placed it on the table. "You'll finish this later, John. Rest now."

The morning sun burst forth like a trumpet blaring through the small window.

"Rain, Kat. Rain." He stared hard to the ceiling. "I can feel it… smell it… and can almost to see it. Drink and taste it as well. Can you…feel it?"

"Certainly not, John," said Katherine, bewildered by such words. "We are in a drought. The fever's making thee full of fanciful notions. But mayhap your vision is a prophesy." She shrugged her shoulders feeling tired of a sudden.

"'Tis what we need." John closed his eyes, staying silent, arms stiff at his sides.

"The rain will come," she told him. "We must have faith." Her husband needed soothing, not scolding.

He opened his eyes again and turned to her. "I must go to the harbor soon…to work all this out," he said. "Remember?"

"Work what out? You worked it out yesterday. Nay, you will not go to the harbor, not today nor on the morrow. Here you shall remain. Until you are well enough to go."

John shook his head. "But…I must go."

"Enough of your rantings. I'm here nursing you." She wiped his forehead with a fresh cloth and pushed back his hair, trying to calm his agitation.

"On the morrow then." John coughed and rolled over in bed, turning his head away from her.

•-•-•

A few hours later, she fed the girls their midday meal, and brought John a mild cinnamon porridge. He seemed asleep, so she set the bowl on the bedside table and gently nudged his shoulder. "John, John, wake up for your meal." She pushed his shoulders back against the bed. His face looked pale and grey with more veiny patches running through it.

"I've made some porridge," she told him. "Here." She cradled his head and spooned a bite into his mouth. She held him like she had held so many soldiers in the battlefield tents.

He shook his head. "Nay, Kat. I need no food now. I'm leaving… leaving for the harbor."

"Leaving?"

"Aye, leaving." There was a long silence. Too long.

She knew what she had to do. Katherine left the room and shouted for Rebecca. "Becca, run to the Gilbert Homestead. Tell the Marshal, Josiah, whoever is home, to get a doctor. Quick now. Your Papa's ailing."

In a flurry the young girl flew down the road seeking help. Katherine ran back to the bedroom to let John know someone would be here soon to help. But once she saw him, she knew it was too late. She checked his pulse, listened for a breath, and pressed her hands to his chest trying to revive him.

But John was gone.

She closed his eyelids, never to see those merry blue eyes again.

"No John—No! God… No!" Her words echoed as if in a hollow chamber. She fell to her knees wailing, and crumpled to the floor, tears flowing down her face. She pounded the floorboards with her fists. Then she screamed; a scream so loud she was certain God Himself had heard it.

CHAPTER 38

Her husband was dead. John, her beloved helpmeet and father of her three children was gone. She had tried to save him. Done what she had deemed right. Yet for all her knowledge, the poultices, salves, and drink worked not.

When Governor Winthrop arrived and officially pronounced John dead, he told her there was naught she could have done; the blight had infected his body and his heart had weakened. But inside herself, Katherine railed against God, twisting her hands together as if she would tear herself—or anyone— to pieces.

Marshal Gilbert and his wife Elizabeth were the first to pay their respects. "'There wasn't a better man round these parts. One of Wethersfield's finest," the marshal said, after expressing his condolences and wiping a stray tear from his eye.

"Please sit." Katherine invited the couple. The girls watched nearby on the settle swinging their legs back and forth, leaning on each other softly crying. "Girls, please go outside for a time." She knew she needed to talk with them, answer their questions, and to be strong for them. Now was not the time. "Let me get you both a mug of ale," she offered her guests. They nodded, and she retrieved the drinks.

"What can we do for thee, Cousin?" Elizabeth asked. "In your distress—and shock—while you mourn?"

Katherine noticed Elizabeth wore a black cap today. "I would be obliged if I could borrow your black cap, seeing I am now a widow."

Elizabeth looked bewildered by Katherine's request. She turned her long nose up and touched the black cap. "Why, of course," she said, removing the cap from her head. "You may wear it for a fortnight. Seeing this *is* my favorite cap, I am certain you will find another—or make thee one yourself." She begrudgingly handed it to her.

Katherine removed her white cap, dropped it into her knitting basket, and placed the black cap atop her head. "Aye, 'tis suitable in my grief."

"It suits you," the Marshal agreed. His voice grew somber. "The authorities will come for the body soon. There's been mention John will be buried in the town's cemetery near the Meetinghouse. After all, he *was* a member of the church." He arched an eyebrow and stared at her. "But you are *not* a church member, Katherine. Perhaps this will change soon."

Katherine shook her head. "Nay, upon my word, John will be buried right here on the land he so loved. Right here on the farm. This way his spirit will ne'er be far from me." A deep cry came forth from her chest. "Please, Jonathan, make it so." She sobbed, tears flowing from her eyes, her body numb to her surroundings.

The marshal pulled at a greying curl near his shoulder. "I will do what I can. And let us not forget John's will. I have taken it upon myself to ask both Governor Winthrop and Magistrate Wyllys to be present next week for the reading."

"Aye. And I want John buried on the knoll at the field's end near the stand of pines next to the cottage."

"I will see to it," he said. "Mayhap the authorities will oblige— for a price."

"Price? I will have our workman Joseph dig the grave for a proper burial. Perhaps an offering to the church will do?"

"Aye, Cousin. You understand."

"And after the mourning period is over, Widow Harrison, what will thee do?" Elizabeth asked.

"What will I do? I will carry on with the farm. This is what John would want. I will have the help I need, for I believe God wills it."

After finishing their drink, the marshal and his wife stood to leave. "We are sorry for your sudden loss," said the Marshal. "I will be back later today. Find the will, Katherine. It's important to present it to the authorities."

"And I will be back in a fortnight," the marshal's wife said. "For my black cap."

·—·

Throughout the day a steady line of townspeople paid their final respects to John. Truly, he was beloved by many. Neighbors Joan and Robert Francis, the Griswolds, the Wellses all stopped by, leaving gifts of butter, milk, puddings, yarn, and cloth, even an extra pail of water! How gracious they were to the memory of her husband.

When Joseph appeared at the door she burst forth into a fresh soaking of tears.

"We heard the news. Harrison man no more. Tribe sad. Good trader and great man. We are sorry...and sad." He pulled forth from his satchel three thick strands of wampum beads. "This is a gift from Tribal Elder. We honor Harrison. Wampum…one for each daughter."

She embraced him. "I thank thee, Joseph. And I have a request," she said. "Would you dig John's grave, his final resting place out back? I know the ground is hard and dry, but we must find a way."

Joseph's dark eyes widened. "I am honored," he said.

"Begin at once. There's no time to waste." She knew she had to keep charge of everything and keep a calm head.

Joseph grabbed her hands and bowed to her. "We send up prayers…for his spirit."

She smiled warmly and opened the door to where John lay. "First, go inside Joseph. To the man who loved thee dearly."

••••

When the mourners left, Katherine finally had time to retrieve John's will. She knew he kept it hidden under the bed in a thick wooden chest. Scurrying about, she found the peg in a back corner where clusters of keys hung like grapes. She espied the small iron key she needed.

After dragging the chest from under the bed, she unlocked it, and the box creaked open. Inside the box, along with strings of wampum, coins, notes, ledgers, receipts, and paper bills, a small scroll lay tightly wound with hemp and a red wax seal stuck on the side. Next to the seal, it was written: '*Last Will and Testament of John Harrison*'

She pulled the scroll out, then closed the chest, locking it up. She stood afore her dead husband now, readying to cover him with a white cloth. "You need not worry, John." Her voice trembled, her chest wracked with sobs, she leaned toward his body and kissed him on the forehead. "And we need not worry. I know you have left us well enough." Katherine placed the scroll in her apron pocket, and secured her husband's body in the white cloth.

·•·

Later that afternoon, Governor Winthrop, Marshal Gilbert, Josiah, and others arrived for the burial. Marshal Gilbert announced her request was granted; John could be buried on the land he so loved. Earlier the marshal had arranged for a simple pine coffin to be delivered to the farm. Meanwhile Joseph continued digging the grave for John out back.

The Reverend Haynes, the interim minister of Wethersfield, arrived with his Bible in hand. The gathering, thankfully, was small. Katherine told Joseph she would like him present as well. After all, he was a part of the family, now even more so. The town's official drummer, Sergeant Hugh Wells, father to Samuel from across the lane, solemnly beat a steady mournful tattoo, as John's body was carried forth to his burial spot.

After the prayer, the coffin was lowered into the wide pit. Katherine and the girls wept openly while people threw dirt on the coffin. Some left wilted sunflowers and drooping wildflowers. Joseph stood strong beside her. Even the marshal had tears in his eyes, letting forth an occasional cough and clearing his throat.

Josiah shifted uncomfortably, and his eyes darted back and forth. Even the cows bawled as if they knew something was wrong; the farm's rooster crowed mournfully this late afternoon.

After the brief ceremony was complete, Katherine suggested the crowd remove to the house. "I need more time with John. There's food set on the table. And Marshal, please take the girls inside with you."

As the group made their way to the house, Joseph stayed behind, sprinkling herbs atop the mound. He took forth a rattle and began to solemnly wail. Katherine watched him do a mournful dance, eyes closed, crying out and singing in Algonquin. He is communicating with the Great Manitou, she thought.

Then a brisk wind blew in from the east almost knocking them to the ground. Joseph opened his eyes and looked up. Katherine did the same. They both watched as dark clouds thickly formed over light thunderheads that rolled like white wheels. The sky began to rumble. "This is Harrison's spirit. He speaks to you…to us." Joseph raised his hands to the blackening sky. "Listen."

It started with a slight drop. Then a single plunk. And then another. Now it was raining, and she could hear the low roar of thunder.

"Joseph, this is what he wanted. Rain. But how?"

"Not how," said Joseph. "It just is. Harrison wanted rain and he got his wish. Good for all now."

"Thank you, Joseph," she said. Both of them, now wet from the rain embraced; then Katherine handed him several coins from her pocket. He shook his head, but took the money.

"No thanks to Joseph. It's Harrison. Wangunk's God listened… and heard his cry."

•—•—•

A week later Governor Winthrop, Marshal Gilbert, Josiah, and Magistrate Wyllys arrived at the house in anticipation of the reading of John's will.

"Let us gather round the table. We have business to conduct," said the Marshal. "Do you have John's will, Katherine?"

"Aye, 'tis right here." She pulled forth the sealed scroll and handed it to Magistrate Wyllys.

He put on his spectacles, broke the seal, and read aloud:

"'*The Last Will and Testament of John Harrison, signed and dated August 1, 1666, a witness being Jonathan Gilbert and Josiah Gilbert signed the same day.*'"

Katherine interrupted the Magistrate. "August the 1st? That's but days ago. What prompted him to change his will? Why did he not tell me? She clenched her fists and glared at her cousins who looked sheepish. "And *you* were witnesses. What did you know?"

"John called upon us," said the Marshal. "Complained the drought was making his heart heavy. Claimed he was tired. We thought little upon this, for although he was tired, he looked hale and hearty enough."

"Please, the seal has been broken. Let us continue with the reading," said Magistrate Wyllys. He read on:

"'*I, John Harrison, leave the full estate of my holdings, including my farm, ten acres or more of land in the meadows, all farm animals, and equipment to my wife, Katherine. I have amassed a total for my wife Katherine, a sum in amount of £975, whereby my daughter Rebecca will receive £60, and my two youngest daughters, Mary and Sarah, will receive £40 each. Signed, John Harrison*'"

Not a word was heard from anyone in the room.

"But what about the girls?" she asked. "Why so little for them?"

"The law states only male children can inherit property," Magistrate Wyllys said.

Katherine stood in shock. Her husband had made known his final wishes.

She was now one of the richest persons in Wethersfield.

CHAPTER 39

September 1666

Three weeks after John's death, Goodwife Gilbert and her old friend, the scold Rebecca Smith, walked briskly up the Sandy Lane. They were heading to the Harrison Farm. Goodwife Gilbert wanted her black cap back. "She's been seen all over town with my cap," she said with a sniff. "And 'tis past a fortnight. The Widow Harrison promised. Forsooth, she can of a certain afford her own. She'll get no further charity from me."

"Indeed. The widow hath more wealth—and nerve—then any person I know," said Goodwife Smith.

They opened the gate and climbed the slight slope to the farmhouse. "She'd best be home," Goodwife Gilbert said. "There be little mercy I'll show her." She knocked impatiently to the door.

Katherine let them in. "How is the widow this morning?" Goody Gilbert eyed her black cap atop Katherine's head. "I see you still wear my cap."

"Aye," said Katherine. "And mayhap I would like to purchase it. This cap is now a part of my widow's dress. What say you?"

Goodwife Gilbert stirred with frustration. "Nay. I beseech thee, I desire *my* cap... *now!*"

Katherine reluctantly removed the cap and flung it toward the marshal's wife. She could not understand the woman's urgency for the cap, nor her unreasoning ways. "I would pay thee double to own this cap," she said, frowning at the two biddies.

"'Tis not for purchase. No thanks I have heard from thee. Why, I let you keep this *longer* than a fortnight." With those words said, Goodwife Gilbert removed her white cap, stuffed it into her bag, and placed the discarded black cap atop her head. Then she tucked her grey thinning hair inside the cap and patted it down.

"We shall take our leave now," she said with a cold flourish. "Come Rebecca. I got what I came for."

•◦•

On the walk back to the Gilbert Homestead, Elizabeth grimaced. "My head aches of a sudden," she said to her friend. "A heaviness afflicts my head to shoulders. Could it be, I wonder—this cap?"

"You mean the cap is making your head and shoulders to ache? Mayhap the widow bewitched it, considering the angry look she cast at thee? Mayhap she placed a spell on it?"

"All I know is mine head hurts; such a heaviness I ne'er have felt."

"Will you tell Jonathan of this?"

Elizabeth shook her head. "Nay, not with the Widow Harrison naming my husband in charge of her estate—should anything happen to her. Jonathan thinks highly of Katherine. Forsooth, with the money she has, imagine begging for my beloved cap. The gall! And now my head feels heavy with such pain. A stranger feeling... I ne'er have felt."

"Best to take that cap off for now," said Rebecca. "Wash it well and try it on again on the morrow."

•◦•

A few hours later looking around the yard, Katherine shouted out for her eldest daughter. Rebecca came forth from the barn, broom in hand with Hoccanum prancing at her heels.

"Run up to the Francis house," Katherine said. "See if Goody Francis has some extra emptyings—the pig trough needs filling." The twelve-year-old found a pail and ran up the lane toward the Francis home.

Goodwife Francis heard the knock at the door. She had just checked her beer cask; all seemed to be settling well. She rushed to the door carrying her newborn swaddled in cloth.

"Why Rebecca," she said, startled to see the eldest Harrison daughter on her stoop, bucket in hand. "What can I do for thee, child? Come in."

"My mother requests some emptyings. Our pig trough runs low."

Joan Francis eyed the young girl, so much like her father in looks and manners. Rebecca was always polite. It was just that Joan had never liked her mother. She and her husband had respected John—and kept quiet about how they *really* felt about his wife while he was alive— as proper neighbors do.

"Wait here. I am busy out back." She rushed through the kitchen to check out back for emptyings. She saw they had but few; just enough for their own pigs. She checked the beer cask; it continued to settle well.

She returned to Rebecca. "We have no emptyings to give thee." Then a great sound like a musket shot rang forth, and the baby began to shriek. Goodwife Francis ran back to the kitchen leaving Rebecca standing with the empty pail. "My beer is ruined," she shouted. "Bless me, the bunghole was loose and now my hops are leaking out. It's ruined. Gone!"

When Goodwife Francis returned to the front hall, Rebecca had taken her leave.

···

Later that afternoon Katherine was out back tending John's grave. With the recent rains, she had managed to find a few fresh sunflower heads to place atop the mound. The girls had written letters to their beloved Papa, and sang him his favorite songs. Each day she would find time to spend with John.

"There you be."

She heard a sharp voice. It was Goodwife Francis, looking as if wasps had stung her cheeks. "Widow Harrison, I will have you know," she said in a huff, "after I told Rebecca we had no emptyings, the bunghole on my beer cask went a-flying. Flew right across the room. All my precious hops sputtered and spread atop my kitchen floor. Methinks you caused this." She placed her hands on her hips, squinting her eyes. "What say you? Mayhap you owe me a barrel of beer."

"I owe you naught," Katherine said, annoyed this woman could think such thoughts. "We merely asked for emptyings. I did naught to your beer, and 'tis not my fault your cask's bunghole flew off and emptied out your hops."

Goodwife Francis shook her head and wagged a finger to Katherine's face. "I suppose you did naught to my ailing child years ago—aye, when John was alive. I never told thee, as I respected your husband. Now that he is gone—"

"I know not what you speak." Katherine frowned as she rearranged the flowers atop John's resting mound.

"Now that *he* is gone, I will tell thee. You'd best listen to me. It was November two years ago when my little James was ailing. God rest the boy's soul. And while my child was stricken and lay ill, I saw *your* shape appear in my house. Aye, I saw you hover near my sick child."

Katherine stood and shook dirt off her skirt and hands. "So you claim you saw a specter of me?" She laughed aloud. "Ha! This is nothing but drivel—hogwash in fact— all fanciful notions."

"'Tis nothing to scoff at, Widow. After I saw your spirit, my child took to fits and died weeks later. I tried to save little James from your wicked spirit, but there you were, standing by the fire staring at *my* child. Nay, more like glaring. And you stared *deeply* at my sleeping husband as well."

Katherine was beginning to feel a pain in her chest; she was angered to listen to such blather. "I did naught, Goodwife. 'Tis all your imaginings."

"Even my husband heard me shout out, 'The Lord Bless me and my child, for there is Goodwife Harrison afore us.' We will ne'er forget it."

"Did your husband see me as well?"

"Your shadow perhaps…I know not," Goodwife Francis said. "But I saw thee myself, standing near the hearth, watching my baby boy. Was thou filled with envy I had a boy child, while you did not?" She sniffed, grasped her neck, and a sob came forth from her throat. "Seeing your poor husband is deceased now—dead of a sudden—and how he *really* died we all but wonder—I can speak the truth to you. Katherine, you came into my house that night and took my child's breath from him. And now you have ruined my beer. Is this not enough?" She wrung her hands in despair.

Katherine had heard enough. "I will listen to no more of these lies. Begone—before I truly do place a spell on thee."

With that said, Goodwife Francis took her leave, running up the lane in a fury.

CHAPTER 40

July 1668

Almost two years had passed since John's death. Katherine, who never remarried, preferred her life as such. People talked, aghast a widow could manage a farm and acres of meadowland without a husband. Yet as much as townspeople gossiped, the farm thrived; between Joseph, the girls, and Thomas and Lydia Gilbert's sons come down from Windsor, she had plenty of help— and needed naught else.

Today Katherine planned to load some wares in her wagon for market: flowers, imported pewterware, cornmeal, linens, and early vegetables. But before she set off for market, she needed to stop at the shop of the joiner, Goodman Nott, down at the corner of Sandy Lane and High Street. He had built a special chair in John's honor, with Katherine and John's initials entwined in the center, and a sunflower carved around the letters. In turn, she had wrapped up some pewter candlesticks, linens, and some of her knitted goods in exchange for the chair.

She decided to walk to the shop tugging a small handheld wagon, a perfect size for the chair. Once she made the exchange, she would bring the chair home and find a perfect place for it in the Great Room.

Goodman Nott's store was crowded today; a line of at least three people stood out the door. She found her proper place behind them and waited. As she stood admiring some of Goodman Nott's furniture in front of the store, she heard a voice from behind her.

"A good morrow, Widow Harrison."

She turned about to see Ann Griswold sneering at her. Katherine never much fancied the woman. Ann reminded her of the dolls displayed in the shops of London, dressed as Puritans with their perfectly small perfect faces, fixed cold eyes, and pursed little red mouths. Katherine remembered what Ann had said to her after she married John, casting slights about her past. Goodwife Griswold had too much to say that was not her business. She was nothing but a highbrow busybody and a gossip.

"And a good morrow to you, Goodwife Griswold. 'Tis a fine July morning. It will be a bountiful harvest come autumn, mark my words," Katherine said.

Ann nodded. "Aye. What brings thee to Goodman Notts's shop today?"

"Goodman Notts has fashioned me a special chair. He carved both John and my initials in the wood. It will prove attractive in our expanded Great Room."

"I see," Ann said.

Katherine turned back in line, anxious to purchase the chair. Then she felt two slight pokes to her shoulder, so she turned around again.

"Yes?"

Ann fixed her with a pointed look. "Do you not think it is time to marry again? Are not thee lonely? John's been gone two years now. You have children. A chair for remembrance is fine, but methinks you need a husband—one that's alive." Ann's small brown eyes and long eyelashes blinked with little expression.

Katherine bristled at such talk. "What business is that of yours, Ann Griswold? What I do with my life is *my* business."

The crowd of a sudden got quiet. Katherine knew she must not raise her voice.

"Aye, but *we* in town know all about *your* business. We have *all* heard about your business— following the soldiers about in that war. I reckon 'tis true." A small smirk rose from her mouth and she tossed her head.

"True? I know not what you speak."

"Aye, but you do." Ann lowered her voice. "It was *your* business to service these men—and not just with your plasters— either." Ann grinned an even-toothed smile, turned her nose up, and smoothed down her cap.

Katherine turned away. She heard tittering noises coming from behind. People were laughing, taking notice, and trying to listen to what they were saying. She did not care. She would stand her ground and defend her reputation.

She felt Ann's breath on her back. "Townspeople claim you are a cunning woman. I say you were—and perhaps still are—a woman of ill repute." Ann leaned even closer and whispered in her ear, "You were naught but a common servant...and before that... a common whore."

Katherine spun about, stomped her foot, and brandished a closed fist to Ann's glazed little face. "And you, Ann Griswold, are a malicious gossip and scold. You yourself are a savage whore!"

What had she just said aloud? Her heart was beating, her skin soaked in sweat, but she did not care. It was too late to care, for the words had flown right from her mouth, flown out like a flock of ill-timed blackbirds to a cornfield.

Michael Griswold, Ann's husband, was tying his horse and wagon to a post when he heard the commotion, and heard the Widow

Harrison insult his wife. He rushed to his wife's side. "How dare you speak to my wife in such a manner? How dare you slander her good name?"

Katherine shook her head. "Nay! She defiles *my* name."

Michael stayed firm as Ann began to shake and sob, wailing, then wiping her eyes.

"I heard what you called my Ann. Aye, 'tis true, Widow Harrison, we *know* your type. We know you have been in league with Satan for many years—well before you landed on our pious shores. Your soul was damned long ago." He sneered at Katherine, his eyes narrowed in spite.

"And you, Michael Griswold, would hang me if thou could—though you have damned a thousand souls before. Why, I know you damned my friends Kate Palmer and James Wakeley before they were warned out."

"Aye, 'tis correct, Widow Harrison. They may have escaped the noose, but they are damned in the sight of God." He paused. "As you yourself are damned."

Never in the last two years had Katherine wished more fervently that John was by her side. This ne'er would have happened if John was alive, she thought. She was alone— so she would tell Goodman Griswold what she really thought. "Your soul was damned long ago, Michael Griswold," she shouted, filled with an angry passion. "Worry about your own soul, and leave mine well enough alone!"

She knew right then she had to step out of line and go home before any more curses flew from her mouth. The chair would wait. She'd retrieve it later when she came to her senses.

Josiah wondered what the uproar was that he heard on the High St., and stepped out the front door. He watched cousin Katherine scurry up the Sandy Lane, towing her wagon, face as red as a radish. He saw Michael Griswold speaking to the gathering crowd. He had never seen Goodman Griswold, an upstanding member of the community, so angry.

"What has happened?" Josiah asked.

He noticed Ann Griswold sobbing like a young child gaining sympathy.

Michael turned to him. "If you must know, your cousin Katherine cursed my wife in a fit of passion. Slandered her good name." He removed his hat to wipe his brow. "The Widow Harrison vexes my dear wife. This is cause for alarm. For your cousin is a dangerous woman—a cunning woman—so they say. I say 'tis even worse— she is one in covenant with Satan."

Josiah hung his head in shame. "I doubt she really *is* my cousin," was all he said.

CHAPTER 41

Fall 1668

The week after the spectacle at the joinery, the marshal paid a visit to the Harrison Farm with troubling news. "Seems the Griswolds have taken to heart what thou said to them," he reported. "I'm giving you a warning, Katherine. The Griswolds have entered a suit against you in court on account of slander."

"Slander? Goodwife Griswold started it. I merely finished it," Katherine said, her hands twisting in a hard fury.

"Did anyone else hear Goody Griswold slander thee?"

Katherine shook her head. "Nay, she whispered it to me. It vexed me so...I lost my temper."

"Expect a summons to appear in court next week. You will be held accountable, and there will be a trial."

After two days in court, the jury found Katherine guilty of both slander and uncontrolled fits of passion. They claimed she disturbed the peace. What angered Katherine were the fines that added up to £40. The normal fine for slander was £15. Just because she had money now was no reason to increase the fines. All over a few scant words she had uttered in haste.

Her mind buzzed like a swarm of angry wasps. She would defend herself. Katherine decided she would appeal the ruling and thus began a long, detailed letter to the Court of Assistance, asking them to review her complaint of slander against Ann Griswold, and that she receive the money due *her.*

After she finished the letter, she spent but a few minutes darning socks and sewing some stitches onto a small quilt for Sarah's bed. Then she heard a low bawling outside the farmhouse door.

Her second daughter Mary, now twelve, ran inside. "Ma!"

"I am here. What is that noise?"

"You need come outside. Quick! Holly is hurt!" Over the months Mary had learned to care for the livestock and worked hard on the farm, feeding the chickens, the pigs, and getting the cows home from pasture. It helped ease the pain of her father's death; she even knew all the animals by name.

Sure enough, Holly, their milking cow stood afore the front door groaning in pain. Katherine gasped at the sight of her prized cow, her udder slashed and bleeding.

"I found her crying on the road trying to find her way home. Someone hurt her in the meadow, I think." Mary turned a bright pink and began to cry tears for the poor bovine.

Katherine stepped off the stoop to see if Holly bore any other injuries. There were none. "You have done well, Mary. Lead her to the barn, and I will prepare a salve and plaster for the udder." She watched her daughter heave out a breath and wipe her eyes. "And don't fret, Mary. Methinks Holly will survive."

But Katherine *was* worried. This was not the first attack on the Harrison farm of late. Other animals were not as lucky as Holly. Since John's death, many injuries had occurred, and Katherine's rage boiled up inside her. She knew not who executed these cowardly deeds; she could only guess. Her neighbors with envy in their hearts, that was who.

Embittered over her losses and feeling angered that no one seemed to listen—or care— she decided she would write another petition to the court. Although she may have lost money in the Griswold case, when the court read of the damage done to her livestock, they would surely provide redress.

She found her inkwell, quill, and a piece of parchment, and wrote out the damages:

- *After my husband John's death, our yoke of oxen at our stile suffered blows on the back and sides.*
- *The summer last, thirty poles of hops were cut and spoiled.*
- *Last year my three-year-old heifer in the meadow was stuck with a knife.*
- *One of my prized cows was spoiled, two ribs and back broken. Had to be put down.*
- *Milking cow's udder, slashed.*

There were many more such incidents; Marshal Jonathan and Josiah knew of these offenses. Time and again she had complained to no avail. Time and again the townspeople and authorities turned away. She demanded the authorities recognize the damage done *to* her, not *by* her.

And to the damage done to her daughters. Not only had they lost their beloved father, they now feared for their lives— and the lives of their mother and farm animals. Katherine vowed that justice would win.

•—•—•

Michael Griswold spent the morning collecting written statements from witnesses testifying against the Widow Harrison. These signed statements would be used as depositions against Katherine if she went to trial. It would not be long before he would deliver them to the Magistrate of Hartford, Samuel Wyllys. Let him read the accusations, he thought.

Michael knew that Governor Winthrop, even Major Mason, would hear of this.

Today he had two stops left. Michael walked down the Watering Lane, passed his own farm, and turned left onto the Rose Lane where his neighbor, Captain Samuel Hale resided. He was certain Captain Hale could provide some evidence against Katherine.

Michael tucked the sheaves of parchment inside his heavy coat. He could ill afford a gust of wind sweeping away his hard-earned efforts. He knocked briskly and waited at the Hale door.

Mary, Captain Hale's daughter, answered. "Why Goodman Griswold. What brings thee about this morrow?" Seeing the distressed expression on his face she quickly let him in.

"I seek your father. Is he in?"

"Nay, he's collecting goods down at the harbor. Mayhap I can give him a message?"

Michael nodded, thinking to himself what a sweet, comely maid Mary was, and how she would make a man the perfect goodwife soon. Just like his Ann.

"I am presently about collecting evidence against the Widow Harrison, due to her troubling behavior. Have you heard anything from your father—? Any evidence would be helpful. Has he seen or heard anything you know of?"

Mary's clear blue eyes rounded and her rosy mouth opened wide. "Goodman Griswold, please do come into the Great Room. Let me take your hat and cloak. *I* do have something to share with thee."

She led him through the short hallway to the great room on the left where he took a chair. Mary gathered herself up, found a stool, and drew close to the man. "I must say, Goodman Griswold, I know *not* what my father hath seen; I only know what *I* have seen—of late."

"Seen of late?"

"Aye. I have mine own story of Katherine. So afeared was I—I ne'er have experienced such fright in all my twenty years. I was scared unto my wits, I was."

"Would you be willing to tell me? And mayhap write it down? Even testify, if the widow goes to trial?"

"Aye, I would. After how she slandered your innocent wife and cursed you, why of course I shall testify... *my* story pains me so." She clasped her hands together as if in prayer, and gazed down with a pained melancholy look. "I shall share what I recall," Mary said.

"Just enough to let me know if your testimony holds merit."

The young woman tearfully told Michael that just a week past she'd been lying in her bed waiting for sleep to come upon her. Then she heard a great noise. "Aye, something heavy fell upon my legs and my stomach, pressing the life from me. Then an ugly-shaped, dog-like thing appeared...with the head of Widow Harrison. I *knew* it was her. She asked me if I was afeared. 'Nay' was my answer. She told me—"

"Stop right there, Mary. You say the widow appeared afore you in the night wishing to harm you and then asked if you were afeared?"

"Aye, it certainly *was* her."

"Do your parents know of this appearance?"

"So they do."

"Then there's no time to waste," said Michael. "For the sake of justice and peace in our community, write it down. For Widow Harrison moves like a fog snaking up the river soaking and clouding this town with her poisons."

Mary feeling important of a sudden, ran to fetch a quill, inkpot, and parchment paper.

Upon Mary's return Michael stood to take his leave. "I have but one stop left," he said. "And I will be back shortly for your testimony. Your parents raised you righteously, Mary."

With these words, Goodman Griswold left the house and quickly made his way to the Gilbert Homestead.

Josiah opened the door. "Michael, what brings thee here?"

Goodman Griswold nodded gravely and asked if he could come in, saying he needed to speak with him in private. It was urgent. "I am collecting testimony regarding your so-called cousin, Katherine. Would you have any evidence against her, you knowing her background? This would give the court more weight, to have someone like you, a relative, testify against her. What say you?"

"I know not what to think—or do," Josiah said, running his hands through his long greying hair. "She has recently suffered losses to her property; her livestock have been maimed; I saw it with mine own eyes." He stared down at the smoothed planks with light sawdust on them and shook his head.

"The widow suffering losses is most likely deserved," Michael said. "'Tis not my business. My business, Josiah, is to see that justice and truth prevail, not just for my wife, but for the good of the community."

"I heard the widow paid a hefty price to settle your slander claim."

"'Tis true, but it makes no recompense for all the troubles she has caused."

Josiah shook his head. "I know not," he repeated. "I need to think upon these things."

"I will return on the morrow for your answer," said Michael, and took his leave.

•—•—•

After Goodman Griswold departed, Josiah marched straight up the Sandy Lane heading to the Harrison Farm. He had heard enough accusations, enough gossip from the neighbors. Would Katherine listen to his advice? He never liked her, but like many others, he had respected John and thought highly of their three daughters. He even recalled the day Katherine helped with baby Ben and his injured arm so many years ago.

He found Katherine in the barn sweeping the floor. "Katherine, I need speaking with you."

She turned about and faced him. "You see I am busy, Cousin. What need you? Another plaster?"

He stared in shock to see how gaunt she had become; new lines etched around her pale weary face, long strands of grey hanging from her cap.

"Take heed, Katherine. I am here to warn you. You need to get out of this town before they swing you on Gallows' Hill. Like they did to Lydia. Leave, I say. Go find Katherine Palmer and the others who escaped."

Katherine leaned on her broom. "As if you cared for Lydia or Kate Palmer? Forsooth! And now you care for me? Bah! Leaving me at Captain Cullick's house years ago? That's where my problems started."

Josiah stood firm and wagged a finger at her. "Your problems started with you—and your bold tongue. All those years ago... bragging of your talents. No proper maid or goodwife boasts of fortunetelling,"

She gripped hard the handle of her broom and shook it at him. "*You* damned me, Josiah, you and your kind," she said, her voice rising with each word.

"*You* damned yourself." He lifted his hat. "You have been warned. Good day."

CHAPTER 42

May 1669

Throughout the previous fall witnesses were called separately and sworn under oath to sign and vow their testimony to be true. The court planned to use these depositions as evidence for a possible trial against Katherine. All had remained quiet during the early months of 1669, the next court session being in May.

And there was a calm throughout Wethersfield, an uncanny calm that lulled Katherine into the feeling all would be well. She still waited for the court to address her damages. Her daughters were now thriving at the new school in Wethersfield, attending a few scant hours each morning, so they could work the fields and help with chores in the afternoon.

Katherine knew what her neighbors thought. She had not forgotten Josiah's warning. But she would never leave the land she and John had toiled on and expanded; his burying place, now with a marker and stone gave her strength. How could she abandon the farm? Why should she marry when she loved no other?

She knew of the numerous accusations against her—all lies and drivel. What evidence could the town possibly have since she had done nothing wrong?

On the morning of May the 11th, 1669, Katherine was officially summoned to the Court of Assistants. Marshal Gilbert delivered the warrant and offered to accompany her to Hartford. The May session of the Court of Assistants, presided over by none other than Major John Mason, was held at the Hartford Meetinghouse, where the Major sat behind a large table afront the pulpit. He held a thick stack of papers in his hands, his specs hanging down his nose. He called Katherine to the front.

"We have gathered evidence against thee, Katherine Harrison. It took months to amass this testimony. We awaited the Hadley depositions for some time. Thankfully, you see here—" He held up his hand and shook the papers. "The Court of Assistants now has *enough* evidence."

"Enough evidence?" Katherine repeated. "Evidence of what?" She glared into the major's cold black eyes.

Major Mason grinned and stared right back. "Enough evidence to cause *more* than enough suspicion of witchcraft. For the time you will be committed to the Hartford jail— to await trial." Major Mason straightened up in his high-backed chair, his beady eyes studying her with smug satisfaction. Clearly, she thought, he had led the official charge against her.

She turned to see Marshal Gilbert slump in the pew behind her. "I must confer with my cousin," she said loudly, leaning over and gritting her teeth at the major.

The marshal limped forward, a look of helpless defeat on his face. She whispered into his ear, while Mason looked on. "Cousin Jonathan, I place you in charge of my estate for now. And for my daughters' care and well-being. I shall pay thee for your service. Watch over my farm. Give my workers the news. I shan't be away long."

"Aye, so I will," the marshal said softly. "They have nothing serious against you—"

As the marshal left out from the meetinghouse, two guards with pikes rapidly approached Katherine, tied a thick cord of hemp around her wrists, then knotted it. They dragged her off to the Hartford jail across from Meetinghouse Square.

A few spectators milled about awaiting the news. When they saw Katherine, they began to whisper, point their fingers at her, and laughed aloud. "From the richest woman in Wethersfield, to a poor prisoner," they jeered and pretended to weep for her.

⁃⁃⁃

After sitting a miserable fortnight in jail with two visits from the marshal bringing news of the farm, Katherine's jailor, Daniel Garrett made an announcement. He was a gruff character, tall like a giant, with pale skin, pale blue eyes, red hair. and a short-cropped grizzled beard; he towered over most others. And because he was impressed with the widow's wealth, he charged her estate his highest rate for keeping her a prisoner.

"You are being called into court today, Widow. Prepare yourself. You have received an official summons." The jailor opened the cell, removed the empty platter of food, and then tied the hard cords around her hands. She walked head down to the Meetinghouse with Jailor Garrett aside her.

Once again Major Mason sat at the grand table and presided over the Court, along with Magistrate Samuel Wyllys, Magistrate William Leete, and Governor Winthrop. Wyllys wore the formal wig of the magistrate, while Governor Winthrop donned his black velvet skullcap of one who holds authority. Secretary Allyn sat along the side of Mason readying to take notes.

Katherine glanced over to the governor, trying to read his face—
and mind. But the governor avoided her eyes and stared straight ahead.

Major Mason stood with paper in hand. "The prisoner, Katherine
Harrison, arise."

Katherine stood tall. There was no John by her side to lean on,
no cheer from her daughters, no singing ballads, no snuff to soothe
her nerves—it was just Katherine—alone.

"*Katherine Harrison of Wethersfield, thou standest here are indicted
as being guilty of witchcraft for thou, not having the fear of God before
thine eyes, hast had familiarity with Satan, the grand enemy of God and
mankind, and by his help hast acted things beyond the ordinary course
of nature, and further hast hurt the bodies of divers persons for which by
the law of God and this corporation, thou oughtest to die.*"

Major Mason raised his head and watched Katherine with narrowed
eyes. "How doth thou plead?"

"Not guilty."

Secretary Allyn dipped his quill to the inkpot scribbling down her
plea. "And I request a trial by jury, Governor Winthrop. And a lawyer."

"The Court will, to a reasonable degree, allow for a jury and
representation," replied the governor. "For now, you shall return and
remain in jail to await further news of your trial."

She had no recourse but to submit; she felt certain it wouldn't be
long before she was back to the Harrison Farm.

All she could do was wait.

CHAPTER 43

May 1669

A week later the trial of Katherine Harrison officially began. Held in Hartford's Meetinghouse, even in May a chill wafted from the high ceilings, descending and spinning a stiff breeze through the pews. The jury chosen by the magistrates was in place: six men of high status. Katherine was appointed a lawyer, Nathaniel Hopkins, who met with her in the jail to plan a defense. Marshal Gilbert brought Katherine the monies she owed Attorney Hopkins—and monies to pay for jailor Daniel Garrett's efforts to oversee her care—if one could call it such.

Wethersfield and Hartford townspeople entered the meetinghouse either as spectators or witnesses. The tithingman escorted them to their seats. She recognized the Wells family, the Griswolds, the Francis family; her neighbors were all lined up in pews, all lined up in rows against her.

Magistrate Wyllys banged his mallet and called for order.

"Oyez, oyez," shouted the tithingman. All was quiet as the first witness was called forth, one Mary Hale. Sworn in with her hand on the great Bible, she stepped up to the wooden box afore the jury. Katherine noticed how much Mary seemed to revel in the attention, face a-blush, smiling, nodding to her family—even waving.

Major Mason stood and addressed the young woman. "Mary Hale," he said, raising his voice. "We have before us your deposition of a disturbing nature. Please share with the jury what you wrote for the Court."

"Aye," Mary began. "It was late fall of 1668. I was lying in my bed, the hearth-fire alighting the room. Suddenly, I heard a loud noise, and a great heaviness dropped on my legs, then pressed my stomach down hard." Mary took a breath and grabbed her throat with both hands. "'Twas terrible. I almost—"

"Answer the question," said Major Mason.

"Then there appeared an ugly shape— like a dog. But when I saw the head arise, Lord save me, but I knew it was the head of Katherine Harrison!"

Gasps echoed throughout the Meetinghouse.

"And then what happened?"

"I saw it walk to my father's room...and then it returned."

"Is that all?"

The young woman shook her head and covered her face with her hands. "Nay. It returned seven nights later...to haunt me further." She began to breathe hard, tears appearing in her eyes.

"And it had the same face as the prisoner?" Mason asked, pointing directly at Katherine. "Is this correct?"

"'Twas the same face."

"What happened after this?"

Mary took forth a handkerchief and dabbed her eyes. "I recall it was a windy night. Aye, she flew in with the gale and whispered into my ear, 'I will not come again, but are you not afeared of me?' Being a good Christian I shouted, "'Nay, never will I be afeared of you.'"

"How did she respond?"

"Aye, she told me then that she would make me, 'very afeared before she had done with me.' I felt my chest go heavy, and called for my parents sleeping nearby."

"Did the Widow Harrison finally leave you be?"

Mary shook her head with vigor. "Nay, the voice told me, 'I have preserved my cart, but I will make it a death cart onto you.' The voice then told me that God had commissioned her to kill me. I told her the devil was a liar, and I would make known to sundry people what she said. I make this known now, as God be my final witness." Mary burst into a sob and rocked her body back and forth.

"So you say that Katherine Harrison came again— and told you she wanted you dead—by God's commission?"

"'Tis so."

"No further questions."

·—•—·

It was Attorney Hopkins's turn to question Mary Hale. He held her deposition in his hands. "Mary, you say during these nightly visits your father and mother were lying asleep nearby, and then you shouted aloud… but they heard you not?"

"The voice told me, 'Though you call, they shall not hear until I am gone.'"

"So… you shouted as if in a nightmare, and your parents were unable to hear you?"

"'Tis true. Just as Goodwife Harrison told me that dreadful night and it came to pass."

Attorney Hopkins slowly paced before the magistrates and nodded to the jury. "Why, Mary, is your story of the death cart and the specter of Katherine Harrison committing you to the gallows *not* in your original deposition?"

Mary started to fret, wiping her neck and fumbling with her cap. "I spoke of this in private to my sister and no other."

Hopkins approached Mary and drew within inches of her face. "Why *is* this?"

Mary held her head high. "Because it upset me so."

"Mary, since your parents heard you not and saw nothing, were there any other witnesses to your vexations regarding the curses you claim were from Katherine?"

"Nay," she said in a resigned voice.

"That is all."

·•·

The next witness sworn in was neighbor Joan Francis. She had been waiting for her chance to testify for months, nay years. She was still angered over the death of little James, and the spoiling of her beer.

"As it please the Court, state your name and affiliation," Magistrate Wyllys said.

"Goodwife Joan Francis, wife of Robert, and neighbor to Katherine Harrison."

"Proceed with your evidence, Goodwife Francis."

Joan took the seat and addressed the panel of magistrates and jury. "It began almost four years ago. One night, my young boy was stricken ill. I said, 'Lord Bless me and my child, here is Goody Harrison.' As God be my witness, she stood afore me. I took the babe and placed him between my husband and myself. Strangely after this he continued ill, and thus soon died." She glared at Katherine with the piercing eye of a blackbird.

"So, you think Goodwife Harrison killed your sick child? Why would you think this?" asked Magistrate Wyllys.

"She was envious of my precious boy. *My son.* I know how Katherine and John longed for a son. But *all* she has are daughters. 'Tis a pity, I know."

Katherine bristled in her seat. Over the years she had done many kind deeds for the Francis family including giving them healing poultices and salves. Now she was being accused of a child killer.

"Is there anything else?"

"Aye, so there is. It's the incident of *her* spoiling my beer—on account of her jealousies."

"Please explain the incident."

"One day a few years ago, she sent her daughter Rebecca for some emptyings; claimed the pigs needed them for their trough. Imagine a rich widow in need of emptyings! Forsooth!"

She flung her arms out in exasperation as if beseeching the crowd for support.

"Please continue and tell the Court what happened next."

"I told the child, 'Nay, we have no emptyings, so run home and tell your mother.' Then within seconds, the bung on my beer cask shot out and released my precious hops all over the floor." She pointed a long stiff finger at Katherine, the glint in her eye as sharp as ice, and announced, "And *she* caused it all, wicked woman that she is…witch!"

Katherine shuddered. Spectators began shouting and sending up loud huzzahs.

Attorney Hopkins jumped up in response. "No need to address the defendant as such. Remove this slanderous comment from the records," he said to Secretary Allyn.

"No further questions," said Magistrate Wyllys.

⋅⊷⋅

Attorney Hopkins began questioning Goodwife Francis. "Did your husband witness Katherine peering at the sick child?"

"Nay. But he heard me call, 'Lord bless me and my child, there is Goody Harrison.'"

"Had you called on Katherine for her healing remedies over the many years you have been neighbors?"

There was an awkward pause. "Perhaps," Joan said with a shrug. "Years ago."

"So she did not heal your child …and according to your statement…she caused the death of your child—all because Goodwife Harrison was envious you had a boy—and she did not?"

"'Tis correct. And I make claims for damages done… to my spoiled beer."

"Thank you, Goodwife Francis. No further questions."

Governor Winthrop announced the Court was adjourned until the following day.

CHAPTER 44

On the second day of testimony the Hadley and Northampton depositions taken in August 1668 were read in court. Secretary Allyn emphasized the words of Joseph Dickinson, that he had heard Katherine call out 'Hoccanum, Come Hoccanum' in the Great Meadow near the Dry Swamp and that her cows, with great violence, tails up straight to the air, rushed to the meadow gate.

Although Goodman Dickinson absented himself from the trial, being a distance to travel, John Graves *did* make the journey from Hadley, the Court having assured him it would cover his travel expenses.

Katherine sat in the front pew of the Meetinghouse, her attorney on one side and Marshal Gilbert on the other. She glanced at Governor Winthrop sitting stiff and expressionless. How could he approve of such a spectacle? Nothing but hogwash, she thought. Why, her cows made more sense than these people.

She grimaced thinking how much had changed since John's death. First a wife, then a widow, now a prisoner at their mercy. She had no choice but to endure this slander and blasphemy to her name and to the memory of John's good name.

John Graves was finally sworn in and questioned as to his oxen's strange behavior from seven years past, when he had paused near the Harrison farm before taking his cattle to pasture in the Great Meadow.

"Why would thou stop and graze your cattle near the Harrison property on your way to the meadow?" Governor Winthrop asked.

Goodman Graves seemed for some moments unable to speak. "In all honesty, Governor, I had heard years before that Goodman Harrison and his wife Katherine were both—witches."

Katherine had heard enough and rose from her seat. "How dare you bring my husband into this?" she shouted in a rage. "He's been dead and gone these many years."

Governor Winthrop glanced over at Katherine. "Please— sit. I will have order in this Court. Continue Goodman Graves."

"As I said before, I stopped to graze my cattle on the row of land by the Harrison's farm. Hearing of how they *might* be witches, I tested this rumor to my cattle and lo, they became spooked on the Harrison land." Goodman Graves had a bold smile on his face, as if he was proud of his actions. He paused to take a deep breath.

"Spooked?" the governor asked. "How so?"

"I tied my oxen to my cart rope, one to one end, the other to another end. As God be my witness, they were securely fastened. Further, I tied five or six quick knots at each end, even tying the yoke between the oxen." He spoke so fast the secretary requested he slow down.

"I see. Go on," Winthrop insisted. Katherine felt she now understood the governor's questioning: make the witness look foolish and get him to admit he trespassed his cattle on the Harrison property.

"I left them there. Then I walked a short distance, I did. When I turned around, I saw they grazed *not*! Nothing but empty bovine stares for me. Spooked they were! Then I saw the knots unloose—by themselves I shall add— like a preternatural force untied them." He wiped his brow and shook his head. "I will ne'er forget the sight, although it be years ago."

"Goodman Graves, what happened next after your oxen refused to graze—on the Harrison property?"

"The knots, they became unloosed," he repeated. He stood and pointed to Katherine. "You unloosed those knots. Witch!"

The crowd murmured aloud in agreement.

"Did you re-tie the knots?" Governor Winthrop asked.

"I tried, but could not. For my oxen became so afeared, they threw off their yoke, it rising some six feet high, and they refused to eat grass from the Harrisons' land."

"Thank you, that is all," the Governor said.

·•·

"Goodman Graves," Attorney Hopkins began. "Is it good and proper you should trespass and allow your cattle to graze on another's property? And further—to use this as a standard to test your suspicions of the Harrison's for witchcraft?"

Graves looked uneasy of a sudden, and began to fidget in his seat. "I thought it good and proper to discover if the rumors be true. Turned out I was right." He wore a smug look on his face and shrugged his shoulders.

"One more question, Goodman Graves. Was there any another witness who could testify to this odd, strange…what you call a preternatural event? Did anyone in the neighborhood witness this incident other than yourself?"

"Nay. It was just me and my oxen."

"That is all," Attorney Hopkins said, and walked over to speak with Secretary Allyn. "Make a note of this," he said. "There was no other witness."

·•·

Samuel Wells, son of Sergeant Hugh Wells, now a resident of Hadley, was the next witness called to testify against Katherine. "Samuel Wells, step forward," Magistrate Leete said, and Goodman Wells was sworn in and took the witness seat. "Please tell the court what happened that day seven years ago as written in your deposition."

Samuel noticed Katherine grimacing at him; her eyes chilled his soul; even her freckles still glowed like Satan's spots. But this time her stare would not get the better of him. He quickly turned away. "One day seven years ago, when I was living in Wethersfield on the Sandy Lane with my mother, helping her with chores, she sent me forth to fetch the cows from pasture. It was milking time. I ventured out, but lo, I beheld our cows making their way up the Sandy Lane. And lo, the Harrison's cows happened to be right behind them; all crowded together they were."

"And according to your deposition, you saw something strange. What did you see?"

"At first, I saw no one. Then from around one of *our* milking cows, I saw Goodwife Harrison arise with a small pail of milk in her hands."

"You saw her milking one of *your* cows?"

Samuel said, "Aye, and I saw her run off with the pail filled with milk."

"And did you call for her to stop? Did you shout out to her about the theft? Did you call the constable?"

"I did not, and could not."

"And why was that, Goodman Wells? You were young enough to chase down a thief. What stopped you?" the magistrate asked.

Samuel pointed to Katherine. "*She* stopped me!"

"Stopped you? How could she stop you?"

"It was an invisible force that stopped me. It was *her* presence that stopped me. *Her* force. It was her stare when she turned to look on me, a look that froze me in place—on the spot. Only the devil and this witch know what spell they placed on my body."

"So… you watched her run away with the pail of milk?"

"Aye, I could not move a muscle until Goody Harrison disappeared over her stile. She placed a hex on me—stuck to the earth I was."

"That is all," said Magistrate Leete.

Attorney Hopkins arose for his questioning. "I have but few queries for Goodman Graves. I will be quick." He sensed the crowd was getting weary. "Was Katherine bringing her own cattle home from pasture that day?"

"Indeed she was. Had her black cat with her as well. Her cows were behind our cows."

"So how did you know if it was *your* cow or *her* cow she milked?"

"Her face arose near our milking cow. I saw it with mine own eyes."

"Was there a witness who could testify to what you saw regarding the spell you allege Goodwife Harrison placed on you?"

"There be no other witnesses… save the cows."

"No more questions," Attorney Hopkins said.

Governor Winthrop announced court was adjourned until four in the afternoon.

·—•—·

The next witness called to the stand was old Rebecca Smith, friend of the marshal's wife. Katherine could not understand why she would testify against her.

Rebecca, now seventy-five, still had her wits about her, and welcomed the attention she was getting at the trial. Since her friend Elizabeth Gilbert would not testify against Katherine, she thought it proper to do so herself.

Using a cane, she hobbled to the stand and was sworn in. She nodded in every direction of the congregation, her blue eyes squinting as she took in the surroundings. Her bony bird-like hands trembled as she remained standing, leaning on her cane.

"Please tell the court how you know Katherine Harrison and explain your circumstances," Major Mason asked, then added, "We have your deposition, Goodwife Smith—if your memory needs reminding."

"Nay," said Rebecca, shaking her head. "'Tis all right here." She slowly tapped a finger to her forehead. "It happened when I went with Elizabeth Gilbert to retrieve her black cap. Weeks before, the widow asked her if she could borrow the black cap. Elizabeth's favorite black cap, I might add. Elizabeth agreed, but just for a fortnight. The black cap was ne'er a gift—it was but a lend."

"Did the Widow return the cap within a fortnight?"

"Nay, 'tis my point. We had to fetch the cap ourselves."

"What was Katherine's response to you wanting the cap back?"

Rebecca leaned hard on her cane, paused, and took a breath. "When Elizabeth asked for her cap back, the Widow told her, 'Nay, I will not give it back.' Then she had the vexing nerve to ask Elizabeth to sell it to her. Ha! Imagine such impudence!"

"Did Goodwife Gilbert sell the widow the cap?"

"Nay, of course *not*. She wanted her best cap back."

Katherine mumbled from her pew. She wanted to stand up and shout she was only trying to be fair to Elizabeth. After all, she had offered her a fair price for the cap.

Major Mason paced the floorboards. "Go on. What happened next?"

"Elizabeth demanded she return her cap immediately. I shook my cane at the widow and threatened I would use it to clip that cap from her head…if need be."

Katherine laughed aloud amid the rustlings of the court—that nervous laugh that she often could not control, the high-pitched laugh that led her into trouble.

The Court was not amused. She received a stern warning from Major Mason, who then continued with his questioning. "Did the widow return it?"

"*Finally.* And she threw it at Goodwife Gilbert…in a fuss…nay, more like a fury—"

"Is this the end of your statement, Goodwife Smith?"

"'Tis not!" she said. "That black cap was ne'er the same after *she* wore it. It became bewitched by the devil and his consort— this she-demon!" She wagged a gnarled finger at Katherine.

"Why would you think this?" asked the Major.

"Why? On our walk back home, I witnessed my friend with the black cap on her head. It made her head to ache. Even burned her scalp, so she told me. I saw how she could not move her head, nor neck and shoulders with that cap on. Fixed her head stiff. That cap burned with the flaming brands from hell. But when Goodwife Gilbert took it off, the aches left her person."

"What happened to the cap?"

"The cap is gone. For God told Elizabeth to throw it into the fire, so Satan's flames would vanish from her head. Aye, I was there when she burned the bewitched cap; she sent it back from whence it came." She stopped to wipe spittle from her lips and then shouted, "From hell…where Widow Harrison will be going someday!"

"Is this all, Goodwife Smith?"

"That is all."

·•—•·

Attorney Hopkins had but few questions for the old woman. He would be brief. "Goodwife Smith, can you kindly explain why Goodwife Gilbert, wife of Marshal Gilbert, cannot testify herself today in court?"

"Because it upsets her so. She ails in bed, that's why. She's not been well of late," she said with a cry.

"Is that due to the malice from the black cap?"

"Aye, you might say this. 'Tis the ill effects of the cap that linger."

"Would you say Goodwife Gilbert has a conflict of interest, her husband being related to Katherine, and a trustee of her estate?"

"Perhaps. I know not. I am only doing what Elizabeth asked of me."

"And without Elizabeth's testimony, we are supposed to believe yours?"

"Aye, I know what she suffered through and still suffers today from the black cap. It pains me to know my friend did a good deed lending the grieving widow that cap."

"Thank you, Goodwife Smith. I have no further questions."

CHAPTER 45

The third day of Katherine's trial began with testimony from Thomas Bracy. Not only had he visited the Wells House years ago he recalled, but after the visit, when he stepped out onto the Sandy Lane, he saw something unusual.

Governor Winthrop began the questioning. "You describe in your deposition, Goodman Bracy, that what you witnessed was strange. What did you see? Explain to the Court."

Thomas Bracy worked hard to recall what he had seen seven years ago. He now lived in Hadley, thus making the memory seem more distant. "I went out from the back of the Wells home to the Sandy Lane for some air. I espied a cart across the way near the Harrison farm, driven by the Harrisons' native helper. The cart was loaded with hay; atop a large haystack sat perfectly a red calf's head. Its ears were standing straight up. I kept an eye on the cart until it came near the barn. Lo! The calf's head disappeared, and to my dismay I saw no other but Goodwife Harrison in its stead."

Winthrop asked Bracy what he did next.

"I shouted by the fence to her that I suspected that she, Goodwife Harrison, was a witch!"

"A dangerous accusation, Goodman Bracy. Did she respond?"

Bracy began to shake and shiver. "Aye. She came forth and told me she would get even with me."

"I see," Winthrop said. "She made a threat against you. Did she, in fact, get even with you?"

"Aye, so she did. She came to me that night. Along with James Wakeley. They stood at the end of my bed, threatened to kill me, choke me, strangle me. And they pinched and afflicted my skin. Frightened me to a shivering wreck." He started shaking on the stand rubbing his arms with his hands.

"That is all," Governor Winthrop said.

·•·

Once again it was Attorney Hopkins's turn to question the witness. "Do you suppose, Goodman Bracy, you might need spectacles?"

The audience burst into a torrent of laughter.

"Nay, I need no spectacles, and I certainly *know* what I saw; I saw a calf's head a-sticking up from the haystack."

"I know not what you saw, Goodman Bracy. Why would you think the Harrisons would lodge a calf's head atop hay?"

Bracy stood up and stared over at Katherine. "Because they were hiding the calf—stealing it from somewhere—covering it over with hay. That's what I think!"

"So, did you see a body along with the head?"

"Nay, it was just the head. That was enough evidence." He pointed to Katherine. "The witch stole it."

"And Goodman Bracy, besides Katherine herself, do *you* have a witness to back your claims?"

"It was just me standing alone." He shrugged his shoulders. "I know what I saw."

Katherine could not help herself. She stood again and shouted, "All fanciful lies, spying on our farm. It might have been a pig for all I know. Methinks people don't work as hard as John and I did... people filled with spiteful envy...and too much idle time."

Governor Winthrop arose and raised his hands to calm the restless crowd. "Widow Harrison, please—you will have your chance to speak." He turned to Hopkins. "Counselor, let us finish the questioning."

"Thank you, Governor. As regards your professed attack from Katherine Harrison and James Wakeley, did anyone else in your household see them? Did they *hear* the pair conspire against you?"

"Nay, but my family saw my bruises. Black and blue they were, dotted all over my arms and legs. No doubt I was pained by them."

"Was this in response to Katherine's so-called curse against you? That 'she'd get even'?"

"Aye, it was. For it happened just hours after her telling me that she'd get even— and then I became sore afflicted."

"I have one last query for the witness." The attorney glared hard at the young man. "Is it true, Goodman Bracy, you were accused and convicted of night-walking about the town—destroying property and overturning the stocks—a few years before you departed Wethersfield?"

"That was a long time ago. Perhaps...my memory is vague."

"'Tis my point as well. 'Twas years ago and your memory *is* vague."

Attorney Hopkins, hands behind his back, paced toward the witness, drew close and stared hard into his face. "Aye, you are afflicted, Goodman Bracy. But not by the Widow Harrison nor James Wakeley. You afflict *yourself* with your notions." Hopkins paused. "That is all."

❧

During the break, Marshal Gilbert commented to Katherine how well Attorney Hopkins was representing her. Even Governor Winthrop nodded toward the lawyer, his round brown eyes no longer so dull. The only authority with a sullen expression was Major Mason.

As the afternoon session was called to order, the next witness, Hannah Robbins, was sworn in and took the witness seat. Hannah, now twenty-four, had affirmed for the court that seven years earlier, Goodwife Palmer and Katherine Harrison were present at the Robbins's home, ministering to her ailing mother. Soon afterwards her mother breathed her last breath.

"Please tell the court and jury, Hannah, what happened that day seven years ago?" asked Magistrate Wyllys.

Hannah nodded, tucking a golden strand of hair inside her cap. "The Palmers lived next door. Henry, the husband was a quiet man. But Goodwife Palmer was a nosy biddy, always trying to sell her physicks to the family. Almost useless she was— she and Katherine Harrison's salves and poultices worked not. My mother believed Goodwife Palmer's claims— for a time." Hannah delicately wiped a tear away.

"Was Goodwife Palmer advised," Magistrate Wyllys asked, "not to enter the house?"

"Aye, on several occasions. On that day both Goodwife Palmer and Katherine Harrison pushed themselves past the door and into the parlor where mother lay ailing."

"Where is Goodwife Palmer now?"

"She was warned out of Wethersfield, and escaped with her family. Her name was mentioned as one being at the Merrymeets in Hartford. There's no doubt in my mind that Goodwife Palmer is a witch. And we know that witches do keep company... with one another." Hannah smiled faintly.

The crowd fell silent of a sudden. Townspeople glanced over at Major Mason who stared coldly straight ahead.

"Do you have direct evidence these women killed your mother?"

Hannah shook her head. "I wrote down what happened years ago. I know not what I did with the writing."

"You lost it?"

Hannah shrugged her shoulders. "Perhaps… I have misplaced… or lost it. I know not." She had a look of a wilting buttercup in need of rain.

"Thank you," said Magistrate Wyllys.

"And I have no further questions, Magistrate," said Attorney Hopkins, noting how people were slumped over in their seats.

"Court is dismissed and will begin nine on the morrow," Governor Winthrop said.

CHAPTER 46

The fourth day of Katherine's trial was underway. Today Josiah sat in a back pew staring hard at his calloused palms raw from all the plowing and planting of the season. He thought of all the work he ought to be attending to. But instead, he worried more about whether he should testify for or against his cousin. Or testify at all.

He knew of her background. He *did* warn her. Yet he had written no deposition nor any complaint. But neither did he wish to be called to Katherine's defense. Her petition noted that he and Jonathan were witnesses to the vandalism of her farm animals. Let Jonathan testify, he thought. He is trustee of her estate now.

He listened to a few of the servants from Captain Cullick's household all those years ago. Some testified that they heard of Katherine reading fortunes, and that she boasted of reading Mr. Lilly's astrology book. Back then, townspeople called her a cunning woman. Now they called her a witch. To Josiah's mind Katherine was filled with a greed that led to her impudence, her bold outbursts, always having to get her way. Everything for a price, he thought. And what a price the widow was paying now.

He ran his fingers through his damp hair and then clenched his fists together. His reputation was at stake due to Katherine's vexing ways. John had tried to keep control of her like a good husband should. He succeeded—for a time.

But now for these many years Goodman Harrison lay dead on the farm. And Katherine, stubborn and headstrong, refused marriage, and refused to share her farm. These thoughts haunted him. For he had always wanted Katherine gone. And now he was no longer alone in his desire.

·—·

One of the last and most anticipated witnesses to be called was Captain Cullick's former maidservant, Elizabeth Bateman, also known as Betty. She stepped up to the front and was sworn in. Katherine admitted to herself that Betty looked stylish and tidy in her blue shawl, bright mustard-colored skirt, white waistcoat, and starched white cap. Even her light brown eyes and rose-pink cheeks glimmered in the sunlight that beamed through the paned windows.

"How dost thou know the prisoner?" asked Magistrate Wyllys.

Betty flounced her skirt and carefully smoothed out the wrinkles. The jury and crowd leaned forward listening with care.

"I worked in service with Katherine at Captain Cullick's house years ago—maybe 1651 and 1652. I taught her everything...took her under my wing, I did. Then she read my fortune and my astrology chart she did...and 'tis odd... how it came to pass."

"Kindly explain."

Betty glanced over to Katherine. "Why, I was engaged and wanted to be wed to Will Chapman. Captain Cullick did not approve. He was taking me to court over Will, he was. Nay, he would not approve. But Katherine told me I would marry a man named Simon. And I *did*!"

The crowd gasped.

"So Katherine predicted you would marry a man named Simon. And you did. What else do you know about her that you can tell the Court?" asked Wyllys.

Betty stood with a flair and pronounced, "Why, she's a notorious liar…and a Sabbath breaker. The devil she knows well… I tell you. I was afeared."

"Are you saying she refused to attend meeting?"

"She made me lie for her when she *did* break the Sabbath." Betty began to pout and sniff as if looking for sympathy.

"She told your fortune, refused to attend Meeting…anything else?"

"Katherine told me all about Mr. Lilly's book on astrology. *Christian Astrology*. Bah! As if there could be such a thing. His book was *her* Bible, not God's good book. Ne'er did I see her read the Bible. She cared naught for the Word of God."

"Anything else?"

"Aye, she spun like a she-demon, she did. I have ne'er seen the wonder of it. Why she possessed a fury at the spinning wheel. There was no stopping her. And ne'er a thread was out of place. 'Tis not a skill from this world, I tell ye."

Secretary Allyn scribbled furiously to a page.

"That is all," Magistrate Wyllys said.

· — ·

Attorney Hopkins watched Betty the way a wolf watches a rabbit. He was ready with questions to pounce on this ex-servant. "Betty, did Katherine offer to read your fortune?"

"Not quite," Betty answered. "But she boasted of her skills. She told me how she read fortunes in England and used astrology to predict the future—"

"Did you, Betty, inquire about a reading from Katherine?"

A long pause ensued.

"If I can recall, aye… perhaps…"

"So you did request a reading from Katherine." Attorney Hopkins eyed his notes, "And were you satisfied with the fortune?"

Betty retrieved a white cloth and dabbed the corner of an eye. "Why of course *not*. I was in love with Will Chapman. I knew of no Simon."

"But you knew that Captain Cullick approved not of this Will. Methinks that after your fortune, *you* went seeking after a man named Simon—until you found one."

The crowd tittered in sing-song voices.

Elizabeth hung her head

"That will be all," the Attorney abruptly concluded.

⸱⸻⸱

During the break Marshal Gilbert approached Josiah. "I will be on the witness stand testifying on behalf of Katherine." He raised his eyebrows. "And you, Josiah? Brother, will you speak on your cousin's behalf? I would suggest you do so. Do what's right and proper."

Josiah stood listening to his brother ordering him with commands. "*You* are trustee of her estate now. *You*, Jonathan have much to gain. I, on the other hand, have much to lose."

The marshal cocked a glance at his brother. "You will lose my respect."

"The other option is I testify and lose the respect of my neighbors in Wethersfield. You are in charge, Jonathan. To think she's of our blood—nay!"

"You would deny her this?" The marshal blew a long breath out in frustration, frowned, and shook his head. "I will be testifying this afternoon…whether you testify or not. We saw the damage done to her livestock. Methinks you may know the vandals."

Josiah knew what he must do for himself and his family. "The Gilbert farm needs tending. You speak what need be, but my voice will remain silent."

With those words he left the church and departed on his horse toward Wethersfield leaving the marshal alone.

·⇢·

The afternoon session allowed Katherine time on the stand. She firmly denied all the charges against her and read her lengthy petition to the court. Although she had written it months before, she had most of the charges memorized in her mind. All the horrors she and her girls suffered through, never mind the wounding of her livestock. When would she get her just compensation?

The marshal testified to the damages done to her estate. Josiah was not even present.

She passionately pled to the jury, "I rebuke all the charges against me. There was ne'er enough evidence. Why, these people testifying do insult my talents, talents such as spinning, that I worked hard to master over many years. Instead of appreciation, I am condemned! 'Tis envy— a far worse sin than I ever hath committed. And when certain persons trespass to my property and those who accuse me of theft—why it's naught but lies." Her voice wavered, but she continued. 'Tis never would have happened if John were alive. I am guilty of naught but being a widow and a woman of means. Have pity and mercy upon me."

The jury seemed moved by her words, one juror fidgeting in his seat, another wiping down the sides of his face and rubbing his eyes.

Secretary Allyn read the charges and directions to them.

Katherine's trial was over.

Now it was left to the jury to decide her fate.

• ► •

Two days later Katherine heard the clattering of keys and was promptly awakened by Jailor Garrett. "The Court has an announcement. Seems they have a verdict, most likely guilty from all I'm hearing." He let out a loud yawn and grabbed her arm. "Let's go."

Katherine yanked herself away. "You are the one who profits most by my being in jail. You are taking money from my estate every day I'm in this horrid pit. I will have little to show by the time I am finally freed."

"You speak right. Perhaps your freedom lies in swinging from the hanging tree. You will be free, and our towns will be free from your hexes!" He led her into the bright sunlight where guards awaited to manacle her. A large crowd had gathered and began heckling the prisoner as Garrett, followed by the guards, pushed her through the square toward the Meetinghouse.

She gathered herself for the verdict trying to read the jury's faces. Their eyes refused to meet hers.

"Order, order!" Magistrate Wyllys banged his mallet. "Foreman, step forward with the verdict."

The foreman stood and read from a paper: "'We the jury, in the trial of Katherine Harrison, accused of witchcraft, could not agree on a unanimous decision.'"

The audience groaned.

Major Mason's face burned like a white-hot stone in the sun, his eyes dark with fury.

Katherine, bewildered and confused, asked her lawyer if she could return home.

"Governor Winthrop is preparing to speak. Let us listen," he replied.

"I demand discipline in the court," the governor began. "On behalf of the Court the prisoner hath been found neither guilty nor innocent of the crime of witchcraft. Therefore, the Court is adjourned until the October session commences."

"What will happen to the prisoner?" someone in a back pew shouted. "Is she to be freed?"

"The prisoner will remain in jail for her safety until the October Court is in session."

Katherine shook with rage. How dare the governor speak such words? She vowed she would not stay in that jail through the summer months. Not when her family and farm needed her. But for now, she had to obey the Court's orders.

"This trial is over," Governor Winthrop said.

Part IV

THE DECISION

CHAPTER 47

Katherine did not have to wait long to be released from jail. She had written several letters to Governor Winthrop in the past weeks. She wrote him that she already had paid a great price, her fines were adding up, and her family awaited her return.

This July morning, she heard a loud banging on the thick, iron-rimmed oak door with the tiny window carved into it. "Release the prisoner immediately," she heard a voice echo. Jailor Garrett opened the door. Marshal Gilbert stood afore him.

"What's all this now?" the tall muscled guard said with a growl. He'd been enjoying the monies from his wealthy prisoner. Of late he had provided her a few extra morsels of food—for a price. But even in jail, the widow struck a hard bargain.

"Per orders of the governor, Katherine is to be released and returned to her farm," the marshal said loudly. He handed the jailor a sealed parchment.

Garrett tore it open and read the declaration aloud: "*By order of the Court, until further notified, the said prisoner, Katherine Harrison is to be released from jail and returned home at once." Signed, Governor John Winthrop, Jr., Magistrate Samuel Wyllys, Magistrate Leete, Major John Mason. Dated July 10, 1669.*'"

Katherine was free—for now. Free to return to her life on the farm with her daughters, to Joseph, and a return to her beloved meadows and farm animals. The jailor turned the key and the cell door creaked open; she ran to the marshal for a steady embrace. She knew she smelled like old straw; she did not care if her cap, hair, and clothes were in tatters. She gathered up her satchel along with her few belongings.

"I will see thee back soon Widow, mark my word—you will be back," grumbled the jailor.

"We shall see," Katherine replied, more interested in taking her leave. She had at last achieved a victory.

"Your daughters will be thankful their mother is coming home. Methinks that black cat of yours missed you too." The marshal grinned at her and raised his broad hat.

"It will be good and right to be back with my family and on my land again." She patted his arm. But a question that had bothered her for weeks rose to her mind. "Cousin Jonathan, how could your wife's friend, Goody Smith, testify about that black cap? I wore it during my time of grieving," she said, an angry resolve coming over her. "What say you?"

"I say I stay out of the affairs of my wife. *You* are plenty my affair now, and you have caused a mighty trouble."

"You are right, Cousin. It will be good to get home again."

⋅—⋅

Not a neighbor nor townsperson was happy the Widow Harrison was released back to her farm. They were angered over the thought that Governor Winthrop favored her. "Why doth she receive special treatment?" was the refrain heard at the nooning-house on the Sabbath, and at the taverns the rest of the week. Townspeople even began a flurry of petitions; like small snowflakes in a storm, they quickly accumulated.

"I cannot bear the sight of the widow, her native worker, even her cows," neighbor Joan Francis said to Ann Griswold on their daily walk. "'Tis wrong she's free." They ambled past John Nott's store on the High Street, crossing to the Sandy Lane. Here they watched with pride as several people marched in protest up and down the Sandy Lane carrying wooden placards, some bearing the letter S for slanderer, others reading, 'Guilty' or 'Hang the Witch.'

"Back to jail she must go," people chanted. Others stood around in little hives, gossiping and buzzing in agreement.

"I would say we need not join this mob," said Ann Griswold politely. "Michael and I did *our* part winning the slander suit against the Widow. Ha!"

"And I said my peace at the trial… for all to hear," said Goodwife Francis.

"Katherine has caused this discord. By God's mercy, may the truth prevail," said Goodwife Griswold, who cast her eyes up to the sky.

·–·

Katherine held herself up against the mob in the summer of 1669. Joseph and a few farmhands, with her supervision and help from the girls, had brought in some profit from this year's crops and exports; the flax, hops, wheat and corn had flourished with the abundant sunshine and gentle rains. She continued on the way John would want and expect.

Until one afternoon in late August, when she received more news from Marshal Gilbert. By Court Order she was required on the morrow to return to jail, a court order signed by Governor John Winthrop, Jr.

CHAPTER 48

October 1669

Katherine sat on her stool, hands on her head, waiting for breakfast. What would today bring? She was tired of waiting in this jail that reeked of mildew, stale urine, and the pine cleanser the jailer's wife used to wipe the bars and floor. Bits of straw from her lean pallet hung off her stained skirt.

Finally she heard the thump of footsteps and a rattling of keys. The smell of biscuits and a faint scent of meat filled her nose. Daniel Garrett stood afore her and slid the plate of food under the iron bars. "A good morrow to you, Widow. A special breakfast for you today."

Katherine's eyes widened. "A rasher of bacon with my biscuit?" She pounced on the hot food with relish. The jailor stared through the bars with a slight grin on his face.

"That's right. Eat up. This may be one of the last hot meals you will ever get." Katherine heard him, but continued to stuff the bacon and biscuit into her mouth. "You'll need your sustenance today all right," Garrett said. "I have just received news the jury has reviewed the evidence again, and has reached a decision. Orders are I am to take you over to the Meetinghouse where the verdict will be read."

Katherine swallowed the last morsel and stared into the jailor's mocking eyes. "Will I be freed?"

"Hardly, I reckon. From what I'm hearing, the folks from Wethersfield will have you swinging on Gallows' Hill. How does it feel to have thirty-eight petitioners sign against you? They want you gone, plain and pure. And then they'll take your land." He chuckled to himself.

Katherine slid the empty platter through the bottom slat, stood up, and wiped her mouth on her sleeve. "They can't take my land, jailor. It's in a trust now."

"Ah, but they will take your life first. Then your land. Mark my words."

"So you say. May I have permission for a wash-up?" she asked.

"Nay, you'll have time after they read the verdict. Before they hang you proper. Even witches need a cleansing before they meet their maker. Go as you are. This will have to do."

Katherine shook a fist at him. "And you expect me to pay for this treatment?" she shouted.

"Aye, you will pay me in shillings. And then you will pay with your life."

·—•—·

The jailor jostled Katherine through Hartford's Meetinghouse Square. People lined up to jeer at the spectacle of the Widow Harrison looking like a wild cat, her stringy red-brown and grey-streaked hair sticking out from her dirty cap. Children pelted clods of mud at her. The dirt and ugly words fell on her faster than the whirling leaves the wind blew down about the square.

The crowd followed her to the Meetinghouse, shouting, "Guilty, Guilty!"

Was this to be her fate, she wondered, a fate by hanging? Like Lydia? Why didn't she pay heed to Josiah's warning to follow Kate to Rhode Island? And for all the readings and fortunes she'd told for others, fortunes that turned out true, she could ne'er foretell her own future, nor foresee the tragedies of her own life.

The Meetinghouse bustled with activity, as the tithing man settled townspeople in pews. It seemed all of Hartford and Wethersfield were present. Witnesses who testified against her were there watching and waiting—waiting for a guilty verdict to be read aloud.

As the last stragglers found their seats, Katherine was escorted by the jailor, manacles tight around her wrists, down the center aisle of the church to her specified box. She noticed her three daughters were in attendance, eyes squinting, faces pinched with worry. Her youngest, Sarah cast a broad smile at her. Katherine vowed to herself she would stay strong for her children.

"All rise!" shouted Secretary Allyn, as the magistrates entered from the right, followed by the six members of Katherine's original jury.

The lead magistrate, Samuel Wyllys banged his mallet thrice to silence the anxious crowd. Governor Winthrop, William Leete, and Major Mason sat aside him. "We are here because the jury in the Katherine Harrison trial, adjourned since May last, hath notified the court that they have come to a unanimous decision," announced Magistrate Wyllys. He glanced at the jury. "Lead foreman, prepare to read the verdict."

Katherine heard the mutterings from the goodwives, those who gossiped and condemned her. She turned and witnessed several of her accusers eyeing her. There was prim Ann Griswold, alongside Joan Francis. They seemed like the evil ones now, grinning with satisfaction and a smug pride.

The lead juryman stepped forward to read the verdict. All was eerily quiet as he cleared his throat. "We the jury, after reviewing all the evidence in the trial of Katherine Harrison for the crime of witchcraft punishable by death, find the defendant guilty on all accounts."

"Liars, all of ye!" she shouted.

The crowd erupted with loud huzzahs, then shouts of "Thanks be to God."

Again, Magistrate Wyllys banged his mallet to silence the crowd.

Governor Winthrop arose from his chair and began to address the magistrates, the jury, and the relieved crowd. "Good people…please… Katherine Harrison hath been found guilty for the crime of witchcraft. Due to the severity of the crime and severity of the punishment, I question *not* the verdict; I question the *standards of evidence* used in this trial against her. 'Tis the law I speak, in particular, English law. And we must respect Biblical precepts. We must do what is deemed proper. Therefore, I will be recommending a panel of ministers to review the standards of evidence against the Widow Harrison, to deem if the evidence meets the criteria of death by hanging."

Silence fell like a dark cloak over the meetinghouse.

"How long will this take?" a spectator finally cried. "We've waited plenty long enough." The tithingman found the man and rapped him with his tithing stick.

The governor spoke with authority. "The next session of the court meets May 1670; the panel will have their findings by then. In the meantime, Katherine Harrison will remain in jail until further notice. Moreover, Goodwife Harrison shall continue to pay her jail debts, and any debts owed to the prisoner will be paid to the prisoner through the marshal. Any debt incurred of witnesses from travel and board will be paid up."

The crowd left murmuring and shaking their heads in confusion. Most were relieved a guilty verdict was in place. But Major Mason sat stiff, his bone-white fists clenched in rage. Here was another delay for the people—and another delay of justice.

Katherine Harrison, found guilty of witchcraft, was going back to jail. She had been given a reprieve by the governor. For a time.

CHAPTER 49

After the guilty verdict was read and the jury and court dismissed, Governor Winthrop knew where he had to go. He pushed his way through the crowds milling about the Square, untied his horse from its post, and rode straight on to Wethersfield. He had to speak to the Reverend Gershom Bulkeley, Wethersfield's minister.

The governor knew Gershom Bulkeley never wanted to be the new minister of Wethersfield. He turned down the position years before in favor of New London. But in 1667, the governor in his persistent manner, had convinced the young divine he was the one for the job. "Wethersfield needs you Gershom, for your intelligence, practical sense, and a quest for righteous truth. I need you to help keep the peace as well," he told the reluctant minister.

He was thankful for their friendship. Both men shared much in common, for aside their primary jobs, they each served as doctors— and part-time alchemists— sharing notes, cures, even recipes with one another. Reverend Bulkeley, although a minister, had a strong law background, and Governor Winthrop thought it fit to use this knowledge. He needed Reverend Bulkeley's help more than ever.

The governor tethered his horse out front, and strode to the back of the parsonage. There he found the minister clearing out leaves and dead stalks from about the grounds. Nearby sat baskets filled with late apples picked from the orchard. He watched how deliberately the Reverend Bulkeley clipped the dead parts off the plants, pruning them with great care.

"How-fare-thee, Gershom? Have you heard the news yet?" Winthrop asked out of breath. "I have just come from Hartford."

The minister arose and greeted his friend. He pulled off his work gloves, so they could shake hands. "John, what news do you speak?"

"Katherine Harrison has been found guilty of witchcraft." The governor watched the reverend's head shake back and forth and his mouth droop low.

"'Tis not a surprise," Reverend Bulkeley said. "The town has much against her." He took up his pitchfork and began to rake leaves from the dead flower beds. "You don't mind if I continue to work?" he asked. "Helps calm me."

"Of course not. But tell me, what do you know of the Widow Harrison?"

"I have been Minister for two years now. I have seen the widow down in the meadows; she hath a commanding presence both to man, woman... and beast. And I heard about the damages to her farm." He paused to rub the back of his neck. "Members of the church have complained about her. I hear what they say...but I know well enough not to pay mind."

The governor sighed a long breath and stroked his small pointed beard. "'Tis why I am here. The widow sits in jail awaiting sentence...a sentence that will surely hang her."

"I understand that this is the traditional sentence for one found guilty of the crime of witchcraft."

"Precisely my point, Gershom. I need to know doth the evidence rise to the legal standards, not just the English court case standards, but Biblical standards."

The lanky minister rose and stood face to face with the governor. Winthrop thought he smelled like the autumn air itself, an air filled with the scent of cracked dead leaves and cornstalks. "What, John, are you saying? What are you asking of me?"

"As governor, I am asking— nay requesting— that you lead a panel of ministers inquiring as to whether the evidence in this trial reflects English law and sound Biblical principles. I was thinking of you, the Minister of Windsor, and that of Mattabasset— would form a fair panel."

"Now I understand your reasoning."

"Aye, and you know of what I speak. During my role as a magistrate in the trial, I have taken note of much of the evidence. As governor, I must ensure the evidence reaches the proper standards."

Gershom bore a pained look on his face. "And what if the evidence is found insufficient for a guilty verdict?"

"That is my point."

Reverend Bulkeley stuttered out the next question. "What will the people of Wethersfield think of my personal involvement? 'Tis a conflict, perhaps?"

"Remember Gershom, the jury hath found her guilty. 'Tis the sentence I question."

The tall, slender minister nodded in agreement. "'Tis a sensible plan." A smile lifted his handsome face. "This is why *you* are governor, and I but your servant."

"Part of my job is to keep order in this Colony."

The friends grasped each other's arms. "I have called a meeting on the morrow. Meet me at Jeremy Adams's Tavern in Hartford at noon to discuss this further," said Winthrop.

"I will be there, Governor."

⸱•⸱

After the discussion the governor's next stop was back to the Hartford jail. He owed Katherine an explanation. He could not promise her freedom; he was a realist, a practical man who sought solutions. But he could gather information from her and give her hope. Let her know her children would be cared for, her farm looked after, and debts paid off.

Stragglers still lingered about the Meetinghouse Square. As the sun set lower in the sky, Governor Winthrop espied Josiah Gilbert glancing toward him. Josiah stood among the Wethersfield folk. The governor shook his head in dismay as the group ambled toward the tavern, clearly in a celebratory mood.

He banged hard on the jail door. The jailor stuck his massive head out. "Greetings Governor. Here to see the prisoner, I presume? Quite the verdict today, eh?" Goodman Garrett smiled, waiting for a response.

"Enough of the banter, jailor. Let me in." The governor marched past the ruffled man and made his way to the large jail cell on the right. Scant light shone through the tiny window near the ceiling, sending needlelike rays and then dim shadows to fill the room.

There she sat, stunned.

"Katherine," he called out to her.

She stared past him and pointed. Jailor Garrett hovered in the shadows watching and listening.

The governor turned and addressed him. "We *will* have our privacy."

"Of course, Governor. Sir." The jailor walked out slamming the door hard behind him.

Winthrop pulled up a stool and sat close to the bars. Katherine began shrieking, "Guilty? How could this be?"

"You have been given a reprieve because of my concerns. If not for this, rest assured, you would be carted away to the gallows come the morrow. Aye, here you sit... but you are alive."

"I *need* to stay alive—for my children and my farm." She balled her fists, put her head between her hands, and rocked her body back and forth.

The governor, grieved, took out a handkerchief and wiped his forehead. "If I were you Katherine, I would get your things in order. *A Last Will and Testament* is needed. We must respect the jury's verdict of guilty. I cannot overturn this. But the evidence needs testing against the standards held up by English law."

The sun was fast setting and Winthrop had little time. "I am gathering a panel of ministers to review the evidence from your trial."

"You mean all the false testimony against me? The spectral evidence? I cannot help the disturbed fancies of these people... imagine... seeing me at the edge of one's bed. And as a dog's head? Bah! 'Tis all hodgepodge, Governor."

"Now is the time for serious examination, Katherine. There are two main criteria that have been upheld for years in England. The first is the two-witness testimony and the other... admitting to being a witch."

"Rest assured I shall 'ne'er admit to being a witch. What of the two-witness rule you speak?"

"Two spectators must witness the same event. In prior cases, this rule had often been overlooked. Be confident the panel will study these cases and findings."

"You saved me once years ago, Governor. Saved my life and that of my third child. Kept my family together you did—"

She began to weep quietly.

"That was but many years ago, in my role as doctor—"

"And mayhap you will help save me again."

CHAPTER 50

The next day in Hartford, Governor John Winthrop Jr., Major John Mason, Magistrate Samuel Wyllys, Magistrate William Leetes, and the Reverend Gershom Bulkeley sat in a back room at Jeremy Adams's Tavern; the door was shut as they discussed Katherine's case in earnest. Each had their own ideas about the verdict and sentencing. The governor was concerned that much of the evidence against her was spectral. Could the widow be hanged on the basis of a night-time ghostly appearance to someone's home? Or repeatedly making threats on someone's life as an apparition?

Major Mason had a different opinion. "Hasn't this woman caused enough mischief—far more mischief that those hanged here in Hartford for witchcraft in 1663?"

"And I had no say, Major, being away obtaining *our* Charter. I understand that you did what you thought right. Remember, *I'm* in charge now," the governor said.

Major Mason, dressed in black, saber hanging from his belt, black steeple hat still atop his head leaned over the table glaring at Winthrop. "Aye, and I was in charge when you were gone. I did it the way I thought best. Remember, it was I who led our militia to the Pequot Fort years back and listened to the voice of God through the prophecy of Reverend Stone. I know how to lead in times of crisis. I did the same for the problem of witches. The people trust me. I have a proven record." He glanced at the men around the table who said not a word. "Governor," he continued, "our good townspeople do not deserve bedevilment and vexations that interfere with their pious lives. Katherine Harrison is far more dangerous than the others, for she has land, money, and refuses to remarry so I—"

"Times are changing, Major," said Reverend Bulkeley. "The governor and I see things differently." The reverend pulled his chair closer to the table, his lanky frame held in by his plain brown doublet. His light blue eyes blinked, and then he stared hard at the Major. He lifted his tankard, downed the remains, and waited for a response.

The serving girl entered and asked if they needed anything else. "We will have another round for the table—put the pints on my bill," said the Major with a grumble in his voice. He sat, legs spread, his knee-high boots shining from a thorough polish and leaned back on his chair. "Only an execution can stop her kind."

"Major," said Magistrate Wyllys, "The standards of evidence must be reviewed. We are conducting a proper inquiry, thanks to the Governor and Reverend Bulkeley."

Governor Winthrop lifted the large, wrapped bundle of parchment papers sitting on the table, papers from the trial. Here were all the witness testimonies, depositions, questions, and Katherine's statements.

He handed them over to the Reverend Bulkeley. "These are for you, Gershom, and for the other ministers to review. Also, I have with me the four legal points that need addressing. I have written out a copy for each person at the table." He grasped his satchel and pulled forth the pages and passed them along, one to each man. "These are the standards of evidence we need to follow." He began to read:

> "*1. Is it necessary that more than one witness testify to the same event, or do uncorroborated witnesses testifying to similar events count as legal proof?*
> *2. Is an appearance of a specter or apparition in the form of the person legal evidence against that person?*
> *3. Is fortune telling evidence of familiarity with Satan?*
> *4. Does the knowledge of things considered secret evidence constitute familiarity with Satan?*"

"Reverend Bulkeley," the governor continued, "these standards must be reviewed and applied in full. Please advise the other ministers to read up in the English law books from your extensive libraries and of course, refer to the Bible for evidence. If, as the jury thought, the standards had been met, the sentence of death will happen within a fortnight of the ruling."

Major Mason shook his head. "There's more evidence against the widow than in any other trial I suffered through. Is she getting *special* treatment from you, Governor?" The Major narrowed his black eyes at the governor.

Winthrop wiped his thin mustache and mouth of any beer, and made ready to leave. "I will not abide by stubborn pride, nor the ways of the past." He glared hard at Mason. "Mark my words, the outcome of the Widow Harrison's trial will be fair and just."

"I *am* fair and just," said the Major.

The governor stood and found his hat hanging on a nearby peg, placed it on his head, and stormed out of the tavern.

"Major Mason, will you not support the governor in this effort for truth?" asked the Reverend Bulkeley.

"The jury decided what was true; *they* decided Katherine's fate," Mason said, with a scowl on his face.

"Nay, they decided her guilt," said the Reverend. "We shall decide her fate."

CHAPTER 51

May 1670

At last Katherine was notified that the ministers had carefully reviewed the evidence against her and had come to a decision. She had waited long enough in jail; it seemed that everyone in Wethersfield and Hartford awaited the decision as well.

The meetinghouse was full. Once again, the tithing man escorted people to their seats and demanded order. The crowd murmured in whispered voices waiting for the verdict. The magistrates filed in as Governor Winthrop and Major John Mason sat at the front table presiding over the Court— along with Secretary Allyn who was preparing to take notes. All seemed ready for the announcement.

The lead magistrate, Samuel Wyllys banged his mallet to silence the anxious crowd. "As you know, due to the complex and long duration of this trial and sentencing, we have requested that a panel of ministers review the evidence against the guilty party, Katherine Harrison. They have studied the many accusations regarding the Widow Harrison, including her appearance as a specter, and if her fortunetelling met the standards of witchcraft, and finally whether she deserves to live or die."

"She was found guilty. She deserves to die!" one spectator shouted.

"Tithingman, remove this man immediately."

Magistrate Wyllys continued. "We of the Court, including our esteemed Governor John Winthrop Jr. and Major John Mason, have conceded to the power of our ministerial body. We trust the right and fair decision hath been made, and further, we will abide by this decision." The Magistrate paused. "Reverend Bulkeley? Are you ready to read the statement regarding the sentencing of the said prisoner, Katherine Harrison?"

Gershom Bulkeley arose from a seat along a side pew and made his way to the podium. His simple, dignified presence established a new power in the meetinghouse. This time, instead of a sermon, he would review the points in question and then announce the sentence.

He cleared his throat and began to read from the parchment paper he held, his long fingers slightly trembling. "This panel and Court, having considered the verdict of the first jury of no-agreement and the second jury decision of guilty, as a representative of the Ministerial Panel, we have come to our own decision, based on evidence, testimony, and the law. Be confident that the panel hath studied the evidence in detail." The reverend paused for a moment. Not a sound could be heard in the meetinghouse, just the spring winds rattling the panes.

"Regarding the first charge—"

Katherine held her breath and grabbed onto the arm of her lawyer. If the sentencing was death by hanging, she would stand proud, and assured herself she would not crumple in a faint.

The Reverend Bulkeley continued, "—we examined the evidence and have answered the governor's first question as to whether it is necessary to have a plurality of witnesses to an event. This is called by English law, the two-witness testimony." He gazed out to the assembled. "After careful review of the testimonies and by assuring this sentencing is Biblically sound, we have concluded that throughout Goodwife Harrison's trial, no two people witnessed the same event. Katherine's lawyer made it known throughout her trial that but one witness experienced each event. Please note from the book of Deuteronomy, 19:15, the verse that states, '*One witness shall not rise up against a man for any iniquity, and at the mouth of two or three witnesses, shall the matter be established.*'"

All remained silent, but Katherine noticed people shaking their heads.

Reverend Bulkeley continued. "Further, we found a passage from John 8:17 that says, '*It is also written in your law, that the testimony of two men is true.*'" He concluded, "The evidence in the widow's trial did not reach the standard of the two-witness testimony. This is how the panel of minsters interpreted not only the English law, but God's law as well."

Hissing and loud muttering sounds arose from the crowd. But no one dared make a comment aloud to a Minister of God.

"The next question brought forth by Governor Winthrop and the Court," Bulkeley continued, "was whether an appearance of a specter or apparition in the form of a person constitutes *legal evidence* against that person. This second point is well connected to the first. Since no two witnesses saw a specter of Goodwife Harrison at the same time or circumstance, and we the panel know not whether the devil himself caused the appearance or not, the host of spectral evidence does not rise to the level of death."

Katherine sighed with relief. Reverend Bulkeley, like the governor, was a man of reason. She thought to herself she would soon be free, free to be a mother again to her daughters, free to rule her farm.

"The third point," continued the Reverend, "specifically deals with the charges of fortunetelling. We know from the evidence that Goodwife Harrison indulged in and even boasted of telling fortunes. Fortunes, in many cases, that came to pass."

She knew this was a troubling point, for she *had* read others' fortunes and they *had* come to pass.

"The question for the panel, 'Was fortunetelling evidence of familiarity with Satan?' We studied the law regarding fortunetelling. And it was found that fortunetelling of death and disaster is considered a crime. This also applies to the use of astrology for dire predictions. The evidence in the widow's case is that she predicted no untimely deaths or destruction; in fact, her prediction in evidence pertained to a betrothal. Although this is considered a wrong in the eyes of the panel and jury, it once again does not rise to the death penalty."

The rumblings grew louder throughout the meetinghouse. Katherine, encouraged by the Reverend's pronouncements so far, thought it would be but minutes before they announced her freedom.

"The last question posed to us, 'Was the knowledge of secret things evidence of familiarity with Satan?' This was the hardest question to understand. Did Katherine work a form of magic? Did she truly know of things to come?" Reverend Bulkeley wiped his forehead, his face now glistening in sweat. Major Mason sat motionless, his face looking stern, cold and hard.

Katherine knew not what to expect.

"Although Goodwife Harrison claimed to see into the future, and we do not condone such behavior, we found no *maleficium* in her knowledge of things to come. We know not the widow's motives—whether she was merely trying to impress others with her knowledge. Further, we the ministers felt that of these things done in secret, this person was in all likelihood pretending this certain knowledge...knowledge that often did not come to pass or that she truly knew. Because of this uncertainty, we the Ministers of the Panel have come to our own conclusion."

People began talking aloud amongst themselves.

"We will have silence." Magistrate Wyllys banged his mallet to keep order. "Reverend Bulkeley, please continue."

"Thus, the Panel of Ministers respects the guilty verdict, but cannot concur with the jury's sentence of death by hanging. Therefore, the recommendation by the panel is for the prisoner to be set free. After she pays her jailor his dues."

Free? Katherine covered her face in her hands and thanked God in His mercy. Her ordeal was over. Now she could get back to her farm and continue to raise her daughters. Some men stalked out of the meetinghouse eyeing her with disgust. Women glared at Katherine, eyes darting like poisoned arrows. Josiah sat wide-eyed in the back stunned by the reversal. But the Marshal and Katherine's daughters whooped with joy. Their mother would be home at last.

·•·

As Reverend Bulkeley retreated from the podium, Governor Winthrop stepped forward. "Please. The Court is still in session. There's more. We are not finished here."

Major Mason sat up, and watched the governor with great attention.

"Although the panel has decreed that the evidence in this case did not rise to the level of the death sentence, we the Court and the panel—for the sake of Katherine Harrison— for her own safety— *and* for the peace and contentment of her neighbors... declare that she remove herself from Wethersfield and from Connecticut Colony altogether…never to return, unless by order of the Court or issues of estate." The governor paused, a pained look in his eyes. "The prisoner is now allowed to go free."

CHAPTER 52

Free to go? But where? Katherine sat stunned hearing the news of her banishment from Wethersfield and Connecticut Colony. Where would she and her daughters go? What would happen to her farm, her animals, and her land holdings?

Still manacled amid the frenzy, she looked around for her jailor. Goodman Garrett held the key to unlock her from these fetters. Her attorney rose to offer his congratulations on her freedom. She, in turn, thanked him. For without his sharp mind and quick thinking, as well as the reasoning of the ministers, she knew she would be preparing for her death.

She watched her jailor come bumbling down the aisle, keys jangling from a pocket. "Let me loose," she demanded.

"Not before I am paid up."

Katherine's attorney searched his pockets. "Here's the twenty shillings owed you. Now unshackle her."

The jailor stuck the tiny key into the manacles, and Katherine felt them released from her hands.

"Free you are. And Wethersfield will finally be free of you too. Good riddance." Then Garrett added, "And take the *devil* with you when you go."

Unfettered, Katherine proceeded to hold her head high, as she walked down the center aisle; she was flanked by Marshal Gilbert and her lawyer, followed by her daughters. Many people remained seated, appalled by the sentencing.

Is my removal not enough? thought Katherine. These people were never happy unless someone was hanged by the noose. Banishment wasn't good enough. But she would not hang. She would live.

Finally she walked through the open doors of the meetinghouse into bright sunlight. Her daughters embraced her warmly, and the marshal congratulated her heartily.

Governor Winthrop also approached her. "May I have a word with you? In private?" He looked tired and gaunt, older by years. He led her to an oak tree set apart from the meetinghouse yard. "Katherine, I did what I could to save you."

"And you did save me, Governor—saved me for a second time. For this I will always be grateful. I do not blame you for the order of my removal." She paused and watched him sigh in relief. She placed a hand on his arm. "Governor, we have no place to go, no other place to call home. Home is my farm. Home is Wethersfield. My husband lies in rest there. My daughters and I…we should not be forced to leave."

The Reverend Bulkeley exiting the meetinghouse saw the two speaking, and loped over to join them. "Huzzah to your freedom, Katherine. The right decision hath been made. Now you can live your life in peace —elsewhere."

"We know not where we go." She felt her eyes tearing.

The reverend looked at the governor askance. "You haven't told her?"

"Nay, I was readying myself with the news. First let me thank you, Gershom, for your fine work. You were a voice of practical sense and wisdom in this decision… even amongst the discord."

"Told me what?" she demanded.

Reverend Bulkeley began. "You see, Katherine—"

"Please," Governor Winthrop interrupted. "'Tis best I share the news with Widow Harrison—alone."

"And I thank thee, Reverend, for your wisdom and courage," she said.

Reverend Bulkeley graciously smiled, wished her well, and walked back to the congregation gathered outside the meetinghouse.

"Come Katherine, let us walk by the river," suggested the governor.

Katherine grasped his arm and the two made their way onto the path along the Great River. She felt stiff from sitting on that hard stool for these long months and sleeping on that lean pallet. At last, she could breathe in the fresh air— of freedom.

They finally settled on a bench. Katherine watched the silver-blue circlets of water flow past her spinning downstream. She looked to the man who had helped save her life twice, the only man besides John and the Marshal, and now Gershom Bulkeley, she respected. "What news have you to share, Governor?"

He pulled out a piece of parchment from his doublet pocket. "The Reverend Bulkeley and I worked tirelessly to find a place for you and your daughters. After much inquiry and review, Captain Richard Panton of Westchester, New York has offered you and your daughters room and board until you get settled on your own."

Katherine thought back to the time she served in Captain Cullick's house so many years ago. Another captain barking orders at her? Nay, she would not abide it. "Not as a servant, I presume?"

"Nay, worry not. The captain has plenty of help. His home is but a starting off place for you. Then you will be ready to find your own…home."

"What about my farm? My land holdings? My money?"

"Your land will be parceled off and divided among the neighbors and your Gilbert relatives." He gazed down the river. "Know that you won't receive half of what your land is worth. I will continue to do what I can. But you are alive, and soon you will be free from this vexing problem, once and for all."

Katherine knew she should be grateful for the removal; her new freedom beckoned like a fresh breeze. But she was being forced from her home. And as to the governor's proposition, staying with another captain? It all sounded like hodgepodge— just a way to rid Wethersfield of her.

Governor Winthrop handed her a piece of paper. "This document represents your release from Wethersfield. God hath chosen to save you, whilst others were not so fortunate."

Why couldn't she be gracious instead of resentful? The thought of the injustices she had suffered still irked her. The destruction of her livestock, the malicious words spread about her—she should be happy to leave.

Governor Winthrop grabbed her by the shoulders and shook her hard. "You have little over a fortnight to get your effects in order. You can take small items— some money—but naught much else."

"Governor, I'm too old to begin again."

"Nonsense! You ran the farm without John for years. You survived Captain Cullick's *and* jail, with the prospect of a noose hanging around your neck for many months. You endured a difficult childbirth, and you endured the scorn and violence of townspeople. *You*, Katherine, are a survivor." He paused to take a breath. "The time is right for you to leave this behind. Time to let go of your old ways. The past is forever gone. And 'tis good for the community… *and* good for you. Leave it behind, I say."

She realized she had lost the battle with Wethersfield. There was nothing she could do but follow the governor's orders. He was right in so many ways. She burst into tears of frustration and of anger— but also new tears— tears of relief. And tears of thanks.

There was little more to say. Katherine stood facing him holding herself proud. "I thank you, Governor. Without your help, I would be dead soon enough. I am grateful."

"Shall I escort you safely to the farm?" the governor asked.

"Nay. Cousin Jonathan awaits me at the meetinghouse. He'll cart me and my daughters back to Wethersfield."

"So be it. I will be by to check on you soon. Remember, you have just over a fortnight to prepare for your departure."

"Aye, Governor, we will be ready."

CHAPTER 53

Two weeks passed. The wagon was packed to near full. Much had been sold or given away. Katherine managed to save some treasured mementoes from her life with John. She knew she'd be starting anew. The girls kept demanding a new cat since Hoccanum finally died of old age while she was still in prison. She promised them the first gift when they arrived to New York would be a new cat.

But she had concerns over two items. She fretted whether to take or leave them.

After much thought she entered her study for the last time. The books she wanted to keep were packed; the empty herb jars from the many shelves in her cupboard given away. Her precious journals with years of handwritten notes were also packed. She remembered to leave out her book of remedies for the governor as a parting gift.

What of these last items? She held them in her hands. One was Mr. Lily's *Christian Astrology*. What had this book brought her but pain and heartache? How could owning a book originally meant as a signpost and guide— turn out so that it had torn the fabric of her life to pieces? She had put her faith and trust in William Lilly's book— too much faith, she now realized.

The other book was John's old Bible. She wasn't sure what to do with this either. She paused and finally made her decision.

She held a spade in her hand, and carried her satchel with the worn books inside. She made her way across the wide field near John's resting place, where a new flourish of spring grasses sprouted up around his marker. She found the right spot nearby.

The clank of the spade's hard metal against the solid earth brought back memories of her beloved John's burial years before. She dug a deep hole, held the book, and then tossed it into its own grave. She thought of the years of study, meeting Mr. Lilly himself, the readings, and considered pulling the black book out from the soil.

Instead, another idea presented itself. She stared up to the heavens, clouds passing in the vast blue sky. "Hear me now," she said with a strong voice, "I will leave this place, my home of sundry years. I leave a part of my past buried in this earth. May it stay buried on this land for all time." She hurled with passion mounds of dirt on the book and patted it down.

Life continued on, and will continue onward, she thought.

Then she pulled forth John's old Bible. Should she leave this here with him as well? She wondered and opened the book to the fronts page. There was the date of their marriage, and the birth dates of each of their daughters written in John's steady hand. Her eyes glanced over the different quotes and markings, until she read something that made her pause. She hadn't noticed it before. She looked again and read the words aloud: "'*My Katherine is far greater than rubies.*'" He had written down what he said to her on their wedding day so many years ago.

Tears welled in her eyes. She shut the book and placed it back in her satchel. John's great book would go with her and the family. She knew those loving memories would help carry her forward.

Then she turned, walked away, and did not look back. What dreams she had in Wethersfield were gone, buried with John, buried with that other book. But she had new dreams. She could still dream of her future, and still have hope for the future of her three daughters.

⸱⸱⸱

The next day the small group huddled around the wagon waiting near the farmhouse. There was Governor Winthrop, the Reverend Bulkeley, Marshal Gilbert, Joseph, and her daughters all awaiting her. Then she noticed Ben, Josiah's son striding up the lane. The May sun felt strong today, the air crisp with fresh breezes and the scent of apple blossoms. New life was beginning in Wethersfield, but her life here was ending.

She greeted the small party with a wave of her hand. "How kind of you all…to wish us farewell."

Governor Winthrop stepped forward. "Godspeed, Katherine," was all he said. His eyes had a look of tender care and mercy. She pulled from her satchel her book of herbal remedies and offered it to him.

"As promised, Governor. To add to your growing collection." He accepted the gift and murmured words of thanks.

Joseph, her faithful farmhand stood stoically in place. He held a large pouch in his hands. "Joseph," she called faintly. The Wangunk, now with three children of his own, handed the pouch to her. She opened it to find a beaded pair of leather moccasins. She noticed John's initials branded on the inside of the shoes.

"These are made from leather Goodman Harrison gave to my tribe many years ago. He knew size of your foot, and I remember."

"Something old from John? Made new?" She immediately took off her old boots, threw them into the wagon, and placed the new shoes onto her feet. "Joseph! How can I thank you?"

"No thanks. Prayers answered…for Katherine's life is saved!" His eyes filled with tears. "Tribe thankful you are alive." Katherine embraced her loyal friend and farmhand, tears rising and falling from her eyes.

Then she remembered something she had packed. "Joseph, I have a gift for you." She dug through the chests and trunks in the wagon until she found the sturdy box. "Here," she handed it to him. Joseph quickly opened it, and stood staring wide-eyed at the inside, for there was John's old blue town crier jacket with the shiny buttons. Alongside the jacket lay his brass bell. Joseph, unable to restrain himself, lifted the bell out, and began to ring it aloud.

"Honored. Truly, I am honored," he replied.

Ben had joined the party. He was now a handsome, well-muscled man of nineteen years. "I truly never thanked you all these years ago for stitching up my arm. No scar remains." He pulled his thick arm up to show them. "And on behalf of my family, the Gilberts, we wish thee fare-thee-well."

Katherine understood now that Josiah had sent Ben to the farmhouse. This small gesture brought a feeling of peace to her, a peace missing for many years.

Then she thanked the Reverend Bulkeley, and turned to her cousin. "Keep me abreast of my estate, Jonathan. You of all, have anchored me through these storms."

She gathered her daughters about her. A special driver assigned by the Court awaited atop the wagon. "The horses are becoming restless," he shouted. She took a long last look at the farm she had so lovingly cared for, then turned her eyes to this group who truly did care for her.

Katherine and her daughters climbed atop the wagon. As the driver clicked the reins, Governor Winthrop shouted, "God hath given you a new beginning, Katherine. Make the best of it." She nodded in agreement.

"Aye, 'tis true," she said to herself.

This was something she knew how to do.

AUTHOR'S NOTE

Katherine Harrison, although found guilty of witchcraft by the jury, was banished from Wethersfield after receiving her sentence by the Panel of Ministers. She was the last person in Connecticut Colony to be convicted of witchcraft and to be released. Thus, she began her new life in Westchester, N.Y. Her reputation apparently preceded her; petitions in Westchester soon began because the people residing there, wanted 'no witch' in their community.

Katherine did reside for a time with Captain Panton. Her eldest daughter, Rebecca soon married, and so Katherine settled in the area. Henry Stiles in the *History of Ancient Wethersfield, Vol I* mentions there's evidence Katherine did return to settle her estate and writes there may be evidence she may have bought and moved to the area of Dividend Road (now Rocky Hill), but nothing substantiates she moved back to Connecticut on a permanent basis.

Katherine's story proved to be a complex one. I did what I could with the dates. She did arrive to the New World around the fall of 1651, and the evidence suggests she was a cousin to the Gilberts. The fact that Josiah in the records mentions he wasn't sure, 'Katherine is my cousin,' and that Marshal Gilbert was left in charge of her estate, and that both Josiah and the Marshal were witnesses to John's will, indicates a familial bond. Other authors have hinted that Katherine was related to Lydia Gilbert, but Lydia was a Gilbert by marriage to Thomas, not by birth.

And besides Jonathan, Thomas, and Josiah, there was another Gilbert brother named John. I make my apologies to my readers and the Gilbert family because I omitted John Gilbert. He seemed a minor character in the story, with the exception that along with the Marshal, he was put in charge of her estate. The reason for the omission is that *The Witch of Wethersfield* already had five characters named John. It can get confusing with the same names…John, Elizabeth, Mary and Katherine were all very popular names for the time period. Once again, I apologize for this.

We know from the research that Katherine *did* work in servitude for Captain Cullick in Hartford, and ultimately got fired due to reading fellow servant Betty's fortune. A few other persons who worked for the captain included Thomas Waples, who stated he had his palm read by Katherine, but alas, this character was omitted due to the many characters already in the story. By focusing on Betty's fortunetelling, and her testifying at Katherine's trial, I established reason enough for her firing and wanted to focus on the main story.

How did Katherine happen to end up at Captain Cullick's home? We really don't know. I speculated she came over to start her new life, leaving the war behind, and somehow her cousin Josiah really didn't want to deal with her. Her reputation clearly preceded her. In the records, it states that she 'followed the troops.' On one level, this indicates she was a skilled nurse of sorts. However, at the time, the meaning of "following the troops" referred to a common prostitute who followed the men for obvious reasons. I insinuated that either or both meanings may have been true.

It was clear during the organization of my research how many witnesses did testify against Katherine. I had to choose carefully who I would include, and who and what I'd leave out for the sake of the story. For those interested in reading about the other incidents and persons offended by Katherine, please see my bibliography.

Most of the characters in *The Witch of Wethersfield: A Cunning Woman* are true to life. I took a few exceptions. Joseph Hawk Wing, the Native American Wangunk was created by me. I realized after reading and researching the story, the Indians did live close by during the planting and reaping seasons. The tribe did spend part of the year on the Island of Merriment off Wethersfield in the Great River and then wintered south in Mattabassett, now called Middletown. Relations were peaceful at the time I write of, so I included Joseph and the Powwow into the story.

John Harrison settled in Wethersfield during the 1640s and was truly a 'lone-man' in Wethersfield—until he met Katherine. The town crier he was, as well as beginning his career as a cobbler, then a farmer, and then onto becoming a wealthy merchant. I imagined Katherine and John being enterprising, industrious, and together they made a formidable couple who amassed a fortune.

In many ways, *The Witch of Wethersfield* is a prequel and a sequel to my first novel, *Days to the Gallows*. Readers of my first book will recognize characters such as Marshal Gilbert, Major John Mason and others. Also, readers may make the connection that during times of unrest, church schisms, quarrels and natural disasters, these tended to arouse the specter of witchcraft.

In both the Hartford Witch Panic and in Katherine's case, we see how these disturbances in the towns created a need to blame someone for the outbreaks. A woman could go from a much sought after healer, someone wealthy and different, to suddenly being a widow, then accused of a witch.

The town of Wethersfield has changed much since those days. Where the Harbor was there's now the Cove created from natural flooding in the 1700s, when rock and debris created a wall and thus allowed the river to run a different course. The old High St. is now Main St. and the Sandy Lane has become "Hartford Avenue." Back in the 1600s it had both names and still leads one to Hartford. Ironically, when I walked up the Hartford Ave. from Main St., to the left is a white church-like building with the name of another Harrison on it. Connection? The Broad Street is still there, and a small street called Robbins Wood is approximately right next to where the Robbins resided.

Wethersfield, in essence, was the first suburb of Hartford. Many townspeople such as Marshal Gilbert owned land in both towns and would go the several miles back and forth on a regular basis. The Great Meadows sadly has been cut and divided by the highway. But you can find little hints of the old meadows, swamps and brooks, if you look long and hard…especially in the fall when Wethersfield is the epitome of New England…with scarecrows lining the streets, lantern gravesite tours, and of course the specter of those hanged as witches from Wethersfield seem very much alive…

I tried to keep to the true chronology of the story (and it proved complicated) and who Katherine really was—a young, brash woman who wanted more in her life, had something to prove, and was determined to get the respect, prestige, and attention she felt she deserved. Obviously, besides her successful marriage to John and the money they amassed, her expectations fell short.

During his life, John was her protector and defender, but once he died, the tides turned on Katherine. For she was a rich widow and refused to marry. Clearly— she was never one to follow rules or protocol.

Katherine Palmer and her Henry did get a "warning out" as the Hartford Witch Panic unfolded and left for Rhode Island. Someone asked me, "Why didn't Katherine Harrison go with them?" My answer was, "Why should she?" At the time, she had her husband, her farm and children, her money and business; there would be no reason for her to leave. Later in the story perhaps. It's clear Katherine was never really involved in the Merrymeets on the South Green, so she felt secure enough to stay. She became in essence, "wedded to her land" and family.

It appeared according to John's will, written a week before his demise, he had a sense it was almost his time. I'm sure the town's treatment of Katherine caused him angst. And that fateful summer of 1666, when Wethersfield suffered through droughts, blasts, and blights to the crops, and a mysterious illness lingered was perhaps what John succumbed to. It was obvious to me he was the victim of all these disasters.

All characters are based on the records with the exception of Joseph, James Robson, the man on the ship, as well as the women on the ship. We know that Katherine had a lawyer, we just don't know his name, so I called him Nathaniel Hopkins. I tried as best as I could to get the dates correct, but looking back, I realized John Winthrop Jr. came into his governorship a few months after he saved Katherine and her child. This was created by me to establish a bond between the two early on. Marshal Gilbert was most likely not marshal throughout the whole story. But he was marshal during the most important sections of the story, so the marshal he stayed. I used my "historical imagination" to fill in many details.

Last but not least, many of you might be still wondering, "Who and what is a Cunning Woman?" The cunning folk, known as folk healers or the wise folk, were practitioners of folk medicine, magic and divination in Europe from the Middle Ages until the 20th Century. I believe that Katherine saw herself among this select group that made a difference in their communities and villages in Europe. Yet the cunning-folk could be unpredictable; they could easily turn and use their magic in a malevolent manner. But Katherine tried to promote herself as a healer, wanting to feel needed, important, and to have that attention she craved.(and she certainly got attention!)

Alas, her efforts proved to be futile, and much was held against her due to her proclamations. Perhaps she never learned that being a cunning woman required one to keep quiet and keep your secrets hidden. She was unable to do this. And although she didn't pay the ultimate price, the costs to her and her family were tremendous.

I hope you enjoyed the tale of Katherine, and that if one is interested in knowing more, there are several books available that address the subject. Often her story is included amongst others, but the best place to start would be John Demos's, *Entertaining Satan.* Many of the records are included, but if one feels compelled to go to the Connecticut State Library, the Wyllys papers hold the depositions and testimony by townspeople against Katherine. Also, Carol Karlsen's, *The Devil in the Shape of a Woman* has an outstanding chapter on Katherine's plight. There's also a great deal of information online, including Katherine reading Betty's fortune at the Captain's house. *Christian Astrology* by William Lily is available, as well as many books on cunning folk.

Please see my selected bibliography.

Once again, thanks for reading!

Katherine Spada Basto

If you enjoyed the book, please leave a review on Amazon and Goodreads. Reviews are the lifeblood of an author, and we count on them. Thank you.

Please check out my website at www.katherinespadabasto.com for updates.

SELECTED BIBLIOGRAPHY

Samuel Wyllys Papers, Connecticut State Library. Hartford, Conn.

DeForest, John. *History of the Indians in Connecticut.* WM Jas Hamersley, Hartford, Conn. 1852

Demos, John Putnam. *Entertaining Satan.* Oxford University Press, N.Y. 1982

Hall, David D. *Witch-Hunting in Seventeenth Century New England.* Northeastern University Press, Boston. 1991

Karlsen, Carol F. *The Devil in the Shape of a Woman: Witchcraft in Colonial New England.* WW Norton and Co. N.Y. April 1998

McDermett, William P. *Wethersfield, 1634-1670, Families, Community and Change.* Kerleen Press, Tolland, CT. 2009

Stiles, Henry R. *The History of Ancient Wethersfield, Connecticut, Vol I* originally published 1904, Henry Stiles. Republished 1974, New Hampshire Publishing Co.

Tomlinson, Richard G. *Gershom Bulkeley, Zealot for Truth.* Self-published, 2018

Woodward, Walter. *Prospero's America,* Omohundro Institute and University of North Carolina, June, 2011.

The *Ballad of Maid Marian* can be found online and is from the 16th century. *No more Maids a-go a Rushing* is from the 15th-16th century.

ACKNOWLEDGEMENTS

I would like to thank the Wethersfield Historical Society to providing me a full copy of the 17ᵗʰ century map of Wethersfield. This map ranges from 1640-1699 and was very helpful locating the land and townspeople's home lots. Unfortunately, I could not include the whole of the map; rather just the land, what streets people lived on, and the general terrain.

Many thanks to my editor, Carol Gaskin of Editorial Alchemy that made this manuscript much better. Thanks to my beta-readers, including my husband Ronald, Jane Sibley, Duncan Eagleson, Trish Truitt, and Paul Francoeur. All of your feedback was very helpful.

Thanks to Alvis for his care. Also, a big thanks to my art cover designer, Duncan Eagleson, who always provides a fitting and attractive cover. It's always a pleasure to work with you. Thanks to Moira Ashleigh for working on my website and FB page.

Thanks to all who asked how the book was coming, and that they were excited to read it.

READERS' QUESTIONS AND GUIDE

1. In the 17th century, Katherine Harrison was scorned by her neighbors. How do you think she'd be treated in the 21st century? What qualities did she have that might be admired today?

2. Explain the role of superstition and envy among the Puritan settlers throughout the novel. Why was it convenient to call someone different, "a witch?"

3. Compare and contrast the old ways of thinking as evidenced by Major John Mason, to the forward reasoning of Governor John Winthrop, Jr. and Reverend Gershom Bulkeley.

4. In "The Witch of Wethersfield" there are many characters. Who was your favorite, and why?

5. How did the power of the mob affect the story? How is it true today that a mob often obtains power. How and why does this happen?

6. Katherine Harrison was the last woman convicted of witchcraft in Connecticut Colony, the last *convicted* 'witch' to be freed—although banished. How did the new standards of evidence change things for those accused of being a witch?

7. Why was a hanging considered almost a celebration to towns-people? Was this a sacrifice of sorts?

8. Describe how the role of history, weather, plagues, in the story are characters in themselves. How did the English Civil War, the Royalists versus the Puritans, the change from a Regent to a Monarch restored to the throne affect life in Wethersfield Colony? Why was it dangerous for John and Katherine to admit they were Royalists at heart? What about the Hartford Witch Panic when Governor Winthrop was away? How did sicknesses, the weather, and church quarrels affect townspeople? Describe how changes such as these affect the well-being and stability of the community.

9. For much of the book, Katherine was often an unlikeable character. Show and describe how she matured at the end, and compare her to the beginning of the story. What adjectives might describe her character?

10. How did the sudden death of John change everything for Kath-erine? Why do you think she didn't remarry? Why were women who didn't follow the rules subject to being called witches?

Made in the USA
Middletown, DE
04 October 2023

40209281R00210